I
XAKATAN

Spiderwize
Remus House
Coltsfoot Drive
Woodston
Peterborough
PE2 9BF

www.spiderwize.com

A CIP catalogue record for this book is available from the British Library.

The views expressed in this work are solely those of the author and do not necessarily reflect the views of the publisher, and the publisher hereby disclaims any responsibility for them.

Copy Edited by Christina Willis 2017

ISBN: 978-1-906352-01-1

XAKATAN I, II and III is a work of fiction. Described events and any part of dialogue attributed to real or made-up characters in the story must not be considered factual or of historical value.

I
XAKATAN
(SCHAKHATAAN)

TONY AMCA

I

Somewhat timidly at first, the wavelets of high tide smoothly rippled over the dry sand, like freshly poured lemonade, looking for the jungle beyond the virgin bay. An early mid-summer mist lingered above the greenery and partly hidden among the frontline of trees, the wooden shack of Pedro Bolivar stood like the brain-child of some shipwrecked mariner.

Halfway from the ocean, a small rowing boat had been turned upside down for safety, and a trail of clothes led to the wooden dwelling; where to the beat of breaking waves, Pedro's loud snoring confirmed this to be the morning after a heavy night of Cachaça drinking!

To one side of Pedro's home, past a wall of dried fish, two young Indio girls emerged from the jungle and walked bare-chested towards his shack, giggling to each other as they collected the clothes he had discarded on his way to bed.

"Do you think we'll find him naked Deedee?" giggled the younger of the two covering her mouth, unable to hide her excitement as they went.

"I hope so Ara… It's about time we discovered what he keeps hiding so zealously…," added the other with amused anticipation.

"It's probably such a *small thing* that he feels so shy about it…?" reasoned the first one, also a little aroused by her thoughts.

1

The shack was built on a wooden platform and the girls went silent the moment they stepped onto the planks leading to the door left ajar, with Deedee claiming the right to have the first peep!

"Is he naked?" Ara whispered impatiently after a while, feeling that Deedee was taking too long.

"Yes, but he's got his back turned to us… He's got a hairy bottom…" She commented, doing her best not to laugh.

"OK, let me have a look then…" Ara insisted, ready to grab Deedee's vantage point, only to be panic stricken soon after… "Oh my God, he's going to turn around…" She almost shouted back to Deedee, whose head suddenly found its way back inside the door!

"Deedee…?" The middle- aged loner enquired as he tried to turn around.

"Are you OK Pedro?" Deedee replied already back outside, pretending to have just arrived "Ara and I have been picking up your clothes from all around the bay… What happened?"

"I don't know I'm not too sure… I had too much to drink last night and I don't feel too good…"

"Are we OK to come in?"

"Not yet… Give me a moment to get dressed?"

Their muddy make-ups and haircuts that could rival Robin Hood's Friar Tuck aside, the two young women were unquestionably feminine; with pretty faces, almond eyes, perfect smiles and sculptural bodies yet to be marked by motherhood. They both stood at around 5.6 ft. tall. Ara was fractionally the shorter of the two and neither looked a day over 16.

Both girls belonged to one of a dozen families that made up a small tribe called the Akazi, whose camp was about three miles further in land. They were Pedro's most regular visitors and somehow looked after him, in as far as keeping his home clean; his clothes washed and sometimes even cooking him the odd meal. In return, Pedro was a bit like the tribe's link to the outside world, often bringing them a variety of supplies each time he returned from selling boxes of his dried fish in the white man's village (Pitimbu), some 30 miles down the coast.

Pedro however was a bit of a recluse, with something of a dark past. Some fifteen years earlier, as a small shopkeeper in São Paulo, he had lost his wife and three children in a fire, for refusing to pay "protection" to a local Mafia gang. Blinded by grief and disenchantment with mankind and the modern world, he soon got his revenge on those responsible, but found himself on the run going north, where he obtained a Provincial Land Concession to use the remote bay as his home.

"How long have you both been standing there?" Pedro enquired suspiciously as he fastened his trouser belt.

"We just got here when you woke up…," replied Deedee.

"We didn't even see you naked or anything like that…," confirmed Ara!!

"I see…," returned the old veteran, amused by the girls' innocence. "You can both come in now".

"Did you drink everything missing in this bottle last night?" Deedee censured him, producing an empty 2 litre bottle of home-made Cachaça from behind her back, as if it were a court-room exhibit.

"Oh yes… there it is…" Pedro attempted some justification that never came.

"Why do you do these things to yourself?" Deedee was insistent and motherly in her reproach, but before Pedro could manage a reply, he had to release a loud fart he could no longer hold, causing the two girls to descend into a fit of giggles.

"Sorry about that…" He looked apologetically at Deedee, as she fought to return to her serious stance, "…there are times when the past creeps into my mind and just seems to stay there… and a good measure of Cachaça often helps to chase those thoughts away…" He eventually justified his behaviour.

"You could come to us when that happens… You know that…" Deedee reassured him, softening her tone, "…Even our tribal Elders offered you their blessing, should you want to keep us…!"

"You're both too young and deserve younger men; we've been through this before…"

"That was a couple of years ago,…" Countered Deedee "The Elders will soon start wondering if you'd rather have one or two boys to keep you regular company instead…," she teased.

"What's wrong with me being by myself?" Pedro complained, desperately trying to keep another *loud explosion* in, but none-the-less amused by the Elders' concerns. "You guys really picked the wrong day to pass by…" He said changing the subject while holding his stomach. "I need to sober up…"

"Shall we come by tomorrow and cook you a meal?" Suggested Deedee letting out a sigh, realising he really needed to be by himself.

"That sounds wonderful…" Pedro tried to be positive as he stood up. "Take some dried fish for the tribe as you go?" He proposed, looking for a carrier bag to give them.

"We'll take them some tomorrow instead?" Deedee decided it was time to go, rather than prolonging his agony.

"It's a deal…"

And no sooner had they left, he took off his clothes to enter the Ocean.

*

Pedro felt revitalised by the time he returned to the shack and after an outside shower, thanks to the power from the single solar panel, he switched on the transistor radio to hear the World news, while making himself a pot of coffee.

"*The stupid leading the stupid…!!!*" He expressed his thoughts out loud to the news reader!

Thinking back to the morning, he was shocked to realise how fast time had passed since he had settled on the bay; especially when Deedee reminded him that two years had elapsed since he considered her to be *too young*… The truth was that although not insensitive to her beauty (or Ara's for that matter), in his eyes he still saw them as they were two years earlier!

The girls were most probably still virgins and the last thing Pedro wanted was to open a new Pandora's Box for the hell of it! His sex life was well sorted out. On his monthly trips to Pitimbu to sell his dried fish stock, he would always visit the local Brothel to spend an hour or so with Madalena, by now his regular, before returning home.

By nightfall however, the sounds of nature were suddenly silenced by those of an approaching Police patrol boat entering the bay.

"PEDRO BOLIVAR…!" An authoritarian voice boomed from a loud speaker when the boat came to a stop just short of the sand. "THIS IS THE POLICE…," continued the voice, backed by a strong searchlight firmly pinned onto the shack. "WALK TO US WITH YOUR HANDS WELL UP ABOVE YOUR HEAD…!"

Brazilian Police were notorious for their no-nonsense general attitude and Pedro wasn't willing to test their lack of good humour, especially with no one to bear witness, and was quick to comply.

"What's all this about?" He asked calmly as he neared their boat, looking a little startled by the whole thing.

"You'll soon find out. Is anyone else with you in the shack?" Their Captain enquired.

"There's no one else…" He accepted a hand to help him get on board. "Am I being accused of something?" He wanted to know.

"We just need to ask you some questions as part of an ongoing investigation and we'll bring you back once we're done." The Captain replied as the boat left the shore.

*

At meal times, the Akazi sat in two separate circles; one for the men and boys above the age of 8, and the other for the women and younger children. Deedee was one of the tribe's favourites and as in relation to the two circles, sat immediately behind Joojoo (the old Witch Doctor) with her back to him.

"There is sadness in your eyes Deedee…," noticed Joojoo as the tribe assembled for their evening meal "Is the white man not responding to your feelings of the heart?" He ventured in a lower tone of voice from the men's circle, without turning around to face her.

"He still thinks I'm too young for him and was ill with firewater today…" She confided from among the human noises of the gathering as they all ate and socialised.

"The only explanation is that he either prefers young men or white women…," hooted Mela (Deedee's mum) with her ultra sharp hearing, from further around the women's circle.

"Maybe he has a little *Dinky* that doesn't work?" Her grandmother contributed with a heavy voice and a matching giggle, ever ready to echo Mela's comments in some way.

"Leave her alone…" Ara came to the rescue from near by, seeing Deedee close to tears. "He just has ghosts from the past in his mind…" At this point, Joojoo turned around to face the women.

"Pedro has always been useful to us and we want things to stay that way…" He looked at the sobbing Deedee. "Maybe you should accept that some things are just not meant to be…," and then continued in a near whisper "There is no man among us that wouldn't gladly have you for a wife, you know?"

"You are always kind to me Joojoo…," she managed a smile, "…but my heart is set on him. He could also be a great chance for me to see the white man's world without being afraid… and perhaps even the start of bigger things for the Akazi?"

"I don't think you'll see much of the white man's world with him! In fact, I sense that he probably wants as little to do with it as possible. Why else should he want to live where he is?"

"Listen to the wisdom of Joojoo and downsize your dreams…," Mela advised. "…Besides: can't you see he is a bit too old for you? Another 10 or 20 years down the line you'd be a widow, just like me!!!"

"Can we talk about something else?" Suggested Deedee, taking in a deep breath

"That sounds like a good idea…," approved Joojoo with a subliminal wink to Mela, "…and let me know if there's anything I can do. Yes?"

"Thank you Joojoo."

It was still day light when the communal meal had finished and to help with the women's chores, Deedee and Ara offered to wash all the food bowls in the nearby stream.

"If you ever get married to Pedro and go to the white man's world… will you take me with you?" Ara didn't want to be left behind! "I would make myself useful…," She promised.

"Of course Ara, you're my best friend." Deedee reassured her.

"Joojoo might even work out a spell…"

*

Deedee and Ara got to Pedro's beach not long after day break, carrying a forest bird they planned to cook.

"He is definitely not here." Ara concluded after looking everywhere for him.

"He's got to be somewhere near, his rowboat is here and

his motor boat for fishing is still anchored there…," pointed out Deedee, beginning to wonder if he might have fallen somewhere.

"He's not gone hunting either," confirmed Ara emerging from the shack "his rifle and pistol are in their place…"

The girls called out for him for over an hour, searching all the likely spots where he could have gone, and eventually concluded that someone had come for him when they spotted an oily patch still present where the Police patrol boat had been.

"What do you think happened?" Deedee enquired of her cousin "He has no friends that we know of and… nothing was disturbed inside his shack." She thought out loud.

"The only explanation is that he probably did something he shouldn't, got so drunk that he forgot about it… and the Police came looking for him?" Proposed Ara, turning detective!

"He is probably in some kind of trouble I agree, but I don't think he has done anything wrong…" Deedee was quick to come to his rescue.

"What do you want to do? Shall we hang around in case he turns up?"

"I think we should. At least until midday…"

To help pass the time, taking advantage of this rare opportunity, the girls went through his belongings as carefully as they could, making sure that each item was returned to its original place.

The memorabilia box was of particular interest to Deedee, finally finding it unlocked; the family photo of Pedro with his wife and children causing her eyes to water.

"What do you think happened there?" Ara asked, looking at another photograph of the same people. "Do you think they are the ghosts he talks about?"

"You could be right…" Agreed Deedee, suddenly distracted by the corner of a magazine peeping from under his mattress.

"Gosh Ara, look at this?" She said, quickly browsing through the explicit pages of the pornographic photos in it.

"No wonder he doesn't need us!!!" Ara seemed suddenly amused "That is probably what he looks at before going to sleep…" She added while memorising each photo!! "Wow, look… at… that!!!"

Noon came and went but still no sign of Pedro and while they dried after a swim, Ara began to wonder how much longer Deedee would want to hang around.

"Shouldn't we start going back?" she enquired

"I think we ought to stay here until he returns, to protect his belongings…" Deedee argued.

"…And what if he doesn't turn up?"

"Well, we'll have to wait and see…," she paused. "But I don't mind if you want to go back…"

"I'm not going back by myself; it will soon be dark… and I'm hungry. Shall we cook that bird?"

"Good idea. I'll prepare it while you start a beach fire… and he might get here soon."

*

Pedro didn't get much out of the crew of the patrol boat and it wasn't until he sat face to face with a Police interrogator in Pitimbu that he learned what the whole thing was about!

"My name is João Guimarães…," the well-built Officer introduced himself with a powerful hand shake. "…And in case you don't know, Pedro, the reason why we need to talk to you relates to the death of Maria Madalena…" He seemed cordial in his manner.

"Oh my God… The Brothel girl?"

"That's the one"

"When…How did it happen?"

"She was found strangled in her bedroom the day before yesterday…"

"In the actual Brothel?"

"Ummmm!" João confirmed calmly while browsing through the original Police report. "Where this gets complicated for you Pedro, is that this happened on the same day you came here to sell your fish. Making matters worse, the Brothel has also confirmed that you were her last client of the day…"

"God help me…! I was indeed a regular client of hers, I can't deny that… but what motive could I possibly have to do such a thing? She had always been pleasant and compliant with me… Am I the only suspect in this?" Pedro suddenly felt he had entered a horrible cul-de-sac.

"You are not the only suspect, but you are certainly the main one at present… If you tell me all you can remember about that day, it may help to clear you of this." He paused "A DNA sample might also assist in establishing if you were indeed her last client…"

"I've no objection João… anything to help clear me from your list of suspects." He paused. "In fact I would be immensely grateful if you were to keep my name out of the public domain on this, at least until you have completed your investigation…? I can assure you I'm not the guy you're looking for…"

"Is that because of your past in São Paulo?" The question took Pedro completely by surprise.

"What do you know about that?" Pedro went a little red in the face.

"All that there is to know my friend, but you have no reason to worry on that particular score… you actually did a favour for the Police there and they are not after you… To be honest, I would have probably done the same in your shoes…" He paused, sounding like a man in full control "Tell me when you're ready, so I can start running the tape?"

"I'm ready when you are."

Pedro's recorded statement lasted the best part of an hour

and was enriched here and there by some direct questions from João.

"Can you take me back home now?" He asked, once João declared the interview over.

"Not yet, I'm sorry. We need to take that DNA sample and I shall have to retain you until we are able to verify your version of events…"

"How long will that take?"

"Normally a day or two, at best… but rest assured; I will not keep any longer than absolutely necessary." And with this, a guard came to escort Pedro to a temporary cell, where he found a bearded unkempt looking man exuding a strong smell of alcohol, fast asleep.

"If I were you I wouldn't strike a match in there…," commented the prison guard locking the cell.

"Good advice… You really are a pal!"

In Brazil, Police treatment of suspects was strongly influenced by their social status, and the norm for borderline social outcasts was: "*guilty until proven innocent!*"

*

"I ate a lot more than I needed to!!!" Ara complained with a burp while rinsing the bowls and implements they had used, in the nearby stream that also passed their camp.

"Me too" Deedee felt just as bloated and was salvaging the meat left from their barbecued bird.

Nightfall came swiftly and no sooner had they finished tidying up than they entered Pedro's shack, making sure the door and windows were securely shut. This was the very first night they had ever spent away from the safety of their tribal camp; and the nocturnal sounds from the wild somehow seemed a lot closer and more threatening…

"Shall we take turns sleeping?" suggested Ara lighting up an oil lamp.

"That's a good idea… Do you want to sleep first?"

"OK… But you will be with me in bed while staying awake yeah?"

"OK little one…"

Between the sounds of the jungle and the occasional rummaging of leaves near the shack, neither of the girls could shut an eyelid until well into the night, by which time they both fell profoundly asleep!!

"DEEDEE? ARA?" Shouted one of the Akazi warriors from outside the shack, in the late morning of the following day.

"Is that you Tamko?" Replied the sleepy Ara, recognising the voice.

"Yes… Is Deedee with you?"

"Yes, we are both fine… just give us a minute and we'll be out OK?" She continued.

"And Pedro…?" Enquired the young warrior once they emerged, surprised by not seeing him.

The girls told him all they knew and he soon convinced them to return to their camp with him, promising he would send a couple of younger boys to keep an eye on Pedro's belongings.

Entering their camp, they passed Joojoo walking towards his hut.

"Come to see me once your mother's done with you?" He invited, with his usual paternal smile.

Immediately after a good cuddle each, Mela was then quick to give the two girls a loud ear full. This went on and on for a good 15 minutes, to the amusement of the gathering tribe, until she managed to get rid of all the stress she had accumulated overnight!

"Hi Joojoo… I'm sorry for making everyone worried over us…" Deedee went to him by herself.

"The important thing is that you are both OK…" He smiled, happy to see her.

"Do you know anything about Pedro? Ara and I think that a motor boat came for him…" She told him all she knew.

"Last night I had a vision that he was in jail… in Pitimbu…," he paused. "Well, these visions are not always accurate as you know…"

"What do you think he has done?"

"Now you're asking! I have no clue as to that. Only that his cell mate had a huge black beard."

Deedee looked at him, wondering whether to take him seriously.

"What would you do in my place?" She then asked.

"All you can do is wait. Pedro appeals to me as being an honest man and if my vision was indeed true, I'm sure everything will soon sort itself."

"And if he is not back by the full moon?"

"Let's wait for the full moon first…," he tried to keep her spirits high.

*

By morning, from the bunk bed below him, Pedro's cellmate started to show signs of coming around and got up, probably wondering where he was, only to be startled by Pedro's presence on the bunk bed above his.

"Who the hell are you?" Asked the bearded man finding his balance.

"I am Pedro" Pedro tried to be civil by stretching out his hand for a handshake.

"I am Luis, Luis Ramos…" He returned the handshake, his eyes doing their best to focus. "What have you done to be here?" He enquired.

"Nothing… They are investigating the murder of a local prostitute and decided to keep me here while they clear a line of enquiries…" Pedro's explanation made Luis laugh with gusto.

"I wish you luck. They often retain people just for the sake of showing they are doing their job!"

"Well…" Pedro did his best not to be concerned by Luis' comment. "…And you?"

"Drunk and disorderly… as usual! I've lost count of how many times they've kept me here; normally for one week…", he said scratching his head before yawning loudly, probably getting drunk all over again, from his own breath this time!

"Why do you drink?"

"I like it." He replied calmly, getting ready to urinate against the wall furthest away from them. Luis certainly knew how to halt a line of conversation in its tracks, leaving Pedro wondering how his cellmate would normally tackle other toilet necessities!!! "I'm sorry about this, but I couldn't hold it any longer…," he apologised.

The food was considerably better than Pedro had anticipated and by the evening, Luis had sobered up to the point of actually looking intelligent!

"How did you end up like this?" Pedro asked, offering his cellmate a rolled-up cigarette which he readily accepted.

"You don't end up like this! You evolve into it…," Luis explained. "I once had everything a man could want; a pretty wife, a steady job, money and my own home… you know?"

"Children?"

"None thank heavens! I even used to go to Church on Sundays!!!"

"Good God! What happened?"

"I worked as a long haul intercity coach driver. From Salvador to Brasilia, Rio, São Paulo, there were times when I was away from home for more than a month…"

"Say no more… I can already picture it…" Pedro got him talking.

"It is actually worse than you think;" He paused to gather his thoughts. "At first, the savings started to disappear, and my wife eventually admitted to having a drug problem. We

14

argued and in the end, she promised to make an effort." He looked at Pedro. "Until… Returning from a stretch of work a couple of months later, I found out I no longer had a house and that the stupid bitch had run away with some drug dealer…!"

"I'm sorry to hear that Luis. But… well, at least you still had a job…?"

"At this point I was left with the option of either paying for all the debts she had left behind or face the prospect of being buried alive…" His voice seemed to falter, as if momentarily reliving his ordeal. "…It took me five years to pay it all off…" He paused again, momentarily raising his voice, but Pedro didn't dare interrupt his flow. "I was living in São Salvador at the time and decided to move to Recife to start a new life…"

"Still keeping the same job?" Pedro had to ask and Luis confirmed it with a nod.

"Anyway, as if this were a curse, on one of the trips I made to Rio, I decided to try a new Brothel, as you do, and there she was… believe it or not, ready to take me as a paying client!!!"

"Fucking hell…! What did you do?"

"I paid…"

"You're kidding! After all that? …Were you still in love?"

"I wasn't in love, but she was as good a lover as a man could get… and after spending years fantasising over every moment we had ever spent together in bed, I wasn't going to let the opportunity pass! I even returned to the same Brothel on my next trip to Rio, but she was no longer there…"

"Was it at that point you started to hit the bottle?"

"No. My back started playing up from all the hours sitting at the wheel and I took a different job with the Government, still driving but for fewer hours at a time and on better paid contract jobs… ferrying Indios from their lands to native reserves or elsewhere in the Country. This was to allow for mining and oil exploration…" He had a hiccup. "I saw some awful things being done to those people during that time…," he was almost emotional. "The worst of all being when we were four coaches taking some native Indios from near the Peruvian border to not too far from here… The Akazi, I think they were called…"

"What happened?" Pedro asked impassively, not wanting to reveal how well he knew them.

"We were 20 seats short of fitting everyone into the coaches… and were told to leave them behind for the "Federais" to deal with…"

"Meaning?"

"They were all shot and buried on the side of the road the moment we were out of sight."

"Jesus! Are you sure of this?"

"I learned from other drivers that this wasn't a first either…" He took a deep breath. "I didn't take on any more jobs after that and that's how I ended up here in Pitimbu… My coach is still on a stretch of the beach where I parked it, some four years ago… and it is where I sleep when I'm not here."

"Wow Luis… but you still don't look a day over 40… Have you given up completely?"

"I've applied for a job in a local brewery, but for some reason they didn't give it to me!!!" And with this, they both started to laugh.

The second day came and went. Pedro also shared some of his life with Luis and somehow both men identified with one another through their life's ordeals. By day three however Pedro started to get restless with the lack of news regarding his case;

"Any news from João Guimarães regarding his enquiries…?" He asked the guard.

"I'm sure he'll let you know if anything changes…," was the reply.

"Should I probably get myself a lawyer? How long are you guys allowed to keep me here?"

"You've seen too many American films amigo!" The

guard laughed. "…We'll keep you here for as long as we see fit… and don't go making matters worse for yourself…," he advised.

"These people are nasty bastards…" Luis commented the moment the guard was gone. "You don't want to be seen as being cocky…"

"What a stupid situation!" Pedro thought out loud.

"I will be out of here in the next couple of days… If you're still here then, let me know if there's anything I can do for you outside?"

"Thank you Luis…" Pedro stretched his hand for a handshake in appreciation, "Let's hope it won't come to that…," he then changed the subject: "Tell me about the Akazi people… do you know much about them?"

"Their homeland was deep in the jungle west of Rio Branco, close to the border with Peru. There are many stories of lost Inca cities around there, of rich gold mines, and of huge oil and gas reserves near the surface… which pretty much sealed the fate of those poor Indios…!"

"Do you think there's any truth in any of that?" Pedro smiled sceptically.

"I don't know about the Inca cities, but a definite yes for the rest… Of course, the last thing the government wants are rumours of lost Inca cities, so as not to draw the attention of archaeologists, preservation groups and all that always seems to follow that type of people…" He then looked probingly at Pedro before continuing. "I personally feel however that if there is another Machu Picchu to be found somewhere, it is most probably hidden in that area… and the Akazi might even know of it…"

"If that were the case, I'm sure the "Federais" would have made someone *sing*…"

"…They did try hard, but I don't think it brought them any joy…"

On day four of Pedro's *stay* in Pitimbu, he was finally taken to see João Guimarães shortly after lunch.

"Please sit down Pedro… It seems I've got good news for you…" João Guimarães greeted him with the same cordiality of their initial interview. "After analysis of your DNA against the sperm found in the body of the victim, we discovered that you were not quite the last person to have sex with her…" He paused. "Your luck is that feeding our finds into our national criminal DNA databank, we managed to trace a match to someone in our Village. He has since confessed to his crime, in fact only a couple of hours ago… once we confronted him with all the evidence we had gathered, along with a couple of slaps…" Pedro let out an enormous sigh of relief. "I'm sorry we had to put you through this," João added standing up, stretching out his right arm for a handshake.

"Thank God for DNA!!!" Exclaimed Pedro shaking the hand stretched out to him.

"Indeed…" Agreed João with a chuckle, as if looking at a lottery jackpot winner… "When would you like us to take you back?"

"I'd like to say good bye to the guy I shared the cell with first…"

"Luis is harmless when sober, but an alcoholic and a diagnosed schizophrenic… unpredictable and dangerous when seriously drunk…," he commented, "It wouldn't surprise me if one of these days we ended up having to shoot him, so as to protect members of the public…" He paused. "Please be quick."

The crew of the patrol boat were a lot friendlier on the return journey and even shared a few jokes with Pedro, oblivious to how much he was enjoying each and every new breath of fresh air.

"Keep out of trouble… and come to see us next time you're in Pitimbu…" They shouted as they left him on the beach.

Back in his shack, the moment the patrol boat was gone,

Pedro was quick to check his money under the floor boards beneath his bed, when from the corner of his eye, he was startled by two shadows that turned out to be two young Akazi warriors with head feathers.

"Shit! You guys scared the hell out of me…" Admitted Pedro, replacing the safety catch on the pistol he had instinctively grabbed, to then gain his usual friendly stance. "Sam and Tok… What brings you both here?"

With big smiles on their faces, they told Pedro how concerned everyone had been over his absence and that it was Deedee's idea that they should guard the shack from marauding robbers.

"Thank you very much to both of you… I think I ought to go and see everyone in the Camp to thank them too… Will you help me take some dried fish as a gift?"

"Gladly…," offered Sam also on behalf of Tok, happy to oblige.

They got to the camp by twilight and suddenly there was a festive atmosphere, crowned by two big hugs from Deedee and Ara, along with a near-toothless smile from Joojoo. Quito (the tribe's chief) also came out wearing a Brazil football shirt… and while some of the Akazi warriors got ready for a welcome dance, the women gathered like spectators; somehow telepathically sharing a guessing game, as if trying to work out what Deedee (Ara, or both) could possibly be missing?!!

"It is good to see you…" Greeted Quito with a handshake "Another couple of days and your two girls would have us all looking for you…" He chuckled

"It is good to be among friends…," was Pedro's reply.

"I can't wait to hear what happened from you…" Admitted the Indio Chief "You must sit next to me while we eat…"

"With pleasure…"

As the whole tribe sat to watch the warriors perform their traditional act, Deedee's eyes couldn't stop looking at Pedro, like a woman seriously in love and unafraid of showing it to the world, always ready with a smile each time his eyes were on her.

Quito was fascinated by Pedro's account of his *stay* in Pitimbu, which omitted the fate of those Akazi left behind, and found it ironic that one of the drivers should have settled so close to them in the end.

"Would you ever settle back there if you had the chance?" Pedro asked, while sipping some of the tribe's own firewater.

"Personally, without a second thought. But I don't think the tribe would follow me on that one. Some of the men have been learning how to read and write, intent on settling down among the white folk, and most of the others seem fascinated by everything white; from mobile phones and television to the glamour of the big cities and everything in them...," he paused. "What made you ask?"

"Mere curiosity..." He lied, to Quito's amusement.

"I was tortured and beaten by the "Federais" when they took us from our land, trying to get some information out of me concerning the whereabouts of Inca Gold... They even destroyed one of my testicles in the process, but got nothing out of me..."

"Is there really something of significance out there?" Pedro's bluntness caused Quito to hesitate.

"There is...But it is cursed gold that belongs to the Inca dead..."

"Have you actually seen any of it?"

"Not personally no... but my father's father was in XAKATAN... and died there, surrounded by wonderful artefacts of gold, so I was told."

"Is that the lost city Luis hinted at?"

"Well, it's the only one I can think of..." He chuckled.

"I suppose you have never seen it either..."

"I did see it once. My father took me there when I was a little boy. We walked over mountains and passes for nearly a week before we reached it." He then smiled broadly and did his best not to laugh. "To answer your next question; I wouldn't have a clue how to get there…"

"That was a good guess…" Complimented Pedro amused with how obvious he had been! "To be absolutely honest about this, my thoughts were that if it exists, it will only be a matter of time before someone finds it… whereas if we were the ones to find it and profit from it first, the entire tribe could become so wealthy as not to have to play second fiddle to the white man forever…" Pedro also knew of Quito's vulnerable points and how to strike a few right chords.

"And what about the curses that would come with it…? A lot of these stories are not just based on superstition and folklore; you can be sure of that…"

"Well, look at it this way: death is unavoidable for all of us regardless, and the end of life no more than a brief moment in time. Given the choice, wouldn't you rather die rich?"

"I could argue with that, given that we see life as part of a much bigger process, but I can see your point…" He seemed reflective. "It was good of you not to have mentioned your acquaintance with us to Luis. You've given me something to think about over the next few days anyway…and I may have to confer privately with some of the Elders. I'll let you know."

The gender divide was kept as the evening evolved beyond the meal, but Deedee still found ways of sneaking the occasional smile at Pedro, unaware that his vision had started to betray him. The tribe's firewater had a strong after-kick and it was already late into the night when Pedro found himself following *three Quitos*, on his way to a swing bed in the Akazi Chief's hut!!!

**

II

Two days had passed since Pedro's return from Pitimbu and it felt like an autumn day, with large drops of rain quickly exposing the flaws in the shack's roof. The weather forecast predicted a full day of the same and rather than go fishing, Pedro decided to stay in-doors, making plans for a second shack. Deedee had stayed the night and looked at him cosily from inside his bed, completely naked.

"What' you doing?" She asked sleepily, her eyes and voice denoting she wanted more from him. She didn't quite have the experience of Maria Madalena of course but she had the love..., exceeding Pedro's wildest expectations, perhaps thanks to the magazine still hiding under his mattress!

"I was making plans to build a shack for Ara...," he looked at her. "I think that's what the three of us want... isn't it?"

"Do you reckon you could cope with both of us?" She covered her face below her eyes.

"Well, not at the same time... but perhaps on different days? I think that among the Akazi it is customary for men with more than one wife to make a home for each?"

"Yes...," bypassing his question, she kept the lower part of her face covered, and eventually got him to join her under the thin blanket, eager for his lips and the weight of his body.

They were both famished well ahead of lunch and after some barbecued fish, Pedro returned to the Akazi camp with the beaming Deedee, looking for volunteers to help him build the second shack.

Mela was delighted to see her daughter looking so radiant

and approached him the moment she could do so with some privacy;

"You should take Ara with you today…" She almost whispered. "…She spent the night crying her eyes out…"

"It was my intention to take her… are you OK with that?" Pedro replied in the same tone and she just smiled, not quite sure of what to say.

Pedro left for the bay with Ara in the late afternoon, after Quito agreed to provide three strong Akazi warriors to help with the construction effort the following day.

"I was afraid that after spending the night with Deedee you would forget about me…" She admitted as they followed the most direct trail to his place.

"What a silly thing to say!" Pedro censured her with an amused face and she squeezed his arm excitedly as they walked.

Some thirty minutes later they had reached the shack and Ara threw her arms around Pedro the moment they entered… and then kissed him passionately before he could even think!

"Wow Ara… You are quite a kisser…" Complimented Pedro a little disconcerted but definitely aroused from the unexpected experience! She was delighted with his reaction, of course.

"Will you make love to me? I've been waiting for so long…," she didn't have to ask twice and after another of her speciality kisses, Pedro was more than ready to comply… from start to finish in record time! "Was that it?" She asked just as surprised by the speed of the whole thing!

"It won't be as quick next time," promised Pedro, feeling a bit like a rabbit, "It had been building up the whole day… and you made it extra special…"

"I never thought you'd be so romantic…" She teased with a happy smile, pleased with herself.

Pedro spent a night of passion as never before and when

the Akazi warriors arrived in the morning; he could hardly stand upright!!!

*

In the four weeks that followed, while building Ara's shack, Pedro also decided to build one for Deedee, so that the three of them could have their own private space, even if only yards from each other. Pedro's helpers had been steadfast to the task and once the building of the shacks was completed, he rewarded them with the tools they had used (should they ever wish to build their own), as well as a variety of home ware equipment.

"You didn't have to give them anything..." Half heartedly censured Quito in a quiet voice while inspecting the quality of his warrior's workmanship. The whole tribe had come to see the finished job and Joojoo looked busy adding his magic spells and good omens to all three dwellings.

The Akazi were also there to add a more official seal of approval to *the marriage* of Pedro to Deedee and Ara. Everyone had contributed towards the celebration in one way or another; and as the evening wore on, most of the revellers gathered around beach fires to sample a variety of meat and fish barbecues. Some of the younger couples would occasionally escape into the jungle, perhaps inspired by the giant full moon or the theme of the gathering.

As night fell, once the alcohol began to flow, the women were not short of good humoured sexual jokes between themselves!!!

"If Deedee and Ara are not enough, you just let me know yeah?" Sniggered Mela with loving inebriated eyes at Pedro, not too sure what she was talking about, but none-the-less ready for anything going, after a few shots of home-made Cachaça...!

"Exactly" Confirmed the even more *far-gone* granny in her funny voice, smiling at the heavens!

"I think he's got enough trouble as it is Mela…" Quito was near-by and came to Pedro's rescue with a chuckle.

"Thanks Quito…" Pedro whispered, just as drunk, but then felt brave enough under the *protection* of the Akazi Chief to tease Mela back; "I'll keep that in mind…"

"Are you trying to get us both killed?" Joked Quito, taking him away to "safety"!

Although well pickled, Pedro sensed that the Indio Chief had something to tell him from the very beginning of the evening, but somehow couldn't either find the right words or the right moment…

"What have you been hiding in your chest Quito?" He asked candidly, as they strolled away from the others along the shoreline.

"I've been reflecting upon a conversation we had a while back…," he started hesitantly.

"About the XAKATAN thing…?" Pedro asked almost inaudibly!

"Yes…," replied Quito, the sound of his voice displaying that he wasn't as sober as he looked either.

"Fancy us going to look for it?"

"I do… But how would we go about it?"

"Well, first we need to have a better idea as to where this place might be; what can you remember from the time your father took you there?"

"It took us about 6 or 7 days to get there… and this place was about half way up a mountain… we went inside a large cave and emerged onto a lake on the opposite side, enclosed by a circular mountain. Most of the city was built around the lake and smothered by vegetation."

"I don't suppose you would remember if this was going North, South, East or West?"

"I couldn't be sure…"

"Were the Akazi still living in the same Camp where the "Federais" took you from?"

"Yes…" replied Quito. Pedro was quiet for a while, seemingly happy with the information he was getting. "I might of course recognise some things if we were to get anywhere near the place but… Was that useful?"

"Assuming that as a little boy with his father you would not walk more than 10 miles each day through dense jungle say… for 10 days, I need to get satellite images of everything within a 100-mile radius of where your Camp used to be; and look for something that might resemble a lake… perhaps inside the crater of some extinct volcano?" Pedro proposed thoughtfully.

"Whatever technology you might be able to use, take also into account that this was more than 40 years ago… The lake might no longer be there, or the jungle could have smothered it since…"

"We'll have to wait and see…" Pedro felt optimistic that with the circular mountain detail and good satellite photographs, he should be able to pinpoint the place with relative ease.

"…But even if you could establish roughly where this place might be however, we'll still have to find it, get there unseen, locate the gold, carry it out of there… and discover enough people with lots of cash willing to buy the goods from us…!" Quito dumped some of the problems he foresaw on Pedro's head, while they walked a wider circle around the beach fires.

"We will certainly need to think of a few things before making our first move…" Pedro agreed, deep in thought, as if suddenly sobered up by the topic.

"At least we won't be short of manpower…I could always get some of our best warriors to accompany us…," contributed the Chief with restrained enthusiasm.

"Give me a few days to sort some things out and… we'll talk more about this then?"

"OK…" He said with a smile.

Already late into the night, some of the Akazi started leaving in small groups back to their camp, with more than half of them deciding to stay till dawn; consisting mainly of young courting couples and those whose legs couldn't walk them anywhere!!!

Deedee and Ara ended up sleeping together in Pedro's shack, as neither felt sufficiently sober to be by themselves in their new homes, and next morning, they all woke full of regret over the excesses of the night before. Outside, the beach resembled a scene from some atrocity of war (!), with some of the die-hard sleeping in all positions by the spent fires.

Over time, there was a point in the nearby stream where a short waterfall had created a small lagoon, and Pedro headed that way for an invigorating bath with his wives, only to find that some of the young warriors were already practicing some serious dives from a large boulder.

"Oh well…," muttered Deedee. "Let's wait till later when they're gone…?"

"Sounds like a good idea…" Pedro agreed, not wishing to compare himself with the boys. Ara's eyes however seemed to linger over the young naked athletes, to the point of bumping into a palm tree, to Deedee's great amusement! "Would you like us to leave you behind?" Pedro asked, causing his younger wife to rush back to them, rubbing a sore forehead.

"It serves you right…," commented Deedee with one of her giggles.

Pedro spent that night with Ara, to try and quench some of the girl's insatiable sexual fire and then left for Pitimbu in the early morning.

*

Luis's bus stood in splendid isolation in the middle of an empty stretch of beach, kept company by a few cacti the wind had scattered.

"Hey…Look who's here…?" Luis said aloud to himself, stepping down from his ageing bus.

"Hey…" Greeted Pedro with a handshake, pleased to see him looking so remarkably sober.

"Good to see you man… What brings you to town?"

"I need to buy a few things and I thought I'd check on you… how's it going?"

"I'm doing good… I've been working in a local factory for just over a month now and even got myself a new girlfriend…"

"I'm so pleased for you… and the bottle?"

"I've not touched a drop in ages…"

"That's fantastic news. And if it's thanks to your new girlfriend, then she must be quite some woman!"

"Time for a coffee?" Luis offered.

"Go on then…" Pedro accepted. The seats from the rear half of the bus had been removed and piled outside the door, to make space for what seemed like a combined bed-living-room-kitchen + a mobile toilet. "Do you think your bus would still work if you wanted it too?"

"It would cost at least 2 to US$3,000 for it to be roadworthy, without counting on the interior and passenger related comforts…" He paused briefly. "What makes you ask?"

"Do you remember this Akazi tribe you talked to me about? I actually know them…" Luis felt a little perplexed, but only to burst out laughing moments later as it clicked.

"Fuck me!!! Are you planning to use my bus for some expedition?" He couldn't stay serious.

"Well… I don't know… While talking to their Chief about the way you and I met, it turns out that he might know where this *Machu Picchu* of yours is…"

"It sounds exciting, but besides the costs involved beyond making this bus reliable, the moment the "Federais" spot a bus load of Indio tribesmen, we could all be dead meat like those on the side of the road…" He seemed to gain a bit of a glint in his eye however… "But on the other hand, if you think this is a certainty, get my bus to work and give me a share of the loot, I'm definitely your man…"

"And what about your job and your new girlfriend…?"

"I'm sure I could think of something like… I don't know… I could always tell them of some family bereavement perhaps…and that I would need to be away for maybe two or three weeks? Once the bus is ready…? …Just in case I should need to come back here, that is…"

"…And to your girlfriend?"

"I'd probably tell her exactly the same thing and surprise her at the right time."

"You realise this could take a bit longer than that…"

"Of course I do… I just hope it will be worthwhile. I'm not really cut out for factory work Pedro; and for nightshift weeks even less!"

In the course of their conversation, Pedro managed to obtain the geographical coordinates of where the original Akazi Camp used to be, and promised to get in touch again within a week or two.

His next stop was the local Police Station, where João Guimarães offered him another coffee and cordial conversation.

"Where do you think I could get some satellite photos of Amazonia?" Pedro asked after a while.

"What on earth would you need that for?" The Police Chief struggled to stay serious.

"It is part of a research project I'm doing for a friend…"

"Well, if you get in touch with the Brazilian Space Centre at the Alcântara Launch Site, with an explanation of what you're looking for, I'm sure they'll be able to help you… or redirect you…" He informed him, a little intrigued by Pedro's project. "Want to tell me more?"

"There's not much to tell… An old friend of mine is considering buying some land to start a ranch, that's all." He then got up. "Anyway João, good to see you and thanks for the information…"

"You're welcome."

To communicate with the Space Centre, Pedro used an Internet Café and was eventually able to download and print the satellite photos he wanted, a bit annoyed with the cost of the whole thing (!). He then enquired in different shops about the prices of the equipment he would invariably need to buy for the expedition, while getting his normal supplies and fuel for his fishing boat.

*

"You must be tired," Deedee greeted him with a loving kiss and then proceeded to help him to unload the boat.

"…And Ara?"

"She went to the pool for a swim…"

"By herself?"

"No. Some friends came to see us this afternoon…" She looked at him and decided to put his mind at rest, "All female…" She tried not to giggle as she said it. "…Want to stay the night with me?" she covered her mouth and looked into his eyes briefly as they returned to the boat for the next lot of supplies.

"Have been thinking about it the whole day…" He smiled back at her, making her feel wanted.

*

Two days later, to try and keep their thoughts private, Pedro got Quito to visit his shack in the mid-morning, so as to finalise the plans for their venture.

"Everything OK?" Quito seemed in good spirits as he greeted Pedro.

"Good news… I think I may have located this XAKATAN city of yours, according to all that you've told me…" He announced proudly, leading the Indio Chief to the empty floor space full of satellite images in the middle of his shack. And with the help of the lantern and a magnifying glass, Pedro explained the process of elimination he used, to eventually conclude where the Inca city was.

"That's exactly how I expected the aerial view of the area to look…" Quito agreed.

"How many men do you think we should take with us?"

"I reckon we'll need at least 10 or 12, should we find the gold…" Quito had been doing some thinking too "…We also need to be armed, have our own transport… Get some white men's haircuts and clothes should we be stopped by the "Federais" at any stage… plus a range of tools, equipment, food and…"

"I've made a list of the logistics involved…" Interrupted Pedro, deciding to tell Quito about the conversation he had had with Luis, "…And between getting the Bus to look the part and all the other anticipated expenses, I reckon we'll need to raise about US$30,000…"

"I suppose that is the bad news?" Quito had to chuckle.

"Well, I've got a little bit saved, but it won't get us anywhere near that…"

"How much would you be able to chip in?"

"Probably half, at best…"

"We've managed to smuggle some of our own gold with us when the "Federais" placed us in Buses…" He said opening a leather pouch he had brought with him, revealing some of the purest gold Pedro had ever seen.

"That will easily cover the other half of the money we need to raise…" Pedro confirmed, fascinated by some of the items. "Does any of this actually come from XAKATAN?"

"I couldn't tell you for sure… my father left me this bag and the tribe when he died…"

"We may need to melt this gold into small unrecognisable ingots, so as not to give away its exact origin, before raising any cash from it."

"Shall I leave it with you then?" Quito closed the pouch and handed it to Pedro

"How shall we go about the business side of this?" Pedro needed to know.

"Straight forward…," proposed the Indio, stretching out his right hand in readiness for a handshake. "You and I are 50-50 equal partners. With my half I'll deal with the tribe and you with yours will deal with Luis, as well as negotiate with the white men all you need, so as to transform the gold into cash that we can use?"

"Sounds like a good deal for us all." Pedro gave him a strong handshake to put a seal on their agreement and then went on to stress the importance of getting the right haircuts and clothing for those involved as soon as possible, to prepare them for their role, while the bus was being fixed.

"It would be good if we also got the guns early, so we could gain some practice with them?"

"That seems like a good idea too…" Pedro agreed. "I should probably rent a car from someone in Pitimbu and buy all the things we need from different towns and cities, so as not to raise eyebrows?"

"I'm sure you'll find the best way to do it…" Quito wanted no headaches with such details!

*

Pedro was back in Pitimbu the following day looking for Luis.

"Good heavens… If it weren't for the bus I wouldn't have recognised you!" Pedro exclaimed, as he came face to face with the beardless Luis. "I suppose your new sweetheart wanted to know what you looked like!?"

"She promised me a few things if I shaved and I really had no option…"

"You look like someone about to come into a bit of money…"

"I wish…"

"Well, if you have a bit more of that coffee you gave me last time, I might have some good news for you…"

"Sounds good already…," replied Luis, getting on with the coffee. "Have you completed the plans?" He asked, while waiting for the water to boil.

"Yes… based on the idea you gave me, when you mentioned about a death in the family as your excuse to be away for at least two or three weeks…?" He paused, while Luis poured them two perfect cups of coffee. "But first tell me, if we were to raise a budget of US$5,000, would that be enough to fix your bus, keeping the first four rows of seats and transforming the rest as a place where 12 guys could sleep, plus equipment storage, etc?"

"It would be more than ample…" He confirmed. "I can do a bit of welding too."

"I've also researched Government Land Concessions in an area situated some 20 miles from where we think this Inca city is. There are no roads beyond that point." He had a sip of the coffee "…I found out that through the local Government there, you could obtain enough land to build a small Ranch for as little as US$5,000, on condition that you used it for some purpose…"

"I'm with you so far… so, what's the plan?" Luis wondered where this money would come from.

"You are going to receive by post an *inheritance* cheque for US$10,000." He paused again, while Luis tried to reassure himself that he was awake! "You will use US$5,000 to apply for the Land Concession and the other US$5,000 to get your bus fixed to fit our needs…"

"…And what if we find no gold? Will I owe you that money?" He looked worried.

"No. The bus and the Land will be yours to keep,

regardless… As a down payment on at least 10 times that coming to you, if it all goes well by the time we're finished…"

"Tell me more…" He urged Pedro to continue, looking like he would dearly enjoy a shot of something strong.

"I will get the Akazi chief and some of his strongest warriors to look like ordinary labourers first, with proper haircut and clothes… In fact, I'll be buying them some clothes and a hair cutting machine today, while I'm in town…" Luis looked stoned from listening to Pedro! "Anyway, the idea is that we will all pose as labourers going to work on your land, in your bus. We will start by building one of two houses before focusing on the land proper…" Luis was about to interrupt when Pedro replied to the question he never asked; "…The houses will be yours to keep too, in the worst-case scenario…" Pedro couldn't help a chuckle before continuing "In the best-case scenario on the other hand, I shall of course discount the bus, the Land and the houses from your share. What do you think?"

"Let's do it…" Luis was clearly super excited. "Anything else?"

"Yes…" Pedro looked at him intently "Not a single drop of alcohol and not a single word on this to anyone, at least until we're finished with it all."

"You can count on me Pedro. This is the best opportunity I ever had to have a life worth having."

"Keep that in mind at all times…" He paused. "…And what of your girlfriend?"

"I'll come back for her once the dust has settled… how soon do you want me to get the mechanics to deal with the bus?"

"As soon as possible. The US$10,000 cheque will be with you in the next couple of days."

"I'll be dealing with it today…" Luis was yet to be back to himself. "Aren't you concerned that I could run away with the money?"

"The US$10,000?" Luis chuckled as he nodded. "Not in

the slightest. I'd just keep your share as well as mine…" The two of them ended up having a good laugh.

*

The short haircuts of the Akazi warriors chosen for the mission soon became a bit like a stupid face contest, with granny actually peeing herself for laughing when she saw the face of her nephew after his haircut!!! And everyone struggled to keep a straight face when Quito emerged from his haircut, the remainder of his face hiding behind his nose…! Dressing up was another pantomime, testing the chosen warriors' restraint to the limit, while taking it on the chin.

To Pedro's delight, Quito's gold had fetched almost US$25,000, and a week later all of those selected had their guns and ammunition too. At this point the bay then became a *shooting gallery*, with the small *Akazi army* looking like a firing squad facing the water, aiming at floating plastic bottles.

"…And what if the "Federais" stop us to demand our travel papers?" Quito asked in between shots, as Pedro walked back and forth correcting the posture of each *sniper*.

"We will tell them who you are and where we live and that Luis became a friend of the tribe after your relocation… and that now at his request, as he is about to get married, we all decided to help him build his new home."

"That sounds OK I suppose…," he replied thoughtfully

"It is not as if we are doing anything illegal… is it?"

"Not until we'll find the gold anyway…," he agreed.

"And even then, if you think about it, your ancestors were probably the rightful owners of that land long before Brazil ever existed…"

"That is probably also true…"

"The main thing if we are stopped, is to relax and to avoid eye to eye contact… and to let me do the talking?"

"I'll let you worry about it…" The Chief gave up.

While waiting for the Land Concession papers to arrive

and for the bus to be made ready, Pedro kept thinking of ways to combat every possible situation, and ended up purchasing a few more hand guns, silencers and telescopic lenses.

It took another month of waiting before they could set off on their adventure, by which time all of the chosen warriors had learned how to shut the correct eye when aiming! And wearing trousers and shirts was now also beginning to look a bit more natural to them.

Not surprisingly, Deedee and Ara were both pregnant. They would be moving back to the Camp while Pedro was away and seemed increasingly tearful as departure day approached. Luis was immensely proud of his refurbished bus and did endless practice runs to help update his driving skills. As for João Guimarães, he could smell something fishy but kept his thoughts to himself.

**

III

Departure day came and with the tribe looking like they were in mourning, Pedro, Quito and the 12 chosen warriors couldn't be out of there fast enough! Luis's bus had been fully loaded and would pick them up by mid morning, somewhere along the main Highway, about 10 miles further inland from the Akazi Camp.

"I've got the feeling we forgot something…" Quito mumbled to Pedro as they approached the Highway, after a three hour walk through crocodile infested swamps, under sun's rays that resembled fiery arrows.

"If we did, let's hope it is something we can buy on the way…," replied Pedro, sweating profusely.

"There he is…" Eventually shouted one of the Indios, the moment he spotted Luis's bus at the arranged rendezvous point, producing broad smiles on all the faces, as if there had been instances of collective doubt!

Going through a mental check-list, what concerned Pedro the most at this stage was if there were any documents missing, should there be random police checks along the way. And once everyone was on board, he gathered all the documents inside a plastic wallet down to Luis's Driving licence, which he then gave to Quito for safe keeping.

Everybody was impressed with the bus and while sorting themselves out inside the vehicle, Luis revealed that he now also had a P.A. system, with a good quality radio and CD player… and it was like party time when they drove off, the moment the sounds of Bossa-Nova came over the loud speakers. This triggered a general Batucada from the "crew" and the occasional chorus.

The Akazi warriors were split into two teams of 6, each with their own leader. They had been trained like commandos and besides knowing how to use their weapons effectively, in addition to their knowledge of jungle life, they could also cook and knew first aid. Luis was responsible for everything to do with the bus and had some knowledge of mechanics, while Quito retained his role as Akazi Chief, as well as being the expedition's Bursar. As for Pedro, he was the overall leader, negotiator and spokesperson.

There were over 3,000 miles of road ahead of them and Luis felt they would probably reach their destination within a week, without pushing it too hard. He had everything well planned down to where to refuel and best overnight stops en route, which basically consisted of a near-straight line going west.

They reached the town of Picos already well after dark, at the end of their first day. Luis parked his bus in the middle of nowhere on the outskirts of town and after eating their food rations, the warriors and the driver had no problem falling asleep.

"You are not tired?" Pedro whispered to Quito, among a cacophony of sleeping sounds.

"I think at least one of us needs to stay awake, in case we receive some unwelcome visitors, don't you think…?"

"I agree… Shall I do the first watch?" Proposed Pedro.

"Ok… and we could alternate each night?"

"Sounds good…"

On the second day, the musical chorus was less lively. The most anticipated moments of the day were lunch and the two Pee & Poo stops by the roadside! …Until they finally came to an overnight stop on the shores of the Araguaia River, by Marabá City. This was probably the longest of the journeys to their destination and everyone welcomed the late departure the following morning, after stocking up on fuel and food.

Itaituba was their day three overnight stop, followed by Porto Velho on day four and Rio Branco on day five; it being the last main city before their destination. Capital city of the Brazilian state of Acre, Rio Branco was a main business centre and particularly popular with Bolivians wanting to keep something away from the hands of their taxman.

Beyond Rio Branco, the terrain and the roads would gradually get tougher as they'd near Luis's future Fazenda (Ranch). The final two days on the road were going to be hardest, with no shortage of *bent* "Federais" and gangs of outlaws along the way. To ensure that they'd all feel rested and alert, Pedro decided everyone could have a free day in Town, providing they stayed together and drank no alcohol.

"…And what if we happen to kill someone trying to defend ourselves?" It occurred to Quito, while walking around town with Pedro and Luis, some twenty paces behind the others.

"We'll bury them as soon as possible." Pedro replied calmly, causing Luis to burst into laughter.

"Including "Federais" …" Luis added, producing an itch on the back of Quito's head.

"Let's hope it won't come to that of course…" Pedro smiled at Quito, trying to reassure him that he wasn't a trigger-happy person, "But if faced with a choice between them and us, we mustn't hesitate."

On day seven, before hitting the road proper, Luis tried to get some updates on the situation ahead from the people in the filling station, and wore a worried frown as he returned to the bus.

"News?" Enquired Pedro sitting behind him, sensing a problem.

"Apparently where we are heading, some "Bandoleiros" robbed and killed everybody in a four-vehicle convoy… a couple of days ago." Luis revealed, turning the ignition on.

"That means that it is probably a lot safer just now...," commented Quito reflectively.

"I agree," concurred Pedro, "but this also means that the road must be full of "Federais" ... and with 15 well armed guys inside the same bus, they could be forgiven for asking us a few embarrassing questions!!!"

"Shouldn't we perhaps wait a few days in case they find the "Bandidos"?"

"No." Decided Pedro. "We've done nothing wrong and we can't live life hiding like mice..."

Six hours later, although still over a hundred miles from the Andes, the air started to thin and the heat of the day seemed to contrast with a cool breeze, turning cold at times. Behind their bus, a convoy of some 12 vehicles had formed and they all seemed quite happy to stay there, no doubt looking for safety in numbers.

"I feel like mother goose..." Luis was amused by this. Later in the day, they encountered two road blocks of "Federais" but in each case, realising they were probably a safety-in-numbers-convoy, they were simply waved on.

"The spirits of our forefathers have probably recognised us..." Said Quito, realising he was also breathing the same air that had once been his. He was not the only one to feel this and although no words had been exchanged, there were some watery eyes from the more senior warriors among them.

By nightfall they had reached the small town of Mâncio Lima. The main road ended there and this was also where they decided to stay the night. From there on they'd be travelling on dust roads to get to Luis's place.

The small town was as lively as a village cemetery in midweek and there was no shortage of shady looking characters eyeing the bus and its occupants. Like the Akazi they were typical Inca descendants and for the best part, probably Peruvian Indios on the run.

"Do you know how to get to your place from here?" Pedro asked Luis.

"It should take us no longer than 3 hours' tomorrow morning, going northwest, assuming the road is good enough for the bus?" He paused. "I'm hesitant whether to ask for information regarding the road in that Café… What would you say?"

"Might as well…" Pedro agreed. "The whole village will know where we are sooner or later anyway… just be wary of anyone proposing short cuts or alternative directions…"

"I'm familiar with the drill…" Luis smiled, almost offended by the advice.

It was going to be Quito's turn to keep first watch, but as everyone settled for the night, looking at some prowlers lurking about outside, Pedro had a weird feeling.

"Do you think these people could be about to try something?" Quito enquired quietly of Pedro.

"I'd be surprised if they tried anything right in their backyard… it is more likely that they might want to suss out if we are armed and if so, how well armed we might be, for future reference…" Pedro took a pause. "But we never know… I'll keep you company…" Quito seemed happy with that.

Around midnight, a boy no older than 14 with three others half his age knocked on the door of the bus;

"What do you want?" Asked Pedro

"There are some people around here that like to slash tyres…" He started. "If you'll give me and my friends a US$1 each, we'll keep an all-night watch…"

"That's very kind of you…," replied Pedro opening the door of the Bus, casually holding his pistol. "There you go…" He said giving the boys 2 US$1s. "Now, if you see someone trying to do something stupid like that, you must let me know so I can deal with them yeah? …and you'll get the other 2 US$1s in the morning. Have we got a deal?"

"Yes sir…" The boys seemed happy with that and Quito chuckled to himself once the bus door closed.

"Certainly a lot cheaper than a big bus tyre…," he commented.

"Indeed…" Pedro agreed.

*

The rest of the night passed without incident and Pedro honoured his agreement with the boys at first light, while the whole party had coffee inside the bus.

"What's your name then?" Pedro asked the older boy, giving him the remaining US$2.

"My name is Nene sir. This is my brother Silvio and those are his friends Raul and Xuxu." He introduced them. "My mother also washes and irons clothes, if you ever need that sort of service…"

"That's good to know Nene… thank you. We'll be seeing you again sometime…"

"Thank you sir."

Back on the road, the first few miles were above expectations, but this soon changed and about 25 miles into the final leg of their journey the bus got stuck in a road ditch caused by a heavy downpour. Everyone got off to lift the rear of the vehicle while Luis did his best at the wheel but to no avail, almost burning two tyres in the process.

"This is so fucking stupid!" He seemed furious with his bus!!!

"How far do you reckon we are from the place?" asked Pedro.

"About 20 miles from here at the most…" He replied seriously frustrated, his words suddenly muffled by the sound of fast approaching 4X4 engines being pushed to the limit.

"Everyone inside the bus quick…" Shouted Pedro to those still at the back of the bus, "…and keep your guns at the ready.

This could be the same people that caused that massacre the other day..." He warned, hurrying them up.

The four Range Rovers stopped alongside the bus, each with a couple of riflemen, but to Pedro they appeared more like rich "Rancheros" than outlaws.

"You look like you are in trouble amigo...," noticed a chubby man in his early sixties with an immaculate white Stetson, stepping down from his vehicle. "My name is George Azevedo and I own most of the land around here..." He tried his best not to sound arrogant as he shook Pedro's hand! "What brings you here?" He wasn't too sure whether to address Pedro or Luis.

"Our friend Luis Ramos bought a small land concession some 20 miles further on... and we've come to help him build his house and get his land a bit under control." Pedro explained, pointing to Luis.

"Well, then let me be the first to welcome you to our neighbourhood..." George stretched out his ring covered right hand to Luis. "My domain stretches from Mâncio Lima and continues for a further 15 miles, on both sides of this road." The man informed.

"Are we trespassing?" Luis tried to look momentarily preoccupied.

"No, no, the road is property of the State; you just have to look at it!!!" He chuckled and then got his men to produce some ropes to help pull the bus out of the ditch. "I presume you'd like some help to get your bus out of there?" He wanted confirmation.

"Yes please, I'd be really grateful" Luis accepted.

"Are we likely to get stuck in other ditches like this further on?" Asked Pedro

"This is the worst one... at the moment...," confirmed George "but each time it rains it tends to alter the consistency and design of the road in different places... So, you might find ditches appearing and disappearing from time to time… you need a 4X4 in this part of the country or you are stuck!"

It took less than 10 minutes to get the bus back on the road and soon after that, the Range Rovers were gone as fast as they'd arrived.

"What could someone possibly do with so much land??" Luis thought out loud, while driving a lot more carefully...

"Cocaine, marijuana, start your own country…," suggested Pedro, to Quito's amusement.

Five miles on, the road suddenly seemed like an A class road for a couple of miles, until it reached a monumental gate on the westside, where a private road bordered by palm trees stretched for at least a mile, leading to a majestic colonial mansion.

"That is what I call wealthy…" Pedro let escape, watching a small plane landing on a strip not too far from the mansion.

"Let's hope he did not surprise his wife with the butler… or some zealous security guard!!!" Luis made everybody laugh.

Two miles further on they were back onto the dirt road again, eventually reaching a coded sign delimiting Luis's property on the south side. Luis found a spot to park the bus away from the road and everyone got out to investigate.

Luis's land seemed a lot bigger than expected somehow, a mile of road front by 2 miles in depth. The place stood in the middle of a plain, and was densely wooded at its remotest half, with a distant view of the Andes beyond the treetops. There was some sort of natural road leading into the more densely forested part of the domain and Luis was quick to take his bus there, well out of sight of anyone using the main road.

The plan from this point on was for the entire team to work on the construction of the first house, to be built somewhere at the deepest end of the property. They would all have a proper place to sleep then, and to eventually follow that up with some fencing and land clearing, before proceeding to build the second house. Only one of the two 6 warrior units would go with Pedro and Quito into the jungle, once the first house was built, while the second unit would stay behind with Luis, working on the property.

"So what do you think?" asked Pedro, when Luis got off the bus in its new spot.

"I never thought I'd like it so much…," he admitted. "It feels like… it's mine…"

"It is yours!!!" Confirmed Pedro with a chuckle

Although half of the property was free of tall trees and well under the light of day, they were at one of the deepest ends of the Amazonian jungle. There was no shortage of wood, and while one of the Akazi warrior units got on with downing half a dozen trees for timber, the others went on to create a clearing where the foundations of the planned two storey house would be dug.

The building process had been well rehearsed before departure and within a fortnight of downing the first tree, they had completed the first house, minus glass windows.

"That was excellent work guys…" Pedro complimented the entire team, while Luis seemed to be daydreaming about the day the whole property would look like the way Pedro had planned it on paper. And to mark the completion of the house, they celebrated by roasting a wild boar one of the warriors had hunted a couple of days earlier.

The Akazi warriors selected to accompany Pedro and Quito on the expedition proper the following day were like a Commando group on the eve of an assault (!); and no sooner had they finished their meal, they got on with their final equipment double checks, from water to bullets and off to sleep. They were the more senior warriors and were clearly built for heavy duty. They all had wives and children back at the Camp and none wanted to delay their return any more than need be. The leader of the unit was Taco and the other five were Zamzam, Toto, Tamko, Zezinho and Cachimbo.

From all that Quito had told him, Pedro had set himself the challenge of somehow finding the trail Quito and his father might have followed some 40 years earlier, in the hope that this could perhaps stimulate the memory of the Akazi Chief at some point.

*

Luis had prepared coffee for everyone by the crack of dawn and the expedition left in a north-westerly direction as the sun rose above the Andes.

The first day trekking was easy peasy and although Pedro reckoned only 10 miles stood between them and the access cave, it would probably take the best part of a week to negotiate the terrain that awaited them, according to the Satellite pictures he had surveyed.

Quito and Taco in particular were very much in their element and with their senses on high alert; they both agreed that something wasn't quite right on day two of the trek.

"Do you think we're being followed?" Pedro whispered in Quito's ear, as Taco's hand was raised for them all to freeze. Quito's face however denoted they weren't too sure.

Using only his right hand, Taco indicated to Zezinho and Cachimbo that they should separately precede the party by half a mile, and to Toto and Tamko that they should fall behind by about the same distance; leaving Pedro, Quito, Taco and Zamzam to continue in silence, whilst allowing time for the other four to follow Taco's orders with stealth.

By early evening, they were moving along one of two parallel mountains, following what appeared to be an ancient trail, with a sharp fall of over a thousand feet down to a meandering river with rapids below. The three Akazi with Pedro would sometimes stop to examine odd markings along the trail, or simply to listen out for anything unusual.

They didn't light a fire that evening and as they got back

on the trail the next morning, it seemed to lead down to the bottom of the gorge.

"I'm looking forward to a river wash I must admit..." Pedro confessed while they continued their descent.

"You are not the only one..." Quito agreed.

Then in the early afternoon, a brief reflection from the mountain opposite seemed to hit the corner of Pedro's eye;

"Did you see something flashing?" He asked Quito, walking a couple of steps ahead of him, and everyone stopped. With his binoculars, Pedro scoured the side of the mountain in the general direction of where he thought the flash had come, but nothing seemed to move, and after a while they decided to continue on, eventually reaching the water by the twilight of day.

"Do you reckon the others are OK?" Pedro asked Taco, as the four sat around a small fire on the river bank, deciding to give up on the game of hide and seek.

"I'd expect so, otherwise we'd have heard a shot or they'd have come to us..." He didn't seem too worried about that. "They know how to move unseen around the jungle..."

"Would you say that we are probably being stalked by other Indios then?"

"If we're being followed, that's more than likely; we'd have spotted any white men by now!"

"Did you use to share this area with any other Indio tribes?" Pedro wanted to know.

"No. On some rare occasions we've had raids from other Peruvian Indio tribes though." confirmed Quito.

"If these are Peruvian Indios, they could well be on the run from their own "Federais"" Ventured Zamzam.

"What we need to know, assuming we are being followed is: what do they want from us?" Quito dropped the question.

"They could obviously assume that we are after

something… and are probably trying to find out what that something could be?" Taco speculated thoughtfully.

Their debate continued for a while into the night, until they finally agreed that the best way of finding out once and for all if they were being stalked or not, was to lay a trap. And in the morning, after bathing in the waters of the icy cold river, they moved out pretending to forget a small bag behind. Zamzam would then fall back into a well camouflaged vantage point from where he'd have a good view of the bag, while the other three would continue on.

*

Toto and Tamko found themselves hiding from a group of some forty or fifty Indios on the trail of Pedro and the others, within half hour of falling behind the rest of the party.

"Shit…" Toto whispered to Tamko as the last Indio passed them.

Neither of the Akazi warriors recognised the tribe those Indios belonged to, but were glad to notice the weapons they carried were knives, spears, bows and arrows.

"Why do you think they are following us?" Tamko whispered back.

"No idea… but I feel we need to be extra careful from here on… They'll soon realise that instead of following 8 people they'll be following only 4 + 2… and that will ring alarm bells in their heads…"

Toto and Tamko continued to follow the group of Indios from a good distance behind and they both eventually agreed that there were 47 of them in total.

"What will we do if they find us?" Toto didn't seem too clear on that.

"If they appear to want to harm us, we'll shoot as many as we can…," concluded Tamko, screwing the silencer on the short barrel of his handgun, prompting Toto to do the same.

Every so often, the two warriors would count the number

of Indios they could see, to make sure they wouldn't be surprised by some of them falling back to look for those missing in Pedro's party, until;

"I only count 42…" Whispered Toto at one point as evening approached "And you?"

"43…"

"Fuck…"

Neither of the two warriors moved from where they were until day break and once the Indios lifted camp, they waited over an hour before taking a much higher and probably longer trail, silently running through the jungle, in an attempt to eventually overtake the Indios and rejoin Pedro's Party.

*

By late morning, Zamzam was cursing the vantage point he had chosen from which to watch the bag, sweating profusely under the midday sun! Little did he know that while watching the bag, other eyes were watching him, and after recuperating the bag, 3 hours later, he spent the rest of the day trying to catch up with Pedro, Quito and Taco.

"Any joy?" Pedro asked Zamzam when he caught them up.

"Nothing moved…," he alleged.

"That's weird…," noted Taco "…Toto and Tamko should have caught up with you…"

"Now that you've mentioned it… That's really weird…" Quito agreed.

"Are you ok to go ahead and catch up with Zezinho and Cachimbo?" Asked Taco looking at the Warrior, checking how tired the man was.

"No problem… and for the three of us to then wait there for you?" He wanted to be sure.

"Yes." Confirmed Taco, giving Zamzam the immediate go-ahead.

"And what about Toto and Tamko?" Enquired Pedro.

"We'll all wait for them once we get to where Zezinho and Cachimbo are." Replied Taco.

Pedro, Quito and Taco caught up with the others by nightfall, and were eventually joined by the missing two well into the night.

"Where the hell have you both been?" Taco seemed annoyed, but the other two were quick to explain themselves. "Are you telling me they could perhaps be all around us by now?"

"It wouldn't surprise us...," confirmed Tamko for both of them.

"What do we do?" Quito confronted Pedro with the question. "There's no point in leading those Indios to the lost city is there?"

"You're right...," Pedro agreed. "It would be good if we could find out what it is that they want from us..."

Dawn arrived before they knew it and Pedro's frustration was clear for all to see, especially since according to his calculations but unknown to the others, they were practically where he expected the access cave to be!

Then to everyone's surprise, on a sandy stretch of the river bank, Pedro stood away from the others and holding his rifle shouted from the top of his voice;

"**HEY**... HEY... Hey...," echoed his call, followed by two loud shots piercing the virgin air.

There was no reply and after a couple of minutes, he repeated the invite. This time around however, an Indio wearing three or four colourful feathers emerged from behind a boulder, on the same side of the river, not too far from where Pedro and the Akazi stood.

"**HEY**... HEY... Hey..." The Indio shouted back, unafraid, followed by an arrow landing near Pedro's feet.

"**Why are you following us?**" Pedro shouted, un-intimidated by the arrow. **"Are you afraid to talk?"** There was no immediate reply but instead, other Indios started to show themselves... and they were considerably more than 47, appearing from both sides of the river and up the two parallel mountains! "Good heavens!!!" Pedro let escape.

The first Indio that stood up then decided to approach Pedro and eventually spoke, but in a language he couldn't understand.

"Do you have a clue as to what this guy's talking about?" Pedro looked to Quito for help and to his surprise the Akazi Chief started talking to the other one in the same language! The two Indios spoke for a few minutes, somehow easing the initial tension. "What's happening?"

"He is saying that we need to surrender our weapons...," Quito translated.

"Why?"

"These people are the actual inhabitants of the City we came looking for...," Quito revealed "And that's the only way we are going to see it..."

"You are kidding me, right?" Pedro almost felt like laughing.

"No... It is apparently for our own protection that we need to surrender our weapons..." He explained, "...Something to do with a defensive system in operation..." Quito tried to look calm and Pedro was doing his best to put two and two together, with little success.

"Are they aware of the world outside this area?" Pedro wanted Quito to put the question to the Indio.

"We are..." The Indio replied to Pedro directly in Portuguese, while a number of other Indios approached them, readily taking their weapons away before anyone could react.

**

IV

"Can you understand any of this?" Pedro whispered quietly to Quito as they followed their Indio captors along a shallow part of the river bed. He looked at the Akazi Chief, "I'm really confused… What did you guys talk about for all that time?" Pedro felt he was being kept in the dark.

"You'll probably find it a little too crazy…" Quito warned him.

"It couldn't get much worse… unless they are planning to offer us to the Gods!?"

"Well… Becchiu, that's the name of the chieftain I was speaking with, he told me that the only reason that we were able to see them is because they wanted us to… and the same about their City."

"Meaning?"

"Meaning that they have the power to make themselves invisible to us… and are able to observe us from a different dimension…"

"Come off it Quito! Can you believe that?" Pedro tried to stay serious.

"The explanation he gave me for having showed up was that there is some sort of protective "*force*", or mechanism, that prevents people from our dimension detecting their City." Quito did his best not to laugh at Pedro's face. "That same "*force*" however, apparently recognised that one person in our party, in this case me, had once laid eyes on the City, and thus automatically assumed that one of us was in fact one of them trying to get back in…?"

"That's crazy alright…" Pedro agreed with an atheist's

52

chuckle. "But if I remember correctly… didn't you tell me that when you saw the City, it looked abandoned?"

"That's my recollection from the glimpse I got of it as a boy…" Quito suddenly seemed tired of Pedro's questions. "They are taking us there now anyway, so you'll soon see it for yourself…"

"What do you think are our chances of getting out of here?" He still had this one question.

"I'd rather not think about it…"

Immediately ahead, the river then seemed to vanish under the mountain, as they continued to walk towards it over shallow water. The closer they got to where the river disappeared however, the blurrier their field of vision… as if they were looking ahead through some intense wall of heat… until the cave was suddenly revealed, like a dark abandoned railway tunnel, leading to a different brightness at the far end!

"Does this seem familiar?" Pedro whispered to Quito as they were about to enter the cave.

"It does…" He confirmed "It won't be so dark once we're inside the mountain" They were still walking through shallow water and Pedro reckoned this to be a stream, rather than the river they'd been following earlier. Then, as Quito had anticipated, there was clear visibility inside the passage, as they continued to follow Becchiu towards the light of day at the far end.

Pedro was not one for fairy tales, even as a child, and the more he reflected upon their situation, the greater his conviction that those Indios definitely needed them for a purpose, rather than the excuse given to Quito.

"Any guesses as to what they might need us for?" Pedro continued to question the Akazi Chief.

"Not a sausage…" The Akazi Chief replied. "And what's worse, I don't think we'll be getting out of here with a ton of Inca gold either…"

"Well, I've already figured that one out…! What language were you guys speaking in?"

"It's a local native dialect that apparently evolved from the original Inca language… I know that you're sceptical, but I'm confident that these people are the real thing…"

"…As in proper, unadulterated Incas?"

"Yes," replied Quito. "The real McCoy, as you'd say." He further clarified!

"Look…" Interrupted Taco, pointing at the workmanship on the ceiling of the Cave as they neared open skies.

"Any museum would definitely be proud to have a piece of that…" Pedro was impressed.

"Wow…" Zamzam breathed as they emerged into a colourful bustling city of thousands of people, encircling a lake of clear waters, about a mile or more across. For a brief moment they all stood in awe looking at the lakeside buildings, at the livelihood of the place and at the things people wore as they went about their business… Pedro distractedly even wondered if they might have accidentally stumbled into some film set!!!

There were numerous floating islets where different types of crops and vegetables grew; and in between, one man vessels resembling gondolas moved from A to B loaded with merchandise, pulled by standing *gondoliers*.

A curious crowd of onlookers soon gathered around the "visitors" and Becchiu seemed to grow in stature as he proudly led the newcomers into a stone plaza delineated by four large pyramids, one in each corner, linked by four smaller ones, defining the 4 sides of the square.

Everything was made of precisely cut stone and calculated to fit into deliberate irregular shapes. Then, about half way up the far corner pyramid, a feathered Ruler (or King) sat on a throne, flanked by an entourage of advisors and masked attendants.

"You must not address our King or look at Him directly," advised Becchiu, briefly turning to Pedro and the Akazi as they walked along an avenue of people. "You will only talk to Him through me and when prompted… Understood?" Pedro nodded in compliance, as did the others.

The procession then became smaller and suddenly it was just Becchiu and Pedro's party walking towards the Inca Leader. Pedro experienced a flashback of a film he had once seen, making him wonder if he was about to be escorted to the top of the pyramid to have his pulsating heart torn out, to a roar of delight from the crowds below…! But instead, once they reached the base of the Pyramid, they were asked to kneel and to remain that way until otherwise told, with heads turned to where the Royal party stood.

Becchiu then proceeded by addressing his king for a short minute, undoubtedly updating Him on the sequence of events, to which the monarch replied with a single phrase.

"Our King wants to know what caused you to come this way…" Becchiu addressed Pedro.

"Gold" replied Pedro "We thought there was an abandoned City full of treasure somewhere around here…" Becchiu passed on Pedro's reply before receiving a second question from his King.

"Had you found the gold you seek, what would you have done with the wealth it would have brought you?"

Pedro explained the plight of the Akazi and how the gold would improve their social condition, in a White-world filled with bias and prejudice… somehow prompting Becchiu to further comment on behalf of the king;

"But you are a white man…"

"My two wives are Akazi…," he answered.

The King seemed pleased with the replies and once the

Royal Party disappeared somewhere inside their pyramid, Becchiu entreated everyone to stand up and follow him.

Pedro and Quito were soon separated from the Akazi warrior unit and escorted to a palatial building with an indoor bathing pool, where some beautiful young women awaited to give them the wash of their lives... as well as anything else they could desire.

"We definitely made a positive first impression on their King...," ventured Pedro to Quito as an aside, the moment four girls, two to each, came for them.

"If you don't tell my wives, I won't tell yours...," proposed Quito with a chuckle, as he was led into a cubicle.

"Sounds like a good deal to me..." Pedro agreed, chuckling as he entered his own cubicle.

*

"I've never been this clean in my entire life!" Quito commented as he eventually emerged from the cubicle, where two young girls made sure the experience would last him the rest of his natural life!

"Likewise..." Pedro looked just as pleased with it all, but unwilling to share in the details...

They were then dressed in simple clean clothes and given a small drink of something that made them pleasantly stoned, just as Becchiu returned.

"Are you both enjoying your stay so far?" The Inca chieftain wanted to know.

"Very much so..."

"Couldn't fault it." Quito added, and then proceeded to ask about the others in their party.

"We are also looking after them, but as we understand it they are of a lower rank to you..." He explained and then continued. "You are both invited to share King Ayar's dinner table tonight."

"We feel greatly honoured…" Pedro was quick to acknowledge. "Will you be there?"

"Of course…" Becchiu seemed a little surprised by the question.

It was still daylight and to help pass the time until dinner, Becchiu offered to give them a mini tour of the city, which they gladly accepted.

Although most buildings were predominantly made of a dark grey stone, as were the walkways and even the lake's edges above the waterline, the colourfulness of just about everything else more than made up for the monotonous grey background. There were no signs of poverty and except for labourers and menial workers seemingly on duty; most passersby were keen to display their wealth and gold to one another.

Becchiu would now and then give them a running commentary explaining what some of the buildings were for, a little about the most important things in people's lives and how it all worked. People paid no taxes, except in times of war in yesteryears. Instead, they worked for the State (or the King) for free, for two lunar cycles each Solar year, and the State provided them with all their basic needs in return; leaving those who wished, free to pursue greater individual wealth accumulation.

"We are extremely impressed with everything… but…" Pedro also spoke on behalf of Quito "…How do you achieve this switch between dimensions?" This was what puzzled him the most! "Do you have geographical… or mobile gateways?"

"Yes and no." Becchiu reflected for a few moments to try and find a simple way to explain it. "Well, let me first talk about the things that are the same and common to your dimension and ours:" He paused, "…and they are the time of day, the moon cycles and astral positions including all heavenly events…," he looked at both, to see if they followed. "There are countless dimensions by the way… not just two…

And in some cases they are so different as to be completely unrelated to the same geography or millennium, within the same space... but I don't want to confuse you."

"I'm with you so far..." Pedro confirmed and Quito nodded.

"As for the rest, I'm going to tell you a story to help you understand...," he paused. "Long before the Portuguese and the Spanish came in search of gold, people from the heavens came to Earth for exactly the same thing: Gold! Not because of its colour or value as jewellery, but because of its conductivity when it comes to electronics, as you name it now." He paused once again to look at them. "Well, through the ages and still today, although very much by stealth, "they" continue to come for tons of the stuff. In fact, the Earth has so much of it, that we could cover the entire planet to the height of a man's chest! ...According to our *heavenly friends*, anyway."

"Now wait a minute;" Pedro tried to cut short where this was going. "Are you about to tell us that for *their* protection and yours they've created some sort of device to allow for your people and your city to remain outside our "reality-zone", so that *they* too could continue to come and go undetected by current day science?"

"I suppose it all comes down to that, really... Although not quite as simple and straight forward as you've painted it..." The Inca Chieftain was a little taken aback by Pedro's quick analysis.

"So... how frequently do these *heavenly friends* of yours visit you?" Quito realised that keeping an open mind about the whole thing was perhaps the best option available to them for the time being.

"Once every five years or so, depending on their needs."

"You've actually met these Aliens?" Quito had to stop to look Becchiu in the eye.

"We all have...," Becchiu laughed. "In fact King Ayar...," he started, but left his phrase in mid sentence.

"Are you Ok to talk about these things with us?" Pedro wanted to know.

"Of course I am. Anyway, going back to the two dimensions we can commute between, a lot of it is down to keeping your mind in tune with the *facilitator device* that enables us to go back and forth almost at will..." Becchiu somehow seemed less at ease after hinting at the origins of his King, but glad for having reached the Ruler's Palace in the nick of time.

Ayar's Palace was built on a gentle slope rising from the lake and about five floors high, with an imposing view over the City from its top floor. Becchiu led Pedro and Quito up a wide stairway to the fifth floor, with guards on both sides every four steps, and onto a huge veranda, half of which stood under a suspended ceiling. There, a U-shaped table had been laid for nine and an open fire added a touch of cosiness to the setting. Three of Ayar's courtiers already sat in line, filling the space on the right-hand side of the U shape, and Becchiu sat opposite them, with Pedro to his right and Quito to his left, leaving the central part of the U for when Ayar and His two wives arrived.

There were no introductions or words exchanged between the six and everyone remained silent, waiting for the last three to arrive. The Courtiers were all male, middle aged, and wore colourful clothing lined with silver thread, which somehow produced a perfect blend against the tone of their golden skin and greying hair. Contrasting with the individuality of their styles however, the three wore identical necklaces, combining onyx and lapis lazuli predominately.

One of the guards then signalled for everyone to stand and Ayar entered the veranda, closely followed by His two wives.

The Inca Ruler looked no older than 30 years of age and was a fine specimen of a man, well built and about 6ft. tall, His long black hair was twisted into three braids and interlaced with leather straps. The only things He wore, besides an identical necklace to those the three courtiers had, were a short golden tunic covering His genitalia and matching sandals, as if he was ready for bed! His wives on the other hand were well covered, very pretty, and could pass for being twin sisters!

There was a natural power and self confidence about Ayar and as they all sat, Pedro felt a little shaken by their first eye contact. It was like having had his soul X-Rayed, with everything changing the next second, as the Inca Ruler adopted an unpretentious-friendly stance;

"I hope to have made you feel welcome in our City…" He addressed Pedro and Quito directly and in Portuguese.

"Very much so…" Pedro wasn't too sure whether to reply directly to Him or via Becchiu.

"Let's leave the protocols behind and talk as friends would?" Ayar's words reinforced by a cordial smile then seemed to take away everyone's initial stiffness instantly. "You must both be puzzled by so many things…" He continued, as if thinking out loud. "…Not least about the reasons why we have brought you into our City, instead of *dispatching* your entire party two or three days ago?"

"The thought did occur to us, while trying to differentiate between what's real and not," admitted Pedro, causing an amused expression to spread over the Ruler's face.

"Everything around you is real I can assure you, even though you may find some things hard to comprehend…"

"I shall take your word for it." Pedro thanked Him for the reassurance and then asked, as the first wave of food and drink arrived. "And so, as you were saying… what is it you need us for, that with all the power at your disposal you cannot get?"

"The case should be rather defined as us choosing not to use the power at our disposal to get it…" Ayar felt the need to rephrase Pedro's words, prompting Becchiu to look at him with reproach.

"That's what he meant to say...," intervened Quito, wanting to keep Pedro in Ayar's good books.

Pedro then noticed that the King's wives also had two identical necklaces to those worn by the others... *Could they all be Aliens*? He wondered, whilst Ayar seemed to be searching the right words to explain his needs. On a casual closer observation of the royals and their courtiers, they did look somewhat different from most ordinary human beings... with wider eyes and finer features... Each side of their faces and bodies seemed to mirror the other a lot more precisely than among humans.

In Pedro's mind, everything around him was beginning to look a lot more real than when he first walked into the City. Although his heart was still set on gold, understanding the new reality before him was gradually gaining precedence over everything else.

A variety of meat and fish dishes were then added to the table, brought in by pairs of women servants who were keen to encourage everyone to taste a little from each of the trays they carried, with their smiles and mannerisms.

"Well..." Ayar cleared His throat just after His first mouthful of a spicy goulash-like dish. "The service I need from someone like you may be beyond your ability and reach... I should warn you," He teased Pedro, without wishing to demean him, "...but should you be able to deliver it, I would reward you with a thousand kilos of the purest Gold... which translated into your preferred currency, would bring you more than US$30 Million..."

Something got stuck in Quito's throat as he heard the figure, to the amusement of Ayar's wives, and it took a heavy hand from Pedro on his back to clear his throat.

"You are obviously well informed about things in the other dimension...," Pedro remarked with a smile, seriously intrigued about the nature of the task that could bring such a reward.

"You cannot rule without being well informed..." He retorted before proceeding. "This City was built on top of a volcano that became extinct over 5,000 years ago. And beneath us lies one of the largest natural gold reserves on the planet..." He paused. "It seems however that an American company has bought a mining concession for this entire area, which includes permits for the exploration of Oil and Natural Gas..."

"And somehow you want me... us, to reverse that?" Pedro wanted confirmation.

"Only if it is something you feel that you could pull..."

"With the right financial backing I'm sure I could pull it off... but while US$30M. is definitely a generous offer for the work involved, we may need considerably more to either buy those concessions, or the actual Company..."

"In the worst-case scenario we could always buy the Company outright, keep the concessions that interest us, and then resell the Company back into the open market..." Ayar seemed as calm as a cucumber as he spoke.

"Do you know how much capital you'd need to raise for something like that?" Pedro scratched his head distractedly.

"We've been preparing for something like that over the past 3 years." He produced a smile. "I know that the Company in question is currently valued at around US$2Billion... and ever since we realised we might have to go that way in the end, we've been increasing our gold bullion stock, should we need to add more liquidity to the existing reserves of our businesses in your dimension..."

"Ok..." Pedro had lost his appetite. Even if only a small-time businessman in his shop in São Paulo, he had been academically prepared for far bigger things, but had traded it all for a happy family life, which he eventually lost. "Then that brings us to the next problem: if I were the right person to pose as the front man for such a thing... how could I possibly explain the provenance of so much Capital at my disposal?"

"We've thought of that too and as far as the world at large is concerned, you would be the chosen representative of an Investment Group. My 3 "friends" here will act simultaneously as your advisors as well as a token sample of those investors, at the appropriate time." He then introduced the three courtiers as Auqui, Pahuac and Ninan. They each stood as Ayar named them, prompting Pedro and Quito to also stand in acknowledgement. The three Inca courtiers suddenly seemed a lot friendlier than when they first sat... almost as if switched on!

"And what about dealing with suspicions that this could be some money laundering operation or just another way of cleaning drug money?" Pedro's question raised smiles on the faces of the three opposite him, as Ayar prepared to put his mind at rest;

"In your "*Real World*", Auqui, Pahuac and Ninan sit at the very top of some very powerful financial institutions and business conglomerates, although they rarely make an appearance."

Pedro then went quiet for a spell, doing his best to digest it all, as he continued to be thrown from one crazy scenario to the next, like in a dream from which he couldn't wake up!

"It seems you've thought of just about everything..." Pedro acknowledged in a trance.

"Not at all...! There are a lot of in-between challenges for you to conquer..." Ayar chuckled. "I will only provide you with some of the most essential tools for the job..."

"With all that you've told me, there is however one thing that makes no sense to me..."

"Why you...?" Ayar anticipated his question.

"Indeed!" Pedro wondered for a moment if he was being made fun of. "From among the people working for Auqui, Pahuac and Ninan, there must be at least dozens that are better qualified and far more up-to-date with the current world of business and finance than I am... not to mention that you hardly know me! What could possibly make you want to take such a monumental risk with a total stranger?" Pedro's outburst caused Ayar to chuckle, copied by the other three.

"You are not the stranger you think you are to us... and there is considerably more to our knowledge and science than the bows and arrows of Becchiu might suggest..." He began. "In the so-called White-man's world you have a thing you refer to as "*Big Brother*" ..." He paused to eat the last morsel on His plate. "We too have our version of "*Big Brother*" but with a difference; ours can look inside yours..."

"So... you know everything there is to know about me?"

"Not quite everything I'm sure; but enough to suggest that we could train and refine you in some aspects, so as to help you succeed in your task, rather than place ourselves at the mercy of those that are able but corrupt, in one way or another..."

"Now you flatter me..." A brief smirk appeared on Pedro's face. "And so... How long have you known about me?" He then asked.

"Not long. In fact, to be precise, only since you left your bus behind to head this way..."

"...Talk about being in the right place at the right time!!!" Pedro thought out loud, putting a smile on everyone's faces as Ayar and His wives got up, getting ready to leave.

"You could definitely say that." Confirmed the Inca King as the others also rose, causing general laughter. "You will be the guests of Auqui, Pahuac and Ninan over the next three days and they'll prepare you." He extended a cordial smile to Quito. "As for the gold you seek for yourselves, some of Becchiu's warriors will help you carry 250 kilos of it back to within a day's walk of your bus... and you will receive the rest upon completion of your task." He paused. "Are you going to be happy with that?"

"Delighted."

"Good." Said Ayar turning to His wives before Pedro could approach Him for a handshake, encouraging the women to leave the room ahead of Him.

With Ayar and His wives gone, Auqui, Pahuac and Ninan suggested that Pedro and the other two regain their seats.

"We hope not to disappoint with our hospitality over the next three days…" Auqui started the conversation while the table was quickly cleared and the meal dishes replaced by a feast of exotic fruits and alcoholic drinks, with a twist of *mind lifting* substances!!

"Judging by the welcome we've received thus far, I feel you are probably being excessively modest…" Quito commented, in the form of a compliment.

"I think he is referring to the girls in particular…" Pedro joked.

"You'll have no shortage of those, don't worry…," commented Pahuac with a chuckle.

"Or even boys… if you feel brave enough!!!" Ninan added, showing his sense of humour.

"…And what about our warriors?" Quito asked, permanently protective of his own.

"We are sure they are having the time of their lives and feeling that they are among friends…" Becchiu reassured the Akazi Chief on behalf of the courtiers.

"We'll probably have to kick them out by the time you're ready to leave the City…" Ninan started everyone laughing again.

"How did you guys manage to be in the financial position you hold in the White-man's world, while living here and away from it all?" Pedro directed the question to all three.

"It didn't quite happen overnight, as you may well imagine…" Auqui offered to reply. "Even if assisted on occasions by converting some of our gold over the past 3 centuries or so, our position is the end product of hardworking generations of Incas and people of all races within our organizations." He paused. "We've had it easy, really! In the way that we've inherited the fruit of their hard work, making our main task to simply keep things going, while making sure that none of our front men and women decide to grow a bit too big for their shoes…"

"How often do you travel to places like Rio or other countries?" Pedro was curious.

"We don't. Those places are dangerous and full of pollution and disease. The people in them are by the greatest part living a life of endless strife, slaves to a nonstop cycle of work to spend… sharing a corrupt view of life. We couldn't live in that environment…" Auqui offered a reply once again.

"Well? How do people live in your world? Don't they work and spend the fruit of their labour?"

"In this City people only need to work to provide the community with their individual share, and the State provides them with all they need. This however does not stop anyone from pursuing greater wealth should they so wish…" Auqui paused "The point I'm making being that they can all enjoy life without becoming slaves of a survival philosophy based on labour-to-spend principles…"

"I meant in your world beyond this City…?" Pedro dared to venture into unknown territory.

"I think we need to deal with your world first…" Pahuac provided the answer this time, somehow stopping Pedro in his tracks, without meaning to sound dictatorial in the way he spoke.

To bring their evening to a close, their conversation then centred on forward planning the three days ahead. Pedro and Quito were to spend a day in each of the Palaces of the 3 courtiers, where they'd deal respectively with: general dos and don'ts at Pahuac's, strategic general planning at Auqui's, and any questions remaining at Ninan's.

Between Pedro, Quito and Becchiu, the latter was probably the happiest to be back on the stone paved street. It wasn't late and only a short walk to the Palace of the Guests but even so, all three seemed to prefer a quiet reflective moment instead of idle conversation. Gondola traffic had ceased for the day and as they walked along the shore, a cool gentle breeze caused tiny ripples to appear on the calm waters of the lake, under the starlit sky.

"Did you enjoy your evening?" Becchiu eventually spoke as they were about to reach their destination, looking suddenly exhausted.

"We feel very much honoured by everything and of course delighted with your welcome, not to mention Ayar's generosity." Pedro replied also on behalf of Quito.

"I'm glad we've succeeded in that…," he found a smile to offer.

Becchiu didn't hang around any longer than absolutely necessary and left soon after wishing them a good night's rest, in the hands of Cuxi (!!!).

Cuxi was a bit like every man's dream mistress, from her looks to her homely attitude, born to please and limitless in her loving ways, she was quick to fix Quito with two young girls for the night, and then decided to look after Pedro herself.

To Pedro, Cuxi provided the added attraction of not speaking any language he understood, which somehow made his night even more exciting, as they communicated through their eyes and touch, with the occasional moan to indicate the intensity of their pleasures to one another. …And he must have felt lost in paradise by the time he fell asleep!

Cuxi spent the night by Pedro's side and in the morning while he still slept, prepared him a fruit feast for breakfast before leaving.

**

V

Pedro was awakened by the sound of approaching cymbals and horns, luring him to the first-floor veranda of his bedroom. A group of musicians were slowly walking around the lake, proclaiming the wedding of a young couple behind them, followed by a short cortège of friends and relatives. A few timid drops of rain were starting to fall and a knock on the door finally convinced him that there was a "working" day ahead.

"How was your night?" Quito seemed rejuvenated by the unexpected flurry of sexual activity the Incas were able to provide.

"No complaints…" Pedro didn't feel in the mood to compare notes. "Are we supposed to meet Becchiu somewhere, or did he say he would come for us?"

"I'm not too sure to be honest… Wow! Are you going to eat all this by yourself?" Quito was suddenly distracted by Pedro's untouched breakfast.

"You are welcome to share it with me…" He pointed Quito to a short stool.

"You must be doing something right… No one prepared me breakfast…!" He complained.

"They were probably too tired…" Pedro did his best to stay serious.

"Now you are taking the *micky*!" He shared in the humour while attacking a slice of melon.

Becchiu arrived an hour later to take them to Pahuac's Palace.

"Do you both feel rested?" He asked, looking like he could do with an extra hour in bed himself.

"Very much so… Quito in particular has not slept this well since he was breastfed!!!"

"Just take no notice…" Quito was chuckling as he turned to Becchiu "He has been like this since he woke up…"

"Nothing like a good breast for a good night's sleep, I agree…" Becchiu ended up joining them in laughing about the topic.

It was only a short walk to Pahuac's two storey Palace near the water's edge. A guard came to greet them at the door and Becchiu left to go about his day, the moment Pedro and Quito followed the security to the upper floor.

Inside, the stone floors and walls were enriched with elaborate Inca tapestries and a scent of fragrant oils and lavender perfumed the air in a pleasant balanced way.

Pahuac stood near the balcony of the spacious first floor room, a little lost in thought, distractedly absorbed by the progress of the same wedding party, by now somewhere on the opposite side of the lake. And once a short moment had elapsed, the guard produced a brief cough to bring him back from his daydream.

"There you are…" Pahuac's seemed to snap out of it and walked towards them ready for a couple of handshakes, looking a lot more relaxed than the previous evening. "Please sit anywhere you like and make yourselves comfortable… one of the servants will bring us some beverages soon" He commented and the guard left the room.

Pahuac had one of those faces that could pass for being as young as 40 or as old as 60, with a naked torso that denoted he still retained some of his prime. Everything about him seemed to suggest that he was one of those die-hard bachelors who'd much rather be in the company of men, without necessarily being gay, or somewhere undecided.

The three of them were soon seated on soft cushions by a

low round table, where a young maiden placed 3 goblets of an icy mint drink moments later.

"I'd like this to be an informal meeting…," started the Inca courtier casually, after a first sip of the drink. "Among other things and in keeping with tradition, I've been asked to tutor you on the strict protocols you'll need to observe when seen in public with Ayar, myself, Auqui or Ninan, for instance, taking into account that the business you are about to take on will most probably lead to a long- term relationship with us…" He paused before talking about those, with Pedro and Quito following his every word. "The inhabitants of our city are of course aware of other parallel realities, but they prefer to stick with the old Incan ways, which incidentally are a lot less savage than what you might have heard!" He had another sip. "Leaving only a few of us to commute back and forth between our two dimensions, primarily to protect the interest of the "State" and the wellbeing of our Citizens…"

"Are you saying that the mass sacrifices to appease the Gods and the Elements are a white-man's fabrication?" Quito asked.

"Mass killings did take place in the distant pass, but not quite for the reasons given by the white-man's historians, when referring to us, the Aztecs or the Mayans. Such events were mostly related to the settling of scores in the aftermath of military conflicts, or as a way of bringing deadly epidemics under control, or in extreme cases, as a way of preventing the spread of specific DNA sequences…"

"Are there some Aztec or Mayan cities like yours still flourishing in parallel dimensions around the Americas?" asked Pedro this time.

"There are… but we are unable to enter their dimensions, just as they are unable to enter ours…," he explained. "In the same way, we keep our people beyond the Earth supplied with a number of natural resources, so do those in Mayan and Aztec Cities that remain active…"

"Are you then like different Companies, different "Aliens" or both…? Using different suppliers of raw materials?" Quito wanted to make sure he understood this!

"As strange as it may sound, we are indeed both different Companies as well as different Aliens, as you would put it. But we don't interfere with one another, as this could affect our common interests."

"So… It takes something like a pass code to gain access to each dimension?"

"That's exactly what this is." Pahuac paused. "Now, as to whether the people from an Aztec or Mayan dimension operate in your day-to-day reality in the same way we do, that's anyone's guess… I would assume that if they did, like us, they would probably go the extra mile to remain anonymous."

Most of that morning was spent correcting and clarifying historical misconceptions, as well as providing a proper glimpse into the real life of the Inca People in centuries past, while after a fish lunch, their afternoon focused on communications and security issues. The strict protocols to adhere to on this were essentially aimed at making life difficult, if not impossible, for those bent on tracing anything back to XAKATAN, or to anyone belonging to the city. And by the end of their session, thanks to Pahuac's easy manner, Pedro and Quito felt clear about all the things he had taught them, and a lot closer to him as a person.

Becchiu arrived as if on cue, to escort them back to the Palace of the Guests and then left, leaving Cuxi and her girls to deal with the needs and *tensions* of the two men!

Quito was soon dispatched to his room with two different girls and Cuxi proposed for Pedro to spend the night with a girl that could speak Portuguese, called Mikay.

"You are very beautiful Mikay," Pedro complimented the

new addition to the boudoir, "…but could you tell Cuxi that I had my heart set on spending the night with her…?"

"What a shame…" Replied the young woman "I really have a weakness for romantic men…" But she passed on the message none-the-less, bringing a happy glint to Cuxi's eyes.

Pedro's time with Cuxi was extra special that night. The woman genuinely liked him too… and to be chosen in preference to someone truly stunning and able to speak his own language was quite something to her…! And until well into the night, they took each other to cloud 9, beyond and back again effortlessly before falling into a deep sleep.

*

The following day, Becchiu arrived looking a lot better than he had done the previous morning, which couldn't be said for either Pedro or Quito!! …And after a few short courtesies they made their way to Auqui's Palace; a mere couple of hundred yards after Pahuac's.

Auqui's Palace was like Pahuac's but with an extra floor. Auqui had a middle-aged wife called Ana and no children lived with them.

"Good to see you looking the part in Inca clothing…" Auqui greeted them, trying his best to sound sincere, and then used both hands to introduce his wife; before taking them up a stairway, into a large room similar to Pahuac's. "Ana is not only my wife, but also my sister and business assistant." He completed the introduction. Her intelligent eye expression reflected her pedigree and her long braided grey hair in no way lessened the beauty she still retained. She also wore an identical necklace to Ayar and the other courtiers.

"It is a great pleasure to meet you…" Pedro and Quito stood and produced a near subliminal bow, as learned from Pahuac the previous day.

"I can see you are fast learners…" She rewarded them with a smile, for the way they observed protocol.

Auqui and Ana looked a little older than Pahuac and as their day of tuition evolved, it soon emerged that the couple were in fact the leading brains at the very top of the Incan financial pyramid outside their City.

Most of the day was spent learning about the labyrinth of contacts, the relevance of some of the processes involved, and how the sequential-domino-line of people used when communicating for specific purposes could radically change the meaning of it all; just like in the spy games played by the Superpowers! At the same time, however, Pedro and Quito were being deliberately denied access to any information the courtiers regarded as irrelevant to their mission.

"We anticipate that there will be times when you will need to have instant access to all sorts of sensitive-updated information, from the availability and general location of funds… to dos and don'ts… and I'm not referring to funds for the actual purchase of the American Company…" Ana stressed and then got up to raise their focus on her words. "You see, when it comes to big business and mega deals in particular, you'll invariably find that suddenly there are key people involved you didn't even know were there at the outset; some real and some others, just bogus opportunists trying to make a fast buck." She paused. "And hence, some lines of communication will be there mainly to assist you in sussing out which are which, and to help you put together untraceable transfers to those genuine ones that will make the difference…"

"It is a dirty world of intermediaries isn't it…?" Quito let escape, looking at Pedro.

"It is a game we need to play well and unflinchingly." Confirmed Ana.

"No worries if you cannot remember everything in one go…" Auqui tried to reassure the expression of concern appearing on Pedro's face. "We'll still give you a few refreshers after today…"

"That's great news…" Pedro smiled, relieved to hear it!

Whilst attentive to everything that was being said, Pedro also kept being distracted by the necklaces they wore, anticipating that they served some purpose besides that of being a body ornament, and by mid afternoon he had to ask.

"Do your beautiful necklaces do anything besides being necklaces?" He asked, unsure whether to look at Auqui or Ana for the answer.

"Ok," offered Ana, after some sort of telepathic exchange with her brother-husband. "Watch this;" She warned and then pressed the front of her necklace in a particular way, and instantly disappeared, to then reappear a second or two later in a different part of the room.

"Wow!!!" Quito was taken aback.

"Is that how you travel between the two dimensions?" Enquired Pedro.

"It is one of the ways we can do it… the lazy way…" She stressed.

"There are also other functions to it, but we're not supposed to impress you with our out-of-Earth technology…" Auqui clarified, before getting back to *business*. "Ninan will tell you all about it."

By the end of dinner, Pedro felt almost frightened by the financial power he would soon have at his command, while doing his best not to think about the likely cost of failure…

As usual, Becchiu's arrival had been perfectly timed, just to escort them the short walk back to the Palace of the Guests. To Pedro's disappointment however Cuxi wasn't around and Mikay seemed to have taken over her role.

"Is Cuxi ok?" Pedro enquired of her, while Quito looked like a little boy lost in a sweet shop, happily selecting the available choices for the night.

"She fell down the stairs and bruised her legs… she won't be back to work for some time…" Mikay did her best to *display* some of Cuxi's mannerisms as she spoke, in the way she felt probably made Cuxi so seductive and appealing to Pedro. And she soon succeeded in arousing him, not because of the *rebranding* but because of her keenness and determination in getting to be in bed with him.

"Is she otherwise alright?"

"She is fine and says hello." Mikay paused to then smile teasingly; "I hope I won't disappoint…"

*

Mikay didn't lag behind Cuxi in any way and even showed Pedro a trick or two of her own, while giving him sex and love in equal measures.

"Did Cuxi give you any clues…?" Pedro asked while taking a break, surprised with how well Mikay seemed to know him, producing a smile on her face.

"She didn't have to… I just instinctively know what a man needs and how he wants it… and I then turn it into my own desires…" She smiled into his eyes, in no hurry to get him going again.

"Have you killed anyone in bed yet?" Pedro had to ask and she seemed amused by the question.

"Only two…" She replied, causing Pedro to pull back a little so as to look at her. "I'm kidding" she giggled and covered her eyes, getting Pedro to join her.

The Inca girl soon had Pedro begging for mercy, only to take pity on him, deciding to gently rest her head on his chest, to encourage him to get some sleep.

"What makes you work in this sort of profession? Does someone own you?" Pedro's question almost shook the girl.

"No one owns me!" She lifted her head to look at him, doing her best not to seem offended. "I enjoy sex and men… and just one husband would never be enough to satisfy my needs…" She admitted. "This way, I also make money with it… and I'm quite rich, if you should know…"

"I'm pleased for you. And… is it the same with Cuxi?"

"You really like her, don't you?" Pedro just smiled but offered no reply, encouraging her to continue, "Cuxi belongs to the "State" and was accepted in payment by the King, when her family ran into a great deal of debt with Ayar Himself…" She looked at him. "I hope you won't get me into trouble for saying this…"

"Not at all… My lips will remain sealed as to any conversation we may have…" Pedro was quick to put her mind at rest.

"What is it that they want with you?" She then asked, distractedly caressing the side of his naked body with one hand as she spoke.

"It's all a bit blurry…," he avoided answering and somehow wondered for a split moment, if Mikay was there to try and suss him out on behalf of Ayar & Co. "Do you get a lot of outsiders using the Palace of the Guests?"

"You, Mr. Quito and the Akazi warriors are the first outsiders I have ever seen…" She sounded sincere. "The Palace of the Guests is otherwise used by the better off, or by people being rewarded for something by the King or the Courtiers…"

"And how did you learn to speak Portuguese so well?"

"It is one of the things we learn in school…"

"So… Cuxi never went to school?"

"No… She became property of the King when she was 7 years of age…"

"Did she start working here from that age?" Pedro was a bit taken aback, but doing his best not to show it.

"Yes…" She confirmed with a sigh…, becoming a little sidetracked!!!

*

It was a fortnight since Pedro had set off with Quito and one Akazi warrior unit, leaving Luis and the remaining Akazi with the task of ring fencing the property, as well as preparing the terrain for a second house.

In anticipation that Pedro would return with a fair amount of Inca gold, the house they had already built had a sizeable basement hidden beneath one of the rooms, where they hoped to store all the gold, which they'd eventually filter out little by little, as the right buyers emerged.

Pedro had estimated that to travel to XAKATAN and back should take them no more than 10 days or so… but now at the start of day 15, everyone was beginning to wonder whether anything could have gone wrong.

"Do you think they might already be living a life of luxury somewhere in Peru?" joked one of the Indios.

"They could have met up with a tribe of headshrinkers…," suggested another to the first one.

"I tell you what I think probably happened…," it was Luis' turn to speculate, as they all sat around a camp fire. They became silent, waiting to hear; "I think they probably found so much gold that they have to double back, to bring everything with them…?"

"If that's the case, let's hope they delay a few more days…," remarked another of the Indios, to everyone's amusement.

"At what point do you think some of us should go looking for them?" asked Tomaz, the Akazi unit leader.

"I think we should stay put…," interrupted another, raising his voice. "I've noticed the same half dozen 4X4s going back and forth a few times in the last couple of days… We should stay together."

"They probably belong to that rich guy… Can't think of his name…," suggested Tomaz.

"George Azevedo…," Someone said, from among the circle of men.

"I don't think so…," Luis had also noticed them and had his suspicions "Those 4X4s have seen better days…"

"What do we do then?" insisted Tomaz.

"Nothing. We just wait and continue the work we've started…," Luis had made up his mind.

"And if none of them turn up after a month?" Tomaz wanted to know in advance.

"Then some of us will go looking for them… but it's too early to do that yet… for all we know they could still be trying to find the place!" Luis paused. "To be honest, I'm more worried about those 4X4s prowling about than about Pedro, Quito and the others…" He looked at the 6 Indios for support. "I think we should all take turns and keep an hour's watch each, overnight, and guns at the ready during the day."

They all agreed and by first light they also pre-planned a few defensive positions, should the 4X4s come suddenly charging through the property.

*

Ninan's Palace was half way around the lake from the Palace of the Guests and was a near replica of Pahuac's. He was a natural joker and the tuition day with him was a light-hearted affair, which he started by declaring himself to be single and bisexual, as they all sat in a similar room to those used by the other courtiers!

"I'm only joking!!!" He then confessed with tears in his eyes from laughing, looking at Pedro and Quito's faces. "Come on guys… we're the ones paying…," Ninan soon got them to loosen up and by the time the beverages arrived, the three were ready to get to work.

Pedro and Quito still retained a mountain of questions at the back of their minds about their newly found reality and most of what surrounded them. But rather than to allow their focus to drift away from the business in hand, their line of questions was funnelled into the ABCD of what could be expected of them, at each stage of the Inca Plan.

78

"The actual plan must be created by you…" Ninan clarified with a chuckle, in case they were under the impression they'd simply be doing things as instructed. "It needs to fit with your personality." He explained as he looked at both. "Your decisions will have to be approved by us at each stage of course, but otherwise you're very much your own masters…" He added, "You will however be able to count on us for providing you with all the data you may need, incidental information, and needless to say; covering expenses and everything else related to cash."

"Did you guys make bets among yourselves regarding this?" Quito decided to mimic Ninan's sense of humour.

"The idea did cross our minds at one point…" Ninan admitted, continuing his chuckle. "But then we felt that it would be tempting providence…"

Pedro had a ready-made list of items of information he wanted to obtain, which included finding out a little more about the wealthy George Azevedo, and Ninan was happy to provide an answer to most, except for one or two which he felt were irrelevant to the case and should therefore remain out of bounds.

"George is white but one of us of course, as you might have guessed, given the size of his Estate and its proximity from XAKATAN…" Ninan paused. "He also owns several other lands in the area and several mines around the country, mostly inherited from past generations…"

"Wouldn't he have been a far better person for this task?" asked Pedro almost irritated, once again a little unsure if they were being made fun of!

"The American Consortium we want would never do business with George. They are fierce competitors and there's been some bad blood between a few of the American shareholders and him in the past…"

"I see…"

"What made you ask about him?" Ninan was curious.

"Well, with the amount of land he seems to own around here, my first thought was that we should perhaps buy him out of the area before the American Consortium does, so as to make access to this place difficult... but if he is one of us, then we are already covered for that..."

"Good thinking anyway...," complimented Ninan. "The Americans however could still outsmart us by buying the local politicians into their pockets... and eventually force George to sell whatever amount of land they deemed crucial to their operation." He paused. "Brazilians don't particularly like Americans but they like their dollars, just like everyone else I suppose..."

"So... you reckon that the first important step is to ensure that the local politicians in power are those that interest us?"

"Absolutely... but why gamble? And not have those in power as well as those in opposition?" Ninan smiled as he tried to get them thinking outside the box.

"Are we already in that position?" Pedro had to ask.

"Well, George is..." replied the courtier with a straight face. "None-the-less, keep in mind that the same principle will apply whenever you need the backing of politicians to get what you want elsewhere..."

"How is he involved in your interests?" was Quito's turn to ask.

"George is one of our front men, even though everything he owns is genuinely his, just as it was his father's and his grandfathers before him." He paused. "To some other front men however, we gave them what they have, and the opportunity to realise their dreams and ambitions, on condition that they'd do as told when called upon... a sort of brotherhood type of unwritten agreement if you like." He had a sip of his lemony beverage "George however has no idea of whom or where we are and knows nothing at all about us here in XAKATAN..."

"So..." It was Pedro's turn to have a chuckle "...If I were

to instruct a particular line of contacts to tell him to put his plane, pilot and airfield at our disposal, would he just do it?"

"Without a question." confirmed Ninan.

"Sweet…" Pedro let escape reflectively and then turned to face the courtier. "Are you then buying us with US$30 Million so that our children's children will become yes men and women to front other future interests of XAKATAN?"

"You don't have to make it sound so awful! You and your future generations will at least have a good solid start from which to enjoy life to the full, instead of an existence enslaved by the most basic necessities."

"He definitely has a point…" Quito agreed 100% with Ninan's assessment. And Pedro couldn't really argue with any of it.

Ninan then informed them that Becchiu would take them back with the agreed amount of gold the following day, but would leave them a day's walk short of Luis' land.

"…And for communications I'm going to give you one of these each…" from a small box, Ninan extracted two necklaces that looked like simplified versions of his own, and then proceeded to explain how they worked.

Pedro and Quito were shown how to get their necklaces to perform 3 different sets of functions by pressing some of the stones in particular sequences. The first function enabled them to switch between the two dimensions, with the option of observing the "white-man's" reality from the Inca dimension, whilst remaining invisible and completely out of reach. The second, allowed for a two-way mind to mind conversation with each of the three courtiers, also making it possible for the courtiers to listen in to any relevant conversation Pedro or Quito should want them to hear. And finally, the third was a bit like an emergency ejector button! It could bring them physically back to the very room where they were in just then, instantly.

"You could eventually become extremely unpopular with

Airlines and Telecommunications Companies you know?" Pedro joked.

"...And not only..." He added.

Ninan gave both men plenty of practice with the device and as usual, Becchiu appeared as if on cue, the moment Pedro and Quito were ready to leave for the Palace of the Guests; and wasted no time in delivering them to Mikay for their last night in the City.

"I'll come for you by first light with the other Akazi, ready to leave." He informed them and then smiled before leaving. "Have a good rest..."

"Good night Becchiu, thank you." Pedro and Quito replied in unison.

Mikay was quick to dispatch Quito to his room, accompanied by two new girls, as usual, and then rather than force the issue, offered Pedro the choice between spending the night with her or with one or two of the other girls.

"Did I disappoint you?" Pedro seemed a little surprised.

"Not at all... I just didn't want to risk being turned down a second time?" She smiled at him reassuringly.

It didn't take her long to get Pedro ready for a good night's sleep and a full body massage finished the job, before he could even attempt to outperform himself!!

**

VI

Becchiu, the Akazi unit and a few strong Inca warriors were ready to depart by first light as promised. The three courtiers had come to wish them well, also on behalf of Ayar, and the girls at the Palace of the Guests stood at their windows waiting to wave goodbye to them all.

"I've never seen your warriors looking so well!" Commented Pedro to Quito as an aside "They even look like they've put on weight…"

"Are you surprised? I reckon they didn't have to scratch themselves for nearly a week…," replied Quito in the same way, keeping a straight face.

A small crowd of early risers started to gather and moments later Becchiu gave his warriors the order of departure, from amid shouts of *good luck* and *come back soon*.

They recovered their guns once they were outside the City and judging by the occasional loud laughter from among the Akazi Braves, they were undoubtedly exchanging notes, recounting to one another their experiences of the previous nights!!!

Their return along the mountain trails was the exact reverse route they had taken to get to XAKATAN. The 3 days' travel to where they had first made camp however seemed to have flown; and by the time Becchiu and his warriors were ready to turn back, friendships had been made and a feeling of camaraderie had grown among them all.

"I look forward to seeing you both again in the not too distant future." Becchiu said with sincerity facing Pedro and Quito, using both hands to touch theirs.

"And so do we…" They returned the greeting, to then wish everyone a safe return home.

The 250 Kilos of pure gold the whole party had carried was made up of 1000 X 250 gram bars, amounting to 10 kilos per each member of the walking party up to that point. But now, although this was their own gold, neither Pedro nor Quito, or any of the Akazi warriors looked forward to the final 10-mile journey to Luis's property, carrying over 30 kilos of gold each, as well as everything else from guns to water.

Quito started chuckling to himself about a mile into the final part of their journey.

"What is it?" asked Pedro.

"I never thought I'd be grateful for having 250 kilos of gold instead of 1,000!!!"

"The good news guys…" Started Pedro, turning to the others light heartedly as they continued to walk "…Is that we are getting closer to Luis's bus by the minute…," his comment was greeted by muted laughter!

It was well into the night when they sighted the silhouette of Luis' house against the full moon.

"Something's not right…" Quito raised his right hand bringing the warriors to a halt and quietly got everyone to place all the gold into a pile, before signalling for them to spread out while moving towards the house. The bus was still in the same place but there was no fire or any sign of life anywhere!

"It smells awful…" Pedro whispered to Quito as they neared the house, almost tripping over the dead body of one of the Akazi warriors they had left with Luis. "Oh Fuck!"

Zamzam was the next to find another dead Akazi warrior and within an hour they had found all seven of them. Each of them had been shot more than once, except for Luis, whom they found with his throat cut wide open inside the house.

"This happened at least two or three days ago," considered

Taco, as the seven bodies were lined up by the front door of the house.

"It looks like robbery…" Cachimbo returned to where the others were. "Apart from the Bus they took everything else of any value."

"Bastards…" Pedro let escape, disgusted with the barbarity of Luis's death in particular.

"What do you want to do?" Quito enquired from Pedro.

"Let's wait for daylight and make sure we keep predators away from the bodies for now." Pedro then had to go and throw up before returning moments later. "We'll give them a proper burial in the morning and will look around for clues… I'm sure they've put up a brave fight." He paused. "In the meantime, let's hide all the gold in the basement room and cover it with earth, as we had planned?"

No one managed to sleep a wink and the feeling of sadness among the men was clear to see. They had all grown together and were as close as brothers.

"Their souls will not rest until we've found the men that did this…" Quito spoke sombrely and suddenly seemed to acquire a second mission, the more the whole thing sank in.

"And so we shall." Pedro tried to reassure him and the others. "But we'll have to be clever and cool with how we go about this, or we may end up losing a lot more than what we've lost already." Quito nodded in agreement but did not reply.

Morning came. And while the Akazi warriors dug seven graves, Pedro and Quito scoured the property for clues. They found shattered glass from car windows and about eight pools of dried blood, presumably belonging to either dead or wounded assailants.

"I reckon this was done by 5 or 6 4X4s… and they definitely didn't leave the place unscathed…" was Quito's assessment after a good look around. "Do you think George Azevedo might have had something to do with this?"

"Even though we know he's got 4X4s, that wouldn't make sense at all! What benefit could he possibly have from something like this?"

"That's what I think too but..." Quito was pensive "Do you think we'd look silly if we used our necklaces to one of the Courtiers, to try and find out who did this?"

"They might be able to confirm that George didn't do it, but I doubt if anything beyond that! As I understand it, I think the sort of information they can provide us with relates more to people and facts within the world of business, rather than this sort of stuff..."

"This could be a way of the mining concession owners scaring people away from the area..."

"It wouldn't be a first... We must think well before making any move." Pedro insisted.

"Could Luis have talked about what brought us here?" He then wondered out loud.

"That's what worries me right now, which makes it even more compelling that we should find who did this as soon as possible..."

By midday they had buried Luis and the others. Pedro gave a brief eulogy and Quito added his voice on behalf of all the Akazi, closing the book of their lives for eternity.

"I think I'll contact Ninan..." Pedro announced to Quito on reflection, as the Akazi Chief joined him on a walk around the property shortly afterwards.

"Why not...? Even if only to update him on what's happening... And then let him take it from there?" Quito further encouraged him to do it.

Pedro stopped to activate a direct link to Ninan, by pressing the right combination of stones on the necklace beneath his shirt:

"Wow!" He let escape looking at Quito's blank face, feeling like his body had been switched on, the moment the sequence was completed!

"Pedro?" Ninan's voice was so clearly heard inside his brain that it startled him further still! Pedro knew as much about sending brain impulses back to Ninan as he knew about Rocket science (!), which seemed to bring some amusement to the courtier for an instant. "It will take a while to get the hang of it… but don't worry; if you talk out loud normally, I'll be able to hear you perfectly."

Ninan was a little speechless by Pedro's news at first, but not entirely surprised.

"Unfortunately, this seems to be common practice by a lot of the mining companies operating in remote areas around the world. It is a bit of a macabre way of discouraging settlers from moving into areas they want to control… But it works for them…!"

"Well, this makes at least two violent massacres in a month around here…"

"All the hallmarks are there… and publicity is what they want of course!" Confirmed Ninan.

"The Akazi want revenge, as you'd expect…" Pedro tried to get some advice.

"You guys need to get out of there as soon as possible…" There was some urgency in Ninan's voice. "The moment those *animals* know that you're back there they'll return to wipe you out… as well as to avenge any losses they might have had the first time around…," he paused. "Would you be able to drive your bus back to George's place?"

"I've got no problem doing that… providing it still works… The battery is probably dead."

"Check for booby-traps too…" He advised. "Anyway, check the bus and get back to me once you've done that… and I'll see what I can do in the meantime, OK?"

"Thanks Ninan."

To Pedro's surprise, the bus was working perfectly and still had almost half a tank of fuel in it, which somehow caused him to hesitate about moving it. Ninan's advice was still fresh in his mind and he ended up switching off the engine. With Quito's help he then looked inside the bus, under it and near the wheels without finding anything suspicious.

"I can't help thinking that something will happen the moment we try to move it…" Quito found the words to express Pedro's gut feelings. "Why else should they have left the bus so invitingly intact?"

"My exact thoughts Quito… Shall we give it another thorough look?" He proposed.

Their second inspection didn't bring them any joy either; except for a small lose screw near the hand brake lever. This attracted Pedro's attention, especially since: "*Luis would have tightened it, surely, had he noticed it…!*" He thought.

"There's definitely something attached to the handbrake…" Pedro announced to Quito.

"I wouldn't touch anything if I were you…" Quito was doing his best to drag Pedro away from the bus.

"What a load of fucking bastards! This means that they knew that there were more of us…"

"…This means that they'll be back sooner or later." Concluded Quito. "I'll place one of the men near the main road as a lookout." He then announced.

"Good idea." approved Pedro. "I think the others were probably caught a bit by surprise…"

Pedro got back to Ninan while Quito went on preparing a defence plan designed to cause maximum casualties among their *Friends*, should they return.

"Hide your gold somewhere safe first…" Rejoined Ninan "Through a line of contacts I'm going to get George to send some men to get you out of there and into the safety of his place, until we find the people doing this…"

"Thanks Ninan. We'll stay put."

By mid-afternoon, a cloud of dust from the main road announced the arrival of several 4X4s, led by the immaculately dressed George Azevedo and his Stetson! They drove into

Luis' property as if it were theirs, eventually coming to a stop by the newly built house.

"Christ Almighty!" he said coming down from his vehicle, looking at the seven freshly made graves. "What happened here?" He enquired and Pedro told him what he knew.

"Any idea of who could have done this?" Pedro asked him, with Quito doing his best to look inconspicuous whilst comparing tyre marks.

"Besides me and another half dozen land owners scattered around the territory, the only sizeable number of 4x4s that we know of belongs to the new mining Company preparing a citadel, about 30 miles from here…" He then looked at Pedro with renewed curiosity. "You must have some very influential friends in high places…" He commented. "I received word that I should take you under my protection," he paused. "Are you working for people opposed to this American takeover of our land?" He enquired.

"Could be…" Was all that Pedro was prepared to say, bringing an excited smile to George's face.

"I can't stand those gringos! You'd think they own the world…" He aired his feelings. "At times, it feels as if the rest of us are some sort of embarrassment to them!!!"

"And what about your hat?" Pedro teased him without malice.

"Just because I like their hats doesn't mean I've got to like them…," he chuckled. "I like their women too… and their currency even more of course." He then turned to Quito and the others, who in the mean time had gathered their belongings. "OK guys, you can climb on board wherever you find space…" He pointed to the other vehicles.

Pedro's eyes met Quito's briefly and immediately understood that the Chief's findings related to tyre marks were inconclusive.

"I'm involved in mining too, in the south of the country," Explained George as they started the drive back to his estate

"Which is why I prefer to live up here and away from it all...
It is a rough and dangerous business at the best of times..."

"Why did you get into it?"

"I didn't...I'm the fifth generation of Azevedos in this
business. My ancestors came from Portugal looking for
fortune, not long after Brazil's independence, and found it."
He looked at Pedro. "I've got two older sons and a young
daughter from my current wife... and if it weren't for them
and the continuation of the family spirit, I'd have gotten out
of this business long ago...," he paused. "And you?"

"Nothing as glamorous as that, even though my means are
probably greater than my appearance might suggest..."

"What line of business are you in?"

"I intermediate on behalf of clients who often prefer
to remain anonymous, when it comes to large business
transactions..."

"That sounds very interesting. Tell me more, once we have
fixed you all for the night?" He proposed, while activating
the electric gate to the avenue of palm trees leading to
his mansion.

"With pleasure..." Pedro agreed, ready to take maximum
advantage of the contact.

George stopped by the main entrance of the colonial
mansion and came down from his vehicle, while the other
4X4s continued on to a group of buildings a mile on.

"Your Indio friends will stay in the Annex... and it would
give me great pleasure if you'd accept my invitation to
remain as my guest at the mansion?" He said, showing the
way inside his home.

"I will be delighted..." Pedro followed George into
his study, from an entrance hall reminiscent of the 1920s.
"You've got a fabulous house..."

George's study was a giant room with well waxed wooden
floors. It boasted a library of valuable books running along
two entire walls, creating a cosy recess where two antique

sofas with matching chairs kept company with a Bernstein Piano. Then, across a strip of Persian carpet linking the two doors at opposite ends of the room, a snooker table and a bar completed the classic ensemble.

"This is Marlene by the way…" George introduced a large black woman servant in domestic attire that came to them. "Marlene is our Head Servant"

"Pleasure to meet you Sir…" The woman acknowledged timidly.

"Good to meet you too Marlene."

"And this is Sebastião, our Head of Security." George introduced a typical commando looking guy in a suit, as this one entered the study from a different door. Pedro shook his hand and George proceeded to briefly instruct his security on the arrangements to accommodate everyone. "Fancy a glass of whiskey before freshening up?" He then proposed, the moment Sebastião was gone.

"I'd accept one with pleasure after a bath or a shower…?" Pedro felt a bit like a skunk (!) and Marlene was quick to accommodate his wishes, after a quick glance from her boss.

"Please follow me Sir?" She smiled at Pedro.

Like most of the communal spaces in the mansion, the wide curved stairway to the first floor was adorned with effigies and portraits of past and present family members, some of which had been painted by well-known artists. And on the spacious first floor corridor, bunches of exotic flowers crowned a colonnade of antique vases spanning its full length. The corridor was then sealed by colourful floor-to-ceiling stained-glass windows at both ends.

"Dinner is served at 8, but Mr. Azevedo usually gets to his study at around 7:30, and breakfast is at 7, unless you'd rather have it in your room." Marlene informed him, taking Pedro into his room, to then show him where everything was, from the private bathroom to the cosy living room with a desk and TV.

"This is lovely Marlene…" Pedro was just as impressed with the splendid view over the avenue of palm trees leading to the main gate of the Estate.

"If you need anything… just press that button and I'll send you someone. OK?" She was pleased to see him impressed and then pointed to the rucksack he had with a load of dirty clothes. "I could get those washed and ironed for you before 7:30…" She offered with a *big momma*'s expression, as if reading his mind.

"Thanks a lot Marlene… You are a star and a life saver…"

Pedro had a steaming hot bath, a close shave, and by the time he put on some clean clothes he was almost unrecognisable! He then timed his arrival at the study for just after 7:30.

*

"What a remarkable change!" George greeted him clearly impressed with the improvement of his appearance. "I didn't realise you were white!" He joked and pointed Pedro to a stool by the bar. "Are we ready for that whiskey?"

"Ready and willing…" Pedro sat on the stool and did his best to remain serious, as George finally removed his Stetson, to reveal an enormous bald patch he seemed keen to hide! "Your hospitality is second to none, I should say!"

"Think nothing of it. I'm pleased to be able to help you out…," he said handing Pedro his glass, before climbing on to another stool near him. "I must admit that when I helped you pull away from that ditch, some 6 weeks ago, I simply assumed you were some labour boss with a bunch of Indios doing a job for… I think his name was Luis?"

"Yes… Luis was his name." Pedro sampled his drink. "… And I compliment your taste in whiskey too…" Pedro opened his eyes and mouth to help him cope with the strength of the stuff, to George's great amusement.

"A Scottish friend of mine sends me a couple of cases every year…," he looked pleased.

"Yes…" Pedro decided to offer George a version of events. "…Luis was a friend of mine who had gone through some rough times in his private life, his wife had left him… and the drama just got bigger until he became suicidal." He paused. "But anyway, to cut a long story short, I tried to help him by obtaining the Land Concession for him, building him a house away from his past… and he was going to help me in the case I'm working on when… well, you know the rest."

"Where were you when the massacre took place?"

"I reckon about half way back from surveying the land where this mining company wants to start digging for all sorts of things."

"You are also a mining surveyor?"

"No, not at all, but I needed to have a clear image of what they are planning to destroy… and please don't go suggesting that I'm a conservationist either!" Pedro made him laugh.

"They are a very big company with mining interests in the U.S., Canada and Australia… What is it you are trying to achieve? Buy their local mining interests or the company itself?"

"Nothing's clear cut as yet…"

"Are your clients likely to want to take up mining in this area?"

"It is my impression that what they want to do is exactly the opposite… prevent any mining activity so as to preserve the region for future generations…"

"What a noble cause!!! Being the greatest land owner in the region I'd very much like to join your clients in their quest, which is also mine, needless to say…" George was definitely suspicious of something and was slowly squeezing Pedro into a corner.

"Are you telling me you'd gladly contribute with a few hundred million dollars just to preserve this region as it is?" Pedro decided to go on the offensive.

"I wouldn't quite put it that way… I'm sure your clients

must have seen a line of profit in this somewhere…" He paused "Come off it Pedro: we are all grown up men…!"

"I'm in a delicate position on this and sworn to confidentiality, as I'm sure you understand… But if you do have a genuine interest in being involved, I'll be pleased to mention it to them… and see what they say."

"Why don't you do that?" He looked at his watch. "Shall we move to the dining room?" He then said, coming down from his stool. "Marlene is very particular about dinner time…," he chuckled.

*

The dining room wasn't much smaller than the study and was in typical Manuelino style, with a very long table at the centre, capable of accommodating over 40 people. No one else would be joining them and Marlene decided to sit them opposite each other, half way up the table.

"Are your wife and daughter away?" Pedro enquired as they sat.

"Yes… They both decided to do a cultural tour of Europe while everything's still standing…"

"Are we expecting some big war?" It was Pedro's turn to chuckle.

"We are going through strange times… The Americans have managed to create such a monumental mess around the world!!! In the hope of picking up the pieces to their advantage of course, but they went too far and I fear they've lost control over what they started, perhaps by thinking that the Chinese and the Russians were done with."

"War is good for you, I would have thought! The demand for iron-ore grows as does its price…"

"That is true, but I no longer think that way. I'm a grandfather now and there's no way I could ever spend the money I've made, even if I lived a wasteful existence over the next 1,000 years…" He paused, making a bib of his napkin around his neck. "I'd much rather see iron-ore used for peaceful purposes…," he paused again, this time to pour some red wine into their glasses. "But anyway, back to us… What's your next move going to be, now that your friend's no longer there?" He chewed a small piece of bread and then continued before Pedro could reply. "I received word from some high up people that I should rescue you from where you were as soon as possible, but that was about it…"

"Have you thought of asking them about their motives?"

"I thought you could fill me in on that… or is that also in the realms of confidentiality?"

"I'm not trying to be awkward George but… How can I possibly tell you about the motives of some person unknown to you and me? Maybe except that it was someone who definitely knew of the predicament we were in?"

"Then that could only be either the perpetrators themselves, which makes no sense at all, or perhaps a mole you or your clients might have placed inside the very company you are planning to hit?"

"I suppose that only leaves the second option…" Pedro agreed, while George passed one hand over his head in frustration, as if letting his fingers run through hair that wasn't there…! "I hope you're not worried about me imposing on your hospitality…"

"Not in the slightest…" George tried to look a little offended.

"Aren't you concerned these people might try something with you?"

"Assuming this is being sponsored by the Americans, no. We've crossed swords in the past, on matters completely unrelated to this, only to recognise that it was in our mutual interest that we should bury the hatchet."

"Well, but only moments ago, you showed some interest in joining forces with my clients against that same company (…?) Or would that not count as unearthing the hatchet?"

"You were the one who mentioned anonymity Pedro! Or did I dream about it?"

"You're absolutely right and I take it all back!!!" Pedro admitted with a smile.

Marlene then entered the dining room at 20:00 sharp, pushing a trolley with two sizzling oval clay dishes, containing a sizeable T Bone steak each. This was complimented by a small pyramid of white rice, a few crispy roast potatoes and creamed spinach purée.

"You're spoiling me rotten Marlene!" Exclaimed Pedro, truly looking forward to his meal. "I'll definitely need a bit of a walk after this…"

"And I'll keep you company…" George chuckled while checking if his steak was as rare as he liked it. "After dinner I usually walk a mile to the staff canteen to have my coffee and then back…"

George got a second bottle of wine halfway into their steak and they both gave dessert a miss, deciding on a couple of large whiskeys instead, before going for coffee.

"Cigar?" Offered George, once they'd consumed a further 4 or 5 large whiskeys each!

"Are you going to tell me you've got a friend in Havana who occasionally sends you boxes of these?"

"You must be having a déjà vu moment!" George found that really funny as they walked towards the staff canteen, causing him to reveal his contagious machine-gun-laughter, instantly triggering Pedro's own!!! They only stayed around long enough to down their small coffee in one and neither could remain serious for longer than a few seconds. "This return walk always seems to take a lot longer… Are we going back the same way we came?" He just had time to finish his sentence before they started laughing again!

*

The arrival of the Akazi at the Azevedo Estate proved to be no different to what they had grown accustomed to. They were immediately directed to a communal shower room and shown an adjacent area where they could all sleep.

For some absurd reason, Brazil was no better than Australia, the USA and others, when it came to the treatment of their original indigenous races, which were automatically labelled as belonging to the bottom layer of society!

Everything changed however, the moment Sebastião arrived to check on how they had been fixed for the night. Away from the *Akazi dormitory*, the Head of Security could be heard having a few harsh words with one or two of the staff, and minutes later they were all brought to the staff canteen for a generous "Feijoada" meal with no shortage of wine.

Sebastião introduced himself to Quito and was quick to apologise for the way they had been received.

"May I join you guys for dinner?" He then requested, having become instantly popular among the Akazi.

"With pleasure... It is your table...!" Quito asked Taco to make space, so that Sebastião could sit opposite him.

"I'm just an employee like everyone else here..." He clarified his position with modesty and while they served themselves, made a point of learning their names, as well as understanding how they ranked among each other. "This was all a bit short notice and I won't be able to improve on your accommodation for tonight... But I'll see what can be done for tomorrow" He promised.

"I wouldn't worry too much about it," replied Quito with an accommodating smile. "To be in-doors is good enough... and this dinner is more than excellent..." He complimented, still chewing his first mouthful.

The wine flowed freely and by the end of their meal, the Akazi were merry, rowdy and ready to sample some of the Estate's Cachaça brews...

"Aren't you concerned that those "Bandoleiros" might come here?" Asked Quito, already a little over the limit!

"Not in the slightest," replied the confident Sebastião. "It is a very big Estate with everything from plantations to herds of cattle and over 500 people split into two small villages…," he paused. "We also have over 40 well trained security men and a fully armed helicopter equipped with night vision and all that we could possibly need to repel any attack…"

"I'm impressed…," commented Quito with genuine admiration.

Sebastião also got the canteen staff involved with a few drinks… and soon enough someone appeared with a guitar, then an accordion, and the inevitable singsongs followed well into the night (!), with everything being used for percussion, from boxes of matches to spoons, glasses and plates! …By the time everyone was ready to call it a day, Sebastião had learned all there was to know about Pedro and the Akazi, except for the Incas and their Gold… but only just!!!

*

Like George, Pedro only had vague recollections of how he got to bed the previous night! The important thing in the minds of both men however, was feeling that neither had revealed to the other sensitive information they could regret. That aside, their carefree evening rewarded them with a rare opportunity to release bottled up stresses, while airing some of their similarities.

George, although far wealthier than the share of Pedro's gold would ever make him, was as much of a loner as Pedro; perhaps in part due to the constant battle to keep everyone's hands away from his money, and this somehow made the sharing of their boyish side even more fun for both.

"How's your head this morning?" Enquired Pedro joining George for breakfast, after an energising shower.

"Pounding…" He admitted but still managed a chuckle.

"It's been a while since I've had so much to drink in one evening… Did you have fun last night?" He then asked, about to have a first sip of the hot coffee Marlene had brought them.

"I've not laughed so much in decades…," replied Pedro, winking a good morning and a thank you for the coffee to Marlene, all in one.

"Today I thought I'd show you around the Estate while we work out how to get your Indio friends to safety?" He proposed.

"Sounds good. Are they OK?"

"They are fine and also had their share of fun last night. Sebastião tells me that you guys came from the Atlantic coast?"

"We did… That's where the Akazi were relocated to by the Government a few years back. Otherwise, this area is their actual ancestral territory."

"I see… So, in a way, to them, helping Luis build his new home also provided the perfect excuse to have a trip down memory lane…?"

"It was a coming together of many things…" Pedro was quick to realise that George probably knew a lot more about him by now, but didn't let that become a cause for concern. "There are three things I need to sort out as soon as possible…"

"What are they?" In contrast, perhaps out of boredom, George was keen to get involved.

"Well… One is about Luis' Land Concession Deeds, of which I have the papers…"

"Does he have any natural next of kin?" He interrupted.

"Not any more, no."

"Well, then that's very simple; you mentioned you bought that land for him, right?" He asked and Pedro confirmed with a nod. "For you to become the rightful owner of it, it will suffice for me to sign a paper acknowledging that I was a witness to him turning the land over to you… as payment of some personal debt?"

"Just like that?"

"Well, no one is going to question my integrity and since you bought it with your own money, it stands to reason that you should have it rather than the Government."

"True."

"We need to inform the Authorities of the deaths though… You cannot leave things just like that!" He paused. "And the other two things…?"

"I need to find the perpetrators of the massacre and get those Akazi home."

"To get them home is no problem… I can fly them to Recife from here; Sebastião told me their Camp is not too far from there…" He poured Pedro and himself some more coffee. "I'd advise you to get the all clear from the Authorities first though. It will save you a lot of hassle later…"

"How long is that likely to take?"

"I have some influence with the Regional Authorities and with things speeded up you might be looking at two weeks at the most. There won't be a problem for them to stay here until everything is sorted out anyway…," he tried to anticipate Pedro's obvious concerns.

"That's extremely kind of you George and I feel increasingly indebted to you…"

"Think nothing of it. But as for finding the culprits, I'd wait for the right time; and the right time is not just now."

"What makes you say that?"

"It is too fresh in the memory of all involved. Minds are clouded by the spirit of revenge and you'd be walking in the dark. Take into consideration that the perpetrators know who you guys are but you don't know them… And that puts you in danger and at a disadvantage." He bit a slice of toast while clearing his thoughts. "If you open up to me about what you are really trying to do vis-à-vis the Americans, we could join forces and, among other things, eventually find out who might have ordered this as well as those who actually did it."

"And then?"

"Entirely up to you… I won't blame you for any decision you might make on the matter…," he chuckled.

"I need to reflect on that George… Do you mind?"

"Take as much time as you need…"

*

After two hours of driving around on dirt roads through hills, valleys and plains, with views of the Andes as a backdrop to the west, George's Estate felt immense.

"Your land is bigger than some countries…" Pedro's comment was like music to George's ears, as they came to a halt by a supply store in one of the Estate's two villages.

"I'm aware of it…" He smiled proudly, accompanying Pedro into the store, "But making it financially self-sustaining is no easy task…" George paused, to give Pedro time to look for the tobacco he wanted. "…especially when it comes to security costs!!!" He completed his phrase already on the way back to the 4X4.

"You need to go into the Brothel business, to recuperate the wages you pay out…" Pedro joked, while doing his first roll up of the day, causing George to go into one of his mechanical laughs.

"We've got a couple of Madams… One in each village… but I've got nothing to do with it." He continued to laugh. "They both come from Mâncio Lima. One day, when they realised how many people worked in the Estate, they asked me if I would allow them to open for business here and…"

"They remained open ever since?" Pedro completed his phrase with humour.

"Joking aside, it is an important service that helps to keep crime down, if you think about it…"

"I couldn't argue with that…," Pedro agreed as they drove on, this time towards the highest point of the property, crowning George's tour with a spectacular view over his domain, as far as the eye could see and in all directions. "All yours?"

"Yes…"

"Wow…How much could it be worth?" Pedro enquired as they walked around the small stone "*Mirador*".

"Currently… Probably in excess of US$750 million, but I wouldn't dream of selling any of it." George then proceeded by driving in the general direction of an area so far unseen, before deciding to explain a little about himself, in the hope that Pedro would follow suit: "The nasty thing about wealth and money of course, is that the more you have, the more you need to have, until you realise you might be missing out on other more important challenges… And this somehow motivates you into going further still, so as not to think about it too much!" He chuckled.

"Do you find yourself imprisoned by it?" Pedro did his best to stay serious.

"It is a silly situation really…! My first wife divorced me alleging I had a mistress in Rio, to then go and live in Florida with one of my drivers, some 20 years her junior…" He paused. "My current wife keeps finding excuses to travel… and I often have stupid nightmares where I picture her being involved with one of my sons, every time she is away… And as for my wealth, I'm bound by sworn allegiance to an ancient brotherhood that made it all possible through my ancestors…!"

"I don't really know what to say…" Pedro wondered about George's motives in having such an open-hearted confession. "Do you feel at times that your life is just about looking after things that aren't really yours?"

"That's exactly how I feel!" He seemed surprised by the ease of Pedro's assessment.

"If that's the way you feel, then why not enjoy life as the passenger, rather than the driver?"

"Couldn't afford that!" he stopped to look at Pedro "The big downfall in all this is the enjoyment of the feeling power brings… It's like a drug that you'll do anything to hang on to. I reckon it is exactly what turns politicians full of good intentions into dictators…" George took a long pause, as if momentarily forgetting what he was about to say. "That's my prison anyway… What's yours?"

"The bigger the prison the harder to escape, I suppose, and mine is considerably smaller by comparison…" Pedro went on to tell him a little about his past in São Paulo.

"I'm glad I've never had to go through anything like that…"

"But tell me more about this brotherhood of yours" The question made George chuckle.

"I had hopes you'd enlighten me on it! You must obviously be involved with them too. I only hear from them once or twice a year, if that, and usually by proxy… And I'm sure they wouldn't have bothered to ask me to rescue you and give you anything you need, unless you were one of them… and a fairly important asset at that…" He looked intently at Pedro.

"It's all a bit too crazy to talk about…" Pedro decided to take a gamble.

"I can take it…" George then went silent, expectantly.

"Well… To do with this American Company… I need to exchange some gold bullion into US$s to grease the pockets of a few people, but it cannot go through bank accounts, which is why I need to use the gold…"

"How much cash are you looking to raise?"

"At least US$7 or 8 million…" The sum involved caused a tickly cough in George's throat.

"That's at least a couple of hundred Kilos…!" George had to burst out laughing. "You're telling me that you came all the way from near Recife with half of the Akazi tribe to be in the middle of nowhere, for the purpose of exchanging some gold bullion into millions of cash dollars?"

"Well, I was told to pick it up from a specific place near here… and it is currently hidden inside Luis's property…"

"Could it be that that was the reason for the massacre…? Only the "Bandoleiros" found nothing, … Perhaps because you had not yet returned with the gold?"

"There's no way they could possibly have known about it…"

"So, you want us to go and get it, to then have me help you raise US$7 or 8 million in cash?"

"…And fly us all back to Recife with the dosh", Pedro added making it sound like this was all included in the "Brotherhood's" plan.

"That's a bit too crazy alright…" He said, returning to his 4X4. "Let's go and get this gold."

**

VII

It was mid afternoon when George and Pedro led a convoy of 8 4X4s, with about 20 security men and the Akazi towards Luis' land. It was in their mutual interest to keep their gold business private and George agreed to stay on guard with his men outside the property, while Pedro and the Akazi placed the gold into 10 boxes under lock and key.

Pedro decided to only part with 210 Kilos of gold in the boxes provided, leaving the remainder 40 Kilos in the same place, but interred a little deeper under the same floor boards, causing a few laughs among the Indios as they did it.

"By the way…" Quito addressed his braves before leaving the house with the 10 boxes. "No more alcohol from this point, until we're back with our families…"

"I'll see to that." Taco decided to put Quito's mind at rest.

"Careful with those boxes…," recommended George to his men, as the boxes were being loaded onto the vehicles moments later. As far as the security men knew, Pedro and the Akazi had found some Inca artefacts of rare value.

"…And no speeding on the drive back." Sebastião added his voice and by 6:30 in the evening, all the boxes had been safely placed inside George's private wine cellar.

"Leave the boxes locked for now." Pedro told George, as he was about to open one. "I've got a sample of what's in them, if you want to analyse it or have it valued… and we'll open them all when it is time to do business?"

"You are very trusting! Has it not occurred to you that I could double cross you or rob you, with all the armed men that I command?" George's question caused Pedro to chuckle.

"You'd be left with a much bigger problem than me, if that were the case…"

"OK, you've succeeded in putting me off!" He joked and then extracted a jewellers' eye piece from his pocket. "Let's see your sample then…"

Pedro handed him a 250-gram ingot, instantly causing George's eyes to somehow grow a little bigger.

"This is pure Inca gold." He acknowledged without hesitation and almost in shock. He then made a closer visual analysis, which he followed with an acid test before weighing the small gold bar. "Do you know how much this small ingot is worth?"

"Roughly… but I reckon you are probably a lot more into this sort of thing…"

"Well, if sold in the *right circles*, this small ingot could fetch as much as US$12 to 15,000…" He paused. "Of course, I couldn't offer you that sort of rate, but to cover my costs, I could give you up to US$11,000 for each one of those…"

"I reckon that at that price, you'd make around US$1.5 million dollars profit out of 100 Kilos…"

"What are you trying to work out?"

"Well, I'm trying to work out that if our brotherhood friends were to tell you to give me US$10million for some valid reason, you'd probably give them to me, right?"

"Probably… What are you driving at?"

"In those boxes, there are 840 identical Ingots to this one, which can be yours for US$10million and will bring you a minimum profit of US$2.5million, instead of a US$10million deficit?" While Pedro spoke, George had his calculator working overtime.

"That's practically US$12,000 per Ingot…," he commented, without raising a complaint.

"…And if you play your cards right, I may eventually offer you more at an advantageous price, should it interest you…"

"How soon will you need the cash?"

"As soon as you're able to take the Akazi and me back to Recife?"

"I'll try and get everything sorted out for you within a week, including the death certificates from the Massacre and your property deeds updated... How does that sound?"

"Wonderful. And to help cover expenses, I'd like to give you this ingot as a personal gift..."

"I couldn't accept that Pedro! My help is given with pleasure to someone whom I trust is about to fight a battle that meets with my full blessing." He paused. "If on the other hand, you want to reward me for probably saving your neck... and for transforming your Inca gold into US$s cash without asking you embarrassing questions..." George did his best not to laugh, "Bring me on board this thing you are about to embark on... anonymously of course." He stretched out his hand and Pedro shook it, after a slight hesitation.

"I'll put in a good word for you... Is that good enough for now?"

"I leave it in your capable hands... and thank you in advance for your valuable endorsement..." George's handshake was lengthy and robust.

*

Pedro was getting ready for bed when he suddenly noticed a shadowy silhouette in the living area of his room... he then saw Quito standing up from a chair, giving him the scare of his life!

"Bloody hell man... You scared the shirt out of me!!! ... How did you get in here?"

"Sorry Pedro... I've been practicing with the necklace..."

"Observing this dimension from the other?"

"And other bits... it's a lot of fun. You should gain some practice too, for whenever you might need to use it...?"

"It's all down to having the chance..." Pedro looked at him

a bit more intently, noticing the Akazi Chief didn't quite seem himself. "You've not done anything improper, have you?"

"I feel a bit ashamed actually…" He admitted.

"What have you done?"

"I've watched this big black woman having a bath…!"

"Marlene?"

"I don't know her name… but I have never seen breasts that size before!!!"

"Easy man… You are not planning to propose to her, are you?"

"Of course not… my other wives would kill me… but Wow…!"

"Quito, you'd better pull yourself together and get back before someone thinks that you've gone missing…"

"I've got my own room now…"

"Don't you even dream about trying to get Marlene in bed with you OK?" Pedro looked at him. "We'll be home in less than a week from now and you'd better start saving some energy for your wives, or you'll never hear the end of it from them! Women just seem to sense those things…"

"You're right, I think I'd better get some sleep… Don't forget to practice…," was the last thing he said before disappearing.

With Quito gone, Pedro felt that the time and circumstances were indeed perfect for practicing with the necklace, and after a few bumps against his bedroom furniture and a head butt against a wall, he felt ready to have a bit of a wander around the mansion, it was about 2 a.m. by then!

There was an eerie silence around George's home. One of the security men was quietly sampling some of his master's whiskey in the study, while another slept deeply on a chair near the front entrance!

George's private quarters were huge. His Stetson rested on the head of a life size statue of himself, near to where he slept, and his bedroom extended into a further 3 rooms: a private living room, a double bathroom and a walk-in vault, with a spiral staircase link to a false wall in his private wine cellar on the floor below.

In the servants' part of the mansion, a young black girl was busy ironing some dry laundry and he even found Marlene's bedroom, with Quito standing in silent observation of the half naked woman as she slept!

"Quito!!!" exclaimed Pedro, almost causing the poor man to have a heart attack.

"I was on my way to bed…" He justified himself. "But… What are you also doing here, anyway?"

"Just practicing… I got here purely by accident…"

*

Between having Luis's property re-registered in Pedro's name and dealing with all the legalities related to the massacre, George and Pedro became inseparable in the week that followed, and even flew together on a couple of occasions to Rio Branco, in George's little Cessna.

In the Estate's hangar, besides his ever-ready military helicopter he also kept a "Gulfstream G200" for longer haul flights, when he travelled with his family or business associates. The plane could take up to 10 passengers and was being made ready to fly to Recife at the end of that week.

Between one conversation and another, George also revealed that he intended to keep the gold for himself, as a "small" nest egg on the side, and that he always kept around US$50million inside a walk-in safe, only accessible from his bedroom in the mansion.

"I sometimes dream that one of these days I'm going to wake up and find that US$s are not worth the paper they are printed on…" George confessed on the second return from Rio Branco.

"That would be quite an event… but they've got it made! Who would go and fleece them?"

"Do you know how much they owe the Chinese?"

"No…"

"It is rumoured it runs into trillions of dollars…"

Over this period, Pedro and Quito had also stepped up their night-time necklace practice, and could now make it do what they wanted without having to think too much about it! The courtiers seemed happy with the way things were progressing and decided to give Pedro a month to get himself organised before going for broke with the Americans; which was their diplomatic way of saying that he also needed to look the part in every aspect!

"What should I do? Get a penthouse in Rio or Recife?" He enquired of Ninan.

"Why not? Get one in each of the two cities… with a couple of fast cars to match. Then get a proper wardrobe of clothes in both places and be seen among the well-to-do…," encouraged Ninan

"The gold share in my hands this far would probably not suffice…" He complained.

"I'm not asking you to use your own money… This could be classed as business expenses."

"That really is generous…"

"I didn't say they would be yours to keep…," Ninan had to chuckle. "…and I'm sure that Auqui and Ana could even authorise the purchase of a Yacht with which to impress your American friends…" He paused. "And one last word of advice before spending our money Pedro; keep your Akazi wives out of sight… remember that a lot of the people you'll be dealing with have hidden views on race…"

"OK…"

With less than 24 hours to go for their flight home, there was great excitement among the Akazi Braves, mixed with a little apprehension about flying:

"It's either that or walking…" From the Inca dimension, Pedro and Quito struggled not to laugh, as they observed

Taco dissuading his Unit from proposing to their Chief to let them travel back by Bus.

Still moving around from inside the Inca dimension (*Inca mode*), it was 1 a.m. when Pedro brought Quito to his room, to show him the contents of two leather cases George had given him earlier that evening.

"I never thought I'd see so much money…!" The Akazi Chief almost hesitated in picking up a neat packet of 100X100 Dollar bills, to then flick through it. "5 million in each bag?" He wanted confirmation and Pedro nodded. "Where are we going to keep all this money safe?"

"Personally, I'm planning to keep US$50,000 with me and to split my share between two banks, in safe deposit boxes."

"In Recife?"

"Yes, as soon as we land, and to keep it all there until I have decided exactly what I'm going to do with it." He paused. "George has already made the appointments and will introduce me in person to the relevant people in both banks."

"I think that's what I should do too." He looked at Pedro. "Why don't you keep my share together with yours in your deposit boxes once we get to Recife? I need to have a good think about the way I'll be using my share too… and I'm not going to bury it like we've done with the 40 Kilos…!"

"I don't mind, if you're happy with that… Just let me know when you need any of it?"

"Yes… It will stop me from having nightmares." He sighed. "My people have never really had much money to spend… and if suddenly they were to be let loose with a few thousand to blow…! Can you imagine?"

"I see exactly what you mean and it is a wise decision… I might even give you a couple of ideas on how to benefit the whole tribe, rather than for you to leave things to chance…"

"It's agreed then and I can go to bed now… I'm not really looking forward to flying tomorrow, I must admit."

"I wouldn't be too nervous about it… The pilot won't be wearing a parachute either…"

"I'll remember that…" He chuckled to himself and then walked out through the door of Pedro's room!

*

It was a smooth 4-hour flight with only a little turbulence on their descent to Recife's International Airport, instantly halting all conversations among the Akazi! …And they all clapped hands to thank the pilot as he landed.

"The bus to take you all home should be waiting where Paulinho parks the aircraft." Informed George turning to face a bunch of happy faces, while they continued to taxi towards the designated alighting slot. "Looking forward to flying again?" The smiles remained, but there was no audible reply!

Unlike the remaining Akazi, Quito was unusually quiet and sombre as they lined up to board their rented bus.

"You OK?" Enquired Pedro

"I'm dreading the moment I have to confront the families of those we've had to bury…"

"It is going to be no easy task; I agree… especially when those same people will be witnessing the happiness of the families of those returning…" Pedro looked at Quito who seemed to have suddenly aged. "And what if we were to give their families some money… as if it were a gift from those who died?" Quito looked at Pedro, a little unsure of what to say. "Something like US$10,000 from each of the dead? …50-50 you and me?"

"It is a good idea, but it is all so delicate…"

"I'll tell you what… no one knows that we've arrived; right?"

"No one." He confirmed.

"I've only got for an hour or so at the banks with George… and they are both on the same street. What if I ask the driver to take you all for lunch at the Parraxaxá and join you there once I'm done?"

"So we can all get to the Camp at the same time?" Quito seemed happy with that, when Pedro nodded to confirm. "Get me also US$50,000 from my pile?"

"OK"

Pedro then got into a waiting Taxi with George, to head for the banks.

"It must be a weight off your shoulders, to see the Indios back in their Camp…?" Commented George, as they both tried to look casual with US$10million in cash!

"They are a grossly undervalued wholesome people, George…"

Both banks awaited their arrival and altogether, it took Pedro less than 40 minutes to part with US$9.9Million.

"After today, when should I expect to hear from you regarding *our venture*?" Asked George moments later, as he was about to get into another Taxi back to the Airport.

"At the most, within the next 3 to 4 weeks… I've given myself a month to get all my bearings and will get in touch with you as soon as I'm ready?"

"In the meantime, should you need anything, let me know yeah?" He stretched out his hand for a handshake, to then offer Pedro a manly hug of friendship.

"Thank you for everything George… and look after yourself."

*

Pedro, Quito and the others got to the Akazi Camp at dusk, to a euphoric reception. Deedee and Ara wouldn't let go of Pedro, nor did the wives of those returning. The night fires had been lit but the party mood soon died down when Quito assembled the families of those who would never come home to one side, for the dreaded moment. The expression of sadness on his face spoke louder than any of his words could... and the wailing started even before he could utter the first sentence.

To try to lessen the pain of wives, children and family members, Quito then manufactured his own epic version of the way they had died; how their lives had contributed towards a bright new future for all the Akazi... and how proud and grateful they should all feel. He then requested that each family should see him privately, to create some sort of closure.

"Shall I give you my share of the money now?" Pedro whispered to Quito as they both waited for the first family of the bereaved to enter the Chief's hut.

"No. I won't give it to them yet... I'll only tell them about it for now..." Quito looked at Pedro. "There's still too much grief in their hearts... they wouldn't appreciate it at this moment in time."

"You know best..."

*

The pregnancies of Deedee and Ara were still not visible to the naked eye, but they already acted *maternally* in some nondescript ways. Neither of them wanted to remain in the Akazi Camp any longer than absolutely necessary. They wanted that feeling of being a special little family again and entreated Pedro to walk with them to their shacks by first light.

"We've got a lot of catching up to do...," warned Deedee, holding Pedro's left hand as they walked, while Ara had claimed ownership of the right one.

"She's speaking for both of us...," confirmed Ara, distractedly inspecting his face when he wasn't looking, as if trying to find if anything about him had changed.

"You are both looking prettier than when I left...," Pedro commented with sincerity.

"We really hope you mean it and feel rested...," Deedee triggered Ara's giggle.

"What sort of plans are you guys hiding from me…?" Pedro forced Deedee to snigger too.

"Would you like to sleep with both of us tonight?" She then proposed in between giggles.

"Wooo… you are kidding me, right?" Pedro stopped to turn to Deedee

"No, it is something we've been thinking about for some time…" Deedee confessed, as they continued to walk. "Would it make you feel embarrassed?"

"We've been practicing some things with each other, to make it more special…" Ara was quick to confirm.

"Where did you get all those ideas from?" Pedro wasn't too sure whether to allow himself to be aroused by the thought, or to be a spoilsport and insist on monogamous nights…

"It is a custom among the Akazi that when a man with more than one wife returns from a long absence, the first sexual night back should be shared equally with all his wives…"

"Poor Quito…!" Pedro thought out loud with a chuckle. "He's got four…"

"We know…," Deedee seemed lost in laughter. "Last night Ara was ever so surprised to see him back…?!!"

Nothing had changed in any of the shacks and after bathing in the stream, Pedro decided to catch some fresh fish while the women cleaned his shack and prepared a fire.

"Tell us what happened", requested Deedee, while Ara and she prepared a fish meal for the three.

Pedro wasn't too sure of what version of events to tell them, especially since the wives of the others would have undoubtedly popped the same question to their husbands; and he felt a bit stupid for not having thought of some official version beforehand.

"How much do you know of our adventure already?" Pedro tried to buy some time to think.

"Well… That you, Quito and the others went looking for some gold belonging to our forefathers, and that it had been hidden somewhere… in our native homeland?" Deedee gave a résumé.

"…And that you found it…," added Ara.

"That's basically it, really… We still left most of it behind… and when some "Bandoleiros" tried to steal it from us, we killed them all… but some of us also got killed in the process…"

"Why don't you just tell us you don't want to talk about it?" Deedee also knew how to be blunt.

"The really exciting thing about this is that we are rich and will soon be able to do things we never thought we would…"

"Such as?" asked Ara.

"Basically, there is almost nothing we couldn't buy or do…," Pedro's mind went a bit blank.

"Could we buy a car and drive around?" Deedee suggested.

"Yes… beautiful clothes… I could bring teachers to the Camp to teach everyone how to read and write and lots more.

"Live in the white-man's city and go to a cinema?" It was Ara's turn.

"That too… among other things. We could even have a big house with servants just for us and your babies…," Pedro was successfully blowing their minds.

"Wow…!" Ara sighed, letting her imagination flow

"Do you think the three of us will still be happy with so many of those things?" Deedee had reservations.

"We don't have to have everything!" Pedro clarified. "To be honest, the thing I like best about this is to know that we can do or buy practically whatever, whenever we may want to…"

"It seems almost evil…" Deedee smiled, a little unsure about the wisdom around this, and somewhat afraid about the things the future could bring to them as a family.

"I don't understand what you're so concerned about," Ara censured "In the end it will always be up to us to generate our happiness or misery…"

Pedro also informed them that he would often be gone for a few days at a time over the foreseeable future, in order to get all the gold for himself and the tribe.

"You don't have to go away to sleep with both of us at the same time on a regular basis you know?" Deedee joked, somehow pleased to see that Pedro's ambitions included her people.

"Gosh... Do we really have to wait until tonight to be in bed?" Ara was suddenly desperate for a way of releasing her excitement about so many things jamming in her mind.

That afternoon provided the girls with one of Pedro's poorest ever performances...! Sandwiched from both sides between the warm naked bodies of his young wives, he was soon surprised by their ability to make him succumb to their touch and kisses... causing him to be horribly premature as to their expectations!!!

"Oh dear...!"

*

"You seem distant..." Deedee whispered, seeing that Pedro was awake late into the night and moved closer to him as Ara slept. "Is something worrying you?" She asked, fascinated by his necklace.

"I might need to go to Recife for one or two days to organise my finances and a few other bits." He announced, putting an arm around her to bring her closer still.

"This is a beautiful necklace... I've noticed one like this on Quito... Did you guys buy it as to mean something?"

"No, it was a gift..."

"A gift?" Her eyes turned to look at him.

"Well, there were these two extremely fat middle aged twins with breasts so big we couldn't even see their faces..." He started, forcing Deedee to block her nose to suppress her laughter, not to wake Ara.

"Come on! Be serious..."

"If I tell you the whole truth of what happened, will you keep it a secret?"

"Of course, if that is what you want…" She squeezed up until she reached his lips. "That's it, I'm ready now."

Pedro emptied his *bag* on her and felt a lot better for it afterwards, realising he would no longer have to find excuses for what he would need to do.

"What do you make of it all?"

"It is a wild story, to say the least…" She looked deep into his eyes as if to ascertain that everything he had told her was true. "As I see it, at best, you'll be forever in debt to those people… But, what if you fail?"

"Failure is not an option. I'm being given all the tools I could possibly need to succeed, be it by hook or by crook…"

"I wish I had an education that would make me useful to you in your quest…" She felt frustrated

"Your love and understanding is the greatest help you could ever give me…"

"You know you've got every bit of me… everything at any time of the day or night…" She looked lovingly into his eyes and whispered, "You wouldn't believe how ready I am…"

*

Pedro, Deedee and Ara arrived back at the Akazi Camp on day three after his return. Pedro had levelled the *score* with his two wives and they both looked happy as they mixed with some of their friends.

"You seem like you've lost weight…" Pedro teased Quito, the moment they were alone.

"Tell me about it!!!" Quito brought him inside his hut with a chuckle. "When do you plan to make a move?"

"I was hoping that you'd keep me company in Recife for a couple of days leaving in an hour or so?"

"That's music to my ears! With pleasure… What are we doing there?"

"We need to get organised for this Inca Project…" Pedro paused. "Would you believe it? I don't even have a mobile phone, or a laptop… or a car… you name it!"

"Well we've got money…" Quito chuckled.

"Indeed…" Pedro looked at Quito as if waking up. "We also need some smart suits and accessories…"

"Give me five minutes to put some white-man's clothes on and I'll be ready… How do you plan to get to Recife?"

"The easiest might be for us to go to Pitimbu in my fishing boat… and we could then either take a bus from there or rent a car…?"

Pedro didn't have a credit card to rent a car with and they eventually reached Recife by intercity bus in the late afternoon, followed by a taxi to the "Onda Mar" Hotel, where they booked a room for the night.

"Would you like a room with a double bed or two single beds?" asked the receptionist with bright orange glasses who could do no more to advertise his sexual orientation!

"I think we'll have the single beds… please…," replied Pedro doing his best to stay serious. "We could always put them together later… I suppose?" He joked, causing Quito to explode into laughter.

Recife was a bustling city of almost 2 million people and one of Brazil's major business centres. It had an impressive skyline, endless miles of sandy beaches and noisy rush-hour traffic jams, with no shortage of entertainment and nightlife distractions. Pedro and Quito however were determined not to be side tracked from their 3-day mission to get things moving.

"It was good of you to think of engaging Joaquim to be our fulltime taxi driver while we're here…," commented Quito as they checked their 7th floor Hotel room.

"We would otherwise be forever stuck looking for places, parking spaces, you name it… We'd get nothing done." Pedro paused to inspect the view towards the seafront and then added. "We need to get two mobile phones before the shops close… and to also have a chat with Ninan…"

"…So as to get our bearings for the next two days?"

"As well as to collect a few contact names and numbers…" Pedro nodded.

"I'm glad we won't have to spend our own money on any of the things we're going to need… Especially when it comes to expensive apartments and flashy cars…," He paused. "I'm looking forward to buying some nice clothes… A big TV for the tribe, mobile phones for everyone, some solar panels… I've made quite a list…" He said proudly, extracting a couple of folded up pages from one of his pockets, which he then showed Pedro.

"Good gracious Quito!" exclaimed Pedro as he checked the Chief's list. "But if I were you, I wouldn't go beyond the clothes, the TV, some solar panels and a few mobiles for now…"

"Do you think it's too much… and that people will ask questions about the provenance of the money?"

"No, I'm not worried about that. You could always say that I gave you the money and I'd deal with that for you…"

"What is it then?"

"I'd introduce things gradually to them… you yourself mentioned that they would probably go crazy if let loose with a few thousand dollars each…" Pedro looked at him. "Besides, I'd like to have your thoughts on a plan I've made for us first… After dinner… once we've bought our mobiles?"

"You're right, I think we'd better get going."

Joaquim was a wealth of useful information on everything about Recife. By dinner time, as well as their mobiles, they had bought two smart outfits each, and Pedro now also had a lap top like one he once had.

"Do you guys want to watch a show or me to find you a couple of nice girls for the night?" The driver proposed as he dropped them back at their hotel.

"I think we'll give those a pass Joaquim, but thanks… we still have a bit of a working night ahead of us and an early morning start… You should probably get some sleep too…" Pedro suggested.

"Good night then… what time do you want me in the morning?"

"Not before 8. I'll call you…?"

"OK Boss"

Back in their Hotel room, they decided to contact Ninan before going down for dinner;

"How are you two doing?" He asked in his usual friendly manner.

"We are good Ninan… and about to get organised, as you've suggested…," Pedro wasted no time in getting to the point.

"I spoke with Ana about giving you access to whatever funds you may need and arrangements have been made with one of our trusted lawyers in Recife. His name is Patricio Mendes and he is at your disposal for anything that you may need as of now, as well as his secretary Thelma. You can also use her as your own secretary and P.R. assistant. I'm told she is very good at everything she does…" He chuckled, as if momentarily reading Pedro's thoughts! "I'd say arrange to meet them first thing tomorrow morning and have them help you in whatever you may need. You can confide in them."

"That is excellent news… Do I have any particular limits on what I can spend on each item?"

"Not really… I presume you'll be using common sense and will try to get value for money, obviously… but to give you a guideline, including your own small private Jet and a Yacht, try your best to stay under US$90 Million for everything." He paused. "And if it all goes well; you might even get a pleasant surprise in the end…"

As on previous occasions, their communication was clinically short, with Ninan also passing on to Pedro the personal mobile numbers of Patricio and Thelma, as well as George Azevedo's.

"I somehow sense that this American company takeover is not the end of the road here...," Quito voiced his thoughts.

"Do you think they are grooming me/us for something else afterwards?"

"I don't know about my part in it but... anyway... It's great news to know we've got some field assistants..."

"Indeed...," agreed Pedro. "Shall we go for a bite to eat?" Quito was more than ready and they were both out of the door less than a minute later.

Although far from being an intellectual academic, Quito was not only intelligent but also very perceptive, when it came to analysing situations; and his comment about the possibility of ulterior Inca plans started Pedro thinking: *what could any of these plans possibly be?*

"I know exactly what you are thinking...," Quito had an amused expression on his face as they entered the Hotel restaurant. "But I wouldn't waste any time thinking about it... it would be just as bad as worrying about what you might be having for dinner on your 90th birthday!!!!" Quito's allegory made Pedro laugh. "If I were you, I'd worry a bit more about the way that receptionist with the orange glasses was looking at you as we got off the elevator..."

"Remind me to have my back against the wall next time we approach the lift?"

"I'll remind you..." He chuckled and they both proceeded to fill their plates from the extensive buffet. "What plans did you want to talk to me about regarding the tribe?" Quito asked, once they sat down to eat.

"In fact, that is something I should check with this Patricio guy first... Which reminds me, do you think it's a bit too late to phone him, to arrange a time for us to meet tomorrow?"

"I'd call him..."

**

VIII

Patricio's Office was in an exclusive area of the city, reflecting the power of his employers. It was tastefully decorated with a blend of "objects d'art" and exotic plants here and there throughout, which contrasted with classic mahogany furnishings against a light grey carpet. The man himself made a point of being the first to welcome them as they arrived. Of medium build with a made to measure suit and an air of affluence about him, Patricio had a thick dark moustache that spread like a beach parasol beneath his nose, each time he smiled.

"Delighted to meet you both..." He readily stretched his arm for a powerful handshake. "I hope it wasn't too difficult to find this place."

"It is our pleasure too..." Pedro also spoke on behalf of Quito as they exchanged handshakes.

"But first let me show you our premises, before taking you into my office;" Patricio offered to lead the way around the spacious corporate apartment.

Taking a short corridor away from the Reception area, he started by offering them a glance into a large office shared by four people involved in secretarial duties, followed by a small canteen and other communal areas for staff use. Returning past Reception, he then continued along a wider corridor this time, coming to a halt by a door about half way along it;

"This is your own office to use as you please..." He announced as he opened the door to an enormous double office with its own bar, library and social living space, complemented by a floor to ceiling glass wall, with a grandiose

20th floor view of the city. Behind one of two internal doors, he was then shown a bedroom with its own bathroom-toilet, should he ever need an emergency overnight stay.

"I'm impressed…" Was all that Pedro could think of saying as they continued to follow Patricio, this time through the second internal door to Thelma's office, where the woman in a business suit stood up from behind her desk, before coming around to greet them with a radiant smile.

"Delighted to meet you…" She stretched her well-seasoned corporate hand to both. "I'm very much looking forward to us working together…" She gave Pedro an accommodating social wink as they shook hands.

"Likewise," Pedro replied on behalf of both once again, doing his best not to show how taken aback he was by the woman's looks and natural ease. She was about 5ft 8in, raised to 5ft 10 with her heals… with a curvy body definitely in its prime, although already in her early thirties. Her dark hair tied at the back, the blue eyes behind a pair of frameless glasses and rich lips were then further enhanced by a touch of Indio influence from some generations past.

"Shall I follow you into your office?" She then asked turning to Patricio, as he opened a second connecting door from her office to his.

"Yes please Thelma, if you would."

Patricio's office was a mirror image of Pedro's own, with a very pleasant vague scent of pipe tobacco, probably emanating from the actual wood furnishings. He was quick to bring everyone into the social area of the office and as if by magic, a young black domestic servant appeared pulling a silver trolley with coffee, tea and biscuits.

Pedro felt comfortable in the white leather couches and while each one got their right measures of milk and sugar, Thelma sneaked a discrete self-confident girl Friday smile at Pedro.

"Well, Pedro and Quito…," Patricio felt more at ease

standing up as he spoke. "Just to make things clear, both Thelma and I are perfectly aware of the mission you are supposed to front, as well as lead in some respects, and our prime role is to ensure that you succeed with flying colours." He paused. "And so, be it for a pencil sharpener, a hit man, legal advice, or anything else you may require, we are your first port of call…"

"You can also count on me as your Personal Assistant; from secretarial tasks to representing you at business meetings, if need be… and more." She looked at Pedro intently. "It is important you should know that by confiding in me fully, I will be enabled to simultaneously anticipate your personal needs as well as assess those demanded by each situation."

"Are you married?" Quito couldn't resist popping the question in Pedro's mind, causing every one to laugh.

"Only to my work…," was her relaxed reply. "Except at weekends…," she then teased him with the full power of her self-confidence, causing the Akazi Chief to retreat at double tempo.

As if to draw a line between the introductions and the business proper, they enjoyed a light-hearted moment for a minute or two, revealing how Thelma could also be one of the boys when she wanted to. They then returned to work.

"Anyway…," advanced Patricio, still chuckling, "I believe the most pressing things just now are to build up your social facade, and to establish some visible historical credentials that will provide a trail of information… and thus add legitimacy to your role." He paused. "Would you trust me to act as an intermediary for you in some acquisitions?"

"On things, such as?" Pedro wanted to make sure they were both on the same wavelength.

"I was told you'd be looking for a penthouse here and another in Rio, perhaps complimented by a Ferrari, an Aston Martin or both… an ocean-going yacht, an executive jet… and maybe a 4X4 to take you back and forth from the

Akazi Camp?" He took a pause. "We could even go as far as dealing with all your other personal stuff like clothes, plus the scrutiny and payment of salaries to any staff you may need to employ… such as domestics to service your penthouses, a yachting crew, a well experienced aircraft pilot… security personnel… and I could continue."

"Have you looked at all the costs of what you've suggested?" asked Pedro.

"We have…," replied Thelma. "And if you were to trust our taste with it all, we could get everything sorted for you within a week at a cost of no more than US$72 Million, including a year's wages and staff related expenses…"

"Where do I need to sign?" Pedro chuckled.

"You don't need to sign anything…," Thelma smiled at Pedro. "Just say yes and it's as good as done…"

"Go for it Thelma, thank you…" Pedro confirmed, a little speechless, and then turned again to Patricio. "There is also a separate issue I'd like you to look into, if you could…"

"Tell me…"

"With our own money, I'd like to see what would be the chances of the Akazi gaining ownership of the land they currently occupy, with a view to creating a proper solid bricks & mortar village with all the modern home comforts…?"

"How many Akazi are there?" Asked Patricio

"There are 12 families totalling just over 140 people, of which about half are children," replied Quito.

"Leave it with me and I will have some answers for you by tomorrow." Patricio was confident.

The four socialised for a further half an hour or so and it was still mid-morning by the time Pedro and Quito left, with the keys and the codes to enable them to gain entry to their office at any time of day or night, plus the 24/7 direct lines access to Patricio and Thelma.

"Do you know what?" Quito started, while they waited for Joaquim to pick them up.

"What?"

"I'm still struggling to find what my role in this mission is!!!" Quito seemed fed up.

"Well, you are my confidante, my adviser and my secret weapon…"

"Secret weapon?"

"Yes… With the two of us having the ability to use our necklaces for the purposes they serve, it allows us to open all the doors we could want…"

"True… I'd forgotten about that…" He paused. "This Thelma is really hot…"

"I thought you were in love with Marlene!"

"Now that's a lot of woman! That's the sort of woman that should be worshiped…"

"OK then, here's the deal: You leave Thelma to me and I'll leave you Marlene, as well as the hotel receptionist. How does that feel?" Pedro made Quito laugh with gusto.

Joaquim arrived in the nick of time and they followed his advice to have lunch at one of the beach restaurants near the hotel. This was apparently the driver's favourite and the two invited him to join them. With a free afternoon ahead, thanks to Patricio and Thelma, Quito saw this as a good opportunity to get something to take back to the Camp… and soon convinced Pedro to join him in buying a further 75 mobile phones (!!!), one for every Akazi above the age of four, including Deedee and Ara. This of course was further encouraged by the fact that Joaquim knew where they could get good value for a deal of that size!

Returning to the hotel with a pile of other things to take back to the Camp, Pedro received a call from Thelma on his mobile, as they were about to go for dinner.

"Good to hear you from Thelma… What's up?"

"Want to go for a test drive?"

"Just now?" Pedro was taken by surprise.

"Yes, I'm sitting in your new black Range Rover… right outside the hotel…"

"…And Quito?"

"Bring him too… safety in numbers…" She made him laugh with her teasing.

"Indeed…"

Thelma stepped down from the driver's seat to give Pedro the keys and then sat in the back, leaving the front passenger seat for Quito. She was dressed casually this time, her hair was still up, but the business suit had been replaced by a pair of jeans and a plain white T shirt, which somehow brought her well balanced bosom into greater evidence.

Getting into the passenger seat, Quito looked at Pedro pretending to be cross eyed for a split moment!

"Once I get my driver's licence I think I'll get one of these too." Quito was impressed.

"I've not driven in years… I should warn you…" Pedro wasn't too sure if this was a good idea, right in the middle of so much traffic.

"I know you can do it Pedro… just go for it. You're insured anyway…," encouraged Thelma.

Pedro managed to return to the hotel unscathed some 30 minutes later.

"Happy with it?" Thelma wanted to know, as the sweating Pedro returned the keys to her.

"Very much so… I like the colour too… Well done." Pedro thanked her. "Fancy having a drink or two with us?" He then offered.

"I'd love to but I still have quite a bit of work to catch up with… You've got your own office parking space by the way… Shall I keep it there for now?"

"Yes please Thelma that would be great… I'll see you in the morning?"

"I'll look forward to that." She replied with her usual self confidence and went.

"You are definitely in trouble…," commented Quito as they returned indoors.

*

Pedro and Quito checked out of the hotel after breakfast and Joaquim drove them to their office.

"If you ever need a taxi just call me, yeah?" The man was almost emotional.

"We've got your number…," confirmed Quito.

"Thank you for everything," Pedro gave Joaquim a little bit extra for his good service.

Thelma awaited them by the building's entrance and helped pack the 4X4 with all their stuff, before taking the two men up to Patricio.

"Do you live in the City yourself?" Quito asked as they entered the elevator.

"No, I live in Porto de Galinhas…," She looked at Pedro. "Much nicer than being in the middle of all the pollution and it is only 30 minutes' drive from here… the best beaches in Brazil…" She boasted.

"Do you reckon it would be a better investment than in Recife?"

"Definitely. Besides, you already have a bedroom here anyway!!! In Porto de Galinhas, you're only 15 minutes from the airport…" She paused. "I'd say go for a penthouse in Rio, but in Porto de Galinhas, you should go for a seaside mansion with all the trimmings… for the same price as a high-rise concrete box?"

"Shall I leave it in your hands?" Pedro said it, somehow touching a chord!

"Yes please…" She replied with a chuckle. "Shall I see what's available?"

"Why not?"

Patricio seemed about ready to depart on some trip, with an overnight case ready packed by his desk.

"Going somewhere nice?" Pedro asked as they shook hands.

"I'll be off to Rio in a couple of hours, to sign for your penthouse... and from there to Seattle the following morning for your jet... and on to Miami the day after that for your yacht...?"

"It sounds like you're not going to have much time to get bored...," commented Pedro, looking through some images of what would soon be temporarily his, for his approval.

"Definitely not... Thelma will deal with everything else in the way of purchases..."

The silver trolley had been brought in ahead of their arrival and Thelma kept busy by pouring everyone their coffees.

"It all looks very good..." Pedro passed the photos onto Quito. "On the more private side of things... Did you get a chance to look at possible options for the Akazi?" He addressed the question to Patricio.

"I did." He said, searching through his notes. "It is a peninsula about 3 miles wide by 6 in length, surrounded by about 8 miles of crocodile infested swamps going inland. Correct?"

"Close enough...," confirmed Quito, passing the photos on to Thelma.

"Well, the local government could offer you a deal whereby they would offer you a concession for the entire peninsula, providing you foot the bill to transform and run the swampland into a sanctuary for a few bird species as well as for the crocodiles there."

"A straight swap with building permits?" Pedro wanted confirmation.

"Yes... Well: the swamps would have to be turned into some sort of tourist attraction..."

"What sort of realistic costs would this involve?" Quito seemed a little sceptical.

"About US$8 million all-told on swampland infrastructure. This would include a basic link road and a small bridge to the peninsula, to which you'd need to add a further US$1.5 million per annum to cover maintenance running costs...," he paused. "With good management however, you should be able to offset the up keeping costs with the income generated from tourism..."

"I'm not really aware of the current value of land in that area...," Pedro confessed.

"I'd say that as things are, the peninsula could be worth about 10 times that to developers, but for some reason this must have escaped their attention..." He looked at Pedro and Quito. "If you have the availability, I'd definitely seriously consider it..."

"And what about the costs of creating some infrastructure for the Peninsula, including a village to accommodate our numbers... with all the standard facilities...?" Quito asked thoughtfully.

"Everything is relative of course. But if we were to think in terms of building some 30 houses with all the comforts for instance, plus say... around 12 miles of private roads... throw in a bit of landscaping and sea defences..." He paused while jotting a few figures." Realistically you'd probably need to find between US$10 to 25 million, depending on the quality of everything." Patricio then turned to the two men. "This none the less would still leave you with plenty of room for some future development projects to at least get your money back, should you want to go that way...?"

At this point, Pedro looked at Quito to try and measure his reaction.

"...50-50?" Pedro enquired of the Akazi Chief.

"I'd be more than happy to go for it, based on Patricio's

figures... but what about your own private plans?" He looked at Pedro.

"Don't worry about those... Our money would certainly be worth considerably more and besides, adding it all up, we'd still be left with a considerable amount of change...," replied Pedro.

"Shall I seal the deal and get a few specialists working on a full project with a proper cost projection?" Patricio suddenly seemed a little pressed for time.

"Please go ahead...," Pedro confirmed and Quito nodded with a big grin. "When will you need some money from us?"

"I'll deal with all that and there's no need for any money for now..." Thelma was pleased to confirm while operating her mobile phone. "You will not need to part with any money until we have evaluated the total costs involved from the specialists, once they come back to us with their proposals..." She then added switching her mobile off. "It's all done."

"I think I really need to get going guys... I'm sorry about this..." Patricio got up, prompting the others to do the same, and picked up his case.

"Shall I take you to the Airport?" Thelma offered.

"No thanks... I've got a taxi waiting..." He said already on his way out.

"Good luck..."

"That's very typical Patricio..." Chuckled Thelma once he was gone "He is ultra precise in everything he does, but when it comes to catching a plane... It's always a mad rush!" She poured herself another coffee, with Pedro and Quito declining a second cup.

"I think we'd better get back to the Akazi Camp and leave you to it." Pedro was ready to go.

"I certainly have lots to keep me busy..." She smiled.

"Keep us updated yeah?" Pedro stretched his hand.

"I'll be in touch daily, don't worry."

*

Turning off the Highway onto the dirt track that meandered through the swamp, Pedro felt he had recovered a lot of his driving confidence, and as he reached the Camp there was no shortage of ooohs and aaahs of admiration for the vehicle!

Quito was soon surrounded by adults and children alike, the moment they realised he had brought something for everyone, while Deedee and Ara couldn't wait to get inside the 4X4. Pedro made the mistake of giving them a short ride, which resulted in him having to give everyone a turn, in groups of 7 to 8 people all squashed up inside!

The trail to his shack was just about wide enough for the 4X4 and he was soon home with Deedee and Ara, both of whom couldn't wait to see what he was hiding inside two neatly folded fashion bags;

"Wow…" They both uttered as they discovered their own mobiles and a dress each. "Shall we bathe in the stream before trying them on?" Ara suggested, continuing to look at her orange and white striped dress.

"Definitely…" replied Deedee, just as proud of her version of the same dress in white and blue. "Do you think I should let my hair grow?" She enquired of Pedro, placing the dress beneath her chin.

"You are both very pretty whichever way…"

"He is definitely asking for trouble…," Ara warned Deedee and then became more serious. "Joking aside… I think that what we'd really like was someone to advise us on the changes we need to make… so as not to embarrass you in the white-man's world?"

"We'd certainly be noticed if we went to Recife as we are just now…" Pedro chuckled. "I think I might know someone actually… leave it with me for a few days?"

"Come on Ara…" Deedee pulled her cousin up excitedly and they both went running towards the stream in a giggly mood.

Their evening was then spent learning and discovering

things about their mobiles whilst wearing their dresses, until they were startled by a call on Pedro's mobile;

"Hi Thelma… Everything OK?"

"I'm fine… I spent most of the day buying clothes for you and I found something along the lines of what we were talking about…"

"About Porto de Galinhas?"

"Yes… If you're not too busy I'd like to show you this place currently available. Tomorrow?"

"No problem… where shall we meet?"

"We could have lunch at the Beijupira Restaurant in Porto de Galinhas and I could show you the area as well as this mansion I've seen afterwards?"

"Sounds good… 12:00 noon?"

"I'll be there… Good night…"

"Good night…"

"Who is she?" Deedee had to ask, and Pedro went on to explain that he now had two specialised people helping him in his quest. "Is she the person you were thinking of… to advise Ara and me?"

"Yes… She is very good at getting things done… and I'm sure you'll both like her…" Ara and Deedee exchanged a silent glance that required no words…

**

IX

Pedro drove to Pitimbu with the first light of day and bought a trailer to take his fishing boat back to the bay.

"Pedro Bolivar?" João Guimarães had to come in person to check that it was indeed him loading his boat on the trailer of the 4X4.

"Good to see you João…" Pedro offered his hand for a handshake.

"Did you win the Lottery?" The Officer enquired examining his vehicle with a frown.

"No…" Pedro looked a bit puzzled. "Is that because you see me with a car?"

"Well, it's not just a car! This is a US$50,000 car… Is it yours?"

"Yes, well… Sort of… Did you think it was stolen?"

"I didn't accuse you of stealing anything… but let's face it; one moment you live in a shack and come to town to sell a couple of dry fishes occasionally to make ends meet… and the next you turn up like a multimillionaire… wouldn't you be surprised?"

"It's all above board João… You've got no cause for concern…"

"What happened?"

"I got tired of fishing and am now working for a company of lawyers in Recife. Are you OK with that?"

"I meant no offence…" He suddenly decided to back off.

"None taken João… We must have a drink next time…"

"OK. By the way…" He took a longish pause. "Whatever happened to Luis?"

"It is a sad story João… He was killed by some "Bandoleiros" while trying to start a new life near Rio Branco… The Police there have all the details…" He paused. "I must rush now though or I'll be late for an important appointment. Do you mind?"

"Not at all… I hope to see you again soon…" He still managed a suspicious smile.

*

Porto de Galinhas was not quite the millionaire's playground Pedro had anticipated, but what it lacked in high roller vitality, it excelled in cosiness. There was something of the "home-made" about everything and even the smallest detail seemed to reflect someone's love.

The restaurant too was a bit like great grandma's dining room turned museum. Dimly lit… this was a place where the power of the spirits, magic spells and Voodoo was taken seriously.

"Mister Bolivar?" Enquired a short middle aged waiter, the moment Pedro walked in.

"Yes?"

"Please follow me." The fellow led the way through near darkness to a table dimly lit by a single fat red candle… and Thelma stood up to greet him with a handshake and a big smile, almost unrecognisable! The glasses had gone and the ebony hair was down, tied to one side. She wore a colourful dress reminiscent of the 1960s and an old straw hat rested on a cushion next to her.

"I would have never recognised you under this sort of light…" Pedro was taken aback by her ability to re-invent her appearance and remain extremely attractive, each time he saw her.

"Did you have problems finding this place?"

"No…" The waiter brought them two glasses of something!

"I had problems parking the Rover though!" He laughed. "Did you order these?"

"I've ordered everything for us…"

"I see…"

"After guessing your taste in cars, shoes and clothes, I thought I'd have a go at testing your taste in food too…"

"Mystery sorted." He looked at her a little more intently. "By the way, you look delicious…"

"Thank you… This place is reputed to be magical and prone to inspiring feelings of love upon its customers…" Thelma's comment almost made Pedro spill his drink trying not to laugh.

"Do you think we'll be safe?" He joked, whipping off a drop of drink that had stuck to the tip of his nose.

"I hope so…" She also found the whole thing funny. "Joking aside, besides the main reason that brought you to Porto de Galinhas, I thought this would be a great opportunity for us to learn a little bit about each other, outside the business environment that brought us together in the first instance?"

"I couldn't be more favourable… and I'm glad to see that you are human after all, rather than just an ultra-efficient wonder woman…," he paused "You must have a good team behind you, I reckon."

"Of course we do…"

"I don't mean to sound obvious but… Are you and Patricio married?" The question caused Thelma to suppress some laughter.

"Not at all. I have every admiration for him though… but I don't think women are his cup of tea anymore…"

"He is gay?" Pedro had to lower his voice and bite one of his knuckles not to laugh.

"Well, as it is often said, he came out of his closet about 5 years ago, after 20 years of marriage and two teenage children… and has been in a steady relationship with someone I've never seen ever since." She paused. "Having said this, he keeps his private life very much to himself… and so much so that I actually found out about this through other sources…"

"I won't say a word…"

"How about you?"

"I'm not gay…" The answer caused Thelma to laugh.

"I meant are you married?"

"I thought you knew everything about me by now…"

"You make it sound awful!" She pretended to complain. "Well, I know that you've been married once and that it ended in tragic circumstances… but with you living with the Akazi, and since there are no records of their marriages, I thought you'd probably have someone?"

"I do have two young wives; Deedee and Ara, respectively 18 and 17 years of age… and both of whom are currently pregnant."

"Wooow…" Thelma was a little disconcerted with Pedro's reply. "And how many mistresses?"

"None I'm afraid… They make sure I've got no energy left for any extras…"

"They must be very pretty…" She pointed to his empty glass "Shall we have another round?"

"Yes please…" He handed his empty glass back to the waiter. "In fact, I was talking about you with them last night when you rang…"

"I hope I didn't make them jealous!"

"Not at all. Anyway; they want to integrate into the white-man's world, as they call it, but feel they'd very much need the guidance… of perhaps someone like you?"

"I don't think I'd be the person for the job, but I know someone who does that professionally."

The first course then arrived, combining fresh scallops and king prawns with a fried banana under a thin line of honey.

"How very exotic!" exclaimed Pedro. "Are you a wine drinker?"

"Red?"

"Of course, I'd better let you choose... I've got the feeling you know me better than I know myself!!!"

Thelma ordered a bottle of wine while chuckling.

"How did you get involved in what you do Thelma?"

"Have you got the violin ready?"

"It's not one of those, is it?"

"Well, I was a Law student in Rio when I became pregnant with my son. I named him Aurelio. The father of the child didn't want to know and my parents somehow, heartlessly, talked me into having the little one adopted right after birth, so I could finish my studies..." She took a pause to compose herself. "Anyway...I never came to terms with that and ended up abandoning my studies. I saw a job advertising a vacancy for the position of Legal Secretary in Recife... and the rest is history. I've worked for Patricio ever since and never saw my parents again."

"I'm sorry to hear that... Have you ever managed to trace your baby?"

"No, I don't want to... It would only destroy other peoples' lives and my own all over again, needlessly..."

"You've got a good point... And what about mister right...?"

"There's no mister right..."

"Mrs right...?" Pedro tried to lighten the mood with a funny face.

"I've tried a couple of those too..." She laughed looking at Pedro's face. "I enjoy a bit of fun now and then, but I couldn't really live with anyone... I get bored easily when it comes to intimate relationships..." She paused "Are you enjoying lunch?"

"Almost as much as the company... and the wine's good too..."

"We've got wild buffalo grilled steaks to follow..."

"My favourite..." He looked at Thelma truly surprised. "Do you find me predictable?"

"All men are predictable… only some more than others… Fancy some more wine?"

"I think I'd better not, or I might become as predictable as to make you die of boredom…"

"You could always have a siesta at my place… I won't rape you…"

"No thanks, I need to keep a clear head. I'm here on business: remember? And I also need to drive back." He chuckled and she joined him in laughter as they looked at each other.

"Could you bring us another bottle of wine please?" She ordered from the waiter.

"Now you're scaring me!" Pedro joked while saying how he really felt!

"It's all bluff Pedro. I've built a hard crust around my heart so as not to risk breaking it again."

"…And so, to protect yourself *that way*, you always try to end up being disappointed with the people most likely to take you to bed… well ahead of the event?"

"I don't do it on purpose." She glanced at him in between mouthfuls. "You're very perceptive."

"That would make two of us…" Pedro smiled, to then change the subject. "Thelma: what do you know about the people you really work for?"

"I know that you work for them too…" She confirmed "Patricio guards that account zealously and doesn't even bring any related documentation to the office…"

"How do you know when you're working for them? Patricio tells you?"

"He refers to it as the "I" Account…" She then stopped. "Are you in the dark about them too, or just curious to find out how much I know?"

"A bit of both, I suppose… Not that it changes anything… but it would be nice to know a little more…"

"This is one of those situations where the closer you get to

140

the actual truth, the less you know about it… and there's a lot of disinformation too…" She topped up their glasses. "Patricio is a bit like a human telephone exchange, if you like; he brings people and businesses together while preventing them from being in touch with each other directly…" She paused. "Also, the other people you saw in the office, for instance, they run their own research and communications teams elsewhere around the globe, while remaining completely anonymous to their own staff."

"Fascinating… But you must be acquainted with the actual names of some of their businesses and a load of other things (!) otherwise, how could you possibly function in the organisation?"

"I'm a bit like the fortress walls around Patricio… That is my primary function." She couldn't eat anymore! "I know of a lot of businesses that belong to "I" of course, but I also know that the real owners could never be traced that way… And that's about it. And you… what do you know?"

"I know a lot less than you…" Pedro admitted. "…Doesn't it frustrate you not knowing who you really work for?"

"Not in the slightest. My salary is greater than that of Brazil's President and like you, there are only very few things in life I couldn't have, if I really wanted to."

"Are you ready for some dessert, or would you like to wait a while, Mr. Bolivar?" The waiter returned after clearing the table.

"I'm just ready for a good strong coffee, if you please… Everything was very nice…" Pedro replied.

"Make that two, please… and the bill?"

They didn't stay long after that and Thelma insisted they should go around in her smaller car instead of Pedro's 4X4.

Thelma's car was a white Porsche Carrera and the alcohol she had consumed seemed to make no difference to her driving, while Pedro would have dearly loved to go for a good afternoon nap!

Porto de Galinhas was bathed by several tropical beaches of transparent waters and could be described as a growing together of several coastal villages, from the hippy home-made type, to those containing the weekend villas of the mega rich, often hidden behind high walls.

"Porto de Galinhas actually owes its name to the slave trade." She explained as they sped through a stretch of coastal road. "When slavery became outlawed, those slave merchants who continued to illegally trade used the word "Galinhas" (chickens) as their coded word for "slaves"."

"Interesting…"

Pedro wasn't overly impressed with the mansion and decided he would much rather use Porto de Galinhas as the home port for his US$30 million-dollar yacht.

"Where would you rather have your main on-land home then?"

"Does it have to be in Brazil? If I eventually get the yacht to port in here, with a penthouse in Rio, a bedroom and office in Recife plus the peninsula near Pitimbu… why not a mansion somewhere in Florida… or a penthouse in Manhattan?"

"Not a problem… Florida or Manhattan?" She looked at him and then turned the car phone on loud speaker to call her office. "Shall I do a search on both to see what's available?"

"Yes please…"

Thelma's call to her office was brief and someone there called Jasmine promised to e-mail her a list of recommendations within minutes.

"Shall we have coffee at my place while Jasmine searches through data?" She proposed. "I promise I'll behave…"

"Are you sure I won't be attacked by some jealous muscular ex?"

"I'll protect you, don't worry…" She chuckled.

Thelma's home was a super deluxe first and second floor duplex apartment in a high security condominium. Spacious and tastefully decorated, the upper floor contained two bedrooms with their own en-suite bathrooms. These were linked by a suspended staircase to the open-plan downstairs; consisting of a guests' toilet, kitchen, dining and living room spaces all in one, leading onto her private swimming pool embedded into a huge balcony that overlooked the ocean, just 50 metres from the waterfront.

"Now here's a place I wouldn't mind calling home…" He complimented her, genuinely impressed.

"Want to live with me?" She joked while preparing the coffees.

"I don't think my wives would approve…"

"Jokes aside… I'd like you to feel free to crash-in whenever… Just give me a warning call before you do?" She invited casually, coming to the dining table to investigate a sound made by her laptop. "Jasmine's e-mail is through." She announced. "Come and sit here…"

They spent a good hour looking through all that Jasmine had sent and concluded that a particularly prestigious Manhattan penthouse would be more useful in the Mission ahead.

"Want to go for it?" Thelma asked, picking her mobile phone.

"What do you reckon?"

"I'd go for it… It looks like excellent value… and cosy." She paused with a smile. "Yes?"

"OK…"

In a weird sort of way, whilst attracted to each other, neither felt it appropriate that they should let go just because they could, for their own different reasons… They seemed to somehow conclude that friendship would perhaps pay better long term dividends, rather than the risks of breaking the magic spell of their imaginings.

"Would you really like me to tutor your wives about the white-man's world, as they call it?" Thelma decided to revisit the topic as she drove Pedro back to the 4X4.

"I thought you said you knew some… specialist? Besides,

come to think of it, how could you possibly find the time?" On second thoughts, Pedro suddenly didn't want to reveal the conditions under which they all lived.

"I know that you've not been living in a mansion or penthouse, Pedro…" She commented with clinical precision. "The fewer the secrets we keep from each other, the greater the pleasures and the fruits of our relationship."

"Very wisely spoken." He looked at her. "You won't be able to get to where I'm living driving this though…"

"It's OK… I also have a car just like yours…" She looked amused.

Going back home, Pedro let out a sigh of relief the moment he was alone on the road, and congratulated himself about not having taken advantage of Thelma's free spirit.

*

From his Recife office, together with Thelma, Pedro spent the week that followed gathering information about the American company the "I" Group had targeted. This included learning about their business interests and about some of the people he would most likely have to deal with. Patricio extended his absence to a week, to fully prepare the Manhattan and Rio penthouses, as well as the yacht with its crew of 7 and 2 pilots for the executive Jet.

Not counting Thelma, Pedro now had 11 full time staff and 4 security personnel. Each of the penthouses had 2 domestic workers and 1 local security man. And of the 7-yacht crew, 2 were also securities.

Deedee and Ara got on well with Thelma and it was decided that once Pedro departed for a get-acquainted-tour of his new properties, the three of them would spend a full fortnight of *intense therapy* at Thelma's.

"I hope you're not planning to change them into bourgeois Brazilian housewives…" Commented Pedro to Thelma, as they shared a quick lunch not too far from their offices.

"I wouldn't do that to you… I know you like their wild exotic side… But you want them to be able to blend and play the part as and when required… right?"

"You really know me, you do…" He looked distractedly into her eyes.

"OK… it's time for us to get back to work…" She gave him a more private personal smile.

Quito had spent that same week trying to find out the things that would be more important to all the tribe members, so as to pass the information on to the urban planners, and as for George; Pedro had it in mind to give him a surprise visit in his own private Jet.

*

"You look rested…" Commented Thelma to Patricio as he walked into her office.

"I feel rested." He confirmed with a smile, shaking Pedro's hand. "Good to see you…"

"When did you get back?" Continued Thelma.

"Late last night…" He then turned back to Pedro "Your yacht won't get here for another week, but you can already use your two penthouses whenever… oh and your jet is at Recife's International Airport… I flew back in it…!"

"Fantastic Patricio… Thank you very much."

"Not at all; it's my job…" He then requested Thelma to update him on the general workings of his office whenever she could, and excused himself to go and play catch up with his working backlog. "By the way, I forgot to tell you…" His head then popped back into Thelma's office. "I got you a Ferrari for your Rio home and an Aston Martin for Manhattan… red and dark brown…?" He added.

"Can't wait to see it all…"

It was now Pedro's turn to go into his office. And after confirming with George that he would be on his Estate the following day, he called the Camp;

"Quito?"

"Hi Pedro...Everyone is calling me today!" He seemed to complain!

"Fancy going on a short holiday?"

"Now you're talking...," he paused, trying to guess what this was about. *"Have you got all your places sorted?"*

"Yes…"

"Wey hey...!!! When are we off?"

"Tomorrow morning?"

"I'd better get a proper haircut again then..."

"Definitely and some smart clothes on too… we're going to start by going to Marlene's…"

"Are you having me on?"

"No…"

"You've got me sweating now!!!" He joked *"I'm even going to shave too, although I've no beard."*

"Good thinking…" Pedro joked back. "I'll see you later."

Arriving at his shack, the girls didn't seem too unhappy to hear the news. They had started to learn how to read and write and over regular mobile phone conversations, Thelma had made them look forward to spending two solid weeks with her, the moment Pedro was gone. They clearly understood this to be an essential prerequisite to being catapulted into the white-man's world and couldn't get started soon enough...

In the early morning, Thelma arrived to pick the four of them up in her 4X4 and then dropped Pedro and Quito off at the Airport, where Patricio waited, before continuing home with Deedee and Ara.

"I thought I'd introduce you to your pilot and co-pilot," greeted Patricio, shaking Pedro's and Quito's hands, and then lead them to Marco and Martha, wearing smart grey and gold uniforms, only a few metres away.

"Good to meet you both…" Pedro and Quito greeted them and they both bowed back slightly with two smiles. Marco was tall with dark hair and clean shaven and Martha was also tall, with blonde hair tied back inside her cap. Both appeared to be in their mid thirties.

"They are husband and wife, by the way…," further informed Patricio.

"Excellent, we'll be able to save in hotel rooms then…," joked Pedro "Any children?"

"No…" They both smiled as they replied in unison.

"Anyway… I won't delay you any longer…" Was Patricio's diplomatic way of leaving, after another round of handshakes!

The jet was a Bombardier Challenger 300 and could carry up to 10 passengers, with kitchen and toilet facilities. Marco and Martha showed them where each thing was and how to operate everything outside the cockpit, down to the well camouflaged drinks cabinet, a life raft and emergency parachutes!

Pedro then discussed with them the travel plans of the immediate four flights ahead, it being: Recife International > George's estate in Acre > Manhattan N.Y. > Rio > and back to Recife International… and less than an hour later they were flying towards the Amazons.

Martha left the cockpit once they had reached cruising altitude, looking a lot more casual, and revealing her Germanic braid tied into a circle at the back of her head.

"Could I get you a drink or something to eat?" She offered.

"Quito?"

"I think I'd better play safe and… I'll have a juice of your choice?"

"And I'll have a whiskey with two ice cubes Martha, thanks."

"This is the life…" muttered Quito while she was gone "And she is nice too…"

"How unusual for you to have noticed…"

The flight was smooth and the landing was faultless.

George was easily spotted with his unmistakable white Stetson, standing up on his 4X4, like a general about to review a parade of thousands!!! He had a great big smile as he came to the plane to greet them with two hugs.

"I'm impressed…" He commented, looking at the plane. "…Yours?"

"You could say that…," replied Pedro.

"Lovely to see you guys… I hope you'll accept my invitation to stay at the mansion this time?" He said turning to Quito.

"With pleasure… Thank you…"

"You are staying a few days, I hope…," he then turned to Pedro.

"Not as long as we'd like George, but there will be other occasions, I hope…," he paused. "Your wife and daughter back from Europe?"

"Yes, they had a grand time and look forward to meeting you both… They've grown to think of you as the local Indiana Jones…" They all laughed.

Paulinho, George's pilot, was soon at hand to make Marco and Martha feel welcomed, and Sebastião and Marlene made a fuss the moment they walked into the mansion. George then led them into his study;

"I've not had a good excuse to have a couple of whiskeys since you left…" He complained.

"We'd better put the record straight then…" Pedro decided to follow on the idea, while Quito dried his forehead!!!

George knew the motive for Pedro's visit related to his possible involvement in getting the American company out of Brazil, but felt in no hurry to raise the subject, anticipating that Pedro would come out with it at the appropriate time.

**

X

"Are you guys looking forward to the three of us spending some time together?" Asked Thelma, the moment they were on the road towards Porto de Galinhas.

"Very much so…" Confirmed Deedee, "Pedro told us of the wonderful home you have…"

"You will soon have homes at least as good…" She replied.

"What sort of things will you be teaching us?" Ara enquired. "We've already started to learn how to read and write…" She informed her.

"So I hear… and I'm ever so pleased…" She paused to look at both of them. "Well, the sort of things I was planning to teach you is basically how to blend in the white-man's world, so that you can be considered and be seen in the same light as everyone else… Dress sense, how to act socially, the things to do and not to do… your hair and face… how to make the best of your pretty features…"

"…How to bring more pleasure to Pedro?" Ara tried to contribute, causing Thelma to chuckle.

"I think you both must be doing very well in that department… he appeals to me as being the sort of guy that would only settle for what he wants…"

"I like it when he really struggles to hold back…" Ara had the giggles.

"Ara!!!" reprehended Deedee.

"He sleeps with both of you at the same time?" Thelma suggested perceptively.

"Not at the beginning, but the three of us have grown to

149

prefer it that way, instead of one of us being by herself in our shacks…," explained Deedee.

"It makes sense, I suppose…" Thelma tried to make it sound as if it were the most natural thing. "Anyway, the first thing we need to do is to have you look the part. I've got a hair stylist coming to deal with your hair once we get home and then we'll need to get you out of those clothes… I got you some jeans and shirts, shoes, socks and underwear…"

"Pedro gave us our dresses…" Deedee started to complain.

"…And they are very nice dresses," Thelma tried to make amends "But you need to try different new things… No one will take those dresses away from you…"

Deedee and Ara were taken aback by Thelma's home and seemed fascinated with everything, from the texture of the carpet to the water closet flush and High-Tec kitchen area!!!

"You must have an awful lot of money…" Deedee let escape.

"Come… let me show you your bedroom. Are you OK sleeping together?"

"We actually prefer it…," confirmed Ara.

Thelma then decided to put some mood music on and casually began taking off her clothes.

"You're going to take a bath in the big pool outside?" Enquired Deedee, fascinated by Thelma's body…

"The hair stylist is not going to be here for another hour and I'm boiling hot…"

"Won't people see you naked?" Ara enquired.

"No, providing you get inside the pool by staying close to the wall on your left… and the same when you come out. Don't be shy, we are all women… Aren't you going to join me?"

The other two soon followed Thelma's example, without realising that the purpose of the exercise was to get rid of everything that wasn't natural to their hair and bodies. And half an hour later they all settled back indoors with some ice-cold juices, inside a dressing gown each.

"This is so soft…," commented Deedee to Ara, feeling the texture of the gown.

The hair stylist arrived at the appointed time and left 2 hours later, after producing a small miracle! The breakfast bowl style of haircuts they had, had now become uneven and shorter, resembling the style of some French models in a magazine.

Thelma then dressed them up in jeans and plain T shirts, drawing further attention to their natural beauty, rather than making them look like something they were not. They then had fun painting their toe nails and got to learn a few things about cosmetics and how to be subtle in their usage, so as to avoid having their faces looking like painted death masks!

"Women like you or I don't really need this sort of thing… I'm just making you acquainted with other things a lot of women use… false eyelashes, false hairpieces, fake skin colour, eye colour lenses… here… look at this… do you want to see me with pink eyes? Watch…watch…"

"Wow!" Ara exclaimed "Can you still see?"

"Yes…" She proceeded to take the lenses out. "Some women use padded bras to make their breasts look bigger… It's never ending…"

"Are we going out to do some shopping?" Asked Deedee

"Not today and not tomorrow. I still need to teach you a few things… but we'll go out every day after that. Sounds good?" They both nodded. Shoe walking, how to wear different types of clothes and table manners was of course what Thelma was talking about.

Deedee and Ara however were not only fast learners and well-motivated, but also on a mission to outdo Thelma in every way they possibly could. Deep down, whilst no words had been exchanged on the subject, they both felt that she was out to get Pedro, sooner or later… and by the third day, they could almost pass for super models that had never seen the bush!

*

It was approaching 7:30. Pedro had lost track of time and found himself rushing out of the shower. Quito had been given the room adjacent to his, but there seemed to be little or no noise at all coming from there…

"Shouldn't we perhaps take out those 40 Kilos of gold before heading to New York?" asked Quito, coming through the wall into Pedro's bedroom.

"Shit man! Next time, would you mind making yourself visible before talking to me like that?" He complained whilst getting dressed.

"Sorry…"

"No, let's leave it where it is… I've got some plans for it… Do you need cash?"

"No… I just thought, since we're so near it…?"

"I didn't mean to snap at you… Are you worried about someone stealing it?"

"Well, I'm a little worried about the transfer of some things from one dimension to the other…" He paused. "I've been making some experiments ever since we were here last time… and when it comes to taking some things from one reality to the other, I've got the feeling it doesn't always work… or that sometimes it works only for a short period, before they disappear back to where they were originally…?"

"Oh, bloody hell! Do you think our gold could come under that category?"

"Well, I thought by getting the 40 Kilos we could be sure… instead of George finding out next time he decided to look inside his vault?"

"Can't you check his vault?"

"I did… and it's not there…"

"He could have taken it elsewhere… couldn't he?"

152

"I suppose…" He chuckled "Well, at least we could never be accused of stealing it…"

"Fuck! When did you find out about this?"

"You know when we were staying at that hotel in Recife…?"

"Yes…"

"While you were asleep, I made the experiment of using my necklace to gain access to a bank's vault on the same street we were… Filled a bag I had taken with money… but by the time I got back to our bedroom… the bag was empty."

"Did you check the bag for holes?" Pedro couldn't stop chuckling.

"Now you're taking the piss!!" Quito was almost offended. "I've made other experiments since, not involving banks, with similar results…"

"We'll have to look into that… I somehow cannot imagine for a moment that Ninan and the rest would take such a gamble as giving us gold that just disappears after a while… and we know that they've probably exchanged billions over the last three or four centuries, in order to get their "Financial Empire" going…," he paused. "Shall we go? It's 7:30…"

"I'm ready…"

They were the last ones to arrive in George's Study. Paulinho, Marco and Martha were already there, as were George, his wife and daughter.

"Pedro and Quito… please meet my wife Lucinda and daughter Filipa…" He introduced them.

"Delighted to meet you both…" Pedro and Quito shook their hands and accepted the drinks George had already prepared for them. Lucinda was slim, elegant and a little taller than George; in her mid forties, with blue eyes and dark hair tied into a net, she seemed to retain the youthfulness of women half her age. Filipa on the other hand was not older than 20 and a typical Daddy's daughter. About the same height as her mother, with brown eyes and a revealing tailored shirt, her dark hair was tied into a braid and was dressed as if having just returned from horse riding.

"George has not stopped talking about you since we've returned from holiday…!" Revealed Lucinda looking at Pedro "And I'm so sorry to have heard about the tragedy involving the Akazi…" She added looking at Quito, who acknowledged her words of sympathy with a slight thank you nod.

"My father refers to you as the Brazilian Indiana Jones…" Filipa looked at Pedro with familiarity and tried to take him to one side, as if she had always known him. "Can you ride?"

"I've never tried…" He admitted. "Can you imagine, Indiana Jones frantically trying to ride a horse that won't move from the same spot?" He made her laugh aloud. "That would probably be me!"

"I can teach you… I'm sure you'd learn in no time…" She said confidently

"Thanks… but we might have to adjourn it for another time… We'll have to leave for New York tomorrow…"

"MUM…" Filipa almost screamed "They're going to New York tomorrow…"

"For how long?" Lucinda came to join their conversation.

"Only a couple of days… I've bought this penthouse in Manhattan that I haven't yet seen…"

"Oh my God… GEEGEE… did you hear that? He's got a penthouse in Manhattan that he's never seen?"

"I told you, he's full of surprises… It wouldn't surprise me if he also had a multimillion dollar yacht hidden somewhere…" Replied George, setting Quito, Marco and Martha into a chuckle.

"I love shopping in New York and we haven't been there for at least… 2 years?" Lucinda looked at her daughter for confirmation.

"Do you fancy going to New York for a couple of days George?" Pedro offered.

"No thanks... I was shot at last time I was there...! But those two might want to go... they are always shopping..." He paused to come closer. "Marco and Martha were saying you're planning to be in Rio in a week's time... I could get Paulinho to pick you up from there?" He directed the question to his wife and daughter.

"No George, I'll bring them back here on my way to Rio... It's no big deal...," offered Pedro, causing Filipa to jump up and down excitedly.

"Dinner will be served in two minutes..." Marlene announced.

"That is kind of you Pedro... Lucinda has a brother who lives in New York...," commented George as they made their way into the dining room.

"He'll be more than happy to put us up for a couple of days...," confirmed Lucinda.

Dinner was an animated lively event and as the evening wore on, back into the study after the traditional coffee walk to the staff's canteen, their numbers began to dwindle until it was just George, Pedro and the first half of a second bottle of whiskey!

"How's your gold?" Pedro decided to risk the question.

"Safely tucked away in my home in England..." He paused to open the new bottle, "I like to spread my wealth around... you never know... you don't want to keep all your eggs in the same basket."

"Absolutely..." Pedro was in full agreement. "In New York... were you by any chance shot at by those same American mining *friends* of ours?"

"Yes..." He chuckled. "They didn't realise I could shoot back... and that's when they proposed we should bury the hatchet..."

"I'm with you..."

"And so…," he raised his glass before taking it to his lips "What's the plan with us?"

"This is a little weird to talk about…," started Pedro. "Where I reckon you'll stand to gain the most in all this, to begin with, is in the purchase of bullion from me, of which I've got a further 800 Kilos or so that are not yet available…"

"It won't be a problem…" He confirmed. "But that was already understood…"

"None the less, as your friend and as promised, I did mention of your interest in getting involved, especially given your position as land owner…" Pedro had a sip "But they came back saying that in view of your historical relationship with some of their main shareholders, this could actually turn out to be a handicap in any takeover…"

"Even while remaining anonymous to the Americans?" George couldn't swallow that.

"I must admit I share your puzzlement to some extent, but I've grown to see this as a blessing in disguise. You see, your Brotherhood is not looking for any financial gain in this. All they want is to get the Mining Concessions, bury the Deeds and sell the American company on to the highest bidder, even if at a loss…"

"How unusual for them…" George became more thoughtful.

"The good news on the other hand, is that there's nothing in my contract that forbids me from using you as a consultant…" Pedro caused George to smile.

"You want me to tell you all I know about those Americans? I can do that for nothing!"

"Not only… I want you to tell me all you know about the mining industry, who's who, how things work, who owns what, how and why?"

"And guide you through every stage of that process?" He looked clearly amused.

"You wouldn't be doing it for nothing…"

"Come off it Pedro! You would be paying me wages?" He seemed a little offended.

"Not wages George…" It was Pedro's turn to chuckle. "Things could be worked out so you could eventually emerge as the highest bidder, perhaps by proxy… get the whole thing for peanuts… and eventually sell it in bits to the Indians and the Chinese." George was shaking his head.

"Doesn't make sense! Why wouldn't they do that in the first place and make money instead of losing it?"

"Believe me it does… Only I cannot explain it to you just now… We could make at least a billion out of this…"

"And what would be my financial commitment?"

"I couldn't tell you for sure right now either, but certainly well below the guaranteed value of what you'll be getting…"

"Regardless of my good will, I'm unable to tell you yes or no without fully understanding what you're talking about Pedro; I hope you'll accept that…"

"I do… and I certainly wouldn't expect you to commit yourself financially at this stage, but if you give me all the help you can from your experience and knowledge in this business, you'll immediately have the proof you'll need at the right time".

"Even if only to satisfy my curiosity, I shall give you all the help I can, but only for as long as it doesn't go against the interests of the Brotherhood. Is that clear?"

"Excellent… I'd suggest that on my return we could go for a drive around your estate, and I'll tell you a lot more about it then" Pedro stretched his hand and George shook it.

"Sounds good" He did his best not to look sceptical or disappointed.

*

Lucinda's and Filipa's bags had already been loaded by breakfast time but George felt in no condition to see them off. Pedro wasn't feeling any better and already slept soundly in

157

a bed Martha had made for him on board!!! And by 8:00 they were flying north, with Quito and the crew as hosts.

The rear third of the plane was made to be easily transformed into a bedroom, with a curtain for privacy; the only embarrassment being that he would have to pass all his guests before reaching the toilet!! Martha had left some clean clothes hanging to one side, an electric shaver and an empty bottle, presumably for emergencies...

They landed in Caracas for refuelling at 12:00 and were back in the air by 12:30 heading for Miami, by which time Pedro was awakened by the scent of roast lamb coming from the plane's micro-oven. He smartened himself as best he could and eventually summed up the courage to open the curtain!

"Good morning Pedro..." Lucinda and Filipa greeted him in unison and Quito laughed!

"What must you think of me?" He tried to brighten up "I hope George is feeling a lot better..."

"At least he slept well... which is a blessing in itself!!" Lucinda's expression said it all! "Martha was kind enough to give me the arrival details and my brother will be picking us up..."

"What time are we supposed to arrive at JFK?" Pedro enquired of her, doing his best to hide a yawn behind a cupped hand.

"Around midnight local time... we'll be refuelling in Miami between 7 and 8?"

"It's not just around the corner, is it?" Pedro continued to move towards the toilet "Excuse me a moment?"

"You OK?" came Martha holding a glass as he neared the cockpit. "I got you an Alka Seltzer?"

"Excellent Martha thanks... How are we doing Marco?" He greeted, sticking his head inside the cockpit before entering the toilet.

"We're doing well Mr. Bolivar... perfect weather conditions ahead" He tried to look lively.

After Miami, Lucinda, Filipa and Quito eventually fell asleep while watching a movie, and they landed at JFK already past midnight, under torrential rain.

"Shall I tell you about the arrangements in place?" Martha came to sit next to Pedro, while Marco taxied towards his allocated gate.

"Yes please Martha..."

"Your local security man is a guy called Giovanni... He is an Italian New Yorker and is currently trying to fast track the four of you through customs. He'll take you home."

"And you and Marco?"

"We've got a room at a nearby hotel where we get special discounts... also because we need to be back here early in the morning to get the plane checked... we want it to be ready at all times."

"That's good to hear... How will I know who Giovanni is?"

"He'll be wearing a black suit and is Italian looking..." She showed him his picture on her mobile phone. "He will see you before you see him..."

"That's reassuring..." Quito grinned.

"And what about your brother?" Pedro turned to Lucinda.

"He's already there waiting for us... I just had a text."

Giovanni had the unmistakable look of the Mafia about him, further accentuated by his dark glasses and black tie, as if on permanent stand by for the next funeral! He stood by two customs officers who immediately waved to them... and the four were through without a hitch.

"Good to meet you sir..." The man took off his glasses and introduced himself with his best smile... "I've got a car waiting outside... do we need to take your guests anywhere or are they coming with us?" he then enquired.

"Good to meet you too Giovanni… Our guests have got someone coming to meet them…" replied Pedro.

"There he is…" Lucinda became excited as she spotted her brother and after saying their goodbyes, the two walked towards him and his family, leaving Pedro and Quito to continue on their way. "Give us a call when you want us for the return journey?" Lucinda shouted as an afterthought and Filipa waved.

A few minutes later, Pedro, Quito and Giovanni were still on their way out of the Terminal, when they heard a commotion of people screaming and a few running past them towards the exit where they were heading.

"What's happening back there?" Giovanni caught a running young back packer almost off the ground.

"There are three or four guys shooting people with silencers on their guns…," squealed the young fellow.

"Thank you…" Giovanni let him go… "Do you want me to check on your friends?"

"Let me try Lucinda's mobile first…" Pedro frowned as they continued to walk towards their waiting car, but by the time they were in, there was still no answer.

"Would you mind having a look Giovanni? She is not answering… and I need to know for sure if they're alright…"

Giovanni returned some 20 minutes later and got in the car, looking frustrated;

"The Police cordoned off the area and the Terminal is being evacuated…" He said, while signalling for the driver to drive on. "I couldn't get anywhere near it…"

"Did you manage to get any information?" Pedro wanted to know.

"Only that it looked like a hit job… and that 3 women and 1 man were either dead or seriously injured…"

"Please stop the car…" Pedro then ordered the driver. "We've got to know for sure if our two guests are OK or not. I'm responsible for those people…" He looked sternly to

Giovanni, while continuing to try Lucinda's mobile... until he got an answer:

"Lucinda?"

"Who is speaking please?" Answered a man's voice.

"It is Pedro Bolivar... Are you Lucinda's brother?"

"Just a moment..." There seemed to be some confusion on the other side and then a different voice came on the phone. *"This is Sergeant Donetski from JFK's Security can I help you?"*

He explained to the man who he was and why he was calling and to Pedro's worst fears, Sergeant Donetski suggested he should perhaps go to the scene of the shooting.

Quito and Giovanni followed him, with Giovanni raising concerns that in the worst-case scenario Pedro could be on the killers' list too, and that there were at least 3 or 4 hit men on the loose.

"If that's the case, they will also know where I live... won't they?" He looked at Giovanni, not too happy with the man's attitude.

"I suppose..." He agreed.

There were blue and red lights flashing everywhere by the time they re-entered the Terminal and it took a fair bit of convincing of two Police Officers, before they were eventually escorted to Sergeant Donetski.

Everyone was asked to surrender their I.D. papers and Giovanni to part with his revolver; and it was at this point that Sergeant Donetski finally spoke:

"We're still double checking on the identity of the victims... Three women and one man have been pronounced dead at the scene... but we are still waiting for the Coroner before the bodies can be removed... would you be able to identify them, if they are indeed your friends?"

"Yes..." The Sergeant then led the way while Pedro wished he had never owned a plane.

All four bodies still lay where they had fallen, covered by

some sort of plastic… and two of them were indeed Lucinda and Filipa.

"The other two I believe are the older lady's brother and sister-in-law…" Pedro then turned to Quito in Portuguese. "…but didn't we get the impression that they were a family?"

"I'm sure they were with a small boy and a girl…" Quito confirmed.

"What the fuck am I going to tell George?" Pedro took a deep breath and twice tried to dial, only to change his mind, before going for it at the third attempt.

"Pedro…? Everything OK…?" It sounded like he was probably asleep.

"We landed less than an hour ago…" Pedro told the sorry tale of what had happened … and there was a long silence from the other end of the call. "…Are you still there?"

"I am…" Was all that George could say.

"Did Lucinda's brother have two children?" Pedro then asked.

"Yes… a boy and a girl… little ones… Why?"

"I think they've gone missing…"

"Could you pass the phone to the Police there please?"

The Sergeant went on talking with George for a good 20 minutes and then turned to Pedro;

"He is flying in… Where can we reach you?" He then asked, returning Pedro's phone.

"Thank you… I'm not too sure… whether to go to my apartment or sleep on my plane…"

"Do you think you could also be a target for these people?"

"I don't honestly know… none of this makes any sense…"

The Sergeant in the meantime received another call on his mobile.

"I know where you live and I'm providing you with an escort home, as well as two armed officers to be on guard duty outside your apartment. Until we get a better understanding of what's going on, I'd advise you not to leave the Country… Or let me know if you absolutely need to?" He handed Pedro his visiting card, their documents and Giovanni's hand gun.

"This was not a very good start Giovanni, was it?" Muttered Pedro as they walked back to the car, followed by two officers. A police patrol car arrived soon after, and then led the way.

"I would have never dreamt of a thing like this in a million years," Commented Quito as they drove on.

"George?" Pedro decided to call him back.

"Paulinho is getting my plane ready…"

"I'm a bit worried about you… and the fact that besides us, only the people on your Estate knew that your wife and daughter were coming here and when?"

"That has occurred to me too… but just now I've no other option than to take a leap of faith…" He paused. *"You stay safe… meet me when I get there?"*

"I will."

The 5-bedroom Penthouse was better than the pictures of it suggested and two black Brazilian maids came to the door the moment they entered.

"This is big Maria and little Maria…" Giovanni introduced them and the two immediately proceeded to show Pedro and Quito around, leaving the two officers outside.

The two maids shared the same bedroom, Giovanni had his own, and the other three were left for Pedro, Quito and any guests they might have. The apartment was then comprised of 2 living rooms, 1 dining room, 1 office, 1 kitchen and 5 en-suite bathrooms + basement parking and storage space.

"Would you like us to prepare you something to eat?" Asked the bigger of the Marias.

"I think we just need to sleep Maria, thank you…" Pedro replied. "However, before going to sleep could you perhaps ask the officers outside if they might need anything?"

"I'll see to them…," offered Giovanni, trying his best to do something useful.

Shortly after retiring for the night, Pedro used his necklace to get into Quito's bedroom for a more private chat, but only to find he was already fast asleep… He then decided to call Thelma.

"Pedro?" She sounded sleepy but also cheerful as she heard his voice. *"Are you OK?"*

"I'm fine thanks…"

"How wonderful of you to think of me at 4 in the morning… are you in bed too?" Thelma gave her voice a touch of complete intimacy… somehow making Pedro feel as if he was in bed with her…!

"I am… and I'm sorry for calling you at this time." Pedro had to laugh! "The girls OK?"

"They're making giant strides… You won't recognise them…"

"Don't overdo it please… I quite like some of their magic exotic ways…"

"I know exactly what you mean… Are you in your New York Apartment?"

"Yes…" He paused. "How are these arrangements with my staff, security etc?"

"Well, you've got 2 staff in each of the penthouses, 5 on your yacht and 2 for your plane. You then have 4 security guards, but they are all part of the same Agency; 1 for each penthouse location and 2 aboard the yacht…"

"Why are the guards from an Agency?"

"There are several reasons: for instance, if one gets killed or injured while on duty, you won't be liable. Then, there is this 24/7 commitment to continuity: to give you an example; what if you get to Rio on your security's day off, or if they are ill? And finally, they can also provide extra secure transport 24/7 to and from airports, etc…"

"I see…"

"What made you ask? Is there something wrong?"

"This Giovanni guy here in New York… I just don't like him. Don't ask me to tell you why. I want to get rid of him. I can't stand the man."

"OK, I get it… Shall I ask the Agency to replace him by a Portuguese speaking security man?"

"That sounds like a good excuse…," he congratulated Thelma's discernment. "It's not as if I want the guy to lose his job with the agency or anything like that…"

"OK I've done that while you were talking… Now: …Are you going to tell me why you're so much on edge?"

"Nothing in particular… I hope to see you in the next few days and then I'll tell you all about my adventures?"

"Ok then… Shall I say hello to the girls?"

"Yes please… I'll call them in the next day or two."

In the morning, Pedro asked Giovanni to check his Aston Martin for devices before insisting on driving by himself to JFK to meet George.

"I feel this would have never happened if it weren't for me George!" Pedro spoke his mind.

"Don't go blaming yourself now… this was on the cards I fear…" He gave Pedro a hug. "Any news about the little ones?"

"I just got here… and I suppose they'll probably contact you before anyone else…"

They were soon joined by Sergeant Donetski and Pedro followed them to a mortuary facility at the Airport, for a more formal identification.

George was distraught and inconsolable about his daughter and after a two-hour police interview, Pedro took him away for a few stiff drinks in his penthouse.

"You know? I've always wanted to get one of these, but every time something got in the way…" George was momentarily distracted by Pedro's car.

"Would you like to drive it?"

"No, no thanks… I couldn't do it just now…"

Getting back to Pedro's penthouse, someone from the Agency came to introduce Sergio. The Brazilian security guard was Giovanni's replacement and seemed to have inherited the same suit, tie and glasses. This one however also had a moustache and a smokers' voice.

"I'm impressed…," said George removing his Stetson as he entered the apartment.

"Make yourself at home George…" Pedro led the way to the bar in one of the living rooms and Quito arrived in the meantime, to sombrely offer George his most heartfelt sympathy.

Moments later they each had their whiskey and the smaller Maria announced that lunch would be served at 14:00.

"If the two little ones were kidnapped, as it seems, how does that relate to you?" Pedro asked the question that had been puzzling him.

"My second wife's brother was my eldest son's father-in-law…"

"Wow…!" Pedro was instantly confused and had to take a moment to work it out. "So your brother-in-law was also the father of the two siblings of your son's wife?"

"Sorry!" Quito couldn't help laughing at all the confusion.

"I reckon it will be my son's wife who will get the ransom demand, as she will now be the new head of her side of the family, given that her siblings are very much under age… And their fortune isn't much smaller than mine…" He paused. "I reckon this was the only way the Kidnappers could ever get access to their money…"

"On the other hand, if those siblings were to disappear, would she inherit the whole thing?" asked Quito.

"As a couple, they would eventually stand to inherit everything!!!" George became a little thoughtful. "My eldest what's mine and his wife what's her father's…" A shiver seemed to run through his spine as he said it.

"And what about your other son?" Pedro was intrigued.

"Too many overdoses when he was a student... he is mentally unstable and will need to be closely monitored for the rest of his life." George made Pedro feel like he should stop the questions!

The two Marias were good cooks and they delighted everyone with a "Caldeirada de Peixe" (a hot pot of mixed fishes).

"I think I will probably head for Rio from here George. How long do you reckon you'll be staying in New York?" Pedro didn't want to hang around any longer than was absolutely necessary.

"I reckon it will probably take me a week to deal with all the protocols... My son and wife will be here tomorrow... but I won't ask you to stay for the funeral. I know of your thoughts and that's what counts."

"You must however promise me that you, your son and wife will use my home as your own, for however long you may wish..." He paused to point at the two maids clearing the table, "Our two Marias here and Sergio will make sure you'll be safe and have everything you could possibly need."

"That is very kind of you..."

"As for our "*business*", that can wait; to give you a little bit of time to try and absorb the impact of all this. But the moment you're ready come to Recife, we'll spend a week or two on my yacht to plan it all out...?"

"So, you do have a yacht after all!" He had a broad smile. "Can I use your car while I'm here?"

"Whenever you like..."

"I hope I won't get too attached...When are you going?" He jokingly made it sound like the sooner the better.

"Tomorrow morning, I'm afraid..." Pedro replied, to the amusement of the on looking Sergio.

*

"How did you enjoy New York?" Enquired Martha with a big smile as Pedro and Quito boarded the aeroplane.

"Don't ask… You wouldn't believe what happened… Hi Marco…" Pedro popped his head inside the Cockpit.

"Good morning Mr. Bolivar… Had a good time?" he replied.

"Very weird… I'll tell you about it once you're on autopilot. I'm looking forward to Rio…"

"The Azevedos not flying back with us?" Asked Martha.

"No. I'll tell you about it later…"

"So, we are going to Rio?" Marco needed confirming.

"Yes please Marco…"

"Okee Dokee…"

The return journey took them through Miami > Caracas > Fortaleza and > Rio, over a total of 18 hours. Marco and Martha were shocked when they found out the fate of Lucinda and Filipa, and Martha shed a tear.

"Poor Mr. Azevedo…"

"I've never been to Rio… What's it like?" Quito decided to brighten up the mood.

"That's our city… and the home of your plane, whenever you don't need it for a while..." Announced Martha, looking at the two men.

Marco and Martha began the descent for Rio with the sun still to rise above the ocean's horizon line, and Martha tried to put everyone in the mood by playing the mellow sounds of slow & hot *bossanova* music over the P.A. system.

"Is it too loud?" She shouted from the cockpit.

"Not at all… Quito is still sleeping…" Pedro shouted back and Quito chuckled.

Salome was Pedro's security guy in Rio. Well-built and black, he was the typical no-nonsense man. Marco and Martha already knew him and considered him a friend.

"Good to meet you sir…" Salome stretched his hand to both Pedro and Quito. "I've got a car waiting.

"Want to come for a drink or two?" Pedro invited the couple.

"If we are not flying tomorrow, with pleasure…" Marco accepted, also on behalf of his wife.

Pedro's penthouse had the same dimensions as his Manhattan home and was right on Copacabana beach, with a wide 25th floor terrace facing Ipanema. The house maids were Isabel and Irene. They were both young and attractive with some black in their genes, about 5 foot7 inches. Irene however had the added unusual feature of having natural green eyes.

"Anything particular you'd like to do while you're in town?" Salome asked Pedro.

"No. Going to the beach, eating well, sleeping and enjoying my car… I need to clean my head of the last couple of days…"

"If you need anything else, just say the word and I can get it for you… no hassle…"

"I think we'll be all right Salome, but thanks for the offer…" Replied Pedro, glancing at Quito.

"I'm OK too…" confirmed Quito "I'm not planning to go beyond alcohol…"

**

XI

It was the end of the first week for Deedee and Ara at Porto de Galinhas and they decided to celebrate by visiting Recife for the day. The two Akazi girls were unrecognisable and their self-confidence grew with each new day. Thelma's focus was now about developing their self-awareness and empathy, particularly where perception of them by the opposite sex was concerned. There had been more than one occasion when this had caused them to take a taxi to escape elsewhere (!!!), stalked by groups of adoring guys full of wishful thinking…

"Do you feel like a pimp?" Giggled Ara on one of those occasions, as the taxi sped away.

"I think it's the clothes we are wearing rather than the way we walk…," concluded Deedee, "It makes men want to see more of our naked skin…"

"The secret is to avoid eye contact guys…" Thelma sighed "…You could also pretend to be on your mobile phones, if it helps to distract you…"

"Have you heard from Pedro?" Deedee then asked Thelma, wanting to change subject.

"I think he is OK and busy working… he should be back in the next three or four days… Do you miss him?"

"Very much… I like being inside his arms…" Ara admitted, with one of her provocative looks.

"Of course," confirmed Deedee.

"Do you cuddle against each other when he isn't around at night then?"

"We sometimes help each other a little bit… but it isn't the same thing…" Ara confessed, her eyes somehow focusing on Thelma's lips for a brief moment.

At the end of a full day's shopping, after stuffing her 4X4 with all that they had bought, Thelma took them to see Pedro's office and hers. They had a plan to go out to dinner at the "Leite" Restaurant, by the shores of the Capibaribe River. To mark the occasion Thelma had bought them two evening dresses, with medium high heels to match! Deedee, in particular, was not too keen on high heels and almost destroyed the shop trying a couple of more adventurous higher heels, while Ara narrowly missed serious injury! But they were determined and after a few goes holding on to Thelma in her office, they seemed to gain the hang of it.

The Restaurant was an exclusive upmarket venue attracting the elite of the city and the ultimate test of everything the two girls had learned in a week of intensive "finishing school". Reminiscent of a bygone age of luxury set in 1920's Brazil, the sounds of live violins in the background and the welcoming "Maitre de" with tailcoat and gloves further added to the theme.

"Please follow me… we've reserved you a discreet table for three… as requested." The man informed them as he proudly led the way with three giant size menus, along a red-carpet on a blue and white tiled floor.

They walked past a small musical ensemble, half hidden by the lush indoor greenery, and caused a few heads to turn as they came into the dining area!

"Do you have something in your shoe?" Thelma whispered to Deedee as they reached their table, noticing the girl was doing her best not to waddle like a duck.

"There…" Whispered Ara, trying only to use her eyes to draw Thelma's attention to what she was looking at. "On the floor…" She continued to whisper. On top of the red carpet, there it was (!) one of Deedee's heels…! "Shall I get it?"

"It's ok I'll do it… you'd both better sit down before this thing turns into something major …!"

*

"Shall I bring you a pillow?" proposed the maid, taking away the ice bucket with the empty bottle of champagne. It was their third day in Rio and after a lobster lunch, Pedro felt ready for a siesta in the shady part of his penthouse terrace.

"I'll be OK Isabel… I'd better get up in a minute and get some work done…" Irene was elsewhere in the penthouse and Quito had gone shopping for his wives with Salome.

"If there is anything else that I can do for you… you'll let me know yeah?" She gave him a carefree smile.

"Thank you, Isabel. I'll keep that in mind…," replied Pedro, wishing to keep his troubles down to a manageable level!

Moments later, Irene came onto the terrace with his mobile ringing loudly, almost as if afraid to touch it.

"Thanks…" He said to the girl, accepting the phone. "…Thelma?"

"Hello stranger… Are we still on talking terms then?" She sounded happy.

"Everything OK there?"

"We're all fine… The girls keep asking for you and complaining that you've not bothered to give them a call…!" Pedro got his well-deserved reprimand.

"You are absolutely right and I'll be calling them after this." He paused. "Thelma… when was the yacht supposed to get to Porto de Galinhas?"

"That's exactly what I called you for… They'll be dropping anchor at Porto de Galinhas by lunch time tomorrow…"

"That's good news…"

"I was thinking of checking if everything is ready for you once the "AKAZI "I"" (the yacht) gets here… and to perhaps pick you up from the airport the day after… in the morning?"

"Sounds like a good plan to me…," He paused. "And what will you do with Deedee and Ara?"

"I'll take them with me, of course… They need to learn how to interact with the personnel… and how to be generally useful to you… also outside the bedroom?"

"You are doing a great job Thelma… Just don't go overboard!"

"Am I supposed to say something to that?"

"No." Pedro chuckled. "I look forward to seeing you the day after tomorrow."

Pedro did call Deedee and Ara briefly in the late evening and got the anticipated ear full from both, mixed with a myriad of emotions from the two mothers-to-be!

*

"Well, at least he called us…," said Deedee turning to Ara afterwards, as they both lay naked inside the bed.

"Do you think he's been having affairs?"

"According to Thelma, he's probably been too busy for that…"

"Hum… it wouldn't surprise me if he had already been between her legs too!" Was Ara's verdict.

"I'm not so sure about that… Have you noticed how Thelma looks at us sometimes?"

"Do you think she fancies us?"

"The thought has crossed my mind, more than once…," confirmed Deedee.

"What would you do, if she made a pass at you?" Ara was suddenly amused by her imaginings.

"I'm not sure…"

"You've got to be kidding! Would you consider it??" Ara lifted her head to look at Deedee, feeling a little bit shocked.

"If what she wanted was to pretend to be Pedro and pleasure

me that way… Why not? It's not as if she could make me any more pregnant…!"

"Yuk Deedee! I never thought I'd hear you say a thing like that!" Ara was speechless.

"I'm just teasing…" Deedee chuckled. "I can't wait to have Pedro back…"

"Me too…" Ara giggled. "Another week without him and I would even consider Thelma!!!"

It took a while for the girls to get to sleep and when they woke up, Thelma had already prepared them some breakfast.

"You both look like you didn't sleep too well last night?" Thelma enquired with a smile.

"I reckon we're probably too excited about having Pedro back and about the big boat house coming today…," justified Ara.

"Yacht… It's called a yacht" she corrected.

"Yes, of course… I'd forgotten the name…" Ara poured herself some coffee "Will we be sleeping in the yacht tonight?"

"Yes, we need to pack…y," confirmed Thelma, picking up her mobile to take an incoming call from the ship. She was informed they had arrived ahead of schedule, prompting them to get on with the packing right after breakfast. "Oh well…" She was amused to notice that even by using all her suitcases they could hardly fit half of their shopping in! "Shall we do it in two stages… and go to the yacht with what we've packed so far?"

"Let's…," agreed Ara.

"I wonder which of us is more desperate to see this masterpiece!" Deedee giggled.

It took them less than 2 minutes to drive to the little dock, where a spacious speedboat awaited them with 2 of their security men on board. There was a strong saltiness in the air from the low tide and an army of seagulls chased a trawler loaded with fish entering the Port.

"Good Morning…" Greeted Thelma, also on behalf of

Deedee and Ara… "These are Fernando and Ze…" She introduced the two security men who nodded politely, on their way to take the bags from Thelma's 4X4.

Dressed in the same style as the other security personnel from their Agency, they could pass for being twins; stout and about 6ft. tall, neither of them spoke much… as if trying to be transparent, or simply blend into the background!

"Is the yacht that big boat over there?" Deedee pointed to the aerodynamic 4 floor vessel, about a mile off shore."

"It is…," confirmed Thelma looking just as excited, doing her best to ignore a few windsurfers trying to impress her and the girls… And moments later they were speeding towards the vessel.

"Welcome to the AKAZI "I,"" greeted the Captain, flanked by his first Officer and crew. The two men were immaculately dressed in white.

"This is Captain Americo and First Officer Raul." Thelma continued the introductions, even though she had never met any of those people in person. Americo was a little chubby, middle aged and about 5ft. 6 and Raul was in his late 20's, tall and slim, with a glint in his eye.

"This is Lucio…" Americo then took over the introductions of the rest of his crew. "Lucio is our Ship's technician guru, from the engines to our on-board computers and the kitchen's cooker, he does it all!!" With a head of grey hair, the man was short and probably the oldest on board. "And finally but not least, we have Marisa and Paula; respectively our Chef and head of Service." Marisa would certainly impress Quito! Black and with an impressive breast line, she could easily pass for being Marlene's sister (!), while Paula was white and appealed as someone who would sunbathe at any given opportunity.

Americo then gave them a tour of the Ship, from the bottom up:

"This is the lowest of the four floors and it's where the

ship's engine room is... the kitchen, staff canteen and quarters for the male crew members." He explained as they walked along a corridor, towards a short stairway to the next floor up. "...This is the sleeping floor... with the Master Bedroom, 4 bedrooms for guests and the quarters of the female crew members..."

"Ara... come and look..." Deedee couldn't help wanting to investigate the Master Bedroom a bit more closely; and Americo was only too pleased to help them discover a few of the hidden trimmings in it. He then took them to the next floor above, once he felt they were ready.

"...This third floor is the leisure floor and includes living rooms, an executive office, dining rooms and open lounger decks... as well as an open air jacuzzi pool for 5." He continued his running commentary and eventually led the climb up to the control room on the short top floor. "And this is my operations room, with its own lounge, should you ever wish to keep us company while we sail?"

"Very impressive..." Thelma let escape.

"Among other things, we also have an elevator to all floors, two speed boats and a mini submarine for two, should you want to explore reefs and marine life without getting wet." Americo then glanced at Paula who seemed to be on stand by. "But for now, I'll leave you with Paula, to help you get organised. Marisa is preparing you some welcome cocktails for when you come to the lounge deck."

"Thank you very much Americo... We still have more stuff to bring on board though..." Thelma mentioned.

"Just let one of the security men know and they'll be pleased to help, I'm sure..."

It took the rest of the afternoon to empty Thelma's apartment of Deedee's and Ara's stuff and to get organised on board, with lunch and cocktails in between.

"Do you like it here?" Thelma asked, while helping the girls to organise their double bedroom next to the Master Bedroom.

"What do you think?" replied Ara with a big smile.

Thelma then pressed two buttons on their TV remote control and a section of the wall moved to one side, revealing the Master Bedroom.

"Wow…" Deedee and Ara didn't know which way to look first, such was the amount of novelty suddenly at their fingertips. And not long after, Deedee had two tears that had escaped her eyes…

"What is it Deedee?" enquired Thelma.

"I feel that we are so primitive and out of touch…"

"Nonsense! Just give yourself a chance. You'll master it all in no time, you'll see… It's much less complicated than it seems…" Thelma gave her a consoling hug, immediately attracting Ara's attention.

*

"Look… Look at *the worker* there…" Ara drew Deedee's attention to Pedro's suntan as he walked with Quito towards their arranged meeting point. "He is the same colour as us…!"

"Don't be too harsh on him guys…," recommended Thelma "He's got more work ahead of him than you might imagine…"

It took Pedro and Quito a few good looks to realise that the women standing next to Thelma were indeed Deedee and Ara!

"Good heavens Thelma… What a transformation…!" Pedro felt a bit stuck for words but clearly pleased with what he saw, doubly confirmed by the gluttonous glint in his eyes. "You two are looking *yummier* than ever…" He finally confessed as he kissed each of them *hello*. "…and you're looking pretty good too, as usual…," he whispered to Thelma…

"You're not looking so bad yourself…" She whispered back. "Marco and Martha…?"

"They say hello… They're dealing with the plane… I may need to fly back to Manhattan in the next few days…" He looked at her "I'll talk to you about it in the office tomorrow."

"OK".

"I didn't realise their full potential until now…" Quito added his own words and then turned to Thelma; "I'd be forever grateful if you could do the same thing for my wives!!!" Everyone had a chuckle, even though he meant it!!!

Pedro sat at the back with his wives as Thelma drove them to Porto de Galinhas.

"Did you like the yacht?" Pedro enquired of the girls.

"We don't want to go back to live in our shacks or in the Camp…," replied Deedee, with Ara's full backing.

"I shall soon be applying for permission to build a house like you've never seen on our bay…"

"At the same time as the Akazi Village is built?" Ara questioned.

"Yes…"

Arriving at Porto de Galinhas, the Speed boat from the AKAZI "I" already awaited them with Fernando and Ze on board.

Quito was moved by the choice of name for the yacht and as expected, immensely impressed by the ocean cruiser… not to mention Marisa!!! Thelma soon realised that Paula had far too much work on her plate; and decided that one of the maids from each of the penthouses should eventually spend a month on board the cruiser on a rotating basis.

"You don't mind me making these sorts of changes, do you?" Thelma wanted to make sure that Pedro didn't feel she was overstepping the mark.

"On the contrary Thelma, I feel grateful for it. Changes were bound to occur to fit the purpose… I know you know what you're doing…," he smiled at her and her eyes met his briefly, as they sometimes did…

"It's amazing the things that money can buy…" Quito joined Pedro at the bar of the Lounge closest to the main dining room area, after a general wander around the ship.

"When do you think I might be able to drop by at the Camp?" He then asked, while Pedro prepared him a drink.

"I was hoping you'd stay for dinner and the night? I'm counting on Thelma giving me a lift to the office in the morning. My 4X4 is there... and I could take you to the Camp by lunch time?" He looked at Quito. "Unless you'd rather we sailed north and dropped you off at the bay where my shack is?"

"No, no, no, that's far too much trouble... tomorrow's good" He chuckled. "I've made a list of the things I need to learn, extended to some of our braves... and it ranges from learning to drive a car and bus to gaining computer skills. I want everyone in the Camp to have learned a trade for when we have the Village... from plumbers and electricians to people dealing with our nature reserve, so we will not have to depend on any one outsider."

"And I'm with you all the way... Let's drink to that." Pedro raised his glass.

"What's the big celebration?" enquired Deedee and Ara passing by, wearing casual robes on their way to one of the lounger decks.

"We're celebrating our first drink on board...," replied Quito also on behalf of Pedro.

"Don't let Pedro drink it all in one go will you," retorted Deedee.

Paula then came to announce that a buffet lunch had been prepared on the lounger deck where the girls had gone.

From among the crew, only Americo and Raul were supposed to join the owners at meal times, if invited, otherwise the staff had their own canteen. On this occasion however, with it being Pedro's first meal on board, he insisted that everyone should eat together.

With exception of his 4 security men, Pedro was well acquainted with the portfolio of every member of his staff, and of them, the one that fascinated him the most was Lucio; for his extensive list of technical qualifications.

"Well, we are not sailing anywhere today…" Pedro toped up Lucio's empty glass of Champagne.

"Thank you… I'm not much of a drinker I'm afraid…," said the man, not wanting more than half a glass.

"I am very much impressed with the scope of your technical expertise Lucio…"

"Thank you, sir… It started as a hobby, working for a general repair shop of an uncle of mine… and one thing just led to another…"

"I would have thought you would do well having your own business…," was Pedro's assessment.

"I've tried that but unfortunately I don't really have a head for business. I like sailing; I no longer have a wife, and being part of the crew of the AKAZI "I" offered me the perfect opportunity to have a home, earn a living, and still have enough time on my hands to further enrich my technical knowledge."

"The perfect job then…?"

"Indeed sir… I hope to be of good service."

"Excellent…" Pedro's mobile then rang. "Excuse me… George?" He enquired, walking away.

"I'm still living rent free in your Manhattan penthouse…" He tried to make a joke of it.

"You know you're welcome to stay as long as you like… are we looking after you?"

"Couldn't fault it…," he paused *"The Americans are dragging their feet and I just heard that it could be a few weeks before I'll be allowed to take my wife and daughter home for burial…"*

"I'm sorry to hear that… and have you had any news regarding the children?"

"Nothing at all…" Pedro scratched his head, not quite sure of what to say.

"What are your plans?"

"I'll be flying to Cuiaba tonight, to try and avert a strike in one of the mines..."

"It never rains... does it?"

"I'll probably pay you a quick visit on my way back to New York?"

"I look forward to that... and let me know in advance, so I can pick you up from the airport?"

"I will..."

Thelma went to Pedro as he finished the call, somewhat intrigued by who could be calling him.

"Was that to do with the New York thing you were going to talk to me about?" She asked.

"Yes..." Pedro told her about what happened in New York and about George.

"I didn't realise you were so well connected...! George Azevedo... that guy is worth about 7 billion US$s... but he is a bitter rival of the main shareholders of the Company you want... If I were you, I wouldn't be seen with him once you start going for it..."

"I realise that... What puzzles me however is... this kidnapping without a word..."

"Most people in George's position have a lot more enemies than friends..."

"I know that..." Pedro filled her glass pensively "Do we have any connections to New York's underworld?"

"Thanks... That's Patricio's *department*... do you want me to ask if he could look into it?"

"Discretely yes," he smiled.

"Of course...," she smiled back, taking him a little further away from the others. "...And your wives? How do you find them?"

"You've done miracles..." Pedro chuckled. "I'm looking

forward to finding out how much more there is to discover…"
He made Thelma laugh.

"I didn't go into the intimate side of things, if that's what you're implying."

"Thank God for that! I think they already know more than enough as it is…"

"What makes you think I could teach them more than what they already know in that "area" anyway?"

"I meant it as a compliment, of course… given that you've surpassed all my expectations in just about everything else…," their eyes met briefly, in what was becoming a bit like a game between them.

"I think we'd better get back to the others, before they think we're plotting something?" She smiled again, as if savouring some lingering thoughts.

"Good idea…"

Deedee and Ara seemed particularly taken with Raul, to the point of making Pedro feel uncomfortable, and the First Officer soon sought help in the company of Americo, to Thelma's undisguised amusement.

"I wouldn't worry too much…" She whispered to Pedro, as they met again topping up their plates. "Americo and Raul are a gay couple…"

"Still…"

Quito and Pedro were back at their bar seats, by now on their own! Quito could hardly keep his eyes open, between the drink and the late afternoon sunset, but had no problems holding conversation…

"Did you ever find out from Ninan about things disappearing… when travelling from one dimension to another?" Quito asked, by now claiming ownership of their whiskey bottle.

"No… I thought you were on the case, since you're the one that noticed it…," replied Pedro.

"I must try and contact him about that when I'm sober…"

"Make sure he doesn't think that we are misusing the necklaces yeah?"

By dinner time, Quito was fast asleep in his bedroom suite! Marisa however left him a tray of cold snacks in his lounge area, should he wake up hungry, and then placed a "do not disturb" sign outside his door! Pedro declared himself more ready for bed than dinner and after a main course, decided to retire to his master bedroom, leaving Thelma to socialise with Deedee and Ara.

"Shall we let him sleep or what?" Deedee enquired of Ara as they were ready to settle for the night in their bedroom.

"Why don't we just go and cuddle up against him…? And IF he wakes up, let him tell us what he's in the mood for?" The way Ara phrased it caused Deedee to giggle.

"Where's the TV remote?"

"I've got it right here…," Ara sniggered.

Deedee didn't get as much out of Pedro as Ara made sure she did, but he certainly redressed the balance in the morning…

**

XII

A week had passed since Pedro's first night on the AKAZI "I". Patricio had obtained the Government Concession for the Akazi peninsula and submitted a full project of development that was instantly approved. It contained the Akazi Village, complete with school and a General Store, Pedro's mansion on the bay, the Nature Reserve Sanctuary and access roads. Quito had never been busier! Between overseeing small alterations to the overall Project and implementing a programme of education for all the Akazi, the man had time for nothing else.

"You've got to get into the habit of delegating… at least the smaller things!" Insisted Pedro on a rare visit to the Camp as the tribe relocated elsewhere in the peninsula, so the village could be built on that same spot.

"I know, I know… but I can only delegate when the others know what they're doing and why…" He looked at Pedro "I'm enjoying this anyway…," he admitted. "Do you still have the number of that taxi driver… Joaquim…?" He then asked.

"Yes… do you need to go somewhere?"

"Not just now…" He chuckled "but I want to buy a bus and a 4X4, so that I and some of the tribe are not stuck here, should we suddenly need something from outside?"

"And you want to employ him?"

"Well, at least until some of us have learnt to drive and got licences."

"Makes sense…" Pedro agreed. "I could ask Thelma to deal with it if you want?"

"Thanks. See how I can delegate when I want to?" He had another of his chuckles.

"I don't suppose you had a chance to contact Ninan did you?"

"Yes I did, and what he told me was that we can only take things from his dimension into ours and not the other way around... and that if we go into their dimension with something we've taken from this one and back again, in reality nothing changes... it is just an illusion that vanishes the moment we return..."

"That's weird... and what about clothes...? I don't remember either of us being naked when switching to their dimension..."

"Funny... I mentioned that to him too..."

"And what did he say...?"

"He replied that the technology linked to the necklace is also clever..."

Later that day, Pedro sat with Patricio in his Recife Office:

"I received the first feed back from the links of "I" to the "underworld" in the U.S...."

"And...?" Pedro looked at him from behind a cup of coffee.

"It seems that the American company you'll be targeting has anticipated that the Azevedos will invariably try to stop them from mining in the Acre region..."

"So, they go and kill George's wife and only daughter on a hunch?" He paused. "Don't you find that a bit over the top... to say the least?"

"It is in fact a little more complicated than that Pedro... and George might even be oblivious to it!" He got up to move about as he spoke. "Apparently, George's eldest son and his brother-in-law were concocting some plan to get the mining concession away from the Americans, using "unorthodox" methods... and keeping the siblings of George's daughter-in-law is probably just an insurance card to ensure that no such plan will ever go forward..." He looked at Pedro. "I would strongly recommend that you are not seen anywhere near George… although it may be a little too late for that…"

"Did your contacts provide any names or any trail we could follow?"

"No. I'm afraid that's as much as we've got…," replied Patricio. "The American's main executive offices however are not in their official H.Q. in Seattle…," he added.

"Where then?"

"They are in Vancouver-Canada, in a high-rise building under the bogus name of Starling Inc. … Do you want the address?"

"Yes please Patricio… Anything else you feel that I should know…?"

"Not at the minute, but I'll give you a shout if anything comes up…" He seemed amused by his own comment!

"Thanks… I may need to take Thelma away for a few days… are you OK with that?"

"The success of your Mission is our current priority… use her and me as you may need."

"Thanks." Pedro smiled at him.

Back in his office, Pedro was quick to contact George:

"You must be psychic! I'm flying towards Recife as we speak…"

"We shouldn't be seen anywhere near each other for the time being George… I've just received a report on that. Your son and his wife should also get out of the U.S. a.s.a.p., or you may end up losing your anonymity… if not a lot more."

"I'm sorry to hear that. What do you suggest?"

"For the time being, let's pretend that our interests are completely unrelated… and I'll contact you the moment the coast is clear?"

"Ok. And what about by phone…?"

"If you are coming to Recife to refuel, I'll get one of the Akazi Indios you've met to pass you a small parcel by the VARIG desk… it will contain a new mobile pay- as-you-go in it. Keep it hidden from your own security and I'll contact you in a few days' time?"

"OK, I should be landing in about 3 hours. Is that going to give you enough time?"

"No problem. Look after yourself and be very careful…"

Pedro then drove to the Camp to pick up Taco, as the best "delivery man" for the job, and headed for the airport, where he also bought a spare pay-as-you-go mobile for himself. Pedro's main worry now was if the tycoon put two and two together and ended up doing something rash…!

"Just pass it to him discreetly…" Pedro instructed the Indio, after taking note of the number.

"It's not going to be easy with that tall white hat of his. All eyes will be on him…!" He chuckled.

"True… Anyway, just do your best…"

Taco did well and with that out of the way, Pedro returned him to the Camp.

"We need to fly to Vancouver in the next day or two Quito…"

"For how long…?"

"Probably a few days… it's important business…" Pedro stressed, before the Chief could complain. "I will be asking Thelma and two of our security personnel to accompany us. I'll get Sergio and Salome to meet us at JFK while we refuel."

"Sounds serious…" Quito raised a brow. "And what about the works here, Deedee and Ara…?"

"I could ask Patricio to keep an eye on things… and as for Deedee and Ara… they will be ok where they are. Fernando and Ze will be there to protect them."

"And about Joaquim?"

"Thelma is dealing with that, as well as with your bus and a 4X4…"

"I'm impressed… fancy a drink before you go?"

"No thanks Quito… we both need clear heads over the next few days…"

That same evening, Pedro decided to have a word with Ninan, to seek approval of his more immediate plan, while Deedee, Ara and Thelma were busy socialising ahead of dinner, on board the yacht.

"It is very adventurous, to say the least… and you could be in trouble if it back fires." Ninan took a reflective pause "Are you sure you could pull something like that out of the hat?"

"I've dealt with Mafia before and I know their ways… as for the rest, I'll be only using the tools you've given me for the job…" Pedro then had an after thought "Ninan… if ever Quito or I should need to use the emergency resource back to you… how will we return to our dimension, or to where I am now, for instance?"

"Well, you'll have to walk out of here the same way you did once before…"

"I see…"

"It is something you should only really resort to in a life or death situation…"

"Definitely…" They both chuckled.

When he returned to the dining area, Pedro broke the news of his impending trip to Canada, and informed them that Quito and Thelma would need to accompany him.

"Do I need to pack tonight?" asked Thelma, doing her best to ignore a few suspicious stares from Deedee and Ara.

"No… we'll only be going the day after tomorrow… I'll brief you on it in the morning?"

"Do you want me to make any hotel reservations?"

"No… We'll only do that at the last moment. In fact…" Pedro had an afterthought, "Is there somewhere where we could stay in Vancouver, or near it, without having to go through the registration razzmatazz?"

"I'll have to check with Patricio on that…," she replied. "We have legal representatives there… of that I'm sure…"

"Can we come too?" Deedee popped the question.

"Not on this occasion Deedee... this is strictly a business trip..."

"We could perhaps just go shopping in this place you're going with one of the Securities?" proposed Ara, prompting Thelma to try and explain that there was a right and a wrong time for everything... eventually causing the two girls to leave the table in tears to go to their room.

"I'm sorry about that..." Thelma also excused herself to go and see to them, leaving Pedro with the dining table to himself.

"Should I take their dinner to them sir?" Enquired Paula, not too sure of what to do.

"Don't worry Paula, they'll come back if they are hungry... did they drink any alcohol during the afternoon?"

"None that I've seen sir..."

"Please let Marisa know that there was nothing wrong with the food." He then said getting up to pour himself a whiskey, before going for a walk towards the loungers' deck.

There was a warm evening breeze and the sky looked almost as starry as from XAKATAN.

"Are you Ok?" Thelma came to sit next to him half an hour later, with a drink in her hands.

"Yes... It's lovely out here...," he paused "Are those two OK?"

"They'll be fine... it's too many things all of a sudden in their minds... and I think they are also probably a bit insecure about you and me?"

"Did I make it look like there was something going on between us?" Pedro seemed surprised.

"Neither of us did, I don't think but... They just need some reassurance from you. If you have any feelings for them, you should perhaps give them some quality time, or they'll soon start feeling like prisoners here..."

"What do you suggest I should do? Take them with us?"

"No, definitely not, if you think we are going to flirt with the monster's jaws…!"

"Well, that's exactly what we are going to do…" Pedro let out a deep breath and then finished his drink.

"Shall I get you another?"

"You've twisted my arm…"

*

Pedro had a Jacuzzi in his quarters and then decided to go to bed, instead of seeking the company of his wives. He didn't feel the patience or the inclination to be with either of them and deep down, he also knew he was fighting a losing battle against Thelma. She was everything he could possibly ever want in a woman and she knew it too… Cool and calculating, she patiently waited for the moment he would helplessly surrender, as in a game of cat and mouse.

In the morning, however, Pedro decided to invite his two wives to have breakfast with him in his private lounge.

"Are you mad with us?" Deedee enquired timidly as they joined him.

"No… I cannot dictate how you should feel. I just wish you could control the way you express your emotions a bit better when we are with other people, instead of acting like two virgin little girls…"

"He is mad at us…," confirmed Ara with swollen eyes.

"Anyway, enough said on this." Pedro then took on a happier expression. "Would you guys like if I took you out shopping this afternoon?"

"To Recife?" Deedee wanted to know, as two big smiles appeared on their faces.

"Ok then. I need to go to my office this morning and I'll ask Fernando to take you there after lunch… In Thelma's big car…?"

"How will you get to your office?"

190

"She also has a little car and she's taking me in it this morning…"

"Can we learn how to drive too?" asked Ara

"Eventually, yes…"

Pedro then left, two or three sips of coffee later.

"I followed your advice and am taking them out shopping this afternoon…" Pedro informed Thelma as he got into her Porsche.

"Simple, isn't it?" she chuckled. "Want to make a woman happy? Take her shopping!"

*

Thelma joined Pedro, Deedee and Ara in a mad shopping spree that afternoon and they even bumped into Quito, doing some shopping of his own!

"How did you get here?" Pedro asked distractedly, while Thelma helped Deedee and Ara choose some hand bags.

"Joaquim is working for us as of this morning… remember?" He said proudly.

"Of course…"

"I now have his taxi, a bus and a 4X4 just like yours and Thelma's… anyway, I heard that this Vancouver place is cold… and I thought of getting some warm clothes…"

"Good thinking…"

"Shall I come by your yacht tonight so we can all go to the airport together in the morning?" Quito suggested.

"I think we should keep our wives happy tonight…" Pedro whispered to him "Get Joaquim to drop you off at the Airport by 10:00 tomorrow?"

"That sounds even better…" Quito agreed. "You can always let me know your plan while we fly there, I suppose…"

"That's the idea… anyway, I'd better let you go, so I'll buy myself a couple of things too…"

*

"The air traffic is slow-moving this morning Mr. Bolivar…," announced Marco as they got inside the jet, with visibility down to 10 yards.

"Well, nothing we can do about that…" Pedro tried to be positive. "Any idea how long this fog might delay us by?"

"From the tower, I'm told a couple of hours, at least…," he confirmed.

"We could always have an early lunch?" suggested Thelma.

"Good idea…," supported Quito.

"Whenever Martha…," confirmed Pedro.

It was early afternoon when Marco finally received the all clear for take off.

"When do you reckon we'll get to New York?" Pedro went to see Marco and Martha in the cockpit, once they were at cruising altitude.

"By mid morning tomorrow, everything being normal." He paused. "You don't want to stay in New York overnight?"

"Not on this occasion…No." Pedro was thoughtful. "I cannot allow you to immediately fly on to Vancouver from there either; it's too much of a stretch.

"Well, if we stayed overnight in Miami, that would be about the half way point to Vancouver…," suggested Martha.

"We could then refuel and pick up your security men at JFK around lunch time tomorrow… and into Vancouver by nightfall," completed Marco.

"Sounds good… I'll ask Thelma to make all the arrangements and contact our securities."

"The Hilton OK?" Thelma suggested while checking her laptop. "I reckon you just want to find out if they've got room, right?"

"Yes please… Don't book anything until we've landed yeah?"

"Are you worried about something?" Quito enquired.

"Not really… I just want to give our *friends* as little

advanced warning as possible of where we're going to be…," justified Pedro.

"I think you are giving them a lot more credit than they deserve…," commented Thelma. "…it wouldn't surprise me if you were being spied upon, but to assume that every single hotel north of the Mexican border would instantly contact somebody, the moment a Mr. Bolivar showed up, seems a bit over the top…!"

"Maybe…"

"Are you going to tell us about this Vancouver plan?" Quito wanted to get on with it, seeing that Martha had settled with Marco in the cockpit.

"Well, there are three parts to this plan…," started Pedro, as the three of them got comfortable at the back of the plane. "In part one, Thelma will fix us with a maisonette in Fairview-Vancouver, by the Marina, complete with harbour space, where we'll be able to dock the AKAZI "I" …"

"Shall I try and do that from here while you talk?" She asked switching her laptop on and Pedro nodded affirmatively. "Are we putting any ceiling on the cost?"

"No. The important thing is for the cost to match value… and it needs to be done in someone else's name…"

"No problem… And then…?"

"Then we'll tell Americo to sail the yacht there, via the Panama Canal…"

"That will take more than a week…," commented Thelma.

"I know…"

"And what about Deedee and Ara…?" She questioned.

"Bring them along…"

"And…?" She was ready to add to Pedro's shopping list.

"We also need an Executive Office in Downtown Vancouver, in the same building as Starling Inc if possible, and a couple of cars…" Pedro took a pause. "By the time Americo reaches Vancouver, you and our securities need to have become fully familiarised with the place, including all best routes in and around the city…"

"You're not going to be there for a whole week?"

"No. Only you and our two securities will be there." Pedro looked at Quito before continuing. "Once we have dropped you in Vancouver, I'll ask Marco and Martha to take Quito and I to Seattle… and from there, we'll eventually make our way back to you…"

"Any particular reason for that…?"

"Quito and I will need to investigate a few things we can only do in person…"

"I see…" Thelma looked at Pedro inquisitively, but he somehow dissuaded her from any further questions. "Is that it?"

"That's the first part of the plan. The other two parts will very much depend on our findings and I see no point in going into it just now…"

"Do you reckon I should perhaps get myself a small handgun?" Thelma probed, doing her best to stay serious.

"It wouldn't be a bad idea, although I doubt if you will ever need to use one…" Pedro confirmed.

"I get it… I'm well trained in that domain too any way… Have no worries about me…"

"Would you guys like a drink?" Martha returned to join them briefly.

It was already late night when they got to Miami. Marco and Martha decided they'd rather sleep in the plane and the other three went to the nearby Hilton, where they had booked two en suite rooms; one for Thelma and the other for Quito and Pedro. Thelma had a good laugh when Quito told her about their previous check-in hotel experience in Recife (!) and also told the two men of some of her own hotel stories…

*

The refuelling stop at JFK was brief. Sergio and Salome were alert to the jet's arrival and on board within 15 minutes of touch down... and all away again some 30 minutes later.

Pedro briefed the two security men on what would be expected of them over the week ahead and Thelma was quick to assert herself as to her role.

"I got us a house on the water front in False Creek, by the way, and everything else you wanted for less than US$2 million... Have a look?" Thelma was excited with it.

"How soon will you be able to move in?" Pedro seemed impressed while also looking at the downtown office photos.

"48 hours at the latest... one of our corresponding firms of solicitors has dealt with everything."

"You always manage to impress me...!" Quito felt the need to compliment her and she gave him a thank you smile.

"Either of you familiar with Vancouver...?" She then turned to the two security men.

"No..." They both replied

"Want to get acquainted?" She offered them her laptop as she got up, ready to move to the back of the plane for a snooze.

"I suppose you are not going to tell me what we are going to do in Seattle until we get there?" whispered Quito with a chuckle, the moment the two security men seemed absorbed with any information they could get on Vancouver.

"You're absolutely correct...," replied Pedro, also closing his eyes.

*

After dropping off Thelma and the two body guards, it was just a short hop from Vancouver to Seattle.

"Do you want us to remain in Seattle or in Vancouver?" Asked Martha, as Pedro and Quito were about to leave them.

"Stay here for three days and then return to Vancouver. We'll see you both in a week?"

Pedro rented a car and less than an hour later they were both heading north.

"Are you going to let me in on the plot now?" Quito seemed a little unsure whether he had popped the question at the right time!

"Well, we are going back to Vancouver… Or should I say Richmond… I arranged for a twin bedroom in a private house in Garden City Road."

"How far is that from where Thelma's going to be?"

"Only 6 or 7 miles…" Pedro looked at the puzzled Quito. "Relax; I've not lost my marbles… I just want to find out for sure if we are being spied upon or not…"

"Is that it?"

"No. We are also going to use our necklaces pretty often over the next few days… and this is something I don't want us to reveal to anybody… least of all to Thelma or Security…"

"We would scare the shit out of them, that's for sure…"

"Anyway… I want us to find out exactly who's in control of our American *friends*, who runs what, who's been ordering all the killings, etc…"

"And then?"

"And then we'll do whatever needs to be done…"

Half way into their 3 hour drive they stopped by a roadside Café and Pedro decided to contact George on his new mobile!

"Hi George…"

"I was beginning to wonder when you'd call… Where are you?"

"Near our *friends'* real H.Q."

"You're in Vancouver?"

"Close enough…" Pedro paused. "George… as far as you know; who's the big guy in all this?"

"His name is Frank Molinari… a third-generation Italian mobster gone whiter than white and originally from Chicago…" He paused. *"There's also Pete Spencer and*

Maurizio Genovese... this last one is another Mafioso from New York."

"Any dos and don'ts to keep in mind…?"

"Yes. If you engage in direct talks with them, make sure they understand that you've got at least as much fire power as they do…"

"Anyone else that comes to mind as being big fish…?"

"No. Unless they've made some recent additions to their team…" He was silent for a moment. *"I can send you some of my boys if you like?"*

"I don't think that will be necessary, at least for now… but thanks anyway…"

"You mentioned before you wanted my advice on your step by step plan… my question however is… have you got a plan as such yet?" George wasn't too convinced.

"I do, but I need to check on a couple of things first…"

"Well, you know where I am…"

Quito wasn't overly impressed either, although he did his best not to show it. Back on the road however, the Indio Chief began to chuckle to himself;

"What is it?" An irritated Pedro enquired.

"I know what the plan is and why you cannot tell the others…"

"Let's hear it then?"

"You are planning to scare them shitless into signing the Concessions over to us… using the powers of our necklaces, aren't you?" Pedro laughed.

"Obviously… why do you think there's a limit to what I can explain to the others?"

"So… we are going to spend a week trying to find the best way of doing it?" Quito couldn't stop laughing!

"I couldn't have explained it any better…" Pedro stretched out his hand to Quito, to congratulate him.

"Are we going to start by going into their offices and taking a look around later today?"

"Of course… By the way, I already knew about those three mafia guys and have their home addresses from my own research with Thelma…"

"Is she aware of your plan?"

"I think she assumes I'm planning to give them a scare of some sort, she just doesn't know how."

"How do those three guys relate to this anyway?"

"Well, Frank Molinari is definitely the big boss and all the roads lead to him. He is the largest shareholder in the company, but only retains majority control thanks to the support of a body of smaller shareholders he needs to satisfy."

"And what about the other two…?"

"Both of them represent other groups of shareholders…" Pedro paused. "Pete is in bed with an Irish bank who procures smaller private investors from among its customers… and Maurizio represents the interests of a few New York *"Families"*, always ready to assist, should the banks ever fail to offer their support…"

"Do you think that Maurizio, or people beneath him, could be the culprits when it comes to all the nasty stuff?"

"It would make sense, wouldn't it? But I'm not so sure. Once they make it into the big time, these Mafias become too obsessed with cleaning their act, even to the eyes of those who work for them…! They wouldn't dirty their hands on anything that could ever get back to them. Somebody from among them will have planned it all and then probably outsourced the whole thing, I'm sure…"

"And what if…?" Quito left his question in mid sentence.

"What if what…?"

"What if this American company was to be an equivalent asset of an Aztec or Mayan group, at a similar level to that of our own Incan friends? …with some guys with *"necklaces"* telling them what our every move is?"

"Now you've hit it on the nail Quito... that's what I'm afraid of and what we need to find out for sure."

"Have you questioned Ninan or the others on this possibility?"

"They believe that there is an unwritten agreement between them all that remains unbroken…"

"Hummn…" Quito seemed a bit sceptical. "Well, that doesn't mean anything, does it?"

**

XIII

The house in Garden City road was owned by an elderly couple, with the husband apparently, an Alzheimer's sufferer.

"If you need anything more just let us know yes?" The sympathetic old lady looked at them as a God sent addition to their month's income.

"That's great Mrs. Yates, we'll be fine…," said Pedro, accepting the keys she had for them.

"Shouldn't we perhaps get some different clothes?" Quito suggested as they returned to the car. "It is a small world…"

"That's a good point Quito…" Pedro agreed and they ended up in a Chinese general store on that same street… emerging soon after with woolly hats, dark glasses and typical Canadian jackets.

"You look like some sort of deer hunter…," commented Quito moments later, as Pedro negotiated the traffic towards downtown Vancouver in the late afternoon.

"And you should count yourself lucky, that hotel receptionist from Recife isn't around…" It was Pedro's turn to have a chuckle.

"I thought you said I looked ok…" He complained.

"I'm joking Quito…! Just try your best to walk normally." Pedro further teased him to lighten the mood, while looking for a parking spot somewhere not too close to their office block.

"Do you realise we could have saved on fuel by simply walking from Mrs. Yates's…?" commented Quito after half an hour walking. "Can you remember where we've parked?"

"Don't worry Quito… It's all under control…"

The premises of Starling Inc were among some two hundred companies using the same prestigious address. The Americans occupied a 22nd floor business suite, while Pedro's offices were a small unit on the 37th floor, under the name "Three Rainbows.com".

There was a strong emphasis on high security all around the building and anyone going in or out of the premises had to be clearly identified by their security personnel. And this meant that Pedro and Quito had to find somewhere private, outside, where they could vanish into *Inca mode* without leaving witnesses…!

Most offices had already closed for the day by the time they passed Reception.

"By the way, we've got to be physically active within our dimension to use the lift…" Observed Quito.

"And if we don't?"

"You'll watch the elevator go and remain on the same spot."

"Shit… Those lifts are bound to be C.C.T.V. wired…" Pedro looked at Quito.

"Don't look at me… If you don't want them to see us, we'll have to climb those 22 floors!"

*

"I hope you're not planning to have a peep at our offices on the 37th floor… are you?" Quito wanted to know, by the time they had reached the 15th floor.

"No… I think we'll wait and be surprised with it in a week's time." Pedro stopped to take a breather.

"I somehow knew you'd say that…"

"We must stay on the Inca dimension throughout our visit…" Pedro warned as they eventually went through the front door of Starling Inc.'s luxury offices.

Overall, their premises were not must bigger than Patricio's, but with considerably smaller rooms. They consisted of 5 executive offices, a conference room, secretarial quarters, toilet, kitchen and a canteen. Three of the offices belonged to the known culprits, but the other two had names that didn't seem to appear anywhere in Pedro's and Thelma's research. They were Maxtla Huemac and Xak Itza.

"Bloody hell…! Have you seen these names?"

"Huemac is an Aztec surname and Itza is Mayan…," informed Quito thoughtfully.

"Don't you find that weird?"

"More than weird, I agree… Especially when not one but two Indios are given high executive positions, when this company has no other interests in South America, besides the Concessions we want to get from them…!" Quito continued while they looked around Maxtla's Office. "It is also absurd that they should go for an Aztec and a Mayan instead of an Incan… when this is about native Inca territory! What do you think?"

"I see what you mean…" Pedro scratched his head. "We mustn't allow our imagination to get the better of our judgement though…"

"Look…" Quito drew Pedro's attention to a piece of paper on the floor by Maxtla's desk, with some Aztec hieroglyphs scribbled on it. "This guy is straight from the jungle… why shouldn't he use common lettering?"

"Can you understand what it says?"

"Not a clue… but I recognise it as being Aztec Symbols…"

"Shall we have a look inside the other offices?" Pedro didn't want to be drawn into a speculative Punch & Judy type of conversation. "It would be good to find out what sort of position they hold in the Company…"

There was nothing of particular relevance to be found in the other offices. Everything was locked and nothing to indicate the job titles of the two Indios.

"Well I think we're done for today. Shall we come back tomorrow and watch them interact? I'm sure we'll learn a lot more then…"

"Nothing like a bit of exercise to keep us fit, I suppose." Quito reminded him with a chuckle as they were about to leave, only to then grab Pedro's arm firmly, causing him to stop.

A thin line of light had suddenly appeared from under Xak's door.

"What the fuck?" Pedro let escape from between his teeth! But before they could react however, an ordinary looking female secretary emerged from that office, to go towards the Conference room holding a few booklets.

"There was no one in there a moment ago!!!" Quito looked at Pedro. "I could swear to it!"

"I know…" Pedro beckoned Quito to follow him into the office the woman had come from. In there, one of the high cabinets was like a door opened to one side, revealing a flight of steps to the floor below.

"I somehow don't think we should go down those steps…" Quito seemed a little insecure as he glanced towards the darkness in there. "Shall we get Ninan involved?"

"Sounds like a good idea…," supported Pedro.

Ninan was a bit taken aback by the two Indio names and within moments was quick to advise Pedro and Quito to get out of there.

"As rapidly as you can… Now…" There was a sudden added urgency in Ninan's tone a few seconds later… and he didn't have to say it twice! Pedro and Quito were quickly onto the staircase, going down as fast as they could… "Use your necklaces to get back to me…" He urged and the two men immediately complied… to find themselves suspended in time and space… and back in Ninan's lounge, a split second later!!!

"What happened?" Pedro was just as confused as Quito. Ninan however seemed happy to find them in one piece.

"You don't know how lucky you were…" The courtier shook his head looking at them. "You've just escaped certain death by a whisker!" Ninan uttered with a loud sigh, as if speaking to himself.

"What's going on?" Pedro wanted to know.

"It looks like the Aztecs and the Mayans have decided to gang up on us by tuning into your Dimension with obvious intent…"

"Don't they have enough raw materials from their own resources?" Pedro was still in a daze and the daunting prospect of a few days walk to get out of there started to weigh heavy on his mind!

"Are you going to be fighting each other with bows and arrows?" Quito was perplexed.

"This might be far more serious than that… Ayar is already on His way to an out-of-Earth meeting aimed at clarifying everyone's positions…" Ninan informed them worriedly. "Anyway, I've ordered a couple of drinks to help you get yourselves back together.

"What should we do?" Pedro felt a bit useless.

"There's nothing you can do for the time being… Becchiu will be here shortly to take you to the Palace of the Guests for the night and hopefully I'll have some news for you in the morning?"

"Will I be able to recover my mobile phones and keys?" Pedro finally enquired, feeling a lot better after downing the drink.

"Once you're out of the City." Ninan confirmed with a smile and walked with them down the stairs to Becchiu.

"Good to see you both…" The Chieftain greeted with sincerity "Shame about the circumstances though…"

"Let's hope nothing too dramatic develops from this…" Mumbled Quito as the three headed for the Palace.

The girls seemed genuinely excited to see them again, although oblivious to the circumstances, and Cuxi was back on duty with her legs fully healed. Mikay was there too and after dispatching Quito with two new girls to his quarters, looked ready to compete for a night with Pedro.

"This is like a dream come true…" Mikay said provocatively to him… "You are my favourite imagining when I'm with some clients you know?"

"You are flattering me Mikay!" Pedro had a chuckle.

"Cuxi and I have not had a single client today and we don't expect anyone else to turn up… would you like to spend the night with the two of us?" Mikay then seemed to translate to Cuxi what she had just proposed to Pedro, bringing a big smile to the other one.

Not surprisingly, Pedro ended up giving the girls not only one, but two extremely poor performances (!) made worse by the strong erotic entertainment they provided him in between!

*

"Do you know what you're going to call your baby?" Ara asked Deedee as they relaxed in their bedroom, heading for the Caribbean and the Panama Canal.

"If it's a boy I'll call him Pedrinho…"

"That sounds cute… I'll call mine Piri-piri…" Ara caused Deedee to explode into laughter.

"He'll have all the chickens running after him!!!" She eventually managed to say. "And if it is a girl?"

"Paprika…"

"Gosh, you're really into spices… I'll call mine Anabela, if it's a girl…"

"…Very conservative…," noted Ara. "Shall we watch a film on T.V.?"

"Why not…?" Deedee agreed. "Captain Americo said it will take us a week to get to this Vancouver place… I suppose Pedro won't bother to phone us…"

"What do you think of those security guys?"

"I've seen the way Ze sometimes looks at you… Do you fancy him?"

"I wouldn't mind... have you noticed the bulge in his trousers? I reckon he would fuck me like a possessed demon, given the chance..." She looked at Deedee. "And you and Fernando?"

"I wouldn't mind him giving me some *dessert*... but that's only as far as I'd go..."

"And if Pedro ever finds out?"

"Well, that's the trouble... Mind you, it would be in the securities own interest to keep quiet..."

"True..."

"The best thing is to let them make the first move... That way we can always feel that it was them rather than us who caused it?"

"That is clever...," complimented Ara. "To talk about this is really turning me on you know?"

"Shall we go for a drink in the Loungers' deck?" Deedee's voice was almost trembling.

"And?"

"Well, at least one of them is bound to be nearby keeping an eye on us..." She paused to look at Ara. "We'll just pretend we're unaware of that... and we'll touch each other a little bit now and then without going over the top, just so they realise we're really hot for it?"

"Bloody hell Deedee, I'm feeling weak in the legs just by thinking..." The two girls didn't have too much to consider and after preparing themselves for all eventualities left their room.

The AKAZI "I" was about to complete its first full day travel north and the warmth of the Caribbean air currents could be felt. The girls had poured themselves a large whiskey each and held hands lovingly as they sipped their drinks, in one of the Loungers' decks.

"Besides Americo on the "bridge" I think everyone else is

probably fast asleep…" Ara whispered to Deedee once they'd finished their drinks. "It is 02:30 in the morning you know?"

"Well… shall we go back to the room? It's getting a bit chilly in here…"

"OK…"

Approaching their bedroom however, they saw Fernando and Ze coming out of Paula's room and instinctively hid against a corridor recess.

"Anytime big boys…," they heard Paula whisper to them cheerfully, before the securities headed in the opposite direction towards their quarters.

"What a cow…!" Ara let escape the moment they were back in their bedroom.

*

Thelma had not heard from Pedro or Quito for two days and after pursuing most avenues decided to contact Patricio.

"Do you think somebody at "I" might know something?"

"You really are worried about them, aren't you?"

"Obviously…" She did her best not to make it sound like her private emotions were involved.

"I'll see what I can do…"

For some reason, because Pedro wasn't gagging for her attention 24/7 like a Recife town-boy would, nor taken any of the open *opportunities* she had presented him with, it made her wonder; were his young wives all he ever wanted in *that* domain? Or was she losing her touch? She didn't think he was in love with them… and even assumed he had probably grown tired of them and their childlike moments, at a time when what he really needed was a woman like her at his side. Delving deeper however, he also appealed to her as being generally shy when it came to women and sex; *could he be the type who probably felt a lot more at ease with prostitutes (?), for knowing he wouldn't have to see them ever again? Or had he become a challenge to her emancipated feminine ego?*

"Should we *wire* Mr. Bolivar's office for his own security, as usual?" Asked one of the "I" technicians, putting the final touches to Pedro's 37th floor P.R. Office.

"Yes please, just as you've done to all his homes and offices…" Thelma then turned to the two security men ready to leave. "Can you both lock up when they're finished?"

"Shouldn't one of us accompany you?" Salome enquired.

"No. One of you could go home ahead of me though… I'm having dinner with my niece in her home… She lives in Vancouver…" She lied.

"If you say so… Just give us a shout if you need us yeah?"

"Ok Salome"

What Thelma really wanted was a bit of space and some time to herself. She couldn't stop thinking of Pedro and decided to have a meal in an exclusive French restaurant before going home, to try to clear her thoughts!

Being in a restaurant by herself however, somehow soon made her the centre of attention, defeating the purpose of the whole exercise, when Patricio called.

"Thelma?"

"Yeah…"

"Pedro and Quito are ok… but you won't be able to reach them for a few days…"

"Why?"

"That's all I know Thel… I've heard it from a good source, so you can stop worrying ok?"

"That's good news Patricio, thanks."

*

Becchiu arrived at the Palace of the Guests shortly after breakfast. Pedro and Quito had anticipated his early arrival and were ready for him. At the back of their minds however, they were beginning to have some concerns about the deal they had made with Ayar. What if the deal was off?

"You two look rested…," he greeted them, as if in a pre-prepared statement.

"Ayar always knows how to make us feel welcome…" Pedro and Quito smiled.

"I'm actually supposed to take you to Him and the courtiers, whenever you're ready?"

To scale up the 5 floors to Ayar's private quarters felt easy, after the 22 floor climb at the Office Tower!

The courtiers were already sat at the U-shaped table on Ayar's veranda, and Pedro, Quito and Becchiu sat in the same places as they had done once before.

They were signalled to stand shortly after their arrival and Ayar entered the veranda without his wives, his naked torso covered by an elaborate red blanket-looking sort of cape.

"Please be seated…" He was friendly and informal, prompting the courtiers to loosen up too. He then gained an amused expression as He turned to Pedro and Quito. "Don't worry about your gold… you are doing well…" He reassured them with an Obama-type of smile! "What happened is something that often occurs when you change management; new people come in with lots of ideas without fully measuring the consequences of transforming theory into practice…" He didn't want to elaborate. "The good news however is that everything is back to normal and both the Aztecs and the Mayans have been forbidden from returning to your dimension with the intent of interfering with our private interests…" He paused. "Ironically, your mission has actually been made easier, in the way that your American *friends* have now been deprived of any support they enjoyed from Aztecs and Mayans resulting from this… You can now roam freely around their offices in our Inca dimension to your heart's content!!!" He caused the Courtiers to laugh full heartedly.

"Is that it?" Pedro found the courage to ask, assuming the King had finished talking.

"Yes…" Ayar replied and then decided to explain further.

"When it comes to disputes between celestial competitors, we each command such power that to engage in open conflict could completely destroy everything we know and benefit from. Therefore, as a safeguard, we are all forced to obey the ruling of a higher Court which arbitrates on any dispute…"

"If that's the situation… what was the point of the Aztecs and the Mayans trying something they themselves knew was doomed from the start?" Quito was making a giant effort to understand this!

"There are also other forces involved." Ayar explained. "Incas, Aztecs and Mayans were once one People, united by the same shield of time (calendar), until we all came along and split them genetically and culturally, to befit our interests." He paused. "The higher Court to which we all obey therefore, acts not only to protect the interests of those in the embodiment of Incas, Aztecs and Mayas, but also of those that represent the ancient union of all three, whom we were never allowed to obliterate for various reasons…"

"Are you then saying that this latest thing was caused by the "*unionists*" trying to pull a fast one, rather than by your Aztec and Mayan competitors operating out of pure-stupid greed?" Pedro asked thoughtfully.

"It is considerably more complex than what it sounds…" Ayar felt He had explained enough.

"I suppose they are all under new management now?" Quito ventured, causing everyone to laugh including Ayar, who this time shook their hands before leaving the veranda.

Back outside with Becchiu, it was still mid morning and the cloudy sky threatened some rain.

"You are most welcome to spend another night with us, but if you are in a hurry to return to your business, I could be ready to take you out of here in an hour's time…" The Chieftain offered.

"With regret… I think we really ought to get going Becchiu." Pedro answered decisively.

"Not a problem… I'll see you shortly"

A few hours later, already on the return trail, Pedro decided to contact Marco, to have him fly to George's Estate, so as to take him and Quito back to Vancouver. He then called George, still stuck in New York, who made every arrangement in relation to their jet and instructed Sebastião to pick the two of them up once Pedro called him.

"And Thelma?" asked Quito… "She must be pretty worried too..."

"I'm about to run out of energy on both phones and we still need to call Sebastião in 3 days' time…"

"You can use my phone…"

"Thanks… I forgot you had a phone!!!" He chuckled.

"Thelma, are you alright?"

"I am now… where have you been? Is Quito with you?"

"We are both fine and I'm using his phone…" He paused. "I'm in the middle of the Amazon and Marco and Martha are on their way to pick us up… I shall be with you by the time the AKAZI "I" arrives…"

"I think I must be cracking up but… What on Earth are you doing in the middle of the Amazon instead of being in Seattle or Vancouver?"

"Cannot really talk much just now… I'll tell you all about it when I see you yeah?"

"Hurry back…" She softened her voice.

"Deedee and Ara…? Why not call them too?" Quito suggested, the moment Pedro was finished with Thelma. "It will make them and their babies happy."

"Have you called your wives already?"

"About an hour ago… The guilt was killing me!!!" They both ended up having a laugh.

Deedee and Ara sounded polite, cold and detached, without any of the anticipated warmth and nostalgia, further cooling Pedro's fire.

**

XIV

Pedro and Quito were back in Vancouver 4 days later, via Mexico City and Los Angeles, and it took them a further day to get organised, which included returning their hired car and reassuring the elderly Yates's that they were OK.

It was 04:00 in the morning; the AKAZI "I" still had at least a day's sailing ahead, and Thelma looked broody as she walked around the kitchen, preparing a very early morning breakfast for her and Pedro. Neither of them could sleep much. Pedro had found the Vancouver "Metro News" of the previous day and distractedly browsed through it while waiting for the promised treat, under the observing eyes of the woman.

"Are you OK?" He looked at her from under his reading glasses.

"I'm fine…" She replied, snapping out of a daydream, and back to the rashers of bacon still under the grill.

"You are not…" Pedro gave up on the newspaper to focus on her, and she came to sit next to him with two plates of bacon, scrambled eggs and toast. "Yummy…," muttered Pedro, ready to tuck in.

"I think you are going to like your office…" She said pouring him some coffee, avoiding eye contact.

"I'm sure I will." Pedro replied confidently. "Are you going to let me know what's bugging you?"

"Nothing's bugging me… I've… I've never been so worried about someone in my whole life… and that by itself worries me…" She admitted and finally looked into his eyes…

"Are we OK to make some coffee?" Sergio and Salome entered the kitchen, ready to start their day.

"Go right ahead…" said Pedro, returning to his plate.

"Morning guys…," greeted Thelma, doing the same.

Quito wasn't far behind and it was still dark outside when they all made their way to the offices of "Three Rainbows.com"!

"Did you choose the name of the company or…?" Pedro asked Thelma.

"I did. Meaning that three parties eventually find their pot of gold… the two parties in a business as well as the go-between?"

"Wow, that's so cool man…?" Salome couldn't hold himself "I've been trying to figure out the meaning of it for days…"

"Are you OK man?" Sergio seemed surprised by Salome's unprompted outburst.

"Yeah, Yeah… Sorry about that…"

Entering the building, after receiving their access passes, Quito was the one with the biggest smile as he got inside the elevator, and Pedro tried to avoid looking at him!

On the 37th floor, the small business suite was made up of two offices, a kitchenette, a conference room and a bathroom-toilet. Thelma had taken care with choosing things she knew met with Pedro's taste, and the whole thing was crowned with an impressive view of the city.

"It looks really good Thelma… cosy but also grand…" Pedro complimented her.

"Couldn't fault it," reinforced Quito, feeling the fluffiness of the carpet.

Thelma then looked at the two security men:

"Now that Pedro's here, I feel that only one of you should move around with us, while the other should make sure that our home is not interfered with." She paused. "I suggest that

Salome should perhaps go home today and leave you two to work out your own schedule from here on?"

"No problem…," said Sergio, glancing at Salome.

"Cool…," confirmed the other, "Shall I go now?" He looked at Thelma.

"Whenever…" She gave him a smile and then added. "It doesn't have to be you specifically, don't take me wrong…"

"Of course not…," he returned the smile and left.

Waiting for his computer to load, Pedro sat thoughtfully at his desk facing the imposing city view, while Thelma had developed a frown checking something on her mobile.

"Everything OK…?" Pedro asked.

"Fancy an early lunch?" She looked at him and winked before turning to Sergio. "Would you mind securing the office while we're out?"

"No problem…"

"Will you join us?" Pedro handed Quito his jacket.

Already outside, while waiting for one of the elevators to come to a stop, Thelma informed Pedro that their Vancouver offices had been broken into overnight, and that who ever did it remained inside for a period of over an hour.

"So, the place must be well bugged…" He paused to turn to her as the elevator arrived. "Ask no questions, take this lift by yourself and wait for me downstairs. I'll be there shortly."

"Don't go calling me from the Amazon in a week's time OK?" She retorted as she got in.

"Could you see what's happening on the 22nd floor?" Pedro then requested, looking at Quito. "And give me a call when you are done, so we can synchronise coming back here at the same time?"

"Ok… leave it with me and drop me on the 24th floor... please…" Pedro looked at him a little puzzled. "It will save me walking all the way down to the 22nd…"

*

"What have you done with Quito?" Thelma was surprised to see Pedro by himself.

"I asked him to check on something for me while we're gone…"

Pedro and Thelma got into a taxi alighting at a "Costa" Café not too far from their office block.

"Well, as you probably know, all your places are *wired* for your own security. The system is quite sophisticated and is also programmed to detect movement of body heat and several other things… Through my mobile I can access system information as well as receive alerts, each time the system detects something it regards as unusual…"

"Very clever… and… You can do that also to the Rio penthouse, the jet, and the yacht?"

"Yes… I suppose you could say that I'm your guardian angel…"

"I think you should have told me that beforehand, not after…! I find it a gross impropriety to be honest…" Pedro wasn't at all pleased.

"I hope you'll accept that I didn't do this of my own accord…"

"Anyway… was this what you wanted to tell me?"

"I'm afraid there is more…" She paused. "Once I discovered we had been broken into, I decided to have a quick historical check on all the other places… Including your wives' yacht premises…"

"Oh crap!!!"

"The two of them… with your security guys…," they both fell silent for a few moments "Would you rather not have known?"

"No no… I thank you for letting me know…" Pedro somehow didn't seem overly surprised "I'm just trying to figure out what to do…" He paused. "Is it tomorrow we expect them to arrive?"

"Yes…" Thelma suddenly felt immensely sad for Pedro. "I'm sorry…!"

"Could you tell if this only took place once or on more than one occasion?"

"It happened on three separate nights and on two afternoons…," she paused "Do you want me to take any particular course of action?"

"Well, you can start by getting rid of the Security Agency… I don't need to be trampling over any of these fucking people… If you cannot find decent professionals, I'll look for some myself…"

"There's no need to shoot the messenger…"

"It's not just those two Thelma… it was that Giovanni guy to begin with, not to mention this Salome! The guy seems constantly high… could he be relied upon in a serious situation? I somehow don't think so…"

"I take your point and… please don't go blaming me for the girls…" she paused. "Do you want the guys roughed up?"

"I can't think straight right now. Do whatever you feel is right…"

"And the girls? They are carrying your children…"

"It's all very delicate… There's Quito involved as well as the whole tribe…" Pedro took in a deep breath. "What a bloody mess!!!"

Pedro's mobile then rang.

"Are you done?"

"Yes. The offices of the Indios are empty and the other three went out for lunch with some Chinese delegation…"

"Quito… I think I'm going to give the office a pass for today and turn in… I'm not feeling too good…"

"Well I'm not going to be doing anything here anyway… I'll keep you company?"

"OK… meet me downstairs in the lobby. I'll be there shortly."

216

Thelma then decided to call Sergio and the four were headed home moments later.

"I've been trying to reach Salome for quite a while now without success…" Sergio informed them.

"Well, let's hope he didn't overdose on something…," commented Thelma.

Arriving at the maisonette, Sergio noticed a small blood stain by the letter box and decided to go around the back… emerging from the front door moments later.

"You don't want to go in there miss…" He looked nauseated as he said it… "I think we should call the police."

"Is Salome…?" asked Pedro.

"They cut his throat wide open and he bled to death… The whole kitchen is full of blood…"

"What a fucking day!!!" Pedro was beginning to run out of socially acceptable words.

The police and an ambulance arrived quickly and after a couple of hours of questions, Thelma booked the four of them into a nearby hotel.

"I was told by my boss that our contract has been terminated." Sergio confronted Thelma as they were about to go for dinner.

"That is correct…" She confirmed. "You've done well though, Sergio… it's the others that were not what we needed…"

"They are bound to fire me too… If you'd let me stay on, I could get you a proper security team like no other…" Sergio proposed and Thelma looked at Pedro.

"How long would it take you to put a proper team together?"

"Only a few phone calls… Two of them have even worked as security personnel in Iraq… They could all be here ready for duty by lunch time tomorrow, if you let me go ahead?"

"Do what you need to do…" Pedro gave him the nod.

"Thank you Mr. Bolivar. I will not let you down."

*

"You look like you've not slept in weeks!" Quito observed as they were about ready for bed.

"I've had a truly bad day…!"

"Want to tell me about it?" Quito invited already inside his own bed, turning to face Pedro.

"Well, we've had our own little share of extra marital activity in XAKATAN but…" Started Pedro, before telling him all he knew.

"I'm broken hearted on your behalf and a bit lost for words…!" Quito seemed in shock.

"What would you do in my shoes?"

"I don't really know… The fact that both are pregnant from you makes it all the more complicated…," the Akazi Chief commented pensively. "Why don't you ask Marco and Martha to fly them to Recife and I'll get Joaquim to take them back to the tribe?"

"And then?"

"I'll tell Deedee's mum what happened and that you don't want either of them back."

"No… They'd be humiliated to death and… I don't wish any harm to come to them…"

"But you don't want them back either. Do you?"

"No I don't… but I need to think about this…"

"You don't have much time; they'll be here tomorrow, so I'm told…" Quito looked at him. "A bit of sleep will do you good man… and you'll wake up with fresh ideas…," he added, getting ready to turn the other way. "Good night"

"Good night Quito…"

"You were probably right when you first thought they were a bit young…" Quito added as an after thought, two or three minutes later. "If you combine that with the full impact of the white-man's world, experienced from a position of limitless wealth… without you being there… Something was bound to give!!!" He said, turning back again to then get up. "I've spotted a few little whiskey bottles in the room's fridge... shall I get us one each?"

"That's the best thing I've heard since this morning...," approved Pedro, also getting up to go into the living area of the hotel suite.

Thelma eventually came out of her adjoining room, also wide awake!

"Were you guys planning to have a party without me?" She said, looking for another little bottle of the same inside the fridge and ending up calling reception for a proper bottle of the stuff!

"We don't want to go overboard with alcohol guys, we've got to get on with business tomorrow." Pedro reminded them.

"No, we don't. We need to sort these loose ends before anything else... or our focus will be distracted..." Thelma spoke with conviction.

"I think she's right...," supported Quito.

The bottle of whiskey arrived and their exchange of ideas on what to do with the girls was viewed from every possible angle, until Thelma came up with a suggestion that seemed to strike the right balance.

"Once they arrive I'll explain the situation to them privately and offer them three choices:" She started. "To go back to the tribe to have their babies and find new husbands from among the Akazi, or to have their babies adopted by the tribe and start a fresh life somewhere else with some financial help from you..." She said looking at Pedro, before having another sip of the drink.

"And the third option...?" Quito wanted to know.

"Be thrown into the ocean with a heavy stone tied around their necks..."

"Wooo!!! You don't mess about..." Quito chuckled. "And if they have some suggestions of their own?"

"I'll listen to them, of course..." She looked at Quito. "I'm only trying to help all parties reach an amicable solution...

I certainly wish no harm to come to either the girls or their babies…"

"Thelma is well qualified to do this from her own life experience…" Pedro clarified to Quito without going into details… And much later, once the bottle was empty, they all returned to their respective beds!!!

*

Pedro decided to stay at the hotel the following day, rather than risk losing his self-control once the AKAZI "I" berthed in the Marina. It was left to Quito and Thelma to sort out the situation concerning Deedee and Ara. Sergio in the meantime had assembled his team and came to introduce them to Pedro in his hotel suite;

"These are Beto and Lima from Belo Horizonte, recently returned from Iraq… and this is Castro from São Salvador da Bahia, previously an instructor for the Brazilian SAS (the Batalhão Tonelero) …"

"Good to meet you…" Pedro greeted them individually. They all looked sharp and beefy, with extremely short haircuts.

"Beto and Lima will take over from Fernando and Ze, the moment they leave the ship. And Castro and I will rotate between the places where you're going to be and your immediate environment."

"Excellent Sergio… I will ask Thelma to come and deal with your employment details before any resumption of duties…" Pedro clarified. "She'll be with you shortly."

*

It was mid afternoon when the AKAZI "I" finally docked against its Marina slot, attracting the admiration of locals and fellow yachtsmen alike. From the loungers' deck, Deedee and Ara could be seen excitedly waving back to a few children, while Fernando and Ze were acting as deck-hands, securing the ship against its private walkway.

"Hi Thelma…" The girls almost ran to her excitedly "We thought we'd never get here!!!" added Deedee seconded by Ara, also looking at Quito. "And Pedro…?"

"We need to have a little private chat in a moment…," replied Thelma.

"Is he alright?" Ara covered her mouth instinctively as she popped the question.

"He is fine…" Thelma reassured them with a smile.

Captain Americo, Raul and Crew also came to greet them, no doubt looking forward to a few days on dry land and Thelma introduced Beto and Lima as the new Security men.

"What will happen to Fernando and Ze?" Deedee enquired.

"They are being recalled by the Agency…," explained Thelma.

"Did we hear our names?" Fernando and Ze came to them looking cheerful and apparently oblivious to it all!

"Yes… You need to leave the ship immediately to return to Brazil. The contract with your Agency was cancelled this morning and our insurance no longer covers you…," Thelma informed them, prompting Ze to check his mobile for messages.

"…And the reasons given?" Ze seemed taken aback.

"That's something you'll need to sort out with your employers. Anyway, you need to be off this ship immediately." She tried not to look harsh. "Beto and Lima will take you to the airport and your belongings will be sent to you…" Thelma then took the girls below deck without further ado, followed by Quito.

"Have they done something wrong?" Ara enquired, as they followed Thelma.

"Quito and I need to speak with you two in private. Shall we go into my room?" She proposed and they followed Thelma, fearing the worse.

The girls were not kept guessing for long and after giving them their favourite drinks, Thelma went straight to the point;

"Well… Pedro is fully aware of what went on between the two of you, Fernando and Ze, and he doesn't want to take you back as his wives…" Deedee was quick to pass out and Ara burst into tears, to then seek the protection of Quito's arms, while Thelma got Deedee back to herself. "Anyway, Pedro doesn't wish either of you or your babies any harm, nor does anyone for that matter…"

"We talked about your interests and those of your babies, among ourselves, and there are some options we'd like to discuss with both of you, to see which you'd prefer…," said Quito.

"I am Pedro's wife as is Ara and he is the father of our unborn children. I will only accept conditions and options directly from him and no one else…" Deedee spoke with a confidence and authority that took Quito and Thelma by surprise.

"He does not want your presence on the AKAZI "I" Deedee… and I've offered to take you back to the tribe, so the two of you can have a period of reflection on the options he is willing to give you." Asserted Quito this time, assuming a Tribal Chief's stance.

"What options are we talking about?" Ara was suddenly curious.

"In the village being built, he is willing to make you a house like Thelma's place, leave you free to find husbands and offer you money to live well every month…"

"That is absurd!!!" Deedee commented, just short of laughing. "He is willing to do all that so as not to come to bed with us? What's the sense in that?"

"If that's what he wants to do and make us free to do whatever, I don't see what we've got to lose…" Ara looked at Deedee. "Will our babies be looked after?" she asked Thelma.

"As if they were Kings…," she replied.

"Will you become his wife instead?" Deedee asked.

"I wouldn't mind to be honest...," she confessed "but I don't think he has any of such plans..."

"You prefer women, don't you?" Deedee looked straight at Thelma, causing Quito to break into a sweat.

"Not at all... do you think I'm that way because I'm not married and live alone?" Thelma paused to look at the two girls, feeling a little hurt. "I'm not against either of you. It's yourselves you need to blame, not me... I'm trying to get you a good deal instead of nothing at all..."

"What would you advise us to do Quito?" Deedee finally asked.

"I genuinely feel that he is offering you a fantastic deal... It is not as if he will go away from your lives completely. The children will always be there and a good friendship would be in everyone's best interests." He tried his best to sound paternal this time. "It goes without saying that you can also count on my friendship and Thelma's of course... But he wants you out of here for now and doesn't want to see either one of you... the whole thing is still too fresh in his mind."

"...And if we don't accept...?" Ara wanted to know. "I don't want to go back to the Camp or the Village... I couldn't live with the tribe anymore... we would be humiliated every minute of the day and night..."

"And what if Pedro bought my home for you, gave you plenty of money each month to live on and go shopping? I'd make sure you learn to drive and other things... as well as ensuring that your children would eventually go to the best schools?" Thelma proposed.

"Could Quito take us to go and live in your place already now?" Deedee asked Thelma while looking at Ara for some support.

At this point, Thelma got up and left the room to call Pedro's mobile, returning moments later.

"Marco and Martha are ready to fly you to Recife when you are..." She announced.

"I'm ready…" Quito stood up and looked at the girls.

"Shall I help you pack a small case and take the rest back with us?" Thelma proposed to the two girls awash with tears. "I will also give you US$5,000 each to keep you going for a week or two."

"Will you come and see us the moment you're back?" asked Deedee. "I'm sorry about what I said to you earlier…"

"I know you didn't mean it." She gave her a hug. "And of course, I'll come and see you both as soon as I return…"

An hour later, Sergio arrived to take Quito and the girls to the airport.

**

XV

Martha came around to check if Quito and the girls were correctly fastened for take off.

"Is this going to be your first time flying?" She enquired of the two girls.

"Can you tell?" Deedee asked, suddenly more concerned with the new experience ahead.

"You don't have to be concerned about anything... We've done it loads of times before..." Martha offered her a confident smile. "Are you nervous too?" She then turned to Ara.

"As can be expected... but I suppose that is normal...," the girl replied.

"I was very scared the first time too..." Martha admitted, on her way to join Marco in the cockpit.

"I almost shitted my pants..." Quito added in a whisper, making them laugh.

Marco decided to go the California-Mexico City way and Martha made the girls a bed at the back of the plane, after refuelling in L.A.

"I cannot get over as to how stupid we've been..." Deedee mumbled to Ara as they both tried to go to sleep.

"It depends on how you look at it and on how greedy you are... I think we've done rather well out of this." Ara turned to face Deedee. "We've got a fabulous place of our own, loads of money, our babies and our freedom to do as we please... What more could you want?" She paused. "...And I think Pedro will be nostalgic for our threesomes sooner or later... I'm convinced of that..."

"I'd like to share your confidence... I really love him..."

"I love him too, in my own way… but I think that until he gets Thelma out of his system we've got no chance!"

"Do you think Thelma might have planned this with Fernando and Ze to get us out of the way?"

"Come off it Ara, you know very well that this was our own doing…"

"Maybe so, but temptation was placed there so we could fall for it… and to be honest, I hope this won't be the last I've seen of Ze…"

"I hope it comes true for you…" Deedee was back sobbing again until she fell asleep.

At Recife Airport, the girls were met by one of Thelma's assistants called Janette. The woman was a middle aged single mother of twin girls of 19 and had been made aware of the situation through Thelma.

"Welcome back to Recife…" Janette greeted the girls as if they were family. "Thelma has asked me to look after you until she gets back…"

"We are not little girls any more…" Ara commented.

"She didn't ask me to babysit you…" Janette chuckled. "You're totally free to do as you please, but you might appreciate being able to count on somebody if you need to, without having to resort to your tribe's people…?"

"That's really nice of you Janette… Take no notice of Ara. I think she is overtired…"

Quito decided to sleep in the office he shared with Pedro that night, rather than to show himself at the Akazi Camp, and was flying back towards Vancouver the next morning.

*

Pedro checked out of the hotel the moment Marco told him he was already flying out of Vancouver with Quito and the girls.

"Good to see you on board…" Pedro was greeted by Captain Americo, seconded by Raul and Lucio. "We heard about what happened to Salome only a day or two ago…"

226

"We're going through crazy times Americo… We don't know who did it, or why, and we've just bought a place no one wants to live in now…!"

"What happened to Fernando and Ze? They seemed nice guys…" Americo was shamelessly inquisitive.

"They were too nice Americo… I'll let you draw your own conclusions…"

"Nice to see you again Mr. Bolivar…" Greeted Isabel in passing, one of Rio's maids, as Pedro looked for Thelma.

"Nice to see you too Isabel… When did you get here?"

"A few moments ago… I landed in Vancouver this morning… I've never seen such a beautiful ship…"

"I'm glad you like it… Is it your turn to spend a month with us then?"

"Yes…" She ended up following him. "Are you looking for Ms. Thelma?"

"Yes, have you seen her?"

"I saw her talking to Paula in one of the dining rooms upstairs…"

"Thanks… Welcome aboard…" He wished to her as he headed for the upper deck.

Pedro caught up with Thelma as she sat at his favourite bar stool.

"There you are…"

"Fancy a drink?" She proposed, going behind the bar.

"Go on then…" He accepted, regaining his usual spot. "How was it with the girls?"

"I'm homeless!!!" She chuckled.

"What do you mean?" He enquired picking up his glass and Thelma told him everything that had gone on with Deedee and Ara. "But that was your own personalised space!"

"Well, at least you have them out of the way. Isn't that what you wanted?" She paused. "You could always buy me a new home I suppose…"

"You make me sound like a right bastard!!!"

"That was not at all intended…" She settled next to him with her drink. "If you want my honest opinion, I think Ara is a complete little cow but Deedee… I somehow think she was dragged into this."

"Come off it Thelma! …For 3 nights and 2 afternoons?" Pedro brought the whiskey bottle to be next to them before returning to his seat. "I can believe that Ara was probably the initial instigator, but Deedee certainly showed no lack of enthusiasm… I'm sure you'll agree!" he paused. "…Do you mind if we give this a rest for a few days?"

"Not at all… I'd like to see you smile and to see you happy… Is there some way I could make you happy?"

"You make me happy already with everything you do Thelma… I can't afford to lose you because of some foolish moment both of us might regret…" Thelma's eyes went a little moist as Pedro spoke. "What I really meant to say is…" At this point she placed a finger gently on his lips.

"This was very unprofessional of me to begin with! I'm sorry. Please don't say anything?"

*

Pedro was in no doubt that the vicious murder of Salome was a message from the "Starling Inc crowd" meant to scare him off! This beckoned some meaningful reply and 48 hours later, it came in the shape of fresh blood being splattered against the family front doors of all 3 main Starling Inc. bosses; in their different cities and on the same night.

"I'm sure they'll be impressed…What do you think they'll do now?" Thelma wanted to know from Pedro, as she shared an after-dinner drink with him and Quito on board the yacht.

"I think they'll calm down… and it is at this point that we enter the second stage of the Plan…"

"Which is?" Quito and Thelma asked in unison.

"We arrange a meeting with all three, aimed at discussing *common business interests*."

"Holly Kamikaze! And where would you hold such meeting?" Thelma seemed horrified.

"In our offices…"

"You can't be serious! Do you think they'd be stupid enough to fall for that?" Quito commented.

"And what if they suggest that such a meeting should take place in their offices instead?" Thelma questioned him before Pedro could offer Quito a reply.

"I'll accept the invitation…" Pedro looked at Thelma and then had a brief chuckle. "And I'm confident that I'll be perfectly safe…" He paused. "They will instinctively know that I have something up my sleeve and in reserve… should they mess up."

"And what about us…?" Quito referred to Thelma and himself.

"Well, you will be with me…" Pedro gave him a meaningful brief look.

"And me?"

"You will be in North Vancouver with Beto, Lima and a Laser Guided Missile locked on me… to be fired on my command, if need be…"

"That's…" Thelma just stopped herself from saying it.

"Crazy?" Pedro said it for her.

"And you expect me to be ready to kill you at any given moment? What could you possibly gain from that?"

"I didn't say anything about being killed… In fact, if I tell you to fire the missile towards me, I won't even get scratched…"

"This is a stupid game you are playing now!" Thelma was getting fed up and almost at the point of leaving the table.

"You don't know what he is talking about but I do… and I can confirm he wouldn't get scratched at all… nor would I." Quito revealed, just short of offering her a demonstration…

"Are you guys going to put me out of my misery or what?" Thelma was clearly annoyed now!

"Well…" Pedro got up, after a moment of hesitation and suggested that Thelma do the same. "Now grab me as tightly as you can…" He made her laugh.

"You didn't have to go through all this you know…" She also made Quito laugh, but in anticipation of the shock she was about to get. "Really tight…?" She couldn't stop giggling… and Pedro wasn't in too much of a hurry to get on with the demonstration either.

"Yes please…" He said, ready to activate the necklace under his shirt and *puffhh,* he was gone… causing Thelma to go into hysterical panic, even after seeing him reappear at Quito's side.

"Ho fuck!!!" She let escape, still trembling. "Did you put something in my drink?" She was as confused as she had ever been. "Are you guys ghosts…?" She managed to say, covered in goose bumps.

"I'm sorry for giving you a scare Thelma…" Pedro apologised, but she didn't want him to come any closer. "Of course we are not ghosts!!!" He tried to reassure her with a chuckle, "But Quito and I… we are able to switch between this dimension and another, at will… and that is why the missile wouldn't even scratch us…?"

"Pedro, you are now making fun of me…!" She looked at both of them. "Go on Quito, let me see you do it…"

"Do you want to hold me tight?"

"No, no, no… you do it from there…" Quito then turned his back to her, so she could not see him press the necklace and… *puffhh…!* "Jesus Christ…!"

"Everything OK…?" Beto came to them, attracted by Thelma's earlier screams.

"Everything is fine Beto…" She tried to reassure him, while becoming increasingly concerned as to where Quito might have disappeared to, and then saw him return calmly from the lower deck!

"You want to join us for a drink?" Quito invited Beto.

"Not on duty sir, thank you… please continue to enjoy your evening…" The man said, returning elsewhere on board.

"Come on Thelma, come back to the table and sit down with us… we won't give you any more demonstrations for today… I promise." Pedro stretched his hand to her apologetically, the moment Beto was gone.

"How is that possible?" She looked at the two suspiciously. "Please tell me? Is it something I can do too?"

"This is obviously a secret that must die with you…" Pedro insisted.

"Have no worries on that, I'd be institutionalised!" She paused. "I'm ready…"

"Well, you cannot do it. Only the two of us can, thanks to a device that is linked to our DNA and biometric details…" Pedro explained.

"But that's beyond anything Human Science has achieved…! Even the mere concept of other dimensions remains theoretical and open to speculation, never mind being able to travel between two of them!" She paused. "You are not E.T.s!!! Are you?"

"Of course not!" Pedro did his best to put her mind at rest, as well as remain serious. "We are however instrumental to some of those…"

"E.T.s?" she insisted and Pedro nodded. "Go on then, tell me, tell me, tell me…" Quito brought a fresh whiskey bottle to the table while she spoke.

"We are not supposed to tell you any of these things nor give you demonstrations like we've just done… can you just trust us for now?"

"…But you will eventually tell me about it yeah?" She poured herself a super large measure!

"Eventually…"

"Well, then that's good enough for me…" She smiled at them raising her glass, silently announcing her intention to get totally legless!!!

*

No one bothered to go to "Three Rainbows.com" the next morning; not because of how much they had to drink the previous evening, but because they couldn't be 100% sure if it had been fully debugged, at a time when secrecy was of paramount importance. Instead, Pedro, Quito and Thelma gathered in the yacht's office after a late breakfast.

"Patricio is going to get a shock, once I ask him for a Laser guided missile and launcher with a 30-mile range; to be delivered to North Vancouver..." Mumbled Thelma while preparing her e-mail, to then stop to turn to Pedro; "...and if we fire the missile... Who are you going to do business with?"

"That will be for the shareholders to decide..." Pedro's reply triggered one of Quito's chuckles.

"I suppose..." She also found it funny.

"Once you're done with that Thelma, what I need to know from Patricio is the actual limit on the capital available for the take over bid, so that I know how flexible we can be, or if I need to find additional resources, just in case?"

"I can tell you those things without going to Patricio..." She said proudly. "Do you want just the total or the detail?"

"Both..."

"You can dispose of up to US$3.5 billion. I'll e-mail you the detail. The company is however only valued at US$2 billion as things stand..."

"Do we have an estimate of what proportion of those 2 billion could be attributed to the concessions we want?"

"Around 25%..." She replied.

"Quito... I'm going to be a pain in the arse but... would you mind spending the day in their offices, to try and assess the chances of me getting the three of them against each one another on this, should the need arise?"

"...And how am I supposed to do that? My English is just about good enough to buy a donut..."

"See how they act together, as well as in the privacy of

their own offices? What they do when by themselves, who they talk to…?"

"And what about that room on the 21st floor we never went into?" Quito asked.

"Be with Ninan and seek his advice on that?"

"OK… Shall I ask Sergio to take me there now?"

"Yes please…"

"Is that Ninan the E.T. guy?" Thelma couldn't wait to find out, the moment Quito left.

"Well, one of them, yes…"

"Oh boy…"

Pedro then went through the "official" credentials he had been accredited with, to make him the worthy acting agent for the parties in the take over bid.

"Where does George Azevedo fit into all this?" She wondered, while Pedro continued to look for any flaws in the data about him.

"Well, his son and daughter in law are obviously involved in more ways than one… and George has shown an interest in picking up the remainder parts of Starling Inc that may not interest us at some later stage…" Pedro paused. "He is also a good friend, the biggest land owner in the Region that interests us… and I will need to call him later…" He looked at her. "Have you recovered from last night's shock?"

"I've recovered from your disappearing act… but not from the feeling of being in your arms…" she tried to avoid eye contact, "I wanted to stay like that forever…" Pedro became a bit stuck for words and somehow got her to hide her face behind her hands! "I'm at it again aren't I?"

*

Castro arrived to pick up Pedro from the yacht, shortly after lunch, in what had become a dull grey afternoon.

"Have you eaten?" Pedro enquired as the man arrived.

"I'm all fixed and ready to go, whenever you are…" He declined politely with a smile.

North and West Vancouver had no shortage of villas surrounded by forestry, often in isolated spots, and the purpose of their car journey was to scout for locations from where the actual missile could be discretely fired…! And eventually discovered an abandoned villa perfectly suited for the job, about a mile or so from the main road.

"I'm surprised this place has not been found by squatters…" Castro commented as they looked around inside the House.

"We must be careful not to leave any traces or fingerprints behind…" Pedro noted, wiping off any impressions left on door knobs. "If we get to fire the missile, the investigators will soon trace it back here…" Castro however seemed to be looking for something as they re-emerged from the house. "What is it?"

"That type of missile you ordered must be fired from a purpose-made launcher vehicle. We'll need to have it here and in place, at least one or two days prior to firing it, to avoid all sorts of last minute snags…" He paused, "We need to find some place where we can hide it…," he said, inspecting a short slope leading from a small lake that was drying out.

"Does that look like what you think we need?"

"It should do it… Let's just hope no one is prowling about at the wrong time, once we have the launcher in place… we shouldn't be using our own cars…" He then added as an afterthought. "I'll get the wheels of this one changed and incinerated…"

"Good thinking…" Pedro approved. "From different garages…?"

"That too…" Castro seemed amused, noticing Pedro's rapidly evolving criminal instinct!

Sergio returned Quito to the yacht in the early evening and the Indio chief seemed more ready for bed than dinner, by the time he sat at table.

"Anything exciting…?" Pedro looked at him inquisitively.

"Regarding the 3 big bosses, my conclusion is that they seriously hate each others' guts… and it wouldn't surprise me if their company is kept afloat by the stimulus generated by that very hatred…"

"Wow…" Thelma let out, "that's what I call an in-depth analysis…"

"Ninan however dissuaded me once again from going into that darkened room…" Quito ignored Thelma's comment, "…and I somehow have the feeling that it is probably where they are keeping the little ones…"

"That sounds like a pretty useful day…" Pedro also seemed impressed by Quito.

"It has also occurred to me…" Thelma booted in, as if not wanting to forget. "Wouldn't it be wise to probably send Castro, or someone to keep a shady eye on the girls in Porto de Galinhas?"

"Castro would be good…They've actually never met him…" Pedro agreed. "Excuse me…"

"George?" Pedro got up to leave the Table momentarily.

"How is Vancouver?"

"Things are about to start moving…," announced Pedro. "Where are you?"

"I'm home… Alberto (George's eldest son) received news from the kidnappers telling him to back off from any attempt to get the Brazilian Government to annul the concession rights given to the Americans…"

"Is that what caused all this in the first instance?"

"Apparently yes… He's offered the Government twice as much as the Americans paid for it… and there are a few people in the System trying to invalidate the original deal, listing a long catalogue of legal irregularities…"

"What would your son do with the Concessions, should he manage to get his way?"

"Add it to the land I already own in Acre and save the

mining rights for a rainy day..." He paused. "*The argument being raised by the Communists in Government, favouring the Americans, is that they have a programme of development for the area that would create thousands of jobs, whereas Alberto proposes the need for preserving the Nation's natural resources, at least for the time being...*"

"How would you rate your son's likelihood of success with the Government?"

"*More than 50-50 in his favour, I'd say...*"

"Shit! ...Are you telling me that I could be trying to buy from the Americans something that might not be legally theirs to sell... and end up acquiring something I don't want for an inflated price?"

"*That's a way of putting it... Yes.*"

"There's one thing that doesn't make sense in all this however...," started Pedro. "Don't the Americans realise that if they were to go ahead and kill the little ones, they'd actually be doing Alberto a favour?"

"*Because of everything from his father-in-law going to his wife...?*"

"I'm sure that Alberto himself must have worked that one out!!!"

"*What are you implying?*"

"I'm not implying anything... except that it makes no sense!?"

"*There are a few things that don't seem to tie up just now... What are your plans?*"

"I need to be sure of what's what before making any move George... Let's keep each other updated and... I'll get back to you over the next few days?"

"*OK. Let me know if there's anything I can do to help yeah?*"

"Thanks George. I'll speak with you soon..."

Back at table, from a parade of silver wear, Marisa

extracted a feast of curried lobster, complemented by all sorts of traditional Indian trimmings.

"This is a fabulous treat Marisa!" exclaimed Pedro. "Are we celebrating anything?"

"We are celebrating the sunset…," she said looking at Quito, who nearly chocked on his drink!

Food remained their talking topic for a while. Pedro's conversation with George however kept hovering in his mind and he ended up sharing it with Quito and Thelma.

"Could George be trying to put you off making any deal with the Americans, so his son could acquire it all for himself?" Thelma suggested.

"Could you ask Patricio to find out if there is any truth in the Brazilian government reconsidering the granting of those exploration Concessions?" Pedro turned to her.

"Yes… I'll also ask him to give us some feedback on the Americans' project of development for the area, as was originally proposed?"

"Yes please…"

**

XVII

Over the three days that followed everyone was kept busy chasing information of one type or another. To Pedro however, the most eagerly awaited news was Patricio's report on the Brazilian Government's actions regarding the American mining concessions. It was on day 3 when the news finally reached Thelma, as she shared breakfast with Pedro on deck.

"You are not going to like this…," she warned, abandoning a piece of toast in favour of Patricio's e-mailed attachment.

"Go on then…" Pedro replied, bracing himself for bad news as he refilled their cups with coffee.

"In short, Alberto's lawyers placed an Injunction, forbidding the Americans from any further activities in Brazil, pending the outcome of the Government's investigation into the whole affair."

"What's bad about that?" Pedro looked pleased.

"Well, this could drag on for years and years…"

"That's perfect…"

"How…?" She tried to predict Pedro's rationale.

"Well, if the Brazilian Government manages to find evidence of foul play by the Americans, either because of bribery or corruption of whatever kind, they stand to lose whatever they paid for the Concessions in the first instance… which I believe was somewhere in the region of half a billion dollars?" Thelma nodded, confirming the figure.

"So, you are planning to make the Americans an offer to buy their Brazilian location, for the *privilege* of taking up the fight against Alberto?"

"And in so doing, save their Company from possible

238

collapse, their bosses from the embarrassment of having to face their shareholders, and as for us, not having to buy the whole company in order to get the part we want." He confirmed.

"That sounds great… but if that fails? Either because the Americans can gather sufficient resources to wait and stay the course… or because they genuinely feel they can win that fight?"

"I somehow feel that they are not as strongly motivated as they were, until a few days ago…"

"What happened then?" Thelma looked puzzled and Pedro told her about the interests of those in the Aztec and Maya dimensions and how he ended up back in the Amazons.

"This is insane! If it wasn't for witnessing the way you and Quito can appear and disappear, supposedly into another dimension…" She took a reflective pause. "Well, still… they can resist any attempts of an aggressive take over from us, through the connections of Maurizio Genovese's New York Mafia… Should they ever need to quickly raise capital from alternative sources…"

"We could go on speculating forever Thelma…" Pedro seemed restless. "Anyway, the moment we feel that negotiations with the 3 bosses isn't going anywhere, that's when you'll fire the dam thing."

"Won't that make you a prime suspect? …And by association also incriminate Patricio's office as well as "I"?" Thelma looked worried. "If you want to blow them up, you should do it now, before becoming officially involved with some take over bid… So that suspicion will fall on Alberto instead of you…" She turned to face him more fully. "You must also consider the innocent people that could get killed in the process, which could include the two kids?"

"I don't think those kids are alive…"

"What makes you come to that conclusion?"

"It is not a conclusion, but more of a weird feeling" Pedro

didn't really want to be dragged into one of his conspiracy theories, but Thelma wasn't going to let go!

"I'm all ears…," she challenged him.

"This is crazy crazy…," he warned.

"I'm ready…"

"OK. What if this whole thing was planned by Alberto, so that his wife would be the sole heir to her father's fortune of some 4 or 5 billion, also ensuring that his father's own billions came to him?"

"…You think there might be some sort of collusion between Alberto and the Americans… or at least with their 3 Bosses…? …And that this whole charade of the Brazilian Government threatening action is just something for show, staged by some politicians in Alberto's pocket…?"

"I'm not ruling anything out… Alberto stands to make billions either way…" Pedro continued, thoughtfully. "He has been staying at my penthouse in New York… and you say that all my homes are wired… correct?" She confirmed with a nod. "Any chance that you, or someone, could go through every conversation there, ever since we bought the place?"

"I'll get my team in Recife to look into it…" She said, typing something into her mobile as she spoke. "I would strongly advise you to abandon the idea of the missile anyway…" Thelma then started to laugh. "If you really want to kill them however, I'm sure you could give them fatal heart attacks just by appearing in front of them out of thin air, under the right circumstances."

"You've got a point…" Pedro agreed, producing a big smile on Thelma's face.

"There you are!" Quito came to join them, still half asleep.

"Good morning Quito… I'm going for a shower while you two catch up?" Thelma excused herself to go to her room, looking cheerful.

"I thought Marisa was bringing you breakfast in

bed on a regular basis?" ventured Pedro cheekily, once Thelma was gone.

"That was a couple of days ago…" The way he said it caused Pedro to chuckle!

"You sound like you are still recovering from it…"

"It was an unforgettable experience, let's put it that way…," he lowered his voice.

"Don't tell me anything, if you'd rather not talk about it…"

"I don't mind… assuming it stays between us, of course."

"My lips are sealed… As you would expect…"

"Well… in a nutshell, she made me feel like a little boy! I didn't know *where I was*… or even if *I was anywhere* at all?"

"Gosh! That sounds dreadful already!" Pedro was doing his very best not to burst out laughing!

"It was!" he confirmed.

"…A bit like being thrown into a ring with a female Sumo wrestler… a few short moments after waking up?"

"I suppose that's the closest way of describing it…yeah…! But that aside, she is a lovely woman and very resourceful, when it comes to pleasuring a man…"

"OK, OK…. Anyway, changing the subject…," Pedro mentioned some of the theories that Thelma and he had been airing over breakfast.

"Do you think George could be trying to be a bit too clever?" He poured himself some coffee.

"I'm confused to be honest Quito…," he paused "George cannot really mess about with "I" because of his sworn allegiance, but neither can his son, since he is the next in line…"

"Well, perhaps neither of them realise that what they might be doing could be against the interests of "I" … I think you should have a word with Ninan and start getting some answers, or soon we won't even know who the hell we are anymore!"

"You're right Quito and I shall take your advice."

"And regarding Deedee and Ara… Do you think that Thelma's assistant will be able to provide enough security, should our *friends* be looking to raise the stakes? They are carrying your children…"

"Blast… We should have done that a couple of days ago…!" Pedro got on the phone to Castro and by evening, the security man was on board a scheduled flight to Recife, with instructions to keep a low profile, while maintaining an eye on the girls at all times.

*

Summer was beginning to fade in Porto de Galinhas. Janette's twin daughters, Mariana and Miguela, had become close friends with Deedee and Ara. They visited them almost every day in their beach buggy, invariably ending up on one of the local beaches, or going out for a meal and a few drinks. The pregnancies of the two girls were beginning to show when they wore their bikinis and this meant they often preferred shopping or eating out, rather than exposing their growing bellies to the general public!

"When's your husband returning from America?" Mariana asked Deedee, oblivious of the situation, while looking around one of the village's small shops.

"He should be back with his yacht in a couple of weeks or so…" Deedee played along.

"It must be nice to be so rich as not to have to look at prices when you buy stuff…" Mariana thought out loud as Deedee went inside the shop to buy an expensive silk scarf, followed by the other three.

"Well…" Deedee smiled at her, not too sure of what to say.

"Mum told us you are both married to the same guy?" Mariana had kept this question at the back of her mind ever since they had met three days earlier.

"He must be really well endowed…" Miguela covered her mouth as she spoke, causing Ara to giggle.

"We cannot really swing from it, but we have no complaints…," replied Deedee, not sharing Ara's amusement. "…But what about the two of you? I reckon that with being identical twins you've probably played a few tricks on your boyfriends?"

"We did, one time…" Miguela covered her mouth once again for laughing…

"And she ended up having to give my boyfriend a blowjob, so as not to reveal what we had done!" Mariana owned up, just as amused as the other was.

"And you got nothing from her boyfriend?" Ara wanted to know more.

"He was too shy, the poor thing…!" Mariana then seemed to get an idea. "Do you both want to go to a "Nite" after dinner?"

"Is that like a dance club?" Deedee enquired, not looking particularly excited.

"We could go to "Downtown" in Recife?" Migela proposed.

"The three of you can go but I think I'll stay behind… I'm feeling really tired today…" Deedee wasn't in the mood for it.

"What will you be doing by yourself?" Ara asked.

"I noticed that Thelma had some knitting wool in the living area and I thought I'd have a crack at making a little hat for my baby?"

"That… is… so… cute!" Migela was impressed and Ara's eyes reached for the sky.

Ara and the twins were keen on going to Recife and after spending the afternoon by Thelma's pool, the three began preparing themselves for their night out.

"I can't believe you'd rather spend the evening trying to knit a woolly hat!" Ara commented to Deedee while the other two helped each other with make up. "…You don't even know how to knit!!?"

"Well, that doesn't mean I can't learn…"

"You're still Pedro's "little wife" aren't you?"

"I probably am… does that make you a better person?"

"Woo…You really are touchy today, aren't you?"

"I hope you have fun Ara! Do I need to feel guilty about something?"

"Ok, ok…"

It was already after dark when the three girls headed for Recife, leaving Deedee behind in the apartment. And the moment they were gone, Deedee was quick to lock everything, down to the veranda doors onto the pool!

She spent the first hour doing culinary experiments and even had a crack at knitting, only to end up watching some T.V.! There was an eerie feeling at the back of her mind, causing her to suddenly turn around to look behind her on more than one occasion, as if something was there lurking in wait… She eventually moved some furniture around to have her back against the wall, before gradually falling asleep as the evening wore on.

Something awoke her around 1:30 in the morning. There was still no sign of the girls and a few faint noises from outside the veranda doors prompted her to switch the T.V. off, to better hear what this was. There was definitely someone outside, but she couldn't sum up the courage to peep to see what was out there from behind the curtains… until she felt something picking on the lock of the veranda door.

"Hey…" she found the courage to shout from behind the curtains…

"Ara?" came a voice from the outside.

"It's Deedee… who are you?"

"It's Ze and Fernando… Will you let us in?"

"You guys shouldn't be here at all… Are you trying to get killed?" She continued to talk from behind the curtains, while

from the other side, one of them continued to pick the lock…
until they managed to get in…

*

Vancouver was well into autumn and the many shades of
browns reds and yellows were now fast leaving the trees
within sight of the Marina.

"Winter will visit us any morning now…," commented
Americo, while explaining to Pedro some of the navigation
technology available to them on board.

"Do you reckon we should start heading back soon?"

"This vessel could sail through any conditions…," he said
proudly as they headed for the main dining room of the yacht,
"the ocean gets a little bit rougher as we get into winter, but it
should make no difference to us…"

That evening Pedro decided to invite Americo and Raul
to join them for dinner, which they readily accepted. Thelma
seemed to be taking longer than usual and Pedro prepared
some aperitifs while they all waited for her.

"We've been meaning to invite you to join us on several
occasions now, but somehow, something always gets in the
way…!" Pedro felt the need to offer some justification to the
two skippers.

"Think nothing of it. We can clearly see that you are very
busy people…" Americo showed his understanding, also on
behalf of Raul.

"Any news on the case involving Salome…?"
Raul enquired.

"Nothing yet… The Police told us that the whole thing
had all the hallmarks of a Mafia style killing…" Pedro took a
pause to greet Quito before continuing. "We think we know
who did it… and I'd be surprised if they were to try something
like that again…" Pedro tried to reassure the two mariners.

"You guys done anything exciting since you arrived in

Vancouver…?" Quito directed his question to Americo and Raul, as he joined them with his drink.

In the mean time Thelma entered the Dining Room, looking like the carrier of bad news.

"You look like you could do with a strong drink…," commented Pedro, trying to lighten her mood.

"Janette has been on the phone to me… and Deedee has disappeared…," she informed them, taking Pedro to one side.

"Disappeared how?"

"They think she has been kidnapped…" Thelma soon told Pedro all she knew and he felt like kicking himself for not having sent Castro earlier. "…Even if Castro had already been in Porto de Galinhas, there's no way he could have been in two places at the same time…"

"I'm surprised to see that the bosses of Starling Inc. didn't take the hint!" Pedro looked at her for clues. "I thought that security in your apartment was something akin to Fort Knox?"

"Well, it obviously wasn't…!" She let out a sigh, "The good news on the other hand is that, like in all your places, I've also wired my home for security… and we should soon get some feedback from that…"

"Any joy from the recordings of the Manhattan penthouse…?" It occurred to Pedro.

"That will take longer… There's a lot to get through…" Thelma somehow felt responsible for the situation, "We mustn't rush into any course of action until we can be sure of the facts… it could well be that Alberto is trying to use us against the Americans, for one…"

"I suppose…" Pedro smiled at her reassuringly.

"We should know a lot more by the time we've finished dinner?"

"And what of Ara and the twins…?" Pedro enquired, bringing her back to the others.

"They are in a safe house and well protected." She replied,

to then engage in conversation with the two mariners while Pedro fixed her a drink.

"Bad news?" Quito whispered to Pedro, getting himself a refill.

"I'll tell you after dinner… we'll know a lot more then…"

"Nothing too dramatic, I hope…?" He probed.

"No… And how did your day go?"

"Well, I've managed to get the private phone numbers of Frank Molinari, Pete Spencer and Maurizio Genovese, as well as the combination of Frank's office wall-safe!"

"I don't know what I'd do without you honestly!" Pedro nodded appreciatively. "Great job…"

"There's more…" Quito chuckled.

"That sounds mischievous already!"

"Well, Maurizio's secretary is also his *Masseuse*…!"

"You're kidding! Right there, in the middle of the day?"

"Complete with happy ending…," confirmed Quito, doing his best to keep his breath, "And what's worse is that Frank has got hidden cameras in each of the offices of the other two… and definitely gets a kick from watching…!"

"And what about Pete…?"

"He seems to be into child pornography during his work breaks…"

"What a collection! And the rest of their staff…?"

"From what I've seen, they all look very much the part…" He took a breather, "However, I couldn't find that woman we saw walking out of one of the Indio offices that famous time we ended up at Ninan's?"

"Could have been her day off, or something like that… She probably works on the floor below." ventured Pedro passing Thelma her drink. He then led Quito away again briefly.

"There is no link to the floor below… I checked it from every angle…" Quito looked at Pedro. "What we saw that other time was probably a glance into either the Aztec or Mayan dimensions... and the woman was most likely someone with the same ability to switch dimensions as us..."

Americo and Raul were good socialisers and not short of light-hearted humour when talking about some of their adventures. Throughout dinner they provided Pedro, Quito and Thelma with a few moments of much needed distraction, until Thelma's mobile rang, not long after coffee.

"Would you excuse me? It's from Recife..." Thelma announced, before leaving the table, prompting the others to do the same.

"We must do this more often..." Pedro thanked them for their company. "Unfortunately, we are in the middle of dealing with another situation in Recife..." He apologised also on behalf of Quito, for leaving the table to join Thelma in the ship's office.

"No problem... Hope it all goes well...!" Americo didn't quite know what to say.

"This was done by Fernando and Ze... and they left a ransom note wanting US$5 million, should you want to see Deedee again unharmed..."

"Is this what you wanted to tell me?" Quito was exasperated by the news.

"Yes... We didn't know who had done it until now..." Pedro justified. "Do you think they acted of their own accord?" Pedro directed the question at Thelma.

"I'd say so... and I'd also say that they are oblivious that we know it's them..."

"The stupid bastards...!" Pedro let escape.

"I don't think I'm doing much here at present..." started Quito. "I could go to Recife and help Castro get Deedee back...," he proposed. "...If Thelma was to give me Fernando's and Ze's addresses, I could look into a number of places without being "seen" ..." Pedro looked at Thelma.

"Well, it will be another week before you'll be able to

do anything with any sense of direction or conviction…" She hinted.

"I may need the jet though…" Pedro warned.

"Just ask Sergio to take me to the Airport and I'll sort myself out." He proposed.

Thelma gave Quito all the information he could possibly need and Sergio came for him soon after.

"How are you coping with stress levels?" It occurred Thelma to ask Pedro, once they were by themselves.

"As well as could be expected, I suppose…"

"Would you let me massage your head and shoulders? …It would also make me feel better through you…"

"You find me at my most vulnerable just now Thelma… If I felt your hands that way, I would probably end up wanting a lot more…"

"And I would gladly give you all that you could want…" Then suddenly as if by magic, they found themselves in each other's arms, with all the accumulated passion they kept denying one another… in a way that not even Ara could. "Gosh…! My legs have turned to jelly…" Thelma chuckled to herself, sitting down.

"What a team!" Pedro was just as amused as he sat down too, unable to hide his physical arousal!

"Will you come into my room in 5 minutes?" She then got up, a bit more composed.

"I'll be there shortly…" Pedro smiled at her without getting up just then.

*

Pedro had never experienced intimacy like Thelma could give him. Everything she did and how was better than he could possibly have scripted… without words or inhibitions, just following each other's pleasure lines as they sought to give one another all the very best they had to give.

"That was so special Thelma…" Pedro uttered trying to

get his voice back, as he finally laid back on the bed, feeling super satisfied. "No one has ever given me so much pleasure and in such a short space of time…"

"That's because we are soul mates… your words could have been mine…" She said cuddling up closer to him, her vocal chords sounding just as rusty.

"I hope I wasn't too predictable…"

"You are not competing against anyone… you're in a league of your own… I only want you to be yourself, so I can enjoy you that much more." She squeezed him lovingly. "I'm going to sleep so deeply…," her voice then faded as she spoke.

Thelma fell asleep as if someone had switched an *off* button! In contrast, Pedro felt nimble and reinvigorated, eventually sneaking out of her bedroom and into his.

"Ninan…?" Pedro was quick to update the courtier with the latest news.

"I'll see what I can find out regarding George and Alberto… Get back to me tomorrow around this time."

"I would also like to know a little more about this business involving the Aztecs and Mayas and how it all relates to the three main bosses of Starling Inc.?"

"I'll see what I can do. One word of advice however regarding your Akazi wives and the settling of scores in general… You must think with your head first, not your heart."

"I'll remember that."

**

Tony Amca

XVII

Quito was met by Taco and Joaquim at Recife Airport in the late evening.

"Everyone's been missing you back at the Camp..." Taco mentioned as the two Indios gave each other a brotherly hug.

"I reckon it will all be finished in two or three weeks, hopefully..." Quito then faced the two of them. "You've kept the news of my arrival secret, I take it."

"As you've requested." Taco confirmed.

"My lips are sealed..." Joaquim was also quick to acknowledge.

"What do you want us to do?" Taco needed to know as they walked out of the terminal towards their 4X4.

"Well, you need to take me to the "Best Western" in Porto de Galinhas where I've booked a room. I'm staying there for a few days..." He paused. "I might need you and a few braves at some stage..."

"Just say the word..." Taco was ready. "But... are you going to be there by yourself?"

"No. One of Pedro's security men will be meeting me there later. His name is Castro..." Quito then told Taco what had happened and the man was taken aback with embarrassment as well as concern for Deedee in particular.

"How Pedro must feel...!"

"I don't think it has quite sunk in yet...," was Quito's opinion. "There's too much going on in his life right now...," he paused. "Anyway, Castro and I will be investigating this and... we'll keep going until I have Deedee back..."

"Will you want Joaquim to drive you anywhere?" Taco asked as they neared the hotel.

"No thanks. Castro will have everything. I'll keep you updated, don't worry…," he tried to reassure the Indio who then left, almost reluctantly!

Quito checked in and after getting rid of the small suitcase in his room, headed for the Hotel Bar to meet Castro.

"Welcome to Porto de Galinhas…," greeted the security man, getting up to shake the hand of the Akazi Chief. "It seems I got here a day late."

"Not your fault…" Quito claimed the next stool to Castro. "Any joy from the things you've looked into so far?"

"I think I've located them…"

"You what…? That was fast!" Quito was taken by surprise. "How did you do it?"

"A bit of a fluke, really… From my army days as an Instructor…, my Instructor I.D. is still valid" he explained. "Well, I contacted a few car rental places at Recife Airport, claiming that Ze and Fernando were on the run from the Military… and I eventually got lucky at one of the kiosks. I obtained their car make and registration number, their satellite location… and soon tracked them to a place they've rented, less than a mile from here…"

"I'm amazed!" Quito looked at him with admiration. "Could you take me there now?"

"I could but… What do you have in mind?"

"I just want to see what the place looks like from the outside… They don't know you anyway and with it being dark already… I'll make sure they don't see me…"

"OK…"

The place was a modest bungalow with a garage and a short front patio with a huge fig tree.

"There's no light but they must be home… their car is there…" Whispered Castro as he slowly drove passed the house.

"Have you actually seen either of them?"

"No. I had a plan to start some surveillance in the morning…"

"Can you drive into the next street and wait for me there?"

"You are not planning to go knocking on their door, I hope…" Castro seemed worried.

"Come off it! There are some things we Indios are second to none at… I won't be long…" Quito got out of the car and pressed his necklace the moment he turned around the corner, to edge into *Inca mode*, and was soon inside the house.

Fernando and Ze shared a bottle of whiskey in a tiny garden behind the house and appeared cheerful as they played cards.

"Shame we couldn't get Ara as well, she's a good cocksucker…," commented Ze.

"What we need is to get this ransom money. After that, we'll be able to get as many cocksuckers as you like…," chuckled the other.

Inside, Quito eventually found Deedee naked; her arms and legs spread eagled and tied to the four corners of the bed. She was asleep and all the signs were that she had been raped repeatedly by the two men, throughout her ordeal.

Quito then looked around the house for something he could use as a weapon, settling for a large kitchen knife lying idle on the kitchen counter. At this point he came out of *Inca mode*, grabbed the knife and patiently waited for one of the men to come into the house.

Another 30 minutes passed and Ze came in, intent on using the toilet, and Quito had no hesitation in sinking the knife into the man's chest, straight through his heart, to then cut his throat for good measure!!! It was a straight kill and such was the surprise that Ze never uttered a sound.

After recovering the knife, the Indio Chief then silently dragged the body from view, and got ready for when Fernando entered… And when he did, Quito gave him exactly the same treatment. He then proceeded to untie the startled Deedee.

"Oh my God Quito… I feel so ashamed…" Deedee looked terrified and cried uncontrollably as Quito picked her up to comfort her in his arms.

"Calm down Deedee… you are safe. Those two are dead and no one is going to hurt you any more…" He paused. "You must be very quiet now… I've got a car waiting outside… Put my shirt on?"

"I want to die Quito…"

"I don't want any of that talk now." He then said sternly, "We all love you and you'll soon be home and well. OK?" she just nodded and wouldn't let go of him.

Castro couldn't believe his eyes when he saw Quito and the half naked girl arriving at the car.

"Well done… and the two?" He enquired, getting out of the car to help get the girl in.

"I think we need to torch that place Castro…"

"Ho shit! The car rental people have my details… and this car is from them too!"

"Then let's just go from here while we think of something. I left all their doors closed anyway."

Quito then phoned Taco so that with Joaquim, they'd return to a particular street in Porto de Galinhas with some clean clothes for Deedee, without telling anyone.

"How will I get clothes for Deedee without telling anyone?"

"Go into her shack…!"

Thelma was next on Quito's phone list and she in turn contacted Janette to tell her to pick Deedee up from near her apartment, at an appointed time.

"I'm so thirsty…" Said Deedee after putting on the clothes Taco and Joaquim had brought her.

"We don't have any water but Janette is picking you up soon and she'll get you some!"

Janette covered her face with both hands as she saw Deedee and her eyes filled with tears.

"This is entirely my fault… I should have known better than leave things to chance…"

"I wouldn't waste time crying over spilt milk miss…" Quito was unapologetically cynical "It is what you do now that matters… Deedee was asking for water a moment ago, do you have any?"

"Yes, I do…" She looked at Quito. "You can leave her with me now… I'll take her home…"

"Thank you, Quito…" Deedee hugged him strongly before getting into Janette's car.

"Don't mention what I did inside that house to anyone… Just say we paid a ransom and they let you go?" He whispered in her ear and she nodded in acknowledgement. …And it was with some relief that Quito saw Janette drive Deedee towards Recife moments later.

"Are you going to tell us what happened?" enquired Taco.

"Not just now, we are still trying to sort some things out. I suggest you could leave the 4X4 in the hotel car park and I need the two of you to come with us to help with something."

Some 15 minutes later, the four of them returned to the same spot where Castro had parked the first time, and leaving the other three behind, Quito went back inside the house for the keys of the car hired by Fernando and Ze.

"I need the two of you to drive their car back to Recife Airport… and Castro will follow you close behind in his." Instructed the Chief, who then turned to Castro. "…and at the close of contract with the car rental people, explain that Ze and Fernando are now in custody, and that everything is normal once again."

"And what about our 4X4…?" Taco asked.

"If you don't mind, you and Joaquim could take a bus here in the morning and then drive me back to Recife?"

"And where do I go from Recife?" Castro enquired this time round.

"Take a flight to New York and from there, pick up a fresh flight to Vancouver?"

"Understood…"

"I'll be dealing with everything else myself…" Quito winked to the security man as he said it.

Once by himself inside the house, Quito then started by smashing the mouths of the two men, beyond any dental record recognition, and made sure the place was set well ablaze before leaving.

It was about 4 A.M. when he finally got to his hotel bed, only to receive a text message from Pedro requesting a call back.

"Well done you…," came Pedro and Quito soon updated him with the details. *"You really are so special, man!"* Pedro just didn't know how to praise him enough.

"It is important that Thelma should ask Janette and the girls to stick to the official version that we paid a ransom and Deedee was then freed." He paused. "To tie up loose ends…?"

"Of course, … It makes sense."

"Anyway, Castro is on his way back to you as we speak and I'll see you in a couple of days…"

*

"Everyone else OK…?" Asked Deedee as Janette drove off.

"Everyone is OK… Try closing your eyes, we'll soon be home. Have you eaten?"

"I'm not hungry… I just need a big bath and a big scrub…" She paused "I want to know if my baby is OK…"

A few minutes later they were at Janette's. Ara was very emotional and it took a while before each of them knew how to act towards Deedee.

"I think you should take her to hospital for a general check…," advised Mariana, looking at Deedee's swollen eye and crusty lips.

"I need to wash myself as soon as possible, before anything

else…" Deedee was far more aware of it all than they gave her credit for. "Afterwards, you can take me wherever you like… I want to have my baby checked as soon as possible…"

No one argued with Deedee and by the time she came out of the bathroom, through Thelma, a physician had arrived, ready to give her all the physical checks she needed.

"I'm Doctor Mascarenhas…" The man introduced himself to Deedee, "Thelma told me of your ordeal and asked me to pass by to make sure you were OK?"

"What about if they stayed in the penthouse in Rio until we finish our business here? Castro needs to be out of there for a while, but we could still send Sergio as their permanent bodyguard… Irene is already there…"

"…And I suppose I could give Janette a short holiday in Rio too…?" She looked at Pedro to see his face.

"That's assuming they'd be happy with that…"

"I reckon they are still sleeping… I'll check with them around lunch time?" She proposed, with one of her hands looking amorously for one of Pedro's, in a silent back-to-bed invitation.

"I was planning to have a jacuzzi…"

"Sounds like an excellent start…," she said coming closer to him for a short romantic kiss. "What would you say if I moved to the bedroom the girls used to have… so as not to have those on board keeping track of us coming in and out of our bedrooms?"

"Don't you think that would make it even more obvious?"

"Well, I'd feel more comfortable about "things" … and I know you like to be by yourself some times…," she added one of her smiles to her words. "Or do you think you might still change your mind about the girls?"

"I feel bad about Deedee… to be 100% honest with you…," he paused. "To Ara I don't think I was ever more to her than a convenient sexual experiment, even though I feel she did care for me to some extent… but with Deedee it was a lot deeper and I reckon that if it weren't for Ara, none of this would have ever happened…"

"I can understand that… but what about your feelings as a man towards her?" She took a breath. "Would you have her back?"

"No. I don't think I could… but I cannot discard her like yesterday's newspaper either…"

"Well… you're still caring for them, as far as I can see…" She realised that Pedro wasn't too keen on the topic of conversation, "Would you rather we didn't discuss it?"

"My feelings for you are definitely what they are, but as for everything else… you need to give the dust a chance to settle."

"You're right and I should have known better…" Thelma was suddenly annoyed with herself and they were quiet for a while.

"Are you still in the mood for that jacuzzi?" Pedro eventually broke the silence to look at her sideways, in a manner that he knew would make her laugh.

"I thought you'd never ask!"

*

As lunchtime approached, Thelma relocated to the girls' old bedroom with the help of Isabel, while Pedro went into the yacht's office to check on Ninan's findings;

"Well, if George is into something dodgy, he is definitely keeping his cards close to his chest… We found nothing to suggest he is doing anything improper…," the courtier seemed emphatic. "As for Alberto, however, even though there's no evidence of any collusion between him and the Americans, it seems that the order to dispose of Salome came from a line of people that led to him…"

"Couldn't the same line of people have *dealt* with his father-in-law and the others?"

"There is no definitive proof of that… as yet…"

"So, would you say that his plan has been to encourage me to assume that the Americans were trying to get rid of me, so as to have me fight his own battle against them? And perhaps to also involve his father...?" Pedro paused reflectively. "Ninan... this doesn't make any sense at all! If he has sworn allegiance to your Brotherhood and you've entrusted me with a specific task, why can't someone tell him to go back to his own corner and to get off my back?"

"Originally, we entrusted him with the task that is now yours, until we found he had his own agenda... driven by political ambition and further encouraged by subservient politicians and others within our own organisation..."

"...And you are powerless to deal with it?"

"I wouldn't quite put it that way..." He considered thoughtfully. "...From the possible disruption of our natural environment through the mining concessions obtained by the Americans, to discovering that the Aztecs and the Mayas were only too happy to give them a helping hand... I feel that we are getting more and more deeply entangled in a web of deceit..." he decided to be candid, "...not to mention the even greater threat looming from within our Organisation of course; Alberto...!"

"Have you considered having him *dealt with*?" Pedro's suggestion caused Ninan to laugh.

"There are two problems with getting rid of him Pedro... the first of which is ethical! We are not supposed to resort to that sort of solution when it comes to people within the upper crust of our Organisation, whatever the motives..." He paused, "Secondly, regarding this particular case, should something happen to Alberto, we would probably remain in partial darkness as to the full list of bad apples in our midst..."

"I see..." *Was Ninan trying to encourage him to find a way of getting rid of Alberto while saying the opposite, for the sake of remaining compliant on record?* Was the question growing in Pedro's mind.

The conversation with Ninan didn't drag on and by the time it finished, Pedro got the distinctive feeling that the courtier was under a tight rein, perhaps due to his position? The other thing that didn't make sense to Pedro was; *why didn't the Americans get rid of Alberto, instead of beating around the bush?*

Over lunch, Pedro explained his various mixed feelings to Thelma, in the hope she would share her own thoughts on events and all those involved.

"The way this thing's going, we'll soon conclude that the Americans are the good guys in all this!!!" She chuckled infectiously.

"Did you manage to get any joy from listening into conversations in the Manhattan penthouse?"

"Nothing of relevance has emerged…"

"Well, then I think the time has come for me to contact them…"

"Don't you want to wait until tomorrow, for Quito and Castro to get here?"

"Why?"

"The girls agreed to the idea of going to Rio with Janette and her daughters… and I was thinking of dispatching Sergio there today."

"…And you'd feel better knowing that we had the added protection of Quito and Castro?"

"Well, that too I suppose…"

In the afternoon, Pedro decided to take one of the cars and visit Stanley Park alone, before heading for the offices of "Three rainsbows.com". He needed to do some creative thinking, to listen to his inner self… and eventually decided to call Patricio;

"Good to hear from you. Everything OK…?"

"All's well. Patricio… now about these politicians assisting Alberto in his quest… are you able to elaborate more, in order to give me a fuller picture?"

"What sort of information are you looking for?"

"I don't know… anything that you can gather about the historical relationship between Alberto Azevedo and each of the politicians involved in the investigation by the Brazilian Government?"

"If what you are trying to discover is the extent of bribery and corruption involving "A", to calculate the likely levels of corruption of "B", I can tell you instantly that both camps are fully corrupt…"

"That's obvious, but I want to go further… I want to know names…, the size and type of deals made… about the amounts of money changing hands… that sort of thing…?"

"There's a limit to what I can offer you on that… It could take years to assemble what you're asking me for…" He paused and almost hesitated, *"Besides… are you not aware that Alberto is one of the untouchables within "I"? And a step or two above his father?"*

"What makes you assume that I should know that?"

"Well, given your acquaintance with George Azevedo for one thing… not to mention that Thelma is perfectly aware of that too… Aren't you using her as your first port of call concerning these things?"

"I'm sure she must have mentioned it at some point and it probably escaped me…"

"Anything else I could do for you just now?"

"Not really…thank you Patricio…"

"Any time…"

Pedro felt annoyed by this and left the car to stroll along the conker littered Marina. *Could Thelma be one of the bad apples in the organisation? What could possibly justify a secretary with a higher salary than the President of Brazil…!!? Was she the ultimate "Mata Hari" at the service of "I"?*

The fresh walk did nothing to further his understanding of the situation, so he then drove to his downtown office. *Why did Thelma want him to wait another day before contacting Frank, Pete or Maurizio?*

Approaching the building however, the police had cordoned off the area and there was a movement of ambulances.

"How can I get to my office?" He asked one of the officers redirecting the traffic.

"Come back in a couple of hours Sir… please move along now…," replied the man.

Pedro tried to contact Sergio, assuming he was inside the building, but instead found that the security man was at the Airport, about to board a flight to Rio.

"I'm just following the instructions from Ms. Thelma… Should I have stayed in your office?"

"Not at all Sergio… We just crossed our communications that's all! I hope you'll find it a lot warmer than here…"

"I'm looking forward to it, to be honest…"

"Have a good flight…"

He then called Thelma;

"Any idea of what's going on at the office tower?"

"According to the local news a group of armed men broke into the offices of Starling Inc. and shot everyone there, before killing a few of the building's security people as they escaped…!"

"Did that include the three bosses?"

"The media has given no details yet… I'm glad you called… they mentioned that a few bystanders were also shot… in fact I'm listening to it as we speak." She paused. *"Please come back?"*

"I'll be with you shortly…"

**

XVIII

The media talked of nothing else, keeping Pedro and Thelma awake throughout the night. The police apparently had to ensure that all the next of kin were informed before releasing any names. Castro arrived very late in the night and Quito was expected in the early hours of the morning.

"Why don't you lay back and let me do something to relax you?" Thelma suggested, when she returned to bed naked, after a quick shower! "We could leave the TV on…," she added, kissing Pedro in the most suggestive way… leaving him with nothing to say or do, but to comply!

They were both drifting to sleep about 30 minutes later, when Pedro's mobile rang; it was 6 A.M.!

"Mr. Bolivar?" A man's voice wanted to know.

"Who is this?"

"Be very afraid…," said the voice before ending the communication!

"What the fuck?" Half muttered Pedro to himself.

"Who was that?" Thelma enquired half asleep.

"No idea…," replied Pedro, feeling a lot more awake!

The TV was still on and a few of the victims' names were now beginning to emerge. As somewhat anticipated by Pedro and Thelma, the intended targets were the three bosses of Starling Inc. and according to the media, the only survivor was Frank Molinari, in a stable but critical condition in a local Hospital.

"Well, at least you know that Frank wasn't the caller…,"

commented Thelma, deciding to make a pot of coffee for both of them.

"That's for sure!" Chuckled Pedro, "How well do you know Alberto Azevedo?"

"I've met him on a couple of occasions and I know he is one of "I"'s untouchables… but I never really had anything much to do with him… Patricio knows him a lot better…"

"Funny you should say that, because speaking with Patricio earlier today, he gave me the impression that you were much better acquainted with Alberto than he was…"

"That's bullshit… Why should he tell you something like that?" She said returning to bed with a frown and two cups of coffee.

"I'm not inventing it… and I did find it strange at the time… Thanks…," he then added, referring to the coffee.

"Patricio can be very secretive at times, especially when it comes to "I". He often guards some of the information on them zealously, even from me…! This annoys me no end…"

"So… what do you think prompted him to say such a thing?"

"He either felt he shouldn't give you any further information on Alberto or… for reasons of his own, decided to make you think I probably had motives not to tell you more about him…"

"Well, I've gathered that already…" He looked at her. "Are you telling me he could be one of the so-called *bad apples*?"

"I could never tell you something like that about Patricio… there is only one thing I didn't tell you about Alberto…"

"What's that?"

"I went to bed with him a few years ago…"

"You're kidding!" Pedro felt amused. "He fucked you first and now he's trying to fuck me…," he mumbled.

"If it's any consolation to you, I was completely drunk at the time…"

"I'm not hurt by the fact that you went to bed with him before we ever met Thelma…"

"Do you think he did all these killings so as to pin the blame on you?"

"That seems so obvious as to make it almost improbable!!! The phone call of a moment ago however could only have come from him, I reckon."

"What makes you so sure?"

"The mobile number he used is only known to George and me…"

"Unless…," started Thelma, prompting Pedro to call George.

"George?"

"You are an early riser…!" He replied.

"Thank God you are OK?"

"Shouldn't I be?" Pedro showed his concern over the fact that someone had access to his mobile. *"I can assure you the phone you gave me has never left my sight…"*

"Well, the problem is probably at my end… Sorry if I woke you."

"Not at all, I'm having breakfast and it's always a pleasure to hear from you… and I'm still ready when you are…?"

At this point Pedro was beginning to have some serious concerns about Thelma. *Could she be the Queen in the chess game being played against some hidden opponent?* Pedro couldn't afford to seem overly suspicious of Thelma, as this would either risk alienating her if she was guilty, or result in the loss of a valuable ally if she was innocent. The sex and the loving however felt genuine, as did the companionship. *Could that also be fake? Was he permanently jinxed in his relationships with women?* He wondered to himself.

"You look so cold and distant…" She remarked "Are you annoyed with me over the Alberto thing?"

"Of course not, we've already been through that…"

"Come on top of me a little bit then… I really need to feel you close…" She invited, pulling him towards her, to then let her intimate loving smile do the rest...

"You're turning me into a sex maniac…," he pretended to whisper a complaint.

*

As Pedro reached the upper deck of the AKAZI "I", he found Quito sharing breakfast with Americo and Raul in the ship's main dining room.

"Welcome back…" Pedro gave the Indio Chief a customary brotherly hug.

"Good to see you well…" They all sat back at table.

"Did you hear the news last night?" Pedro asked looking at the other three.

"We were talking about it just then…," replied Raul

"Which reminds me, we are changing some security arrangements as from today…," announced Pedro. "Castro is going to join Beto and Lima on the ship's security team and we are going to leave the Docks to drop anchor further out to sea…"

"How soon do you want us to act on that?" Americo wanted to know.

"Whenever you're ready."

"Paula and Marisa went out food shopping with Beto…," noted Raul.

"Well, once they are all back, of course…" Pedro clarified.

"We'd better make a move then…," Americo looked at Raul and the two skippers left the table to go to the ship's control room.

"Are we expecting trouble?" Quito enquired quietly as the others left to go to their duties.

"I received a threat this morning…," Pedro updated Quito on the situation and in turn, Quito told him the full details of what went on at Porto de Galinhas. "Bloody hell man! How do you feel about it all?" Pedro looked at the Indio Chief with renewed admiration.

"No remorse what-so-ever... you'd probably have done exactly the same, had you seen the state of Deedee...!"

"I don't know what I'd have done, to be honest... Do you think she'll be OK?"

"Eventually... It will probably take the rest of her life to get over it..."

"I somehow feel this is entirely my fault."

"Nonsense! The whole thing was simply an unpredictable sequence of events. Two unscrupulous guys saw an opportunity to sort out their finances... and the rest is history..." He then glanced at Pedro. "Did you fix yourself with Thelma yet?"

"Well... I reckon that was on the cards, with or without Deedee and Ara... as you'd expect" He paused "But that had nothing to do with my decision concerning the girls..."

"I know that too." He poured them both some coffee. "It is not for me to pass judgement on your morality, but if you want my honest opinion as a friend, I feel that of the two girls, you should perhaps reconsider Deedee...?"

"I had in mind to do just that, once this whole business is over..."

"I knew you would...," Quito gave him a big smile and they then changed the subject, to focus on their more immediate plan of action.

"There's my number one hero!" Thelma joined them, her hair still wet from the shower, ready to make a fuss of Quito.

"Come off it Thelma, now you are embarrassing me!" He chuckled, none-the-less appreciative of the acknowledgement. And they soon got to work about what to do next.

"From all that I've learned about this, I can see three simple important steps to our plan of action at this point in time." Pedro voiced his thoughts after a while. "**A**: we need to make the Americans realise we have not played any part in what happened at the office tower. **B**: we need to make them an offer they can't refuse, for their mining Concessions in Brazil. And **C**: we will probably need further clarification from Ninan as to what should be done with Alberto?"

"I hope you realise that Patricio and I cannot afford to be seen as being involved in part **C** of your plan, should it involve any *dramatic* action?"

"We will keep you completely out of it." Pedro confirmed, "One thing that would be really useful to know is whether this threat came from Alberto or the Americans…"

"Perhaps even more important at this very moment will be to find out who's taken over the helm at Starling Inc.," suggested Thelma. "I feel we should perhaps send him or her, our deeply felt condolences. This should be combined with an offer to help to find the perpetrators, while simultaneously announcing our interest in putting forward a business proposal, as and when they're ready to hear us?"

"That sounds excellent Thelma," supported Pedro.

"…And it also takes care of part **A** of the Plan," concurred Quito.

"Shall I deal with that after breakfast?" Thelma looked at both of them.

"Go for it." Encouraged Pedro, seconded by the nodding Quito.

*

In contrast with the fast approaching winter in Vancouver, it was mid spring in Rio. The city's world famous Carnival was still 4 months away, but preparations were already well under way, as were the rehearsals and the spying between the competing Samba Schools.

Sergio wasn't allowed the Ferrari, but was given the use of an enlarged 4X4 they could all fit in when going around for shopping or tourism. The girls felt safe under his vigilant protection and Janette couldn't hide her growing feelings for the man, to the embarrassment of her daughters!

Copacabana beach was just across the road from the

penthouse building and very much part of their daily routine. The mornings were usually spent on the beach and the afternoons were reserved for shopping or siesta time, or following the touristic routes. And a walk along the Copacabana promenade after dinner was the norm to end the day with.

Deedee felt contented in the cocooned environment she was now in, pampered by the attentions of Irene, who never lost an opportunity to put a smile on her face. She was gradually finding greater pleasure in the company of the maid, rather than in Ara's, Janette's or her daughters', and often preferred to help the servant in her after dinner shores, instead of going around in idle gossip with the others. Ara however seemed constantly frustrated, as if "on heat".

"Do you fancy an ice cream?" invited Ara, when one of the beach vendors stopped by her and Deedee, as they sat a little away from Sergio, Janette and the twins that morning.

"No thanks, you go ahead…," she replied, "The others might want some though…," Deedee suggested, while continuing to spread some suntan lotion on Ara's back.

"They are spongers…," commented Ara in a whisper, "They never say no to anything!"

"They keep us company…," Deedee didn't bother supporting Ara's viewpoint.

"Do you want to come with us for a swim?" Mariana and Miguela came to them in the meantime.

"I'm eating an ice cream…," alleged Ara.

"I'll go…" said Deedee getting up leaving her belongings closer to Sergio and Janette.

The physical traces of Deedee's ordeal were fast healing and beauty was beginning to return to her.

"Is Ara annoyed with us?" asked Miguela as they ventured

into the water up to their necks floating up and down with each wave coming to shore.

"She's a bit weird sometimes… take no notice…," replied Deedee, somehow also lacking the patience to make conversation with the two girls. Janette on the other hand seemed to be doing fine with Sergio, who in turn kept doing his best not to look like he was breaking any rules!!!

Returning to dry sand and not for the first time however, the way Ara had consumed her ice cream had gained her a small group of admirers and hopefuls, probably wondering if she would eat another one! So as to perhaps have something to remember when they were alone sometime later…?

"Ara… are you out of your mind?" Deedee did her best to keep her voice down as she came close. "What do you think you are going to gain from this?"

"It gives me a kick to know how much they'd love to be the ice cream…"

"You are not only embarrassing all of us, anyone can see that you are pregnant! People will start wondering if you are mentally retarded…!"

"That's even better… They might think I don't understand what's in their minds…"

"Carrying on like this, it will only be a matter of time before what happened to me happens to you too…" Deedee was fuming as she warned her, "I'm going home now."

"Would you mind waiting a few moments so we can all return at the same time?" Sergio tried to dissuade Deedee from walking back to the penthouse by herself. "I cannot split myself in two…," he alleged.

"You don't have to Sergio. I only need to cross the road… and if you remain exactly where you are now, you'll be able to see me all the way to the entrance of the condominium… OK?" There and then, Deedee also made a mental note to skip the beach mornings from that point on.

Sergio felt he had a thankless job ahead and foreseeing

the likelihood that sooner or later Deedee and Ara would probably want to do different things in different places at different times, he decided to call Thelma once they were all back at the penthouse.

"I'm sorry about all the trouble the girls are giving you Sergio... I'll be calling them in a moment and will sort it out for you... but do feel free to call me back if there's any more trouble. OK?"

"Thank you, Ms, ... I'm sorry to have bothered you with this."

"You've done the right thing...," she reassured him.

Deedee was quick to put herself in the clear, but Ara got a good earful from Thelma and was in tears by the time the call had ended. This was then followed by an adult sized tantrum that scared the life out of Janette and the twins, sending all three packing voluntarily.

"Here, have some of these...," Deedee walked into Ara's room with a couple of her own pills and a glass of water. "What the fuck's with you?" She then asked calmly, once Ara had swallowed the pills.

"I need something to distract my mind with... I feel like my arms and legs are tied against my body...," she paused; "I feel I am such a horrible human being...," she then broke down.

"Do you blame yourself for all this mess?" Deedee enquired and Ara nodded while sobbing.

"I'm so very sorry Deedee...," her compressed feelings of guilt were finally being released, along with a river of tears.

"I'm just as much to blame...," Deedee put her arms around Ara to try to bring her some comfort. "I should have known better and stopped us both..."

"Have the other three really gone?"

"Yes... Sergio is downstairs waiting with them for a taxi to the Airport..."

"I'm not too sorry to see them gone, to be honest... they were beginning to get on my nerves..."

"I could say the same…," Deedee chuckled.

"Do you think Thelma will fire her?"

"Of course not! But she won't be too happy either…"

Fifteen minutes later however they were all back in the penthouse and about to unpack…!

"Thelma is on her way from Canada to be with both of you and asked me to stay here until she arrives." Janette explained, somewhat embarrassed by the last-minute U turn.

*

It was late afternoon before Beto and Lima untied the AKAZI "I" from its docking pontoon and Americo raised anchor, to then slowly negotiate their way out to sea.

Pedro kept company to Americo and Raul on the ship's bridge and Thelma seemed busy on her mobile in the main Lounger's deck, while trying to balance two whiskey glasses in one hand!

"How far out do you want us to go?" Raul asked, ready to type some coordinates into one of the Yacht's computers…

"About half way between here and Bowen Island…," suggested Pedro.

"If you want us to drop anchor at the half way point, it will take one of our speed boats about 20 minutes to get back to our docking pontoon." Americo commented, looking at his chart.

"Yes, that's what I expected."

"Bowen Island itself looks lovely…," commented Raul, showing Pedro some of the Google images he was looking at.

"Indeed…," agreed Pedro, making space for Thelma to join them.

"Wow, you can feel the power of the engines, even though we're not going fast…," she noted, handing Pedro one of the whiskey glasses.

"2,000 HP Bentley engines…," explained Americo with pride.

"And if you are worried about being boarded during the night, we have a system of sensors that will alert us if any human shape comes within 200 metres of the yacht from above or below the waterline." Raul informed them this time. "Of course, we couldn't have had it on when we were docked!"

"Obviously…," concurred Pedro then turning to Thelma as she was about to start her third sneeze… "Shall we go to the lounge?"

"Fancy joining us for dinner?" Thelma invited the other two.

"With pleasure…," replied Americo, also on behalf of Raul.

Pedro knew that Thelma had something to tell him; by the way she gave him his whiskey glass!

"What's the bad news then?"

"They are just like children…," Thelma told Pedro all about the mayhem in Rio. "Sergio won't be able to handle them, Janette has had enough and… I think I should go before something happens that we'll all regret." She looked at Pedro and then continued. "I can still be just as useful to you from there… if you need anything, just call me?"

"When do you want to go?"

"Marco and Martha could probably take me in the morning?"

"This is a nuisance at a time when we are about to go for the push Thelma…" Pedro moved about nervously. "Would you rather we left things to chance?"

"That's not what I'm saying but…"

"Couldn't you get Janette and the girls to kiss and make up? Make them understand the importance of what we are about to do?" He paused. "Couldn't you bribe Janette with a holiday anywhere of her choice after this, or something?"

"I could try…"

"Besides… I enjoy your company…," he teased her.

**

XIX

To Pedro's surprise, the Chairman of Starling Inc. replied within 72 hours of when Thelma dispatched their message. In the letter Pedro read out loud, he thanked "Three Rainbows. com" for their heartfelt thoughts and included suggestions for a written outline of the proposals prior to agreeing to any meeting; signed Jean Claude De Vigny.

"I don't think they've taken us that seriously…" Commented Pedro to Quito and Thelma as they shared breakfast in the main dining room of the yacht.

"What sort of a reply were you expecting?" Thelma was surprised by Pedro's disappointment.

"If you want my opinion, it sounds like this was the very first time they've ever heard of us…!" Quito shared his impressions.

"I think Quito could be right…," concluded Pedro as he reread the letter.

"It could also be that A does not talk to B… and with Frank in intensive care…," suggested Thelma.

"True…," admitted Pedro.

"You really are convinced that Alberto is the one and only devil in all this, aren't you?" Thelma looked at Pedro, somehow feeling he had developed a grudge against him.

"I wouldn't say the only one, but most probably the biggest one…" Pedro had his convictions.

"What about you and me giving this guy a visit?" Quito suggested quietly.

"Sounds like a good idea…" Pedro agreed and Thelma

got her mobile working, to discover the whereabouts of Jean Claude.

"His office is in Seattle…" Thelma informed him. "It was probably not even him that replied to our letter…"

"It wasn't signed *per proxy*… and it is his name underneath the signature…," confirmed Pedro inspecting the letter once again.

"It wouldn't surprise me if he was here in Vancouver though, with it all being so fresh. I'd say that he'd probably want to be seen as being in control." Quito also had a point to make and out of frustration, Pedro decided to take matters into his own hands, by using his mobile to their Head Quarters in Chicago;

"Hello?"

"Good morning… How may I direct your call?"

"Good morning, could you please put me through to Mr. Jean Claude de Vigny? My name is Pedro Bolivar…"

"Does he know you Sir?"

"Not personally no, but he knows who I am…"

"Just a moment please…"

"Good Morning Sir, this is Emma Johnson… I am Mr. de Vigny's secretary, may I help you?"

"Yes, I'm calling Mr. de Vigny in relation to a letter I received from him this morning…"

"You can tell me; I handle all his correspondence… he won't be back in his office for the next two or three days… due to the tragedy in Vancouver that you might have heard about…?"

"Yes… I'm in Vancouver as we speak, would I be able to reach him in any way?"

"The only thing I can suggest sir is, if you tell me what this is about and leave me your number, I'll pass on the message…" At this point, Pedro started to chuckle.

"I've got it…! Do you think this is a Sales call?"

"I cannot really add anything further sir… I'm offering to help you with your enquiry…"

"OK… then please take my name and number down and if you'd be so kind as to ask Mr. de Vigny to call me back the moment he can? He knows what this is about…"

"Is that it?"

"That is it Emma… Many thanks and have a good day…"

"That wasn't easy was it?" Quito sounded amused as Pedro ended the call.

"You wouldn't believe the calls corporate secretaries sometimes get…!" Thelma commented to Quito, to then turn to Pedro. "Do you think he will call you?"

"Not sure… assuming his secretary gives him the message, I'd say if he doesn't take us seriously he won't bother calling me back, given that he has already replied in writing." He paused. "But if on the other hand he might be desperate for options, I think he'll call back…"

"Ok US$5 he won't call you back…" Thelma was ready for a bet.

"Easy on the cash Thelma…!" Quito almost collapsed in laughter!

"You're on…" Pedro accepted.

Thelma managed to persuade Janette to stay in Rio, but her daughters returned to Recife, to be with their friends.

"This Bowen Island looks really nice… Fancy spending the afternoon there for a change?" proposed Thelma, switching off her laptop, as Quito needed to go to his room. "We could take one of the speedboats and have a wander round?"

"I suppose it could help us kill a few hours until Jean Claude gets back to me." Pedro teased, only to be startled by a call from his mobile.

"Pedro Bolivar…," he answered.

"Mr. Bolivar… It is Jean Claude here; I'm returning your call…" Thelma had to leave the table for laughing at

Pedro's face, as he stretched out his right hand, ready for his *winnings…*!

"Thank you for getting back to me Jean Claude, please call me Pedro…"

"Ok Pedro…," the man waited to hear what prompted the contact.

"I take it that you are aware of my letter to you?"

"Not really, you must forgive me… I get so much unsolicited mail that my secretary deals with it all for me… however she did mention something about a business proposal. Am I right?"

"Yes. Well, so as not to beat around the bush, I'll go straight to the point: I am interested in your Brazilian Mining Concession. And since everything has its price, I'd like the opportunity to make you an offer for it. Would you be the right person for me to engage in dialogue with?"

"Ultimately yes, I suppose, but Frank Molinari would otherwise be your man… unfortunately he is in a coma as we speak… I presume you might have heard about what happened?"

"I did indeed… In fact, my office is on the very same building as Starling Inc. and I am in Vancouver just now…," he paused. "It would give me great pleasure if I could invite you to dinner tonight or lunch tomorrow on board my yacht… and maybe talk face to face? It is the AKAZI "I" …"

"Pedro, let me get back to you in the next hour or so? I'm going through hell just now between the Police, Shareholders, the families of the bereaved… you name it."

"No problem at all… I understand. I hope you'll find that a couple of hours in my yacht could well provide you the perfect escape to all that…"

"I shall get back to you shortly…"

"There you go…" Said Thelma handing him a US$5 bill! "Now he is going to X-Ray everything with the name Bolivar in it, on both sides of the Atlantic…!"

"That's not surprising; especially after what happened...," he paused, "For now, I think we ought to postpone our Bowen Island adventure and head back to our Vancouver Berth, wouldn't you say?"

"Definitely... I'm going to check with Marisa on menu options." She said getting up to go two floors below.

"Sorry to mess you about Americo, we need to return to Vancouver...," Pedro went to the Bridge to inform him.

"Can we do it in about 30 minutes? Raul went to have a peep at Bowen Island on one of the speed boats... and I'm about to call him back...," he said, dialling Raul's number.

"There's no rush, providing we go within the next hour or two..."

*

Jean Claude's 1 hour became 7 and he finally called as Pedro shared a round of aperitifs with Quito and Thelma, about to go for dinner.

"I'm sorry I only now managed to get back to you Pedro. How about lunch in your yacht tomorrow at 12...?"

"Sounds great. Do you know where to come to?"

"Yes. I can see your magnificent vessel from where I am..."

"Excellent. Well, I very much look forward to our meeting..."

The three of them moved to the table immediately after the call. Thelma seemed unusually quiet and without comment.

"What do you think?" asked Pedro.

"You're either on a lucky streak or this guy has a screw loose...," she eventually spoke.

"Quito... Any thoughts...?" Pedro enquired, after a brief translation of the phone conversation.

"That is what I thought I understood...," he paused. "I don't think he has a screw loose... but he appeals to me as an older gentleman who refuses to learn how to operate a computer... with a strong focus on the humanity of those around him..."

"Wow Quito!" exclaimed Thelma. "I'm going to start making notes on your assessments!!! Any ideas on his shoe size…?"

"9 and a half…," replied the Indio Chief without hesitation and with a serious face, to Pedro's great amusement. *What was Thelma so frustrated about?*

"There are a few things that I'm confused about; since you seem to have a clear mind about what you're doing all of a sudden…," she started. "If George is aware of his Son's designs on the mining concessions… and is therefore not interested in making a separate bid for it himself; what's his personal interest in all this?"

"Curiosity mainly, I would say…" Pedro chuckled.

"Come on, be serious…," insisted Thelma.

"Well, should we end up buying the whole of Starling Inc in order to get their Brazilian bit, George did show an interest in the remainder assets of the American company…" Pedro revealed.

"I somehow think that he and his son are together in this to some extent, but also that unknown to George, Alberto has a couple of ulterior agendas of his own…" Quito spoke his mind.

"…And that it is convenient to both that we should remain on the scene… should they need to pin the blame for their actions on another party…?" completed Pedro. "Which brings the question;" Pedro turned to Thelma. "What is Alberto's end game? Does he aspire to become a Trillionaire? …To be in control of "I" …? Or rule Brazil…, at least?"

"Don't look at me…" Thelma felt under pressure. "Why don't you give him a call?" She tried to be ironic.

"That sounds like an excellent idea… the only problem is; I first need to find out if it was George with his small army of commandos or Alberto that did all the killings at the office tower.

"What's the relevance of that?" Quito asked.

"Well if it was George, it means that he is still oblivious as to the extent of his son's plans…"

"And if it was Alberto?" asked Thelma.

"Then that means he will be trying to pin the blame on his father…"

"And why not on you…?" Thelma was quick to conclude. "You were in fact the main beneficiary of the office tower shootings… in the way that instead of having to contend with 3 tough negotiators, you now have a much softer opposite number, whose primary concerns might be an easy life for himself and a minimisation of risk for his shareholders…"

No sooner had they finished dinner, Thelma excused herself to go to her room, on account of not feeling too well.

"Should we call a Doctor?" Pedro asked her caringly before she went.

"I've got a strong period…" She whispered in his ear, while Quito went to get the whiskey bottle and some glasses from the bar.

"I think there's an appendix to our mission…," speculated Quito, once they were by themselves.

"Ninan wants us to get rid of Alberto?" Pedro ventured quizzically.

"Yes." He paused. "Do you think George would do it, if he found out his son killed his wife and daughter?"

"It's hard to say… what would you do in his shoes?"

"I don't know… I was wondering about that throughout dinner…" Quito mumbled thoughtfully. "Let us suppose this Jean Claude guy was to be favourable in doing business with you and would eventually accept an offer from you, how do you think George and Alberto would react?"

"It depends, I suppose…"

"Pedro… There's one thing that has been bugging me ever since the incident with Fernando and Ze, but I don't know enough about computers to be able to do this…"

"What's that Quito?"

"Who owns the Security Agency originally contracted by Thelma?"

"OK…" Pedro went to get his laptop from the yacht office. "What is on your mind?" He then asked, switching the machine on.

"Mere curiosity…," Quito didn't want to commit.

"Here we go… Globoseguro Ltd….," Pedro mumbled as he went along. "Irmãos Dimas organisation … Diniz Gomes Ninjas… papapapa… Wow… Quito, you are a genius!!!"

"What have I done?" Quito glanced towards the screen.

"Alberto Azevedo Corporation…!"

"Fuck me!!!" Quito had to get up.

"Let's not jump to conclusions too hastily…," Pedro advised. "Indirectly, it is an "I" Company… and as such, it is natural they would choose one of their companies rather than a competitor for any type of job, big or small. Wouldn't you agree?"

"This is very delicate…" Quito let escape.

"What?"

"Without meaning to sound funny… In percentage terms, how would you rate your trust in Thelma?"

"About 95%..."

"What's with the other 5%?"

"She slept with Alberto a few years back…" Pedro confessed, causing Quito to bring both hands to his head.

"I'm glad I didn't mention anything about getting rid of Alberto when she was still here…!" He chuckled. "…You do have a knack with women!!! Anything else along those lines that I should be aware of, so as not to say the wrong thing at the wrong time…?"

"Nothing that I can think of, no…" Pedro sounded annoyed.

"We definitely need to get rid of Alberto, before he gets rid of us…!"

"I'm inclined to agree with you on that one." Pedro concluded.

*

Ara seemed a lot calmer since the twins had left and to everyone's delight, was developing an addiction to computer games and spending most of the time in her room! Janette and Sergio no longer attempted to hide their romantic involvement, although Sergio always made sure no one could ever accuse him of laxity in his duties. And as for the friendship between Deedee and Irene, it continued to grow, with the two girls spending a lot of their time together in each other's rooms, especially once Irene had finished with her daily tasks.

Most of Deedee's and Ara's shopping was now starting to concentrate on their babies, with Irene always keen to share in their excitement, going through each of their new purchases in Deedee's bedroom, or contributing with ideas while looking through specialised catalogues. Also on occasions, Deedee would go into the maid's room to look at her endless collection of family photos.

Janette however had no volume control when it came to sex and with her room being right next to Irene's, it was as if Deedee and the maid were sharing every intimate moment of the "action" next door, whilst going through the umpteenth photographic album!

"I'm impressed… You're the only person I've ever met with 6 grannies!" Commented Deedee, going into the third Album of the evening…

"4 of them are borrowed…" Irene explained. "When my father died, my mother got together with one of our neighbours in the Favelas for a while, but he also got killed, before my mother married a second time…"

"But you continued to accumulate Grannies?"

"Yes…" Irene covered her mouth to suppress a giggle, as the noise next door began intensifying… until Janette finally climaxed (!) to every one's relief!!!

"Gosh, that wasn't easy, was it?" Deedee pointed towards the wall, trying to keep quiet.

"A couple of days ago they were at it the whole night…," Irene informed her in a whisper.

"The whole night…?"

"Yes. He's got some special pills in his room that can keep "him up" for hours… regardless."

"Poor Sergio… How embarrassing! Can you imagine if somebody tried to break in, in the middle of the night?"

*

A black limousine stopped near the start of the private pontoon walk. Two security personnel emerged from the vehicle ahead of Jean Claude de Vigny and all three walked towards Beto and Lima, ready to escort them onto the yacht.

Tall and well built with a good head of white hair, Jean Claude appeared to be in his mid seventies. His face had all the hallmarks of someone who had lived a life, but his mannerisms were those of a man who had finally found peace. He was also on time.

Castro directed the trio into the main living room and Pedro emerged from his office seconds later.

"I am delighted to meet you Jean Claude." Pedro approached the man with a stretched arm, ready for a powerful handshake.

"The pleasure is also mine… what a magnificent vessel!!!" He praised, looking at everything around them, to then accept the invitation to sit down, before focusing on Pedro with renewed curiosity. "You know, after reading about you, I find it hard to understand how I never heard of you until now…!"

"Well, sometimes you have to know what you are looking for, to find it."

"I suppose…" He chuckled.

"Will you join me in an aperitif before business?" Pedro also added an amused chuckle to his proposition.

"Why not? I've got a new liver that works perfectly… It came from China…," he announced.

"They really are into everything aren't they…?!"

From one subject to the next, the two men clearly enjoyed each other's company while sizing each other up, in preparation to defend their respective interests.

Their lunch took place on a more private table, away but within view of all the guards, who also ate together on another table. And Pedro waited for the coffee to arrive before touching the main reason for their meeting.

"Well, Jean Claude, when it comes to business, I'm not one to beat around the bush." He paused. "Regarding the Concession that interests me, I am fairly well informed of the situation; from the Injunction on your activities and the possible loss of your investment via the Brazilian Courts, to all that this has cost you so far… not to mention the programme of development you promised the Brazilian authorities, which we both know is not realistic…"

"I'm listening…" Jean Claude looked impassive and mildly amused. "And you want to know how much my shareholders want for it?"

"No. I want to know if not you, who would be the ultimate decision maker on this."

"Any certified offer from you would have to go through our lawyers before being approved or rejected by the Board of Directors. Private consultations with the main shareholders will follow, before returning the original proposal with the Board of Directors for a final analysis and decision, which I'm supposed to endorse, or veto."

"Well, I'm not proposing a takeover of your company… in fact not even a part of it!" Pedro paused. "I'm simply prepared to reimburse you the money you have spent on this, saving your company a likely loss of at least 25% of its value…"

"Pedro… I can understand that you want this Concession. But for you to want to buy it, with all the information you've been gathering, it will be obvious to our shareholders that you have anticipated that we have no case to answer to the

Brazilian Government…" He paused to have a chuckle. "If you want my advice on what could be a stronger argument in your favour, I reckon would be for you to mention the number of years this could possibly drag on for… which to you would make no difference, since you want it for conservation purposes, whereas to our shareholders it would mean a substantial paralysis of capital with no guarantees of a return…"

"Should I assume that you would favour selling the asset?" At this point, Pedro got Ninan to hear the conversation.

"For the correct amount of money yes, of course...! I've always felt this venture was cursed from the very outset." He made the brandy in his glass rotate playfully as he thought. "I can get you a deal signed for US$1 billion…"

"Double what you paid?" Pedro tried to look alarmed.

"Not quite, we've had a few related expenses since…"

"Did you know what I had in mind?"

"No…"

"To reimburse your company of the half billion it cost them to acquire the Concessions… plus US$50 million towards your retirement fund in a Swiss Bank Account…?"

"I've got a counter proposition… And if you'll agree to this I can guarantee you'll get it." His forehead had become a little moist.

"Shoot."

"US$600 million for the Concessions plus US$100 million for my so-called retirement fund?"

Pedro was of course delighted with that but didn't want to jump to it like a rugby player for a try.

"And you'll pay all the legal fees?"

"Could be done…," Jean Claude's smile began to broaden as did Pedro's who then got up with a stretched hand.

"You've got a deal."

Patricio was immediately informed and took over from that point on behalf of "I". He would be flying to Seattle later that day, as would Jean Claude, for a private meeting with his directors…

Once the party of visitors was gone, Pedro brought Quito and Thelma into his office and gave them the news, before opening a bottle of champagne. Quito was ecstatic and was rowdier than a football hooligan, while Thelma seemed a bit too thoughtful.

"This really is a bad period…," she whispered to Pedro. "Otherwise I am delighted for you…" She gave him a light kiss on the lips.

"Man…I can't believe it!" Quito was stoned by his imaginings!

"If you guys don't mind, I think I'll go and lie down…" Thelma looked pale.

"Is there anything I can do?" asked Pedro as she went.

"I'll be OK. I just need to lie down," she managed a smile.

"When will we go home?" Quito asked as she left.

"Tomorrow soon enough…?"

"I can't wait to tell my wives…"

"We're not done yet Quito…"

"I know we'll still need to get our gold…"

"…And Alberto… we cannot afford to leave him lurking about…"

"Ah yes… and that!"

"Anyway today, we celebrate."

Quito was legless by dinner time. Thelma insisted on staying in bed and Pedro decided to go for a drive, to get Thelma a huge bunch of flowers to brighten her up. He then entered Thelma's room through their en suite link, hiding behind the moving bunch flowers, making her laugh.

"I know it's you…," she half sang. "What a gorgeous bunch…," she tried to get up to smell them and then got back inside the bed, looking shivery.

"You are definitely not well…" Pedro commiserated, tucking her in.

"I'll be OK... Do you need me?"

"No, no... you have a rest..."

"I don't feel right sleeping next to you when I've got my monthly...," she explained.

"That's fine..." He smiled at her looking for a good night kiss he instantly got. "Give me a shout if you need me?"

"I will... Thanks..."

The more Pedro tried to dismiss the idea that Thelma could be one of the "bad apples" in "I", the more the evidence seemed to point in the opposite direction. *Could she have been working for Alberto all along? What if she was the ultimate weapon in Alberto's arsenal?*

How safe was he in his bed? Was paranoia getting the better of him?

He wasn't too sure whether to go out or call it a day and was about to fall asleep when he heard the faint sound of the en suite partition opening, causing his right hand to instinctively touch his necklace.

"Are you awake?" whispered Thelma.

"Yeah... changed your mind?"

"I can't go to sleep...," she paused to touch him. "You still have your clothes on..."

"I'm undecided whether to go out or not. Have you tried some pain killers?"

"You've been looking at me suspiciously for a few days now and I don't like it." She confessed, ignoring his question.

"I think you are being probably a bit over sensitive..." Pedro switched the light on.

"Since I told you about Alberto and me you seem to have changed..."

"Nonsense! The past is history... and we can only learn from it." He paused. "However, there are a few weird things that keep piling up... and that's probably what gives you that impression."

"Such as...?" Pedro was honest with Thelma and told her

of all the loose ends that raised a few questions in his mind. "Well, with all that fucking list it is not surprising you've been looking at me in a funny way! Why did you keep the whole thing bottled up?"

"It was unintentional… I simply assumed there had to be some logical explanation for each thing sooner or later… but now that you've opened the bottle, can you save me the wait?"

Thelma tried to offer Pedro a simple explanation for each of the things his suspicious mind had somehow enlarged, according to her. Yet in so doing, she inadvertently revealed knowing a lot more of Alberto's plans than previously admitted.

"Thelma… Alberto's days are numbered, with or without me, and there is nothing you or anyone can do about it… Don't allow yourself to sink with him…!" Pedro then took the opportunity to tell her everything else about XAKATAN he had previously omitted, and how "I" functioned behind-the-behind the scenes.

"So… he crossed a line from which there's no return. Is that it?"

"He did… and in many different ways…"

"And what do you expect me to do?"

"Continue to play Alberto's game but switch sides now… and once he is no more, continue as before? After all, only Ninan, you, me and the spying system you've put in place are witnesses to this conversation…"

"As well as Alberto…" A silent tear escaped one of her eyes as she said it, prompting Pedro to instinctively touch his necklace to switch dimension and quickly head for the pontoon walk through the ship… just in time to hear a vague distant boom behind…! He then returned to his natural dimension, to find himself among the chestnut trees that overlooked the Marina. There was nothing left of the yacht, as Pedro stood powerless on what remained of the pontoon!

Pedro was glad to find he still had the keys to one of the cars and his two mobiles on him, as fire engines, police cars and ambulances began arriving on the scene from all directions.

"What the fuck happened?" Quito enquired from behind him, trying to think clearly, giving Pedro the scare of his life.

"QUITO!!! I'm so glad… how did you manage to escape?"

"I went for a walk to try and sober up for Marisa… Jesus Christ!!" It then dawned on him. "Is it just you and me left?"

"It looks that way…"

Pedro was quick to call Patricio, who was obviously devastated by the latest news. Pedro avoided any allusion to Thelma's complicity with Alberto and agreed to meet him in Seattle the following day, so he could then proceed to dispose of the assets remaining in Vancouver.

"Don't drive either of the cars, don't go to the downtown office and don't use the jet, ok?"

"What about Marco and Martha?"

"Ask them to fly by themselves to Seattle and I'll deal with the rest."

"OK."

George was next on Pedro's list of the calls he needed to make.

"Pedro… Thank God you are OK. Is it your yacht that went up in smoke?" Pedro wasted no time in giving George the full list of his son's deeds, from his wife and daughter to the AKAZI "I". *"You expect me to have my own son killed?"*

"It is not for me to advise you on such a thing George, but if he dies now, his children, you and your continuity might be spared. Otherwise those going after him will be going for his entire family, not just him… You or someone needs to beat them to it, or lose it all to the benefit of the State."

"I don't even know whether to thank you for the information…"

"For all its worth, you too are on Alberto's list… and he knows that the cat is out…" Pedro paused. "I'm sorry for bringing you such bad news George. Save yourself and your legacy."

"I shall be in touch..."

"It seems that this is already on the world media Quito... you'd better contact your wives and the Tribe so they know we are OK?"

"I'll do that."

Pedro then contacted Sergio who already knew of the news from Janette, after a call that she received from Patricio.

"Janette will be flying to Recife this morning, back to her post..."

"The girls OK?"

"They are fine. They've calmed down..." Sergio told Pedro all he knew. *"Do you want me to put a new security team together?"*

"Maybe hire one or two extra people to help you protect the Girls and get them out of there and into a hotel... the whole place is bugged... and probably also filled with well hidden high explosives."

"Say no more. I'm getting them out of here as we speak..."

"Call me if you have any problems?"

"I will..."

To complete his round of calls, Pedro then called Jean Claude to reassure him that he was ok and that the deal was on course.

"Even if only for destroying such a marvellous ship, the perpetrators should hang..."

"I have it from secure sources that it was actually the same person that caused the office tower incident that killed a few of your staff..."

"Alberto Azevedo?"

"I see you've got some good informants too..."

"We couldn't be 100% sure... the guy is a maniac and needs to be stopped at all costs..."

"Anyway, take care of yourself..."

"You too…"

Not for the first time, Pedro spent most of the day giving evidence to the Canadian Police! And by the evening, he and Quito were driving to Seattle in a hired car.

During the journey, they decided to contact Ninan to update him on all that was happening.

"We are of course saddened by all the loss of life but also delighted with the way you've successfully accomplished your Mission… my only concern now is for your safety. There is no need for either of you to see Patricio in Seattle. Just let he and your wives know that you are going to have to disappear for a week or so… and come to us." He paused. "Your gold is ready. We hope you'll want to share in a week of celebrations with us… and I think Ayar might have a surprise for you both."

"OK" Quito also agreed with a nod.

They did as they were told and shortly after returning the hired car, they were in XAKATAN.

**

XX

George's Estate was on "red alert", although the man himself had not revealed to anyone the likely source of any threat.

"Was it an anonymous tip?" Sebastião probed.

"Yes… sort of…" Replied George, trying to get through to Alberto's mobile. "…Al?"

"Yes dad…"

"Where are you?"

"I'm home… Any news…?"

"Are you able to come to see me tonight?"

"What's up?"

"I'm being threatened by the Americans… and I fear they are planning to attack the Estate…"

"You with all your army having fear?" He chuckled from the other side. *"Do you want me to send you one of the maids to help protect you?"*

"It is not a laughing matter… and I've also got the feeling that probably some of my men might be working for them…," he paused. "Word apparently got out that I have over US$ 1 billion in cash in my strong room here… and I could use some extra men until I know exactly where this threat is coming from…"

"You've got to be kidding! You've got a billion dollars in cash sitting in your strong room? What's going through your head?"

"I'm being blackmailed by people who say they've got enough evidence to put you in jail for the rest of your life…"

"What do they allege?"

"Just about anything you can think of and what's worse, they also seem to have evidence that you were behind the abduction of your wife's half siblings…"

"And you believed them?"

"I don't know what to believe anymore Al. Will you come to see me and come clean with me? They've also threatened to let your wife see the evidence herself within the next 24 hours…"

"Dad… You've always been a lousy liar, which cost you your first marriage… Why don't you come clean instead and tell me what's really going on?"

"Well, suit yourself. If you've got nothing to hide, I'm not going to pay any more money to keep things quiet… and you might as well stay where you are…"

"Thanks for warning me anyway…"

"You are welcome… say hello to Mary and the kids?"

"I will."

George was probably a bad liar under normal circumstances, but he could also be a good Poker player when it really mattered… and within 10 minutes, Alberto was on the phone back to him.

"I'll be landing on your airstrip with a dozen of my men in 4 hours' time… and I'm bringing Mary and the kids with me…"

"Look forward to seeing you all…" George however had mixed feelings about having the kids involved.

*

It was late afternoon. Ninan wore a more formal outfit and had his biggest smile, when Pedro and Quito emerged into his lounge. Becchiu was also ceremoniously dressed and stood by the courtier, holding two similar costumes.

"Well done…" Ninan shook their hands effusively.

"Thank you Ninan… It couldn't have been done without your help and that of the other Courtiers…" Pedro replied modestly, also on behalf of Quito, causing their host to acknowledge the compliment with a small nod of the head.

"Congratulations…," seconded the Inca Chieftain, "It's good to see you both."

"It is good to see you too…," Pedro continued doing the talking.

"You'd better put these on, before doing anything else…" Becchiu looked cheerful as he led them into a changing room, to then hand them their new outfits.

"Truly beautiful clothes…" Quito looked in admiration to his orange and brown costume, enriched with gold thread and typical Incan patterns, clearly made to fit him. Pedro had a near identical costume, also made to measure, but his had a light sky-blue colour instead of the brown in Quito's.

"You both look magnificent…" Approved Ninan as they returned to the lounge, reinforced by the expression on Becchiu's face. "Come…" he encouraged them to follow him onto the balcony.

A huge crowd had gathered below and erupted into a roar as they appeared on the veranda, eager to express their thanks. Pedro and Quito felt a little humbled by all the fuss at first, but waved back in acknowledgement, perhaps only then realising the true significance of their accomplishment, as to the inhabitants of the city.

"I hope you are not too tired…" Ninan checked with them, almost as an aside.

"We are OK…" Pedro glanced at Quito, wondering what Ninan could possibly have in mind…

"What's the plan?" Quito enquired while continuing to wave back enthusiastically, enjoying his unexpected level of popularity!

"The other courtiers will be here shortly… and on to the King's Palace for dinner…" He explained. "And afterwards we'll all go to the Square of Pyramids, together with Ayar and His wives, for a People's Show in your honour."

"Sounds exciting... Anything along the lines of Protocols that we should know...?" Pedro wanted to make sure they'd be doing everything right.

"Nothing of significance... Just stick to everything you learned...," he reassured them.

From inside the lounge, a security guard warned Ninan of the courtiers' arrival and they re-entered the room, after a few final waves.

Auqui, Pahuac and Ana were just as splendidly dressed and following the customary acknowledgements and protocols they left to go to the King's Palace, along a path the crowd cleared for them as they went.

On Ayar's balcony, the "U" shaped table had been enlarged to accommodate Ana on the Courtiers' side of the U, and they all stood when the imminent arrival of the Ruler and His wives was announced.

Ayar was formally dressed on this occasion, as were his two wives, looking ever more attractive and regal. The three walked straight towards Pedro and Quito as they arrived, ready to express their gratitude.

"You've not only succeeded in your mission, but also saved us a considerable amount of money and bother..." Ayar stated with sincerity, holding the hands of both men and looking at them in the eye. Each of His wives then followed immediately behind, repeating the same gesture with a few words of acknowledgement, but somehow causing Pedro and Quito to experience endless sensations of pleasure as their skins touched...! At this point, given half a chance, Quito would have gladly missed the entertainment in favour of the Palace of the Guests (!), but that would have to wait!!! The two women then smiled at their husband as they headed for their usual sitting places and He returned their smile, as if sharing in some secret understanding. "Please be seated..."

A line of servants then entered the balcony with a feast of food and drink, while Ana avoided looking at Pedro and Quito, still recovering from their influx of pleasures...! Inspecting the trays closest to him, Pedro also found himself a little lost in thoughts, wondrous over the many undiscovered things about these Star People, until the voice of Ayar brought him back to reality:

"As you may have gathered, there are several reasons for Ninan to have recalled you now. Three to be precise; the first of which being your own safety..." He started, but then decided to wait until the servants had left the balcony, leaving them free to serve themselves. "Much blood will be spilt over the next few days and you would have found yourselves right in the middle of it all...," he explained. "The second reason is to show you how appreciative XAKATAN is for what you've done, which includes your just reward of course, but also the freedom of the city, allowing you to live among us whenever you may wish..."

"We are very much honoured...," acknowledged Pedro, before his host could continue.

"And the third?" enquired Quito after a while, seeing that Ayar seemed to stop there.

"I shall come to that one later in the week, once the mayhem and all the razzmatazz has died down in Seattle and elsewhere..."

Pedro's main interest was now focused on understanding the extra-terrestrial side of these people. *Who were they?*

"Ayar... will you tell us a little about your World?" Pedro felt he had earned the right to ask. His question however produced some amused faces.

"My World is the same as your World Pedro... I was born on this Earth, just like the others at this table..."

"I think you know what I'm referring to?" Pedro insisted.

"Each of us was born and bred to play a specific role and to fulfil a particular function, on behalf of something far greater than one single World could ever be… and you are a part of it too." He paused. "…The main difference between you and us being that we are fully conscious of what we are and why."

"And what about those who live in other Star systems…?" Pedro rephrased his question. "The gold you mine here does go somewhere… Doesn't it?" At this point, Becchiu was about to intervene, when Ayar raised His hand, so as for the Chieftain to allow Pedro to proceed.

"My knowledge and understanding of life relates mainly to my role and functions Pedro. As I see it, much of everything else is purely of academic interest and could even be speculative, for all we know…," he paused reflectively, trying to find a way of expressing His wisdom. "I'd say: enjoy your pleasures and your privileges and be grateful for your own ignorance on some of the things you can only speculate upon…" He paused again before regaining a smile; "Did that help?"

"It did… Thank you…" Pedro felt he should quit his questioning for the time being.

The remainder of the meal then evolved into a light-hearted affair, with Pedro and Quito delighting the others as they recounted some of the more amusing moments of their adventures. Each time Ayar's wives' eyes met theirs however, it seemed to re-ignite their earlier sensations of pleasure… keeping the two heroes well glued to their seats!!! *Why were they doing that?*

With dinner over, one of the Guards then led the party through a secret passage, bringing them straight onto one of the Pyramids that overlooked the Square. The crowd below immediately acknowledged their arrival as they emerged to take their seats and Ayar His Throne, a little above the others, and well sandwiched by His two wives!

Walking drummers using various types of percussion instruments then appeared from inside the smaller Pyramids, playing loud rhythmic combinations as they advanced

298

towards the centre of the Square, pushing the audience behind the well-defined spectator lines.

They were gradually joined by other musicians and at a signal from a Master of Ceremonies, the whole show began with an explosion of music and song, in the midst of contagious hypnotic rhythms that complemented the movements of colourful acrobats, jugglers, flame throwers and stilt walkers. Now and then, distractedly, Pedro's and Quito's heads bobbed to some of the beats, causing Ayar's wives to give out the odd giggle.

"Are you enjoying the show…?" From behind him, one of Ayar's wives enquired of Pedro.

"Excellent entertainment…," he replied, doing his best to avoid eye contact!

"The day after tomorrow there's going to be a game of "Tlachtli" … which may last a day or two…," informed the other, just as keen to make conversation.

"What will happen to the losers?" Pedro had heard about that game and all about the fate of the loosing team in bygone days…

"They won't be killed, don't worry…" She was quick to put his mind at rest.

"Is the entertainment going to be… sort of continuous for a week?" Quito whispered to Becchiu after a while, causing the Chieftain to chuckle.

"No… Today it will only last for another couple of hours…," he revealed, still chuckling! "Tomorrow will be a day of rest and after that will be games and competitions for four days, before the closing show…"

Ayar wasn't one to engage in idle conversation, but seemed to draw some pleasure from seeing His wives enjoying themselves, and towards the end of the evening's show, suggested to Pedro and Quito;

"Would you like to join us for breakfast tomorrow morning… before the start of the day's programme?"

"We will be delighted…" Pedro accepted also on behalf of Quito, leaving Becchiu unable to hide his surprise at the invitation.

Eventually at the Palace of the Guests, Quito was finally able to disappear into what had become his usual quarters there, taking with him a couple of girls he had been with before.

"You look tired Pedro…," noted Mikay, as always keen to please, flanked by the smiling Cuxi. "Shall we give you a nice bath and then play the flower and the bees' game… to send you to sleep?" she proposed.

"Flower and the bees…?" Pedro couldn't be sure of what she meant.

"Well, you are the flower… and we are the bees?" she hinted, "…looking for the nectar?"

"I get it…" Pedro had a chuckle, "It sounds like the perfect game to end the day with, I agree…"

*

Deedee and Ara were traumatised by the news concerning the yacht, adding to everything else they had been through of late. People were dying like flies around them and they lived in constant anticipation that they could be next. In a way, however, this was making life easier for Sergio, who no longer had problems getting the girls to do as they were told! He felt that Irene would be safe to stay where she was and after packing a few essentials, he and the girls climbed onto the 4X4 to head out of Rio.

"Where are we going?" Asked Deedee opening a packet of crisps, soon copied by Ara on the seat behind them.

"We are going to drive to São Paulo and then take a plane to Recife…" He replied.

"You are not planning to take us back to our Camp I hope…" Mumbled Ara from the back in between munches.

"I won't take you there if you don't want me to… but right

now it is probably the safest place where you could possibly be…," he alleged, without wanting to sound forceful.

"We would both die of shame, given the circumstances…," reasoned Deedee.

"When did you last speak to your mother?"

"Ooh… a few weeks back…"

"Why don't you give her a call, let her know you are both alright and feel the ground?" He paused. "And afterwards you can tell me what you want to do?"

"The problem is that we don't want to be stuck there afterwards…" Ara had something to say about this idea.

"You both know and I know that Pedro is a reasonable man, or I wouldn't be paid to be here; He definitely cares for both of you and would not force you to be anywhere against your will … Right…?"

Sergio reasoned with them for a while, as a friend would, and Deedee was soon convinced she had nothing to lose by calling her mother.

"Mum?"

"Well, it's about time… where the hell have you been? Taco and Joaquim have been tight lipped ever since their return from Porto de Galinhas… and I know nothing… I even thought you and Ara were dead until this moment…" She paused to let out a sigh of relief. *"Come home and let me hug you?"* Mela burst into tears, getting Deedee to start crying too, as she felt the warmth of her mother's love, and in turn triggering Ara, sobbing quietly in the back seat.

"We are going to fly to Recife later today and I'll call you when we land at the Airport?" Deedee managed to say in a single breath.

"And I'll send Taco and Joaquim to pick you up?" Mela was suddenly euphoric.

"Yes please… I'll talk to you later OK…?" She finally turned to Ara, who showed no objection.

Taco and Joaquim were already at Recife Airport when Deedee phoned her mum to say she had arrived!

"Good to meet you Sergio" Taco greeted him as one of his own and they were soon on the road to the Akazi Peninsula. "You will hardly recognise the place..." Taco warned, looking at the girls. "We even have a proper road to go into our concession with a raising bridge... like in the ancient castles?"

"Sounds exciting..." Deedee was still trying to psyche herself up, "Everyone OK?"

"Well... everyone is ok... except..., Joojoo has left us to join our ancestors..."

"Oh, poor Joojoo..." Deedee's eyes went moist yet again.

Deedee and Ara were impressed with the modern private road over the swampland and even more so with the border-style barrier that preceded a small drawbridge. The "Border Post" was being manned by two young Braves (Sam and Tok), who immediately made a fuss of Deedee and Ara.

"Ho my, ho my!" exclaimed Tok, impressed with the girl's new look.

"Take it easy guys...," warned Taco with a chuckle.

"Welcome to the Akazi Peninsula sir..." Sam greeted Sergio as the barrier was raised.

Inside the peninsula, the road crossed the new modern village nearing completion, in an architectural style reminiscent of "The Flintstones". It then branched east towards Pedro's bay and continued south towards the interim Akazi Camp made up of mobile homes.

"The place really is unrecognisable!" Ara was impressed.

"Do you like it?" Taco also wanted some feedback from Deedee.

"Very much... the village will look lovely when it is finished...," she confirmed.

"It will have a school, a church, a general store and a cinema...," further informed Taco.

"And a café…," added Joaquim, as they reached their journey's end.

Mela emerged from among the gathering tribe with hysterical sounds of joy, somehow bringing everyone to a stand still, paralysed by what this woman could do (!), and was immediately followed by granny, shouting some things no one could understand!

"My babies are home again…" Mela took them both inside her arms… "You both look posh…" she eventually said as she stood back a little to better inspect them. "And those bellies are starting to show…" she added with a singing voice, before giving them another cuddle.

"And where are Pedro and Quito?" Granny enquired, after giving both a far more casual hug.

"They'll be here in about a week…," informed Sergio, who then introduced himself as the girl's body guard, arousing granny's curiosity.

"Like James Bond, are you?" Granny seemed interested.

"Almost…" Sergio confirmed with an amused chuckle, before Taco came to rescue him.

"Shall I show you your temporary home among us?" He invited the security guard to follow him to a small but clean mobile home with all the things he could possibly need, including a stove!

"This is lovely Taco, many thanks… Are you the current Chief of the Tribe?"

"No, no… Quito is the Chief. I'm only keeping his place warm while he is away…" He chuckled "I hope you will join the rest of us for dinner once you've organised yourself?"

"I shall look forward to that… Thanks."

*

At the Azevedo Estate, George went into his strong room with a laptop, keeping an eye on the time while writing a long list of e-mails he planned to send, the moment his son was with him. Then, with 30 minutes to go to Alberto's expected time of arrival, George called Sebastião to his private cellar/strongroom and handed him an envelope.

"May I ask what's in it?" asked his head of security with a frown.

"It is my Will Sebastião... I'm entrusting you with it, should I not live beyond today...," he paused to hand him a small briefcase. "And in here is a million dollars in cash, to thank you for your loyal service over the years..."

"What are you planning?"

"This is only a safeguard Sebastião...," he chuckled, "Should I still be alive tomorrow morning I shall ask you for that money back..."

"I assure you we can protect you and the Estate with confidence, especially with Alberto also joining us... unless you are expecting the U.S. Army to come in full force!!!" He made George laugh.

"I have every confidence in you Sebastião..." He paused. "Tell Alberto to meet me here when he arrives? I still have to prepare a few things for him and time is short..."

"OK...," he then chuckled as he was about to leave the cellar and turned around. "I'm not planning on shooting you by the way..."

"That's the first good news I've heard today... Don't go changing your mind now..."

Alberto's plane arrived almost an hour behind schedule and George awaited him in his Strong Room, sweating profusely by now. Next to him there was a half bottle of whiskey with two glasses and his briefcase, containing his personal hand gun with a screwed-on silencer.

A few minutes passed and as George wiped a few drops of sweat from his forehead, he recognised the walking gait of his first-born nearing the strong room.

"Dad...?" Alberto shouted from the outside, unsure if it was OK to enter.

"Come in Al…" He greeted his son with a customary kiss on each cheek.

"Gosh, it's like a sauna in here! Sebastião said you wanted to see me here?"

"Yes, sit down Al," said George calmly as he opened his briefcase, to then pick up his gun and shoot Alberto on both arms, before closing the door.

"Have you lost your mind? Dad? It's me… what's wrong?"

"Don't move a muscle from where you are…" Alberto ignored his father's warning and George shot both his legs.

"Jesus Christ! Will you please tell me what's going on?"

"Yes, I will…" George got up to lock the door and then replaced the spent cartridges, knowing his son could no longer move from where he was. "Al… Why did you kill my wife, your sister and all the others?"

"I don't know what you are talking about…"

"You take me for a fool?" George this time shot Alberto in the stomach. "Your liver and your intestines will be next…"

"I'll confess to whatever you say, but please stop… can't you see how much blood I'm losing?"

"I wouldn't worry too much about that son… we'll both be dead in the next few minutes."

"Can I do anything to stop you?" Alberto was now haemorrhaging from two of his wounds.

"No… the only choice you have in this matter is to either die in peace by telling me the truth… and I shall be swift… or take the truth to your grave, after spending your final moments in agony." He reloaded the spent cartridge.

"I wanted our family name to be etched in the history of our country, instead of us spending generation after generation hiding like mice, in fear of transgressing the unwritten rules of a ghostly Brotherhood…"

"Al… I'm doing this so your children will be spared… and so that what is yours and mine will go to them once we're dead…" Alberto knew the moment had come as his father approached him unscrewing the silencer from the hand gun.

"I forgive you Dad…"

"I love you son…" were the last word George uttered before shooting Alberto in the temple, to immediately turn the gun on himself.

**

XXI

Becchiu came for Pedro and Quito shortly after dawn.

"It is a very special honour for Ayar to invite someone into his privacy… I've never seen it happen…" The Chieftain was still coming to terms with Ayar's request, as they walked towards His Palace.

"I'm sure that with all the training He received for His role, there must be a pretty valid reason!" replied Pedro, trying not to sound too clever.

"Is today a bit like a Sunday for you guys?" Quito enquired changing the subject.

"Yes… It is the weekly day of rest for those currently working for the State, going through their Annual Tax Payback Period…"

The topic of conversation then evolved into the annual calendar of Inca celebrations, until they arrived at Ayar's Palace. There, Becchiu left Pedro and Quito with one of the Palace Guards, who took them through a small labyrinth of passage ways and into Ayar's private terraced garden.

"Please come through and join us…" Ayar greeted them with complete informality, from a garden table laid with a feast of fruits of every colour and shape, flanked by His two wives, as usual. "By the way, my wives are Bachue and Cava…" Pedro and Quito finally learned their names and acknowledged them with a respectful nod each. "…And if you think we just got out of bed, you are absolutely correct." He got everyone laughing.

"It is good to see you in such high spirits…You all look

so much more human when you get out of bed…" Pedro's sincerity triggered a general chuckle.

"We look just as human when we get inside it, I can assure you…," confirmed the amused Ayar. "And inviting you here this morning was also meant to show you that side of us, among other things…"

"Please feel free to tuck in…," invited Cava with a mystic smile.

"There's no way we can eat all this!" Bachue showed her sense of humour, sending Quito into a sustained chuckle also because of the way she looked into his eyes!!!

"Anyway, the main purpose of us meeting here today, relates to the third reason for your recall." He paused. "A precipitation of events last night meant that I was able to bring this meeting forward… and to be honest, there are some matters I'd rather deal with you in privacy, instead of placing your private business in the public domain." Ayar then went on updating them with the latest developments in Pedro's and Quito's dimension, which included the tragedy at George's Estate.

"What will happen to the huge wealth accumulated between George, Alberto and Alberto's wife's side of the family?" Pedro wanted to know.

"It will all go to Alberto's wife for the time being, Mary, and eventually her children. Alberto's brother was also found dead with an overdose, a couple of days ago…"

"She'll be worth at least a dozen billion…," noted Pedro.

"Twenty billion dollars to be precise… and she is your next assignment…" Ayar looked at Pedro, leaving him a little speechless, which seemed to inspire a caring expression on Cava's face. "But we'll talk about this later…" He paused. "To wrap up everything related to the Mission you've both accomplished, thanks to the savings we've made on this, we are able to pay you the equivalent number of US dollars George would have given you for the remainder of the gold you sold him. And so, Patricio will open two Bank accounts for you with US$22.5 million dollars each…"

"That means you won't need to chip in for the works on the Peninsula." Interrupted the excited Quito looking at Pedro, almost startling him.

"Oh, but I want to…," he contradicted, bringing some amusement to the Inca trio. "And what of Thelma's Estate…?"

"It will all go to her son, whom Patricio traced a few years back." Ayar then took a longer pause, to allow for some coffee to be served, and recommenced His speech the moment the servant was gone. "Through one of our Insurance Companies we will recover the cost of the yacht and from the sale of all the other things that were bought to help your mission, we will actually make a small profit. Altogether, we'll get around US$90 million dollars back, which Patricio will add to your 22.5 account… as a down payment for your next Mission."

"Am I supposed to woo this woman into marrying me… and then kill her and the kids so that "I" can eventually get all the billions back with interest?" Pedro hazarded a guess, causing an eruption of laughter from all three Incas.

"You are very close…" Ayar congratulated Pedro. "Marrying Mary, yes… but we won't ask you to kill anyone… and she is a very attractive woman, by the way…"

"And what about my Akazi wives…?"

"Well, that's something you'll have to sort out yourself. Your Indio marriage to them is not recognised by Brazilian Law anyway. Officially, you are a widower from your only marriage in São Paulo…"

"I will try to help you with that…," confirmed Quito, without stopping Ayar's flow.

"For all she knows, you are already a friend of the family; even though you've never met… She has even slept in your ex-Manhattan penthouse on more than one occasion. Remember?" He paused. "Your wealth will not be comparable to hers in any way, but what you may lack in billions you will be able to balance with your power status inside "I" … And that's something she'll recognise."

"By taking her husband's position at the top of the organisation…?"

"Indeed…," confirmed Ayar. "You will have a full team of expert advisors to guide you, of course, as well as the full support of us all and Auqui and Ana in particular…"

"Revenge is sweet…" Quito had a smirk on his face.

"How soon would you want me to start this?" Pedro didn't see any point in discussing salary!!!

"Use George and Alberto's funerals as the point of rapprochement...?"

"Could I keep Patricio as my personal aid?"

"Of course…, and I think you should too. The whole organisation will eventually become your embodiment… but don't go giving yourself sleepless nights on account of making the right or wrong business decisions… 99% of those will be made for you…"

"Where did Alberto go wrong within the organisation then?" Pedro's mind was now racing…

"He never got to know us as such… which is perhaps our fault. In hindsight, probably none of this would have ever happened…" He poured Himself a second cup of the strong coffee. "He was good at his job, no one will deny him that. But rather than a natural born leader, he was a natural born dictator with his own agenda. He felt so powerful after a while that he started to believe he had a right to own "I" and to use it as his personal vehicle to attain personal political ambitions, putting at risk and neglecting the core purpose of the organisation... creating partisans and several pragmatic supporters of "isms" within it. All that would invariably lead to an implosion of the whole thing…"

"Not to mention some of the methods he was starting to use to get his own way…," reinforced Bachue.

"We cannot afford for "I" to be identified as an organisation.

"I" must remain an invisible link between many different organisations, preferably with unrelated shareholders, whenever possible… and that is what gives us an edge over any branded multinational institution…"

"So… he wanted to bring the whole thing under an identifiable umbrella?"

"Among other things, yes, so he could then float it on the world's Stock Markets, multiplying its value several folds… And in the process, to use this as an economic-political credential…"

"Wouldn't that serve your interests too?"

"Only in the very short term… and we would lose control almost instantly." Ayar confirmed.

"We were in fact almost at that point when we took the decision that Alberto had to go…" It was Cava this time that passed comment, causing Quito to chuckle.

"So… "I" is definitely an organisation you don't resign or get fired from…" Quito continued his chuckle.

"Obviously…" Pedro looked at Quito with some reproach, but none the less as amused as the others, for the naïve comment of the Indio Chief!

The remainder of that morning was spent with Ayar filling in the gaps on Pedro's next Mission, with a few comical moments coming from Quito, and sometimes from Bachue or Cava, both of whom were far from being the submissive wives they appeared to be in public. In some ways, the three Incas were finding the company of Pedro and Quito a breath of fresh air, from their day-in-day-out pomp and protocols. And given that there were no planned activities to keep their two guests entertained, they also invited them for lunch and proposed an afternoon tour of the immediate territory surrounding the city, still part of the XAKATAN dimension.

Bachue and Cava were two big flirts and a strong temptation to anyone they came in contact with. Pedro and Quito were no exception to the rule, but for the fear of treading on Ayar's toes… The Inca King knew this but enjoyed testing the will power of both men to their near limit, especially following the break they all took ahead of lunch, after changing into clothes more adapted to their planned afternoon activities.

"What do you think?" Pedro asked Quito, as they sat by themselves with a couple of drinks, waiting at a round table on Ayar's eating balcony.

"This whole thing is like a dream… and his wives…!!!! I've never seen anything so hot! Bachue is keeping me almost in a state of permanent erection!!!"

"We really need to stick to our brains on this Quito…" Pedro warned.

"Have no worries… I'm aware of that too…," he paused. "I just hope I don't have a major *accident* during the afternoon tour…!" He got Pedro to laugh with gusto.

A guard then announced the arrival of Ayar and His wives, so they could stand.

"I hope we weren't too long…" Ayar was clearly looking forward to the afternoon. He simply wore trousers, a belt, high boots and a leather gilet.

"Not at all…," replied Pedro, who remained standing until the others sat.

Bachue and Cava also wore trousers, belt and high boots, but instead of a gilet, they had something like a revealing blouse each, made of a straw type of material, which allowed for their breasts and nipples to be perceived through it.

"Holly Pope!!!" Quito seemed to mumble in a near-inaudible whisper as they sat.

Lunch wasn't anything like the lavish feast of dishes in previous meals at Ayar's, but a speciality of small Inca sausages in a white sauce. Quito's eyes remained glued to his own plate throughout the meal, in spite of Bachue's attempts to attract his attentions; instead, causing Pedro to release a short painful "*Aahh*", when she finally bit one of the sausages!

"Are you OK?" Ayar enquired, seemingly oblivious of Pedro's troubles.

"I'm fine Ayar..." Pedro chuckled. "I thought I was going to sneeze..."

They didn't linger at table any longer than absolutely necessary. Outside, 20 muscled Inca Warriors stood by 5 Royal Litters, and they were soon out of the city moving up a mountain trail, coming across the occasional caravan of llamas, bringing food and other supplies into the City.

"Where do you plant the crops those llamas carry?" Pedro was curious, given that all he could see was dense Amazonian forest everywhere he looked.

"Underground..." Ayar explained. "We have been mining this place for almost 5,000 years and so you can imagine the endless miles of empty tunnels this has left behind." He paused. "Some of those tunnels we refill with the waste from the new ones being dug... and in the more stable ones, we create controlled environments where we grow different types of crops, rather than become reliant on weather conditions..."

"And on the lake...?"

"There, we just grow fresh vegetables on artificial islets. It simplifies the irrigation process..."

As they neared the top of the extinct volcano they came down from the Litters, to loosen their legs and give the Litter carriers a rest. The air seemed thinner, but the view down to the city was breath-taking, as were the vistas over the Andean chain further west.

"Do you ever wish you had a different life?" Pedro asked Ayar, while the others were involved in conversation a few yards behind them.

"Do you ever wish you had a different body?" Ayar was amused by the question. "Everything is preordained Pedro... we are all robots created to fulfil specific tasks. And when we interact with one another, it is to help fulfil each other's tasks..." He stopped to look at Pedro. "Your conscious self is no more than a helpless passenger riding on a body you think is yours… deprived of all knowledge as to what needs to be done by you… driven forward by instinct, emotions, and forever influenced by surrounding events…"

"Don't you find that depressing?"

"Not at all… What makes life depressing for some, is when you waste time and effort wishing for what you don't have, rather than making the most of what you've got…" He paused "…And there are pleasures to be found in the simplest of things…! Even at the very moment of death… the excitement of a new existence ahead, based on all that you've learnt in life…"

"Then… who benefits from all that we do?"

"The Universe… God… the very force that recycles us into the endless dimensions… worlds and existences across infinite…"

"You guys seem to be having a serious conversation…" Cava came to them, closely followed by Bachue and Quito.

From where they were it was only a short walk to one of the main entrances to a labyrinth of mines and underground plantations. In contrast with the archaic caravans of llamas and Royal Litters however, it was state of the art technology below ground, with huge elevator shafts servicing over 300 floors of gold mining and crop tunnels.

Ayar took them deeper into one of the control rooms where in mid-air, 3D holographic maps provided in-real-time information of all on-going activities in the interior of the volcanic mountain.

"Anything in particular you'd like to see?" Enquired a smiling controller with finer facial traits, wearing a similar necklace to Ayar and the others.

"I'll leave that up to you…," replied Ayar, after introducing Pedro as the future top man at "I" and Quito as his friend.

Being a little claustrophobic by nature, Pedro was clearly pleased to see that this was going to be a virtual tour, as the controller started to manipulate expertly other smaller holographic extensions he *fished out* from the main maps.

"How does the gold leave the Earth? Is it teleported?" Pedro enquired of Ayar.

"Not quite…" He replied, giving the controller permission to show the others one of such operations in progress.

The controller then proceeded by revealing a large reinforced dome deep inside the mountain where a strange looking vehicle was being manually loaded with ingots of various sizes.

"How does it come out of there?" Quito couldn't work it out.

"The same way you travel when using your necklace on "emergency", but only up to the Earth's stratosphere… Then, from around 50 kilometres up, it goes into an Interstellar vessel and on to its final destination."

"And where is that?" Pedro asked.

"That depends on the Buyer. Our Clients are many, far and wide…"

"The craft you see being loaded sometimes also brings new people in and takes us away once we die… we are genetically modified to be sterile and are generated from incubator machines, even though the original embryos are from real fertile people…" Cava tried to satisfy Pedro's thirst for more information.

"But you still have sex, I assume…?" Pedro looked at her.

"Plenty of that…," she replied sensually.

"Did you know that the pleasures we all crave for and enjoy when reaching a sexual climax… are in fact a trick of the brain as it experiences pain beyond endurance?" commented Bachue.

"Are we all masochists then?" Pedro chuckled, ready to believe anything.

"It looks that way, doesn't it?" Ayar was just as amused by Pedro's thoughts.

The return journey back to the city followed a different

route, passing half a dozen small villages of necklace wearing people.

"Have they also been artificially incubated?" Pedro wanted to know.

"Yes…" replied Ayar. "They all work in the mines… The people from the City never go inside the mountain, except to collect supplies brought to the surface for them…" He explained further.

They reached the city by early evening and Ayar and His wives left Pedro and Quito by the Palace of the Guest, on their way home.

"Thank you very much. We had a most enjoyable day…" Pedro also spoke on Quito's behalf.

"We all did… we must repeat it some time…," replied Ayar.

"See you tomorrow at the games…," Cava added and Bachue waved and smiled.

*

Following the completion of the transaction between Starling Inc. and one of the "I" Companies, Patricio received the news of his latest promotion with mixed feelings, especially now that he no longer had Thelma at his side. He had been working with "I" for over 20 years and although not yet 50, he was ready to take it easy in some peaceful location with his Italian boyfriend and a vineyard! A keen lover of the arts and antiquity, he had bought a Romanesque Villa and some land near Florence, intent on enjoying the few millions he accumulated over the years, under a Tuscany sun.

"Could I get you both some more champagne…?" The stewardess enquired in the Navigator Class compartment of the VARIG Jumbo to Recife.

"Yes please…," Patricio replied, also on behalf of Dan (Daniele).

"I'm never going to see you now with this promotion…," his boyfriend complained.

"My salary is going to double Dan... think of how much fun we're going to have once I reorganise myself..."

"You'll never find another Thelma...," he sulked.

"I will, you'll see..."

"What's this Pedro like? Should I be jealous?"

"He is straight..."

"You could still fancy him...," alleged Dan.

"Well, even if I did, I don't think he fancies me at all... and you are giving me a headache!"

"Sorry."

It was a rainy day in Recife and as often happened, Patricio's ex-wife insisted on picking him up from the airport. They still retained some sort of friendship, perhaps helped by the generous alimony he voluntarily paid her each month, in spite of their teenage children rejecting him outright, ever since he came clean with his true sexuality.

"Hi Dan..." She greeted with a little wave, while kissing her ex on both cheeks. "You guys had a good trip?"

"He slept most of the way...," Dan replied on Patricio's behalf, before going forward a few steps, to allow them a moment of privacy.

"I tried to...," he corrected, before turning to Bela, "You and the kids OK?"

"They are growing so fast... another year or two and I'll probably be on my own...," she said, grabbing Patricio's briefcase, leaving him free to drag his suitcase. "Are you going to tell me about this promotion?" She decided to be positive and cheerful instead.

"It's going to be a lot of hard work without Thelma at the beginning... but it should also bring you some benefits once my rise in salary comes through..."

"You've always been thoughtful..." she thanked him in her particular way. "I could perhaps help you like I used to in the old days, before Thelma came along?"

"Thanks Bela, but its more complicated than that...

there's so much technology that… you'd be forever playing catch…," he said it in the friendliest manner. "I myself get lost with it at times."

Patricio and Dan shared a villa in the outskirts of town and it only took Bela 20 minutes to get them home.

"Thank you darling… want to come in and have a drink with us?" Patricio invited as they got out of the car.

"Not today, thanks… give me a shout next time you need a taxi?"

"It's a deal." He smiled to her as she drove off.

Dan was a Pharmacist by trade and one of the first things he did as they got in, was to fix them with a mind soothing concoction, a drink and mood music!

**

XXII

In XAKATAN, the week of celebrations continued to be socially hectic for Pedro and Quito. Their full days in the company of Ayar, Bachue and Cava was immediately followed by private working dinners at each of the courtiers' palaces, in between events, and would invariably end with the pleasures of the Palace of the Guests.

Ayar and His wives were becoming ever closer to Pedro and Quito with each passing day, to the point of inspiring a little jealousy from the courtiers and Becchiu, as they continued to watch all the scheduled events together.

The King still showed no signs of trying to restrain His chatty wives from flirting with Pedro and Quito… and at times, Pedro even wondered if He was perhaps encouraging them in some way…! *Could Ayar have some twisted fantasies involving them? Or could it simply be some sort of innocent assumption that they were untouchable, regardless?*

"Do you think they are just having juvenile fun with us?" Quito asked Pedro as they debated this on a rare moment to themselves, while getting ready for dinner at the Royal Palace.

"It would be madness for us to see it in any other light…," confirmed Pedro. This was supposed to be their final formal working dinner with the usual collaborators, prior to returning to their own dimension, although their very last night of the week would be spent as private guests of Ayar and His wives.

"Would you go to bed with either of them given the chance?" He wanted to know.

"That's a silly question Quito!" Pedro chuckled, triggering the Indio Chief into peals of laughter.

"Women, women!!!" He shook his head, "I've been with more women since we started this thing than... in my entire life!"

"Don't go blaming me for it now...!" Pedro continued to chuckle.

As had become the norm, Becchiu came for them in the late afternoon, and they were at Ayar's "U" table by the twilight of day. Bachue and Cava were at their most radiant, even if keeping the low profile demanded by protocol. The courtiers looked ready to play the predominant part throughout the working meal, and Ayar was poised for the observer role.

No sooner had the servants left the balcony than the courtiers wasted no time in recapping all they had covered in the 3 previous working dinners. This was so that those present could comment on it, or point out whatever they felt might have been missed.

"One final thing...," contributed Ana. "Your expenses budget is unlimited and you are to decide on your own wages, providing it does not exceed 1% of "I"'s gross Annual profits... and I would suggest that you meet with Patricio to agree matters..."

"I couldn't possibly have asked for more..." Pedro felt humbled by the offer, to which Cava somehow added a caress, in the form of an intimate glance to him alone.

"Well, the teams of advisors already working for you in your dimension have been briefed on all the points raised..." Ayar confirmed to Pedro at the end of the courtiers' exposé, in an effort to wrap up the evening. "And from within "I", we have found a worthy Thelma replacement. Clara in no way lags behind her predecessor and has been working for Patricio since this morning. Although extremely bright, none-the-less, I should give her a few days to get acquainted with her new role." The Inca ruler smiled, as if amused by thoughts He wasn't sharing. "Any last questions for us to clear...?"

"Nothing comes to mind just now...," replied Pedro.

Pedro was on top of the world that very moment. For once he understood how Alberto must have felt (!); *bored to tears, with only the impossible left to achieve!!! **What could this Mary look like?** Might he have seen a portrait of her in George's stairway? Did Cava see him as some sort of male prostitute, ready to do anything for money and position?* He ate with no appetite, and the best thing about the evening's entertainment was that he was now a step closer to being back in Recife… with his balls still attached to the rest of him!!!

"Are you OK?" Cava enquired from behind him, as they watched the show in the Square below.

"I'm fine Cava… too much excitement I reckon…" He replied without turning back. "Are you?"

"I feel great… and you've got nothing to be afraid of…" *What could she mean? Was she on the same wavelength?*

"Hang in there man…" Quito whispered to Pedro in between his teeth, while the crowd's applause filled the air at the end of the show.

"We are all looking forward to dinner tomorrow night…" Bachue eventually said it as a good night when they all parted.

"Likewise," replied Quito.

At the Palace of the Guests, Cuxi was off that night for some reason, and Pedro decided to spend the night with Mikay only, in the hope of learning a few things.

"You look tired tonight…" Mikay smiled at Pedro as they got to his bedroom.

"I'm a bit stressed out…" He admitted as they entered the warm pool.

"I know exactly what you need once we're dry … and you can tell me all about it afterwards?" She proposed, her naked breasts touching his back as she soaped him lovingly. …And it wasn't long before they relaxed with a drink each!!!

"What are you so stressed about?" She then asked, pleased with herself.

"Stress is perhaps not the right word... there are some things I feel frustrated about not knowing and others for not wanting to risk asking the wrong person about it...!"

"Can you give me an example? I won't tell anyone..." She turned to face him, as they lay against the back of the bed.

"Well... say; ...what sort of rules are there in Inca Marriages?"

"Is that really so important?" She looked amused.

"Well, you asked me to give you an example..."

"Ok. Now that's a question with different answers...," she started, sitting up. "First you must make a distinction between the true Incas and people generally classed as Incas, either because of their Indio origins or their place of birth." She paused. "Even in ancient Inca days, going back to the time of the Conquistadores, the Inca population was then established at around 10 million. But of those, only around 4,000 were actual true Incas. The others were Indios and Indio tribes within the territories dominated by the Real-Incas." She had a sip of her drink. "So, talking about the Incas in general, men could marry several women, but a woman could only marry one man..."

"And in the case of the true Incas...?"

"Like Ayar and His wives?"

"Yes... I suppose."

"They had no set rules on that, or so it seems. A man could marry several women, just as a woman could wed several men... Those rights would normally be dictated by their wealth and social ranking among themselves... and I would assume some sort of agreement between the parties involved."

"Therefore, could true Incas create their own marriage rules, so that extra marital affairs would be accepted by both the man and the woman in the same marriage?"

"I suppose...," she looked at him suspiciously and then confronted him with a simple question: "Are you trying to find out how you would stand if you had sex with one of Ayar's wives?" The question was so direct and Pedro's reaction so obvious, he didn't need to reply... "Fuck!!! Which one?" she had to cover her mouth, trying not to laugh.

"You're coming to the wrong conclusion Mikay..." Pedro pretended to have some of the drink gone the wrong way, in order to gain time to think of something to say! "It was a question of curiosity, merely because... at times, they act as if they were available... well, maybe I get the wrong impression, I don't know... Do you understand now?"

"I didn't mean to embarrass you... and people actually speculated the other day... when you and Quito were their private guests for most of the day..."

"What did "people" say?"

"Some felt it was out of place that they should mix privately with commoners... and others assumed they wanted sex with you both, perhaps to satisfy their curiosity...? A bit of novelty?"

"That's ridiculous...! To satisfy their curiosity they could simply ask you, Cuxi or the other girls that have *serviced* me, Quito or his braves..."

"I think this calls for another drink..." Mikay had her convictions; "Do you want a top up?"

"Not yet, thanks."

"Would you like me to go and get changed to make myself look just like one them?" she proposed. "I could even sound and talk like them..." Mikay's vocal demonstration was now giving Pedro the shivers.

"No Mikay, please don't. I'm not really into the "*let's pretend stuff*" ..." He resisted temptation.

"Pedro, if you want my advice on the matter, don't take needless risks. You've got everything to lose. On the other hand, if you are so desperate to *give it* to her... let me go and get changed? You won't believe how much I can look and sound like Cava... and it will help you get her out of your system."

323

"How did you know it was Cava and not Bachue?"

"You are a romantic and I reckon so is she. Whereas Bachue appeals to me as someone who would probably milk you from any position just for the hell of it, given half a chance!"

"If she made a clear pass at me and I was to turn her down for fear of consequences… what do you think could happen… as to the way it works among the true Incas?"

"Well, that would very much depend on any agreement they might have with Ayar…," she paused. "You should also realise that among the true Incas, women are often more powerful than men, and for all we know, Ayar could well be a front man for one or even both His wives…"

"I think I'm ready for that top up… but I'd rather have you as yourself…"

"You really are a romantic!!!" She gave him a caring smile.

*

"I'm not looking forward to all that walking back to Luis' place…!" Quito mumbled as they shared breakfast. "…And how are we going to get to Recife? Have you thought of that?"

"I'd assume the courtiers must have something planned, surely!"

"Do you think they'll still allow me to keep their necklace, now that I'm not part of your next Mission…? I've grown attached to it…" Quito made Pedro chuckle.

"Who said you are not part of my next Mission?"

"Well, no one said anything…"

"OK then. In that case, I've just made you my personal under cover assistant. How's that…?"

"If you insist…"

Pedro and Quito decided to venture out of the Palace of the Guests for a walk by themselves, only to find Becchiu striding towards them within a minute of stepping out.

"Did you want to go anywhere in particular?" The Chieftain enquired, trying to appear casual.

"Not really… we were planning to do a full circle of the lake and probably have a look around …Assuming there isn't a problem with that, of course," replied Pedro.

"No problem at all. Except that V.I.P.s are not supposed to venture out unescorted…"

"I see. So… What do we do if we want to go out and you are not around?"

"Just walk out as you've done now and I'll come to you within a minute or two."

"Sounds great…" Pedro suddenly felt more like a prisoner than somebody with the freedom of the City! "Becchiu… are we going to have to walk out of here with you tomorrow?"

"I don't know... I've not yet been instructed on that." He paused. "I'm sure there are some plans in place and… I can only assume that Ayar will tell you about them later today."

Although friendly and servile, Becchiu was beginning to feel like an umbilical chord. *Were they tagged? Did their necklaces possess a multitude of other functions they were unaware of? Could they be listened to through them?* Pedro wondered to himself.

"Are there things we are not supposed to see?" Quito asked, bringing a smile to Becchiu's face.

"You think that's why we don't want you to venture around by yourselves?"

"Well… I'm just wondering…" Quito smiled back.

"There's nothing we're hiding from you! It's a courtesy from all of us, should you feel unwell or need something?"

"I didn't mean to be offensive…" Quito was apologetic.

"Especially now that Ayar seems to have taken both of you directly under His wing…"

"Would you say that people feel resentful about that?" Pedro asked candidly, suspecting Becchiu to probably be among those.

"Not really. Surprised, I'd say. We have never seen the King take such a personal interest in anyone!"

"Well, only a few more hours and you'll have your King all to yourselves again…"

"I was only trying to answer your question honestly…"

"And you did well Becchiu… Thanks." Pedro was not feeling particularly patient just then and Quito decided to provide the perfect excuse to cut their walk short.

"I think we'd better turn back…," he said, passing one hand over his stomach, "It must have been something I've eaten…"

Becchiu was quick to comply and they were back at the Palace of the Guests in double time a few short minutes later.

"I think I'm going to have a nap, Quito… I want to be in a good mood for tonight…"

"The girls here have some really good tonic to "pick you up" …"

"I'll try the natural way first, thanks."

Weather wise, the afternoon was just as dull as the morning, with a little rain on and off. Thunder clouds however were now beginning to fill the sky, in what promised to be a stormy evening ahead.

Becchiu was nowhere to be seen at the appointed time. But instead, two Royal Litters and their carriers waited patiently for them outside the Palace of the Guests. A few people had gathered for a glimpse of Pedro and Quito and then waved to them as they emerged.

As if timed by the Gods, their arrival at the Royal Palace coincided with a flash of lightning and a loud rumble of thunder, followed by a torrential downpour.

"That was lucky…," observed Ayar as He came to greet them, to then lead the way into the more private side of His Palace.

"Cava and Bachue OK?" enquired Pedro, casually.

"They are bathing, which they always do before dinner…" He said as they walked passed the pool area, towards a passage that brought them onto the dining balcony. The usual "U" table had been replaced by the smaller round one. "Shall we have a drink ahead of dinner?" He proposed, as a servant came to them holding a tray with three glasses.

"Thank you…" They readily accepted it and Pedro tried to identify its origins unsuccessfully, after a small sip. "…Very pleasant and fruity… what is it?"

"It is not a type of Chicha (*) …" Ayar clarified. "It is a blend of fermented Amazonian wild fruits with coca and a few secret ingredients…"

"I remember trying something like this in my youth…" Quito recognised something about it. "I've never felt so nicely stoned!!!" He admitted, causing Ayar to chuckle.

"This is our own brew… and it is probably a milder version of what you had then." He clarified and then sat, suggesting with one hand they should do the same. "Anyway… so as to complete our business relating to "I", I've had something new made also for Quito, assuming he continues to work with you in some capacity?" He looked at Pedro who confirmed it with a small nod. Ayar then extracted two small boxes from under the table, containing two identical necklaces to His own. "Could I please have those you are wearing back?" He requested and they complied.

"What's different about these?" Quito was keen to know.

"They work exactly like the other ones, but they have additional functions. On this occasion, I'll show you a two-way combination that will take you from this room to your office in Recife, and from there to this room. And each time you come to see me I'll show you a new combination."

(*) Chicha are various versions of an ancient Inca drink made from corn, supposedly chewed and spat by virgin girls.

"What guides it to our office and back here?" Pedro was intrigued by the technology.

"This…" Ayar showed them a small metallic cube well hidden inside one of the balcony's columns… "You will find another one like this inside the wall safe in your office… and by the way; Alberto never met us, knew of us, or had anything like this at his disposal…"

"I understand that…" Pedro was pensive. "And if we were to change the location of that metallic cube by placing it somewhere in the Akazi Peninsula, for instance… would we end up there?"

"Theoretically yes… However, I'd suggest that you do not disturb it…"

"And if you were to come and visit us some time… Could your necklace use that same link?" It was Quito's turn to fire a question!!!

"Yes… although a visit from me is not very likely." Ayar was amused by the question.

"And what about the mobiles we had with us when we got here? Can we take them travelling this way?"

"You can, but I should avoid travelling with electronics in future…," replied the King.

"Are we travelling back using these later tonight?" Quito enquired.

"That's the idea…" He smiled and the three of them then rose, as a guard announced the arrival of Cava and Bachue.

Like Ayar, His wives decided to abandon the Royal dress code that evening, in favour of the complete informality of some everyday shirt and trousers, in an effort to bridge ranks. Still, they both looked just as regal without any of the paraphernalia.

"Could we have another round of those?" Cava requested from a servant, pointing to the empty glasses on the table.

"Wow, come and look at the storm over the lake…," proposed Bachue excitedly, when a bolt of lightning produced a longer moment of daylight all around them, prompting the others to follow her to the edge of the balcony's roof.

The storm had grown in intensity and each crack of thunder now echoed menacingly all around the volcano basin, with the lightning turning everything into a shade of near-permanent blue.

"Do you get these often?" Pedro asked, admiring the spectacle.

"Not really… but when they come, you do notice them," replied Ayar, leading the way back to the fresh drinks on the table.

"You've no excuse not to visit us regularly now that you've got those…," commented Cava, noticing their new necklaces.

"You don't have to stay at the Palace of the Guests if you don't want to…," added Bachue with one of her smiles, "You can be our private guests here in the Palace, whenever you like…"

"That really is kind… I just hope that our friendship doesn't cause the resentment of some others in XAKATAN…" Pedro reminded them.

"Well, we don't have to justify ourselves to anyone here, and no one could possibly accuse us of being unethical in any way within our role…!" Ayar felt He needed to say it.

The food then started to arrive and to Pedro's and Quito's relief, there wasn't a sausage or a meat ball in sight!

"Do you ever go out shopping in our dimension?" Was Quito's question to the three, as they were left to serve themselves.

"It is not safe for us to be in public places in your dimension… there are a lot of unpredictable people about. In fact, generally speaking, it is said that over 75% of people in the cities are either mentally disturbed of emotionally unstable…," informed Ayar.

"That's a staggering figure!" Quito commented.

"It doesn't surprise me:" Pedro didn't feel the figure was excessively farfetched, "Between anti-depressants, the rat race, survival and social frustrations, not to mention genetic fault lines…" He paused. "How would you say that compares with XAKATAN?"

"We've been refining the genetic codes of the people here for millennia, through a process of natural selection, rather than via genetic manipulation… and they are all pretty healthy and generally sane…" He paused, seeking a sign of support from His wives. "Of course, there are the odd cases now and then, but those tend to be the result of extreme circumstances or changes caused by an accident…"

"Sooner or later, your governments will have to start restricting the procreation rights of people with severe genetic disorders… especially now that the global population is set to double every 20 years or so… with so much interactive opportunity available to almost anyone…" Bachue contributed thoughtfully.

"I think there are some aspects of human rights that cannot be ignored though…" Cava had a more conservative view on the matter.

The conversation then gradually evolved into righting the world's wrongs, within Pedro's and Quito's dimension. They each had a viewpoint, but the debate remained friendly and respectful, occasionally cooled by someone's touch of humour, or a discrete intimate look.

Pedro then decided to drop a "bomb", as they all shared a round of stronger after dinner drinks, still "high" from the earlier brew:

"Last night I questioned one of the girls at the Palace of the Guests, about married life among the Incas… but while she was able to satisfy my curiosity regarding ordinary Incas, she seemed a bit at a loss when it came to those she defined as the "true Incas", such as you; how does it work among you?" Cava and Bachue exchanged a subliminal glance.

"It is not an unexpected question…" Ayar looked amused, as He reflected upon the best way to answer it. "The simple answer is: there are no set rules." He paused. "We are all individuals and therefore different… and so, it is often left to the interested parties to decide on the parameters within which they would have a happy relationship." He paused again. "Things however can change with time… and divorce also exists in our culture, for when things don't go according to plan."

"I think Pedro is referring to our particular case…" Cava turned to Ayar, causing Bachue to chuckle.

"Our case is even more complicated!" Ayar started, causing His two wives to laugh. "Because we are sterile and unlikely to raise a family with children of our own, the whole thing becomes more liberal in some ways, although far more complicated in others…" He signalled for one of the servants to top them up. "Agreed parameters still have to be observed, of course, but the balance between doing the right and the wrong thing often becomes far more delicate, from everyone's perspective." He glanced at His wives briefly. "Between Cava, Bachue and I, for instance, our priority is that we should enjoy every moment of life, without hurting each other's feelings through disrespect, betrayal or hidden actions of the heart…" He looked at Pedro and Quito this time "…and we've actually grown to enjoy having no secrets whatsoever from each one another… down to our thoughts, feelings and fantasies…"

There was an unexpected moment of silence where no one really knew whose turn it was to say or do something… and they all eventually started laughing, knowing perfectly well that the fundamental question in Pedro's mind was: *"How would you feel if we fucked your wives?"*

"And there is of course also the right and the wrong time for everything…" At this point, Cava decided not to confuse Pedro and Quito beyond their endurance. "On this visit to XAKATAN, our focus should remain on the celebration of what was achieved and on the goals ahead, complemented by the start of an honest and transparent friendship without barriers… but also without going beyond the point we have reached… at least on this occasion…" she smiled directly at Pedro.

"That was beautifully said…," complimented Quito glued to his chair, avoiding Bachue's eyes(!)

"I can't take him anywhere…!" Pedro apologised jokingly, causing general laughter.

*

Mela had a good cry when Deedee told her everything she had been through, in the 3 months since they had seen each other.

"Life really is strange at times…" Her mother eventually spoke, the burden on her spirit lightened by the truth. "Do you realise that had you not split up from Pedro, you, Ara and your babies would have been in that boat… and most probably dead by now?" She covered her mouth.

"Jesus," Deedee almost screamed. "I never thought of that!" Her right hand distractedly caressed her bulging belly.

"God writes through crooked lines…," she reminded her daughter.

"Do you think he'll ever have me back?"

"I don't know. I think you and Ara hurt him badly, but I also think he still cares for you… If you could somehow prove to him over time that the whole thing was no more than a crazy phase and that you can be the devoted wife he always wanted…," she left her phrase in mid air, "I don't really know what to suggest my little angel…"

"I think I know what to do, but it will take time…," she then displayed a happier expression. "Will you show me the house he has been making for himself on the bay?"

"I'll ask Joaquim if he can take us there…," she said, getting her mobile.

Joaquim never had it so good! Between his work as a driver for the tribe and mediating on a variety of subjects for the Akazi - from electronic gadgets to prostitutes, his income was growing with each passing week.

"I heard one of the builders say that Pedro's house should be finished in four weeks…" Joaquim informed them, as he drove along the new road.

"Are the three shacks still there?" Deedee wanted to know.

"Yes, they built the house a little further up the slope inland, by the stream's pool."

"I know where you mean…" Deedee was pleased and even more impressed when she saw the place, moments later. 6 or 7 men worked in the construction and a further 2 or 3 had started to landscape the immediate surroundings of the house. Deedee then went to look into the shacks and was surprised to find Ara in hers!

"What are you doing here?" She asked.

"I'm trying to find something I can fit in…!" Ara replied, showing a slightly bigger belly than Deedee's, and making it look even bigger as she spoke.

"We could ask Sergio to take us shopping…," proposed Deedee.

"Not today. It's his day off and he's spending it with Janette…"

"You can use some of my clothes for today…," offered Mela.

"I'm not 9 months pregnant yet!!!" She joked, to then giggle away while Mela chased her around the bay.

Joaquim in the meantime received a call from someone else in the peninsula and took them home on his way.

**

XXIII

It was late Sunday night when Pedro and Quito found themselves in their emergency office bedroom in Recife. Pedro arrived first and Quito a minute or so later.

"That wasn't so bad, was it?" Pedro commented when Quito materialised.

"Yeah..." Quito sounded like he was wondering if his body was all there! "I think we should perhaps travel a bit further apart?"

"You could be right... you can go first next time."

"Deal." Quito checked his mobile. "Do you still have your 4X4 downstairs?"

"I'd expect so... I'm sure Patricio will have had it checked. I have the keys for it. Why?"

"I'm about to touch base with Taco, to see what's going on..."

"Ok..." Pedro decided to have a look around while Quito chatted away with Taco. When he peeped into what was now Clara's new office however, he immediately noticed some light coming from under Patricio's adjacent office door, prompting him to switch to *Inca mode*, to verify who was in it, and it was indeed Patricio sitting at his desk, surrounded by piles of folders.

Pedro then quietly retraced his steps back to Quito and into his natural dimension. The Indio Chief was still on the phone to Taco and Pedro signalled for him to speak quietly.

"Somebody inside...?" He whispered back to Pedro, keeping Taco on hold.

"Patricio's in his office..."

"Don't you want him to see us?"

"What if they have changed the locks for some reason, with all that has been happening?"

"You've got a point…," he agreed, to then tell Taco he'd call him back shortly. "Gosh you are really developing a criminal mind!!!" He did his best not to chuckle and soon after they left the place in *Inca mode*. "Deedee, Ara and Sergio are in the Peninsula by the way…," commented Quito, as they drove out of the building in Pedro's 4X4.

"I'm not ready to see them Quito…," Pedro eventually stopped the car.

"Should I ask Joaquim to pick me up?" Quito tried his best not to look disappointed

"Yes please. I need to get my head straight on that…"

"When should we touch base?" He then asked, getting back to Taco.

"I'll need a good few days to get organised with Patricio and Clara anyway… and I'll give you a shout when I'm ready?"

"OK… Are you going back to the office?"

"Yeah."

Joaquim arrived with Taco a few minutes later and Pedro headed back up to his office. The locks hadn't been changed and he was soon inside.

"Patricio?" he called shortly after, from outside his office door.

"Pedro?" Patricio sounded surprised. "Please come in…"

"It is Sunday man…! You should be resting or having fun…" Pedro censured him in a friendly way, while shaking his hand. "How are things?"

"Hectic. I've been playing catch for a week! Congratulations on the new position by the way…"

"It's your entire fault… I wouldn't have made it without your help Patricio and so, I specifically requested to have you as my right-hand man in the organisation…" Patricio thanked Pedro's words with a small nod.

"And Quito…?"

"He's gone to the tribe for a few days, while you and I get organised. How's this Clara?"

"Not quite the "Bombshell" that Thelma was, but every bit as efficient…"

"That's good to know and… Any news on George's and Alberto's funeral arrangements…?"

"It's all taking place in George's Estate next weekend. I've sent your condolences to the widow, of course… and you are among the V.I.P. guests expected to attend."

"Any chance you could fix me up with a new plane and a yacht along the lines of what I had before?"

"I've already done that, but neither will be here in time for the Funeral, I'm afraid… I could always get Marco and Martha to charter one for a week or so, until yours arrives though?"

"Yes please."

"Your new plane is a Legacy 500 and your yacht is the twin sister of your old one. By the way… I took the liberty of naming the yacht the "AKAZI II""

"Excellent. Good work Patricio… Any idea as to what this Mary looks like?"

"I'll show you…" He said opening his laptop. "She's got a boy and a girl. Alex is 7 and Gemma is 5… and this is what they all look like." He turned the laptop around, so Pedro could see. "She comes from a family of Irish Aristocrats who settled in the US in the early 1900's, also in the mining industry. Her marriage to Alberto was practically an arranged thing… a way for both families to retain their wealth and interests…"

"The kids inherited their mother's red hair…," commented Pedro as he looked at various photos, also pleased with the appearance of the woman, in her early thirties. "Who's in control of her wealth?"

"We are, except for the part that is yet to come from her father's side…"

"Have you met her?"

"She is very pleasant… and I think I could perhaps persuade her to let us also handle the rest of her estate… I know that she is very happy with the way we've looked after their interests this far…"

"Any idea of what her general future plans might be?"

"Not really, not yet anyway, I've got an appointment to see her in Minas Gerais on the Monday after the funeral." He then looked at Pedro. "Our main problem is going to be fighting off the army of romantic suitors and opportunists lining up…" Patricio had no doubts as to what Pedro's plans were! "You can expect some fierce competition… she is quite a catch in every sense of the word…"

"Where is she just now?"

"I believe she is at George's Estate dealing with all sorts of Funeral arrangements…"

"Could you get Marco and Martha to fly me there later today?"

"It's 2 A.M. …"

"It's 2 P.M. in Tokyo…"

Marco and Martha were at Recife Airport by lunch time, with an identical plane to the one Patricio had bought for Pedro, and Pedro was headed for George's Estate by mid-afternoon.

"You must both be tired…" Pedro was apologetic as he went to see them in the cockpit.

"It's good to be back at work…!" Marco sounded cheerful.

"We had an early night last night, anyway…" Martha had a smile to give. "Can I fix you with anything?"

"I'll be OK Martha… I need to make a couple of calls and I'll have a nap afterwards…"

"Sebastião?" Pedro rang George's head of security.

"Mr. Bolivar, good to hear from you…," he then changed tone. *"I assume you've heard the news?"*

"I did and I still can't believe it! I arrived from Europe in the early hours of this morning and I'm on the way to you as we speak…"

"Mrs. Azevedo is with us… in fact, she is next to me… would you like to speak to her?"

"Yes please…" There was a brief interval as Sebastião introduced the call to Mary.

"Mr. Bolivar… How good of you to come to see us. I hope you'll give me a chance of returning your hospitality in New York?"

"It was a pleasure… and Mary, please call me Pedro, unless you'd rather I called you Mrs. Azevedo?"

"Pedro… when do you expect to get here…? It's all a bit chaotic at the minute…"

"I can well imagine… I should be with you in a couple of hours…"

"I look forward to meeting you…"

"Likewise…"

Pedro prepared himself a whiskey and then took a nap.

*

Mary waited for Pedro where Marco brought the plane to a halt and wore black from head to toe. She was aware that he had officially taken over from Alberto at the top of "I" and as such, he was probably the most important V.I.P. among the guests arriving later that week.

"I'm sorry we should meet under such circumstances…" Pedro kissed the hand she offered, in an old-fashioned way. "…And I would have come earlier, if it weren't for some immovable business appointments that had been long standing…"

"You were never under any obligation…," she reassured him.

"Well… George and I had become close friends, as you're aware, and the least I felt I needed to do was to offer you

338

some help to try and ease the added burden these preparations must place upon you..."

"You are kind...," she smiled at him as if assessing his long-term plans... "Fortunately I have a small team of professionals dealing with all those things...," she paused, leading the way into an open top beach buggy type of car. "There is however something I'd welcome your help with..."

"Fire away..."

Far from being the homely housewife her photo suggested, ever ready to accommodate her husband's every desire, Mary was sophisticated, independent minded and self-assured, and certainly not the type of woman Alberto could have pushed around. Yet, she was pleasant and approachable, while surrounding herself with an invisible moat.

"Alberto always kept me away from his business acquaintances within "I" ... and as a result, I hardly know any of the V.I.P.s that will be coming this weekend...," she paused to look at him as they sat inside the vehicle. "I'd be grateful if you'd help me with the public relations side of the Funerals?"

"With pleasure... providing you give me a list of those you are expecting. I probably won't know them all, having just come into the position recently..."

"Oh, I thought you'd been promoted from within the organisation..."

"There are two branches to "I". There's the financial branch, the one your husband used to work for, and there's an upper branch of the Organisation that oversees a wider range of business, of which the financial branch is one..."

"And you come from the upper bit?" She seemed amused.

"I suppose you could say that... Although not totally accurate...," he tried his best to appear unpretentious. "And... How are your children coping?"

"They hardly ever saw Alberto, always busy travelling and in meetings for one thing or another. In fact, when we stayed at your Manhattan penthouse, those few days were probably the longest period we had spent together in the last couple of years…"

"Good grief! I'd have thought that with your personality and good looks, you'd probably have to force him to go to work in the mornings!!!" He made her laugh.

"You are a kind man…," she said almost compassionately, "But if I can trust you to share a secret, the birth of Gemma left me a different woman from the time before that… and… I was actually grateful for his absence, a lot of the time."

"I'm sorry… it just goes to show how naïve men can be…!" He covered his face in a funny way, making her laugh again.

"Well, I'm not completely deprived of emotions; I should add…," she chuckled. "But anyway, let's talk about you…"

They were soon at the mansion, and after greeting Sebastião and Marlene on the way to the study, Pedro combined the true story of his life with a hefty amount of bullshit, as per the manufactured information on him in the public domain. The last thing he wanted was to give her the impression he was after her in some way, having immediately understood that what she really needed just then, was someone to talk to who wasn't an employee, or a pretty boy eager for a chunk of her wealth.

"Mister Quito Ok?" Marlene asked on the first opportunity, realising he wasn't there.

"He asked me to say hello to everyone Marlene…," he said, accepting the whiskey Mary poured him and then turned to her. "Has any light been shed on what precipitated these events yet?"

"George sent me an e-mail, only moments before doing what he did, where he tried to explain his actions. It said that what he was about to do was the only way my kids and I would be spared and also that he loved his son dearly… and that he wanted to be together with him in death…" A shiver ran the full length of Pedro's spinal cord.

"What do you think could possibly bring a father in George's position to take such action?"

"I've asked myself that question countless times over the past few days... And I can only assume that Alberto did something that placed us in mortal danger... Probably Mafia related or something linked to all the family deaths of late... which could include the fatal overdose supposedly taken by his demented brother..."

"I'm sorry I brought up the topic..."

"Not at all... The quicker I come to terms with everything, the quicker I'll be able to start looking ahead..."

The children were already in bed by the time they sat at table. Marco and Martha were dining with Paulinho (George's pilot) elsewhere on the Estate and floral tributes continued to arrive even at that late hour of the day.

"Patricio told me he's got an appointment to see you next Monday in Minas Gerais... are you flying out right after the Funerals?"

"I don't know... I'll probably stay here a few more days instead and ask Paulinho to get him from Recife..." She paused. "Everyone on the Estate is wondering what's going to happen to them... And this place is really a headache I could do without..."

"Are you considering selling it?"

"Well, I don't need two sets of planes, pilots, two small armies of security men... the waste of resources is horrendous!"

"I'm sure Patricio will help you sort out those things to the best of your interests... But should you ever consider selling it, I'd probably consider buying it, rather than let it go to outsiders..."

"I'll keep that in mind..." She smiled at him, somehow impressed, and Sebastião arrived moments later, to give him two pages of printed paper.

"I was told you wanted a list of the guests…," the Head of Security explained quietly as they ate.

"Thanks… Sebastião…"

"I really am glad you came…" Mary admitted in between munches. "You wouldn't believe how nice it is to be able to talk to somebody who is not going to ask me to contribute towards some cause, or some charity after 5 minutes!!!" She paused. "Even now, when people call me to express their sympathy… total strangers, they manage to integrate some begging in their message!"

"Why don't you ask Patricio to set a small annual fund for that sort of thing… and start telling those beggars to go to him?"

"That's a good idea… You know, I've even considered going back to my roots in Ireland…"

"Because of the begging…?"

"It's the security of my children that worries me… I get all sorts of threats sometimes. Most of them empty of course, but there's no shortage of desperate people out there who will do anything to get a fast "buck"."

"Does Patricio have a full list of your financial assets?"

"He's got a list of everything tied to Brazil, including the assets that were originally mine, as well as Alberto's and George's at their time of death. The list of the US inheritance bundle from my father's side is still being assembled…"

"George told me he had a home in England… Do you know anything about that?"

"That's not included in his Will… and I suspect it is a home he bought for a mistress he kept throughout his two marriages…," she had a little smile. "Well, that's what Alberto once told me."

From the dining room back to the study, their conversation continued to be focused on her wealth and on ways to improve her quality of life, while maximising her revenue and security.

"I hope you don't get the impression I came here to talk about your finances… I just thought of reassuring you that all your interests are going to be thoroughly looked after, assuming that was one of the things that were weighing on you…"

"No, no… you are OK…," she smiled at him. "And now that we've got that out of the way, are you going to offer me your friendship?" she said it with a vague hint of sarcasm, causing Pedro to chuckle.

"Do I really sound so much like a déjà vu?"

"I didn't mean for it to come out like that! I'm sorry, I'm a little over sensitive at present…"

"It is understandable… regarding my friendship however, you've always had it anyway…" Pedro realised there and then that Mary was going to be a tough bone to chew… and that he probably had a mountain to climb ahead. "I think we are both tired too…"

"I've some caterers coming tomorrow morning for the buffet planning and we need to stock up on aircraft fuel." She agreed. "Not including yours and mine, we anticipate the arrival of a further 9 private jets, including my father's New York solicitors…"

Pedro was given the same room he had had before.

As expected and even at that late hour, Patricio was still in his office; and Pedro e-mailed him the list of guests, in the hope of getting some feedback on each.

*

Quito's 3 A.M. arrival in the Akazi peninsula was meant to be a quiet affair. He hardly recognised the place and for fear of awakening his wives, he readily accepted Taco's invitation to spend the night in his mobile home! He had however forgotten to tell the "Border Control" Braves not to announce his arrival… and by the time he reached Taco's mobile home, the whole tribe was awake and ready to celebrate his return!!!

"Oh well…" Was all that Quito could think of saying as he looked back to Taco.

343

Quito immediately knew which mobile home was his, because that was where everyone had gathered, as if expecting to hear a speech! And before he could do anything, somebody handed him the latest tribal gadget; the Chief's megaphone!

"**One, two… One two…**" Taco tested the device ahead of a few words from their Chief.

"**Hello everyone…,**" started Quito, receiving a general echoed *Hello*. "**It's good to be back and the good news is that we are all very wealthy.**" He paused to clear his throat. "**Taco tells me that we'll all be able to move into our new homes in about 3 weeks…,**" he tried to think of something else to say. "**I'm tired just now and I need some rest, but tomorrow night… we will party…**"

All the Akazi seemed delighted with his speech and with that, he went inside his mobile home, trying to look a lot more tired than he actually was!

Quito couldn't quite go to sleep, accustomed by now to more comfortable beds and got up with the first rays of dawn, intent on seeing the progress of the works in the peninsula. He was soon joined by Taco and the sleepy Joaquim, ready to give them a tour.

Two lorries with a dozen workers each had arrived while they looked inside the new village. Quito was clearly impressed with everything he saw and after spending some time inside the house he knew would be his, they took the road leading to Pedro's bay, to look at his house from the beach.

They got out of the 4X4 when they reached the sand. The early morning air was moist and full of a strong marine surge from the low tide, and with the builders yet to resume work, the only audible sounds were from the breaking waves, and a few seagulls looking for any fish that would have washed ashore.

"Quito!" Ara came out of her shack, awakened by their car.

344

"Why aren't you with Deedee and Mela?" Quito took her fatherly in his arms as she ran to him.

"I feel more at home in my shack...," she justified, squashing her head against his chest.

"Are you by yourself?" He then asked suspiciously.

"No... one of the labourers missed his lorry ride home yesterday... and I offered to put him up for the night..." she alleged.

"I see..." Quito couldn't hide the disappointment on his face. "Well, he's going to have to start work soon... shall we give you a ride back?"

"Yes please..." She tried to show an innocent little girl's face.

**

XXIV

Shortly before going down for breakfast, Pedro received Patricio's e-mail with the full details of each of Mary's guests. Ironically however, it also emerged that it had been Patricio himself who had prepared the list at Mary's request, in the first instance.

"Your preparation for the meeting with Mary on Monday must take precedence over the rest..." Pedro decided to remind him with a phone call.

"I understand... do you need me there?"

"No, no... thanks. Instead, I would like you to take a day off and get some rest..."

"I think I'll take your advice... My partner has also been complaining..."

"Take her shopping..." Pedro suggested, pretending not to know about his gay side!

"I'll think of something..." Patricio didn't give anything away either.

It was obvious that Mary had a closer business relationship with Patricio than he first thought. Pedro found this weird, since Mary had told him that Alberto kept her in the dark on most things related to "I"; and given her husband's position within the Organisation... *"Could it be that it was Mary who dealt with the family's finances?"* But if that were the case, then... *"Why would Patricio not have told him so?"*

"Good morning Mr. Bolivar...," greeted Marlene, as Pedro reached the dining room for some breakfast. "Mrs. Azevedo is with the caterers...," she explained Mary's absence when she brought him a pot of coffee.

346

"Has she had breakfast yet?"

"She always has an early breakfast in her room...," Marlene revealed.

"Before... Mrs. Azevedo used to come here often?"

"Once or twice a month... and always when the other Mrs. Azevedo and her daughter weren't here..."

"They didn't get on?"

"Now that I couldn't say...," Marlene made a face like she knew more than she was saying. "Please don't say I mentioned anything..."

"Don't worry Marlene... you can tell me anything, my lips are sealed." He paused to cut a small homemade roll and lowered his voice. "And Alberto...? Didn't he come with them?"

"Not since the accident..."

"Accident...?" Enquired Pedro with renewed curiosity. Marlene went to have a quick peep outside the dining room before replying.

"About 8 or 9 years ago, some 2 years into their marriage, Alberto had a serious riding accident that kept him in a coma for over a week..."

"Did he bang his head?" Pedro lowered his voice to a whisper, somehow encouraging Marlene to tell him more.

"He'd gone out riding to one of the villages in the Estate... He was with a bunch of people he worked with... celebrating a promotion, I think it was... and apparently, they all got seriously drunk. It is even said he went into the bushes with one of the women... if you see what I mean...?"

"I get it... and?"

"It was also rumoured that the accident involved his private parts..." She whispered faintly towards the end of her phrase.

"Good heavens!!!..." Pedro looked at her. "Still... he produced some beautiful children..."

"Yes..." Was all she said with a side glance, to then remind him to keep his lips sealed. Pedro showed her a thumb up, trying his best not to look in a state of shock. *The old rascal!* He thought. *Could George be the father of Mary's kids?"*

Mary came with her children and a young woman to meet Pedro, as he was about to leave the mansion to go for a wander around. She was all in black once again, but the more formal garments of the previous day had given way to trousers, boots and a shirt, complemented by a fiery-thick red braid at the back.

"Good morning Pedro… I'm sorry for not keeping you company over breakfast…"

"Not at all… You did tell me you had some readymade commitments this morning…"

"Are you going to say hello to Mr. Bolivar?" She instructed her children, who complied with stretched hands and the end of stretched arms.

"How do you do?" They both said, trying not to fight over who'd be first to shake hands.

"Very good…" Pedro was prepared with two lollypops, which he pretended to extract from inside their sleeves, prompting Gemma to stick her arm inside one of her brother's sleeves, while the boy inspected the other…!

"And this is Miss Nelly, their nanny…," Mary introduced the woman with blonde curly hair.

"Hi…," Pedro shook her hand. "With a name like that, you've got to be Irish…!" Pedro commented in a nice way.

"I'm Brazilian… but my grandparents were Irish…" She informed him with a broad smile.

"Excellent…," Pedro let escape, while their nanny started taking them away.

"Bye Mister Bowvar…," said Gemma.

"Bye Mister Lollypop…," Alex returned Pedro's wave.

"It looks like you've made an impression…," Mary commented quietly with a smile.

"Was that a test then?" Pedro replied between his teeth in the same way, causing her to chuckle.

"Definitely…," she seemed to have mellowed from the previous evening. "Did George show you much of the Estate?"

"He drove me a little bit around and we also got to a "Mirador" from where we had a long view of it in all directions…"

"Well… I'm going to show you the Estate properly… should I ever decide to sell it…," she led him to her buggy-car and then drove down the landing strip, coming to a stop by a hangar that housed their military helicopter.

Paulinho, Marco and Martha were there, presumably talking about planes, and Paulinho had a good guess as to what Mary had in mind.

"Are you going to take "her" out?" He referred to the helicopter.

"Yes please Paulinho… is "she" good to go?"

"Always ready…," he confirmed, using a remote to operate the tall doors of the hangar.

"You can fly this thing?" Pedro turned to Mary, suddenly wishing he hadn't had breakfast!

"Mrs. Azevedo is an Ace Pilot in that machine…" Paulinho confirmed on her behalf.

"You are in safe hands, don't worry…," she said leading the way up to the cockpit of the craft.

Pedro wasn't going to chicken out, taking comfort in the thought that if this was going to end badly, at least he would die together with "presumably" the richest woman in South America!!

Mary seemed more attractive and at ease as she drove the complex machine out of the hangar, to then bring the craft's engines to full for a while. Pedro felt like he was sitting on top of a bomb, especially once the giant propeller began to turn! …and suddenly they were airborne, as if by magic. Mary looked at him to see if he was alright and gave him a reassuring smile.

"I've had more than 2,000 hours of flying time in this

craft in all weathers…," she said as they continued to climb, heading for the very centre of the Estate.

"I can see you are a natural…," Pedro replied with a smile, suddenly beginning to enjoy the experience, such was the confidence she exuded.

"Have you ever flown anything?"

"Only a kite I'm afraid…," he tried to keep a serious face, to immediately regret his stunt, as Mary closed her eyes for laughing!

"You really are a refreshing company from all the stiffs I seem to surround myself with." She chuckled and then gained a thoughtful expression. "I feel as if I'm living my life in a morgue some times."

"You could change all that while simultaneously increasing your level of financial control…"

"How…?"

"Well, late last night, Patricio e-mailed me the details vis-à-vis your guest list. And I took that opportunity to ask him how he was doing in his study of best management solutions for your entire Estate…"

"And what was the juice of that?" She was back on a defensive mode.

"He has apparently come up with a number of options. The one I found perhaps most exciting however, was a total management solution guaranteed by "I", and therefore risk free, which would increase your total wealth by something in the region of 4 million dollars per day, 7 days a week… including Bank Holidays, of course…," he added with his usual touch of humour.

"Did that include an estimate on what's to come from my father's Estate?" She was thoughtful again.

"I believe so…"

"And what do you stand to gain from all this?" She delivered her question candidly.

"As you probably know from Alberto, since he used to

hold a similar position to mine, one of my prime roles in the Organisation is to ensure that the assets we've helped our clients build will remain within our management sphere..." He looked at her. "But that's not the reason why I came here... Although we invariably seem to always end up talking about your finances!" Pedro chuckled.

"So... What's your main reason, besides attending the Funerals?"

"You... obviously!" He succeeded in making her laugh yet again.

"You want to marry me?" She tried to embarrass him jokingly.

"Alas, I think there might be a long queue for that...!"

"You are kidding!!! You fancy me?" She was chuckling away while getting a kick from the tease.

"I wasn't planning to have this conversation but..." Pedro felt somehow amused as well as genuinely embarrassed. "What do you find so surprising about that? Needless to say, I'm not planning to make a fool of myself... this is neither the time nor the place..."

"Are you being serious?" She looked at him through different eyes for a short moment.

"About fancying you?" Pedro was about to get seriously stuck!

"Well, me... my money... or both...?"

"I'm too old for you, anyway Mary... Can we pretend we didn't talk about this? I essentially came here to pay my dues and to try to be a source of strength to you..."

"You don't think I'm strong enough..." Mary was now having fun and almost laughing at him.

"I don't think of you as being weak, but rather than living life in a morgue, I think you are being imprisoned by people, lies, rules and protocols that have little to do with what life's about...," he paused. "We've just met...! But I feel that our friendship could help you escape those heavy chains you drag, without you having to commit to new ones…" Pedro looked at her. "And all the while, knowing that your wealth or mine wouldn't change life for either one of us…"

"Are you trying to get me to sell you this place cheaply?" She was back in a joking mood, but also enjoying Pedro's company more than she would ever admit.

"So you could then get it back again through marriage?" Pedro followed suit.

"I think we are two of a kind in many ways… and that's exciting…" She decided to leave it at that, having reached the spot she wanted to start the tour from.

The estate was considerably more diverse than George's tour had suggested. From coffee and cotton plantations to tropical orchards and herds of cattle, the variety of natural resources comprised vineyards, trout farming and all the processing industries that derived from those including dairy products, wine making, cloth weaving and more.

"I'm truly impressed…" Pedro commented on their way back to the hangar, the moment Mary took off from their final short stop.

"There is also a small logging industry and the subsoil is rich in iron ore…," she added. "George however had always been against any mining in the property…"

"I can understand his viewpoint." He paused. "And somehow I don't think you should ever part with this thought. It should remain a legacy to be passed on to your children… I think George would have wanted it that way."

"You say that because you probably can't afford it…," she teased him.

"What figure did you have in mind?"

"You go first… Make me an offer?"

"George reckoned it is worth around 500 million US dollars… but he also reckoned he had to subsidise some of the running costs…"

"If I was to part with it, I wouldn't let it go for less than twice that…," she was serious.

"Can I think about it?"

"Of course you can… I've not decided to sell it… Yet." she continued toying with him!

At the mansion, they then parted, Mary's P.A. had arrived from Minas Gerais for a late working lunch, and Pedro requested for Marlene to prepare him a small snack for him to eat in his room.

"Are you sure you wouldn't like me to cook you something?" She enquired as she placed a small tray of sandwiches and home-made crisps on the en suite living room table.

"This is just what the doctor ordered Marlene… thanks a lot…," he smiled at her, gratefully.

No sooner had she left, Pedro went into *Incà mode*, ready to hear what Mary and her P.A. had to say to one another.

Mary's personal Secretary was a guy called Mike Murphy. Middle aged, definitely Irish and with a boxer's nose, the man looked more like an I.R.A. Operative than the skilful research analyst type! He had a pile of papers for Mary to sign and they didn't talk much as Mary browsed through each paper before adding her signature to it. It became immediately clear that "I" did not control all the assets of the Azevedos, or at least not all of Mary's.

"You've also asked me to look into this Pedro Bolivar guy… but what I found makes little sense. Overnight, from being a sort of hermit fisherman he became head of "I" … And no one seems to know how he got to be in that position… not even Patricio!"

"That is absurd…!" She looked at him. "And what about personal assets…?"

"The trail on that is also vague… although he does have a few million clearly in his name…" Mike went on to tell her Pedro's entire life story, including his jail retention at

Pitimbu! "Do you want me to fabricate some scandal around him? I've got a few things in place already…"

"No, not yet… we need to know for sure who's propelled him through the ranks of "I" and why."

"I'm sure you could get it out of him, if you decided to…," the P.A. hinted, with familiarity.

"He seems keen enough… but I've got to play the mournful widow, at least until the end of this week…"

"There's no rush… is there?"

What was he stumbling upon? Pedro did enjoy some aspects of the High-Life, but he was also starting to get ever more nostalgic of the times when it was just him, his fishing boat and his shack. Besides Quito; *was there anyone he could trust?*

Mike left in the late afternoon and by 7:30; Pedro found Mary, Paulinho, Marco and Martha in the study, sharing some of George's whiskey ahead of dinner.

"Where have you been?" Mary had prepared him a glass of whiskey.

"I closed my eyes after lunch and slept until a moment ago!" He seemed disgusted with himself, causing Martha to giggle with the face he made.

"Did you have your meeting?" Pedro enquired from Mary. "Yes…"

"You should meet Alan…" Martha turned to Pedro, already on her second whiskey. "He is a laugh and a half…"

"He is Mrs. Azevedo's Pilot…," explained Marco.

"He is Irish and tells jokes…?" Pedro guessed, giving Martha the giggles back!

"It's all so predictable after a while!!!" Mary chuckled. "Alan went to take my P.A. back to Minas Gerais… Mike, my P.A., is flying to Dublin in the morning…"

Marlene called them for dinner at 8:00, as usual.

The meal was an animated affair, with Martha being the life and soul of the evening, and probably high on something…

She was ready to go to sleep by coffee time (!) and shortly after, Mary and Pedro were left alone in the study.

"I think I'll probably fly back to Recife tomorrow and return for the weekend... It's still Tuesday and I'm doing nothing here..."

"On the contrary... you are doing a great job. You are brightening my days with your company and your sense of humour, in between messages of condolences...," she refilled their glasses, her voice getting a little cloudy.

"You really make it sound bloody awful!" Pedro chuckled.

"Life is a macabre sequence of things painted in different colours...," she took a pause. "I think I might have drunk a little too much Pedro... Will you help me upstairs once we've finished this drink?"

"Of course I will..."

"You really are a gentleman... and a fisherman among men...," she had a brief giggle.

Going up the stairs was not exactly straight forward! Mary held on to Pedro, in a way that gave him a good feel of her breasts, whatever he did... until they came to her bedroom door.

"Will you help me get inside the bed?" She requested, opening the door.

"I'll get Marlene to help you..."

"No... I want you to do it. Please?" Pedro helped to take her shoes off after opening the bed, somehow suspecting she wasn't quite as drunk as she made out to be. "Your hands are so warm..." she commented, followed by a genuine hiccup while trying to take some of her clothes off (!) ...Triggering another giggle as she got inside the bed half dressed. "Would you keep me some company?" she added, making some space so he could join her under the covers...

"Not when you are drunk Mary...," Pedro smiled to her.

"Don't be boring Pedro... I thought you fancied me! I

had to get a little bit drunk to find the courage to bring you into my bed…"

"If that's the case, then come into my bedroom instead…?" He said standing up, before she could attempt to unbutton his shirt. "You know where I am… I will leave my door unlocked…." he finally said, deciding to leave the room before she could try something else.

"Everything OK?" Sebastião enquired, walking along the corridor outside. Pedro gestured for him to speak quietly and that Mary had had too much to drink, causing a smile to appear on the Head of Security's face. "Should I get Marlene…?" He uttered in a whisper.

"No… I think she just needs a good sleep Sebastião… Good night…"

"Good night Sir…"

Although aroused from his imaginings of Mary being sexually unchained, he half hoped she wouldn't turn up… just as he half regretted not to have taken advantage…! *Would she be resentful in the morning?* Or *pretend not to remember anything?*

Pedro couldn't be 100% sure if Mary would remain in her room and decided to go into *Inca mode*, to find out what she was up to.

As expected, Mary was perfectly sober wearing a nightgown in bed, and on her mobile phone to someone. A short straw on her bedside table suggested she might have done a line of cocaine since he had left…

"Did you manage to film anything worthwhile?" she enquired… *Did she have cameras in her bedroom?* Pedro wondered to himself while looking around for them. "Wow… She really is hot! Bloody hell…!" She continued, obviously taken aback about someone else, but finished the call before he could get close enough to hear what the person on the other side was saying. Mary then opened her bedside table drawer from where she extracted a ready made "joint" and a small vibrator, before switching the lights off!

Back in his room, the thought of Mike Murphy cooking up some scandal to discredit him at the right moment kept going around his mind. *What motive could Mary possibly have to do such a thing?* This somehow prompted Pedro into trying to find something that he could pin on Mary: something in reserve to trade with, at the right time.

*

Pedro no longer trusted the walls of the mansion and went out for a short walk ahead of breakfast, to give the Akazi Chief a call;

"Hi Quito…"

"Where are you?"

"Not too far from Marlene…," he teased. "Everything OK there?"

"Yes… another 3 weeks or so and your new home will be ready, as well as everything else…," he paused *"The village is looking really good…"*

"Excellent…"

"Did you phone to invite me to your wedding?" He joked.

"I've got the feeling she's the mother of all spiders…"

"Well, well… what do you need me to do?" Quito was no fool.

"We need to see what we can find about a guy called Mike Murphy. I think he is Irish from Dublin… and in Brazil he operates from Belo Horizonte; I'd expect… he is Mary's P.A.…."

"Wouldn't Patricio be your best port of call for this?"

"I think Patricio might be a little too close to Mike for comfort…"

"I see, so… what should I do?"

"Go into our office and use the necklace to XAKATAN… preferably to Ninan… and find out what your best investigative contact in Belo Horizonte might be, without going through Patricio... and once you're back in Recife, take it from there?"

"You want me to deal with that right now?"

"Whenever you have a chance... Try not to be seen by Patricio or anyone else in the office?"

"Ok... I'll let you know how things progress..."

To Pedro's surprise, Mary sat in the dining room, as if waiting for him to come for breakfast.

"Good morning Mary... how are you feeling this morning?"

"I couldn't wait to apologise to you for my behaviour last night...!"

"Think nothing of it! I'm surprised you even remembered anything!" He chuckled.

"I must compliment you on your restraint though..."

"I know... I spent the rest of the night regretting it!!!" They both burst out laughing, nearly making Marlene spill the pot of coffee she was bringing.

"Sorry Marlene..."

"You really are a free spirit..." She looked at him warmly.

"Had you been sober...," he informed her casually, lowering his voice...

"I'll remember that...," she said between her teeth, suppressing a giggle, causing a smile to come to Pedro's face.

"Another two days and you'll have the place full of guests...," he reminded her.

"600 people in total, without counting the 500 who live in the Estate..."

"How are you going to do it?"

"We will have a big catering tent outside... It will be an open-air service and a private Chapel will be built around their burial place, at the back of the mansion...," she paused. "Everything's in place and the whole thing will be managed by professionals."

"I'm impressed… and what commitments do you have today?"

"Today I'll be selecting the animals that will feed our guests… would you keep me company?"

"Of course… it will be a new experience…"

"We won't take the helicopter, don't worry…," she chuckled. "And since I believe you cannot ride a horse, I thought we'd go in my buggy?"

"Sounds perfect…" Pedro didn't allow himself to be intimidated by the things he couldn't do.

*

XXV

Joaquim drove Quito to the Recife office after nightfall and once inside the building, the Indio Chief used his necklace to get into the emergency bedroom, to check the place was empty for his return. He then pressed the coordinates to go to XAKATAN and emerged on Ayar's dining balcony, scaring the life out of the Guard on Balcony duty!

"Good to see you mister Quito... are you all right?" Greeted the Guard, not quite sure of what he should do.

"Good to see you too... I was trying to get to Ninan's Palace..."

"I will take you there..." He offered and requested a colleague to take up his post.

Ninan was amused to see him arriving escorted by one of the Royal Guards.

"I see you took the long route..." Ninan chuckled as he shook Quito' hand, to then remind him of what to press to get directly to his Palace. "It's unusual to see you without Pedro... is he OK?"

"He is fine and asked me to come to you, instead of using telepathy..." Quito then explained the purpose of his visit, leaving Ninan a little pensive.

"If Pedro no longer trusts Patricio, then Patricio needs to be replaced at the earliest... It is extremely important that we should find out what prompted Pedro to bypass his right-hand man, before anything else..." He seemed clearly concerned. "Patricio is a strong key person within "I" and one who has absolute control over billions of dollars..."

"I can see why you are concerned... Pedro however didn't

offer me any specific reasons… I don't know what to tell you on that…"

"Don't worry… I'll provide you with what you've asked anyway, but tell him to come to see me as soon as possible?"

"Ok…"

One of Ninan's servants then brought him a drink while the courtier went somewhere inside his Palace, to deal with the information requested, to return a while later with a contact name and a phone number in Belo Horizonte.

"His name is Rafael Schneider. He is an International Private Eye and is semi independent of

our Organisation. We sometimes use his Agency to investigate our own…"

"Many thanks, Ninan… and I shall pass on your message to Pedro shortly."

*

Mary's buggy driving was considerably more hair-raising than her helicopter skills.

"Do you think it's too late in life for me to learn how to ride a horse?"

"Of course not…! You can learn it at any age… besides, you are only about 10 years older than me… what's the matter with you and with this old man thing of yours?"

"You are a flatterer…," Pedro smiled at her.

"Not at all… But you are suffering from having little virgin girls as wives… to them, you must appear like a bloody relic from antiquity…," she made Pedro laugh.

"I wouldn't go that far, but I see your point…"

"When are they both due to give birth?" Pedro looked unimpressed by the fruits of her research.

"They are about half way into their pregnancies… why?"

"Just curious…"

"We are separated…"

"From both of them?"

"Yes… In my previous yacht, already pregnant, they cheated on me several times with the men I entrusted to protect them…"

"You've never cheated on them?"

"Well, I wasn't 3 and a half months pregnant!!!" He paused. "And you?"

"If I ever cheated on my husband?" She wanted to make sure that's what he meant.

"Hum-hum…," he confirmed.

"I did… but out of compassion…" She went on to tell him what he already knew from Marlene and confessed that her kids had been fathered by George, so that his blood line would not end with him. "Please keep this to yourself… You are the very first person I ever admitted to this…"

"That makes me feel very special. But…Couldn't George have produced more children with his second wife…?"

"She didn't want any more children and like his first wife, had affairs left, right and centre…"

"He couldn't satisfy them?"

"Well, he wasn't particularly well endowed to be honest, and rather clumsy when it came to sex, to say the least…"

"But you must have been with him loads of times…! Was that the compassion bit?"

"To talk plainly, it was the closest to a proper fuck that I could get. My husband became as flat as a eunuch after the accident… even though, he still did his best to try to satisfy me in any way he could… God rest his soul…"

"…And what was this problem you said you had after the birth of Gemma?"

"Well, I had to have a hysterectomy after the birth, due to complications… and that left me a little bit numb *down there…*"

"You didn't appeal to me as being numb at all, last night…," he chuckled.

"I don't know what you did but I was on fire… I even

considered calling Sebastião to my room!" She covered her mouth for laughing.

"Holy Gates of Heaven…!!! Is that what they say in Ireland?"

"I don't know…," she tried not to burst out laughing. "Shall we stay sober tonight?" She then proposed, as they came to a halt by the Abattoir.

"It feels good to talk with no holding back, doesn't it?" Pedro asked.

"You know…? I was thinking just that… you were right about me living in a prison… I've not felt this free in years…"

Pedro followed Mary around as if learning a new skill, but felt a funny tingle at the back of his neck, each time she sprayed a green cross on an animal, after giving it a cuddle!

On the way back to the mansion, Mary decided to go for a little detour, so Pedro could see the process of marking new born calves, and it was lunch time when they returned. They both knew how the day would end but neither wanted to precipitate *things*. Pedro in particular was dreading the thought of having one of his *poor* performances, at a time when he most wanted to impress.

They had lunch on the run. Mary had an appointment with some dress stylists, to look just right for the ceremony and the media that would be present on the day, and Pedro went for a walk around the spot chosen for the burials and future Chapel. There, the volume of floral tributes continued to grow by the hour, and as he read a couple of the messages, Marlene came to lay down yet another wreath.

"In the 20 years I've worked for the Azevedos, I don't remember seeing more than maybe 10 of their friends… and now all of a sudden there are hundreds of people that go and waste a fortune on flowers and cards, when they are no longer alive to see it… how ridiculous is that?"

"It is comforting to see someone deeply spiritual like you Marlene. Are you a religious person?"

363

"Probably not… but I believe in God in my own way…"

"Deep inside, we all need to hold on to something… don't we?"

"Well, right now I hope I can hold on to my job… I've got some weird feeling about the way things are going…"

"I wouldn't worry too much… you'll see."

"Well I'd better turn in, the weather's changing. Would you like an extra blanket on your bed?"

"I'll be OK Marlene, but thanks."

Alan was back that evening. Mary's main pilot was short and chubby and spoke like a cattle auctioneer; meaning that a lot of the jokes he told were for his own entertainment only, which in itself made every one laugh…! Paulinho however, seemed more concerned with the amount of air traffic the forthcoming event was going to create, and the increased likelihood of some accident occurring over the Estate.

"Why don't we redirect all the guests to Rio Branco airport and use the planes we have to ferry them here and back?" He proposed.

"That makes sense Paulinho… but if you add 10 that you can carry with 10 from Alan and 10 from Marco and Martha times 60 minutes going both ways times 20, it would take us a minimum of 20 hours to transfer everyone here and at least another 20 to take them all back… and we don't have room to accommodate them overnight…" was Mary's opinion.

"And what about chartering 2 or 3 normal passenger jets from Rio Branco here and back?" suggested Pedro.

"The runway is not long enough for those to take off or land…" Marco was quick to reply.

"I think a combination of things would probably be the best solution…," proposed Alan. "Allow a manageable number of guest planes to land here and the rest in Rio Branco, which we could then ferry, halving the time it would take us to get them all here and out?"

"And what about housing some in Rio Branco the previous day and getting them here by coach?" proposed Martha.

"Or even a combination of all three…?" Contributed Mary.

"A coach from Rio Branco would take about 7 hours…" Alleged Paulinho.

The discussion continued until well after dinner and they ended up deciding to arrange for the Brazilian Air Force to transport all the guests from Rio Branco to the Estate and back on the day, using 12 troop carrier helicopters.

"All we now need is for the Brazilian Air Force to agree!" Pedro had a chuckle once the pilots had left.

"I've got some good connections for that…" Mary was confident.

"Are you tired?" Pedro looked at her, as she hesitated whether to get them both one last round.

"Not overly tired…," she smiled to him, reading his thoughts.

"I think I've had enough booze for one day…" Pedro admitted, getting down from his stool. "I'm going to have a shower, get into bed, leave the door unlocked… and hope for the best!!!"

"Sounds like a good plan to me…," she looked into his eyes, before replacing the cork on the whiskey bottle. "I'll walk up with you…"

They parted on the upstairs corridor to go to their respective rooms and Quito rang just as Pedro was about to get into the shower:

"Is this bad timing?" The Indio Chief enquired, feeling guilty about the late-night call.

"Another few minutes and it could have been…" Pedro made him laugh.

"I'll go straight to the point then;" Quito passed on the message from Ninan, along with the courtier's concerns.

"Well can't I just set the necklace so that he and I can

exchange our thoughts, like we've done on a number of occasions?"

"I suppose you could try that... but I got the impression he'd rather see you in the flesh."

"In fact you could have probably tried that, instead of going all the way there!" he chuckled.

"I did try it when I got to the office, but it didn't work... I reckon I've probably forgotten the combination..."

"When will you be going to Belo Horizonte?"

"I'm taking the first morning flight there..."

"Thanks Quito... Have a good trip."

By the time he got to bed, Pedro was a lot readier for a good night's sleep than anything else, and wasn't too sorry to see that Mary didn't seem to be in a hurry to get to him either... and was soon asleep!

*

"Hi..." Mary whispered in his ear, snuggling against him from behind.

She was naked and the warmth of her breasts pressing on his back revived him instantly.

"Hi...," he said as he turned to face her, to then find her lips looking for his, in a slow lingering kiss. "Did you just get here?" he managed to ask in between the first and second kiss.

"Hum-hum..." she confirmed without interrupting her kiss... To then slowly bring him to be on top of her with no further ado. Neither of them managed to last past the second minute and they were both gasping for air for a while afterwards... "Where have you been my whole life?" She half moaned, keen on another slow kiss... somehow prompting Pedro to lie on his back.

"That really was intense!" He confessed, still flushed by the whole thing.

"It was definitely worth waiting for...," she came really close to him, to rest her head on his chest. "I'm cold..." she said with a little shiver. "Don't let me fall asleep here... will you?" She added, coming closer still, "Marlene is supposed to bring me breakfast at 6:30..."

"Why so early?"

"I've got to contact the Brazilian Air Force in Brasilia to arrange for those troop carriers... and I may even have to fly there at some point in the day..."

"Well, I'm going to have to fly to Recife to deal with a small emergency in the morning too..."

"But you'll be back by dinner time, I hope..."

"I hope so too..."

Between a kiss and a caress, neither of them could *switch off*, and it took a repeat performance to eventually tire them out.

"I could so easily get used to this you know...?" She uttered turning to Pedro, her head resting on an elbow.

"I could say exactly the same... but we need to be discrete, given the circumstances..." Her face had acquired the beauty of a broody woman, but with an hour to go till breakfast, she felt it wiser to go back to her room.

"I agree..." She then gave him a kiss to keep him *thinking* throughout the day and left.

*

 Pedro slept throughout the flight to Recife and got a cab to his office.

"Pedro, please meet Clara..." Patricio was quick to introduce her as he walked into his office.

"Good to meet you Clara and welcome... I hope you'll be happy working with us..." Pedro shook her hand with genuine warmth.

"I'm delighted to meet you sir." Clara was Latino-American looking and immaculately dressed, with long ebony hair and well manicured hands. Quite plump and touching 30 years of age, her very pretty face was supplemented by an intelligent glint in her eye.

"This is going to be just a flash visit Patricio… I need to deal with a few things from my office before returning to George's Estate…," he paused. "But first, may I see you privately for a moment?"

"I was about to leave…" Clara excused herself to go to her office, so they could be alone.

"She is very pleasant don't you think?" He enquired of Pedro.

"Indeed… she also came highly recommended…" Pedro agreed, to then go straight to the point. "Simple question:" Pedro stopped, to gain his full attention. "What's the story with Mike Murphy?"

"Mike and I go back a long way…" He smiled without looking particularly concerned. "He was the best man at my wedding… and also works for us on and off…"

"In what capacity…?"

"Well, an Organisation like ours needs to have its fingers in many pies, which also includes some clandestine political movements… in case things were to suddenly change?"

"Like the I.R.A., E.T.A. and that sort of thing?"

"Exactly… we all need one another on occasions and Mike is the perfect middle man that all sides seem to trust. He is also a friend of the Azevedos, of course… Alberto was a keen contributor towards a number of causes with his own personal wealth… perhaps out of his known political ambitions… and Mike was the guy in the middle, so that no dirt would ever stick to anyone's hands…"

"Did you know that he is Mary Azevedo's Private Secretary?"

"Not hers! He used to be Alberto's part-time P.A…. unless Mary offered him some employment continuity of recent…"

"I overheard a conversation where she seemed to give him charge of finding or perhaps creating something related to me, should they ever feel they needed to bring me into disrepute…"

"Well… I know nothing about that…! Sometime ago, Mike did ask me if I knew something about the way you came to be involved with "I" and who your internal sponsors were…," he paused. "And I told him I didn't know, which is the truth, anyway… but I never thought anything of it…" He paused again to look at Pedro. "My prime allegiance is to "I", rather than any individual within the organisation, and you have no reason to suspect me of any wrong doing…" Patricio seemed somehow offended.

"I'm glad you've cleared the confusion Patricio…" Pedro was un-intimidated by the man's reaction. "And this is what happens when we deal with half truths and second hand information… we get wrong footed, and that's the last thing I need. Otherwise, you've got nothing to be offended about. I'm trying to do my job just as I'm sure you are trying to do yours and that's what we need to stick to."

Pedro seemed to grow as he spoke, which somehow placed Patricio back in his shell.

"As for Mike to want to find some dirt on you on behalf of Mary, it is not necessarily because they want to blackmail you…," he paused. "Among the extremely wealthy, it is often part of their policy to do that sort of thing to the people closest to them, as a way of safeguarding the possibility that they might be blackmailed at some point in the future…," he paused again. "Alberto was one of those…"

"So his wife inherited the same habit… Oh well… Anyway Patricio, anything else that I should know so as for us not to revisit this type of conversation…?"

At this point, Patricio decided to come clean with his sexual orientation, and further revealed that it was Mike who introduced him to homosexuality!

"I probably should have told you this before…"

"It is not a crime Patricio and I certainly respect your right to have a private life… what concerns me however is if Mike or someone else was to use that as a way to blackmail you, for whatever gain…"

"Have no worries at all on that Pedro! I don't go around soliciting sexual favours from anybody and have been in a steady relationship for over 5 years… And I still support my ex-wife and children… whom none-the-less still despise me for having come out of the closet, as they say."

"What can I say?" Pedro smiled at him. "Except that your honesty has raised you in my esteem." Pedro offered him a handshake which he took, almost overcome by emotion. "I'll see you before going anyway…," was the last thing Pedro said on the way to his side of the office apartment.

"Could I get you anything Mr. Bolivar?"

"I'll be OK Clara, thank you. I'll be unreachable for the next hour or two…," he then added, before closing his office door… to emerge in Ninan's living room moments later.

"It is good to see you Pedro…" Ninan walked to him to shake his hand. "Will you join me for lunch?"

"With pleasure… What good timing…!" Pedro replied with familiarity.

"I thought I could hear a stomach rumble as you appeared…" joked the courtier.

Pedro was quick to put Ninan's mind at rest regarding Patricio, attributing the root cause of suspicions to a string of unfortunate coincidences.

"Do you realise that "we" support a number of so-called terrorist movements?" Pedro mentioned as they sat to eat, causing the courtier to laugh with gusto.

"They are all terrorists… and the so-called legitimate governments often the biggest terrorists of them all! It is a complex clever game to distract people's minds and to keep them where they are Pedro! There are sinister forces at work behind the world your eyes see… and there is a delicate balance to be kept by all major players involved, should they want to remain in the game."

"So… what's the end game plan for "I"?"

"We don't want to be much stronger than we are now, but not much weaker either… just enough to protect our core interests when we may need to do so, and enough to make a difference, should we be called upon to contribute towards maintaining the right global balance of things among the Players…"

"That is where I seem to lose the plot! To be called upon by whom?"

"That is something that is transmitted to us through Ayar…," he paused. "The King is like an intermediary between the people and a higher authority… or at least the "office of the King" is…"

Pedro let out a sigh of frustration, somewhat disappointed for not making any in-roads into the same old mystery.

"Aren't you happy with the quality of life we are providing you?" Ninan was calm and collected.

"I'm not complaining about that…"

"What is your complaint then? You want to know everything? More than everybody else…?"

"Just take no notice. Quito mentioned that you wanted to see me in person…"

"Well, I was obviously concerned with the situation with Patricio… and should that have persisted, we would definitely have had to examine things in detail. But since you tell me that the whole thing was just a pile of misunderstandings, it gives me pleasure that this should be a social visit instead."

"Everyone else OK…?"

"Yes. Ayar and His wives are really fond of you and you should try to visit them now and then, whenever you might have the chance…"

"Of course… and I'm particularly fond of them too…," replied Pedro, checking his fish for bones, "As well as everyone else in XAKATAN, I should add…," he smiled at Ninan and then turned to him again, after finding the bone he had been chasing. "Where do you see me in five years' time?"

"That's a good question… I suppose it all depends on how this Mary *business* turns out I'd say…" he sipped some of his drink. "Is she responding well to your passes…?"

"We were intimate last night… and I'd say we are both looking forward to a repeat tonight!"

"You are a fast worker!!!" Ninan was laughing with gusto.

"I actually like her… although I'm finding it hard to trust her…"

"People in her position can be as volatile as the wind at times… You need to keep her under you and to make her want to stay there at all times… Don't take anything for granted."

"Sound advice…" Pedro acknowledged and then had a chuckle. "Have you had much first-hand experience in this sort of thing?"

"Definitely a lot of the first hand, but not a lot of experience I'm afraid!" He laughed loudly and contagiously, to the point of setting off the guard on duty! "My knowledge on the ways the human mind works however is only second to a few…," he added modestly.

*

Pedro was back in George's Estate by 9 in the evening. Paulinho and Alan had already dined, as to Marlene's timetable, but Mary decided to wait to have hers with him.

Marlene seemed unusually happy to see Pedro back and even cooked them a fresh meal; apparently something of a rarity!

"I'm sorry I couldn't get here any sooner…," he apologised to Mary and Marlene as he came into the dining room, leaving Marco and Martha to join the other pilots in the study. "The other two ate on the plane…," he further explained, looking at Marlene. In her eyes however he could do no wrong.

"I am saying nothing on this occasion…" The woman replied returning to her kitchen, hiding one of her big-momma smiles.

"You must have made quite an impression on her…!" Mary eyed him lovingly. "I missed you…"

"I didn't. Not even one little bit…," he teased her. "How was your day?"

"Good… The Brazilian Air Force will provide us with all we need on the day…"

"Did you promise them a donation?"

"What do you think?" She sighed. "…And what about your day…? Did you sort out your little emergency?"

"Yes… Patricio says hello, by the way…"

"That reminds me, I still have to finalise my appointment with him…" she said looking for the organiser section on her mobile phone. "What are your plans for after the Funerals?"

"My new yacht should reach Recife by Monday… and I was planning to kidnap you for a couple of weeks in the Caribbean, to help clear your mind from all this…"

"Gosh…! And what shall I do with the children?"

"Bring them and Miss Nelly too… there's plenty of space… and I could even have a playroom made…" he paused. "I'd suggest that, once you have seen Patricio on Monday, we'll give ourselves two or even three days to get organised and then go?"

"I can't wait…" Pedro had become her new priority and he felt powerful for it.

From Marlene's body language, it didn't take much for Pedro to understand she knew what was going on between him and Mary. The question in his mind however was: *could she have reached that conclusion from making his bed? Or was Mary so obvious in the way she acted?* He somehow didn't want their relationship to become a source of speculation before the burials of Alberto and his father, to avoid conspiracy theorists from coming forward.

"Do you ever take your necklace off?" She asked, inspecting it with curiosity as they relaxed after making love, much later that night. "It is a beautiful piece of jewellery…" she acknowledged.

"I always keep it on… apparently it has some medicinal qualities…," he explained.

"You don't believe in that sort of thing…! Do you?" She lifted her head to look at him, with an amused expression on her face.

"Not really… I just like it… I could have one made for you…"

"How do you take it off?" She then enquired, looking for some sort of lock.

"That one doesn't come off… but I could have one made with a lock for you?"

"It is some sort of bond with your Indio wives isn't it?" She seemed to lose interest.

"Nothing to do with them, I can assure you…" Pedro had a chuckle.

"Do you ever miss them?"

"No… my heart is frozen in that direction…," he paused. "But I wish them well…" He added, causing them to be silent for a little while. She then bit her bottom lip, as if excited from her imaginings.

"Did you use to have threesomes?"

"Can we talk about something else?" Pedro turned to face her.

"You are going to think I'm weird, but talking about this is turning me on like mad…," she admitted with a little giggle.

"Yes… not at first, but it became the norm after a while…" Pedro explained some of the Akazi customs to her.

"Would you believe I've never had sex with anyone besides Alberto and George?"

"Well… you certainly don't lag behind other women in any way…," he confirmed.

"I'm not suggesting that I am naïve or innocent in that domain… Especially with George…! He might have had a little dick but he was a first-class pervert, I'll give him that…"

"What can I say?" At this point, Pedro was ready to resume his love making, and she readily brought him to be on top of her, but without halting her conversation!

"He took me through the *alphabet*…," she alleged, but her speech then suddenly slowed, coming to a full stop as Pedro's lips found hers.

*

Quito had arranged to meet Rafael Schneider in his office, but given the source of the recommendation, the Private Eye decided to come and meet the Akazi Chief in person, at Belo Horizonte Airport.

"Good to meet you Mr. Schneider…"

"Good to meet you too… please call me Rafael." The tall Germanic looking fellow proposed to lead the way. "First time in Belo Horizonte…?"

"It is and I'm very much impressed… it looks immense, from the air…"

"Not many people know that Belo Horizonte is in fact the business capital of Brazil…" he boasted. "Shall we deal with our business over lunch perhaps? …and maybe continue in the office afterwards, if need be?"

"It is your city and I shall follow you…," replied Quito.

Rafael took Quito to the Porcão Restaurant for lunch, by which time the Indio Chief had already fallen in love with the City.

"I believe the main subject you want me to investigate is a guy by the name of Mike Murphy?" Rafael wanted confirmation, once they finished ordering their meal.

"Absolute discretion must remain your priority… there's a delicate network of people involved in this…"

"That goes without saying…," he interrupted.

"Your investigation might eventually take you to Europe and Ireland… but all your expenses will be amply covered, of course. There are five thousand dollars inside this envelope to cover for that, but just let me know should that not suffice." He paused. "Plus your fees, obviously…"

"Thank you…" Rafael accepted the envelope, which he placed in the inside pocket of his jacket. "Anything specific that you are after regarding this person…?"

"I believe you've already received some information to help you start?" Rafael confirmed it with his head. "Well, basically everything about him since he was born, his business connections, his habits and in particular, the people he may be involved with outside the Azevedo Family…"

"You realise that the Azevedo Family is extremely powerful in Minas Gerais…"

"Indeed… and in some ways, I could actually say that I'm acting on their behalf."

Their meeting didn't last longer than the time it took them to eat. Rafael was quick to understand that Quito needed to find some dirt on Mike, for whatever purpose, and after exchanging contact details and a few other particulars, took him back to the Airport.

*

The long-awaited day for the Funerals of George and Alberto was finally here! The Brazilian Air Force Helicopters had done the first part of their job and suddenly there was over a thousand people circulating in and around a very large catering tent, ready to pay their last respects to two men who had probably shaped their lives.

Behind the mansion, where the Chapel would be built, an open air Altar had been created for the farewell mass, at the centre of a sea of floral tributes. To one side, the two caskets rested on their stands, side by side, but due to the poor presentation of the heads of the defunct, the coffins had already been sealed. Ironically however, placed on top of George's coffin on the correct spot, his unmistakable tall white Stetson stood out like the mother of all erections! *Was he having a final laugh?*

Mary sat on the front row as they all began gathering for mass, behind a black netted veil. The grieving black widow in mourning…

"Don't you think that Stetson looks terrible where it was placed?" Pedro managed to comment in between teeth to Mary, returning from seeing a few of the guests.

"Oh Gosh… I see what you mean…!" She had to use both hands to stop herself from laughing. "I can't even look at it!!!" She tried to compose herself. "Has anyone passed comment?"

"Not that I heard anything… but I noticed one of the press photographers happily snapping away at the hat and coffin from various angles…"

"I can't wait for this day to be over…," she then said, as her children and Nanny arrived to stand next to her.

The service was short and Sebastião was chosen to deliver a brief Eulogy of behalf of all the employees from the mines down south to those on the Estate.

It was well past midnight when the last of the outside guests left, and those from the Estate were asked to take home whatever food had not been used. Inside the mansion, Mary had taken her shoes off and sat on one of the study's sofas with a full glass of George's favourite whiskey, while Pedro served himself at the bar. Sebastião and Marlene were also there at Mary's request.

"Can I get you anything?" Marlene came to her.

"No Marlene thanks… you and Sebastião are not on duty just now. I want you both to grab a drink of your choice and then come to sit with me?" She requested, looking tired.

"Are you going to tell us we no longer have jobs?" Marlene was ready to explode in tears.

"What a silly thing to say Marlene!" Mary felt compelled

to get up to give the woman a comforting cuddle, causing tears of joy to freely flow from her instead. "On the contrary, I've decided I shall be making this my principal home…," she then turned to Sebastião. "And please let everyone know that their jobs are safe and that we are going to make things work on this Estate, bring investment where it's needed and improve pay and conditions…"

"And Mr. Bolivar…?" Marlene had suddenly lost all sense of proportion!!!

"All in good time Marlene…" Mary was a little unstuck.

"We are very happy for you…" Sebastião couldn't hold back and added his bit. "We know all that you've been through over the years…"

"In that case, please let it be a secret for the time being…" She said and then looked at Pedro who simply smiled.

**

Tony AMCA was born and raised in Lisbon-Portugal.

Very much a free spirit, he travelled the World extensively and experienced several cultures at close quarters, facilitated by his fluency in 5 languages, although England remained his home for most of his life.

Among his many real-life adventures, he lived in Brazil in the late 1980's, and his affection for the Country and its Peoples remains to this day.

XAKATAN is Volume 1 of 3.

Other works by the same Author include;

The Vluvidium Collection & *La Suite*